Arilyn's throat tightened in foreboding, for at her side the moonblade glowed with an ominous blue light.

"What's all that about?" Danilo asked, pointing.

"A danger warning," she explained tersely, looking around for whatever the moonblade sensed.

"A glowing sword. How very quaint," he drawled. "Tell me, does it come in green? If so, where can I get one?"

The lack of concern in the nobleman's voice infuriated Arilyn. "There are goblins about," she stressed in a quiet voice. "Surely not even you could find such creatures amusing."

Danilo pursed his lips and considered this. "Actually, there *was* this little fellow down in Cormyr. . . ."

Her retort was interrupted by an unearthly screech. It split the air and hung, reverberating, over the marsh. Then, from behind the ridge of a nearby hillock rose half a score of enormous, scale-covered nightmares. Arilyn had heard tales of the lizard men of Chelimber Marsh, but the reality was a horror beyond telling.

⊙ ⊙ ⊙ ⊙ ⊙

THE HARPERS

A semi-secret organization for Good, the Harpers fight for freedom and justice in a world populated by tyrants, evil mages, and dread creatures beyond imagination.

Each novel in the Harpers Series is a complete story in itself, detailing some of the most unusual and compelling tales in the magical world known as the Forgotten Realms.

THE HARPERS

THE PARCHED SEA

Troy Denning

FANTASY ADVENTURE

ELFSHADOW

Elaine Cunningham

TSR Inc.

ELFSHADOW

First Printing: October 1991
Printed in the United States of America.
Library of Congress Catalog Card Number: 90-71501

9 8 7 6 5 4 3

ISBN: 1-56076-117-2

TSR, Inc.
P.O. Box 756
Lake Geneva,
WI 53147 U.S.A.

TSR Ltd.
120 Church End, Cherry Hinton
Cambridge CB1 3LB
United Kingdom

For Andrew,
my firstborn and my friend.

Acknowledgements

I would like to thank Bette Suska for teaching me that words could be both toys and treasures; Marilyn Kooiman for suggesting that someone so weird ought to write fantasy; and Jim Lowder for his guidance, good humor, and astonishing patience.

Prelude

The elf emerged in a glade, a small verdant meadow ringed by a tight circle of vast, ancient oaks. His path had brought him to a spot of rare beauty that, to the untrained eye, appeared to be utterly untouched. Never had the elf seen a place more deeply green; a few determined shafts of early morning sunlight filtered through leaves and vines until even the air around him seemed dense and alive. At his feet, emerald droplets of dew clung to the grass. The elf's seeking eyes narrowed in speculation. Dropping to his knees, he studied the grass until he found it—an almost imperceptible path where the dew had been shaken loose from the ankle-high grass. Yes, his prey had come this way.

Quickly he followed the dew trail to where it slipped between two of the giant oaks. He parted a curtain of vines and stepped out of the glade, blinking away the bright morning sun. Once his eyes had adjusted to the dim light of the woodland, he saw a narrow dirt path winding through the trees.

His quarry did not know that they were being followed, so why wouldn't they take the easiest way through the forest? The elf slipped through the underbrush and set off down the path. There was little to indicate that other footsteps had preceded his, but the elf was not concerned. The two he sought were, despite their deplorable origins, among the best rangers he had encountered. Very few could walk through the thick, deep grass of that sheltered glade and leave behind no more than a dew trail.

The elf glided silently along the path, his blood quickening at the thought of the victory that lay ahead, so long awaited and now so close at hand. Elves, particularly gold elves, were not hasty people, and behind this morning's mission lay years of planning, decades of discussion, and almost two centuries of waiting for the proper means and moment. The time to strike had come, and his would be the first blow.

The path ended at a stone wall, and again the elf paused, alert and observant. He crouched in the shadow of the wall and examined the scene spread out before him. Beyond the wall was a garden, as lovely as anything he had ever seen.

Peacocks strutted about an expanse of lawn, some with tail feathers spread to flaunt dozens of iridescent blue-green eyes. Brilliantly colored kotala birds chattered in the spring-flowering trees that ringed a reflecting pond. The elf's innate love of beauty welled up within him, pushing aside for a moment the urgency of his mission. It would be easy, he mused as he observed the garden scene, for elves to be seduced by such splendor.

As indeed they had been, he concluded as his gaze lifted above the garden to a distant castle, a marvel of enspelled crystal and marble. His golden eyes glittered with hate and triumph as he realized that the trail had led him to the very center of gray elf power. The ancient gold elf race had succumbed to the rule of their inferiors for far too long. With renewed purpose the elf began to plan his attack.

His situation could hardly be better; no guards patrolled the outer palace gardens. If he could catch his prey before they got close to the castle, he would be able to strike and withdraw undetected, and return another day to strike again.

Between him and the castle was an enormous maze fashioned of boxwood hedges. Perfect! The elf flashed a private, evil smile. The gray wench and her pet human had walked into their own tomb. Days could pass before the bodies would be discovered in that labyrinth.

The arrangement did have its disadvantages. The maze itself did not worry him, but its entrance could be reached only through a garden of bellflowers. Cultivated for sound as well as scent, the flowers sent faint music drifting toward him in the still morning air. The elf listened for a moment, and his jaw tightened. He'd seen such gardens before. The flower beds and statuary were arranged to catch and channel the slightest breath of wind, so that the flowers constantly chimed one of several melodies, the choice depending on the direction of the breeze. Any disruption of the air flow, however faint, would change their song. In effect, the garden was a beautiful but effective alarm system.

Since his quarry was undoubtedly in the maze and heading for the castle, the elf knew he would have to take a chance. He vaulted easily over the low stone wall and raced past the inquisitive peacocks, then glided through the bellflower garden with an economy of motion only the best elven rangers could achieve. As he had feared, the tinkling song subtly altered with his passing. To his sensitive ear, the disruption was as glaring as a trumpet's blast, and he ducked behind a statue and steeled himself for the approach of the palace guard.

Several silent minutes passed, and eventually the elf relaxed. To his surprise, he had reached the maze without detection. A last glance around the garden assured him that he was truly alone. His lips twisted in derision as he pictured the palace guards: oafs too stupid and common to recognize their own musical alarm. Tone deaf, as were all gray elves. With a soundless chuckle, the elf slipped into the maze.

Garden mazes, he knew, tended to follow a common pattern. After a few confident turns, the elf began to suspect that he had found an exception. This maze was like nothing he had seen before. Vast and whimsical, its convoluted paths wandered from one small garden to another, each one more fantastic than the last. With a growing sense of dismay the elf passed exotic fruit trees, fountains, arbors, berry patches, tiny ponds filled with bright fish, and hummingbirds breakfasting amid vines of red trumpet flowers. Most striking were the magical displays depicting familiar episodes from elven folklore: the birth of the sea elves, the Green Island dragonwar, the elven armada landfall.

He pressed on, running to the entrance of yet another garden clearing. One glance inside, and he skidded to a stop. Before him was a marble pedestal topped with a large, water-filled globe. Surely he couldn't have passed that globe before! He crept closer for a better look. A magical illusion raged within the sphere, a terrible sea storm that tossed tiny elven vessels about. Before his horrified eyes the sea goddess Umberlee rose from the waves, her white hair flying in the gale like flashes of lightning. By the gods, it was the birth of the sea elves again!

There could be no doubt. Surely not even *this* ridiculous maze could have two such displays. The elf raked both hands through his hair, tugging at it in self-disgust. He, a renowned elven ranger, was running around in circles.

Before he could castigate himself further, the elf heard a faint clicking sound, not far away. He trailed it to a large, circular garden, ringed with flowers that attracted clouds of butterflies. Many paths led out of the garden, which was dominated by pale blue roses in a bed shaped like a crescent moon. At one tip of the blue-rose moon stood an elderly elven gardener, snipping away at the rosebushes with more vigor than expertise. Again the elven intruder smiled. By all appearances, this was the maze's center; surely his quarry had passed through. The old gardener would tell him, at knife point if need be, which path the wench had taken.

The elf edged into the garden. As he entered a flock of the butterflies took flight, and the gardener looked up, his silver eyes lit with gentle inquiry at the disruption. His gaze fell upon the intruder, but he merely waved and cleared his throat as if to call out a greeting.

No, not that! thought the intruder in a moment of panic. He could not alert his quarry now!

A dagger flew, and a look of surprise crossed the gardener's face. The old elf's hand came up to fumble with the blade in his chest, and he fell heavily to the ground. His rough cap tumbled off. From it spilled an abundance of long, dark blue hair shot through with silver threads.

Blue! Excitement gripped the assassin, and he sped across the distance between him and the fallen elf in silent, bounding steps. As he crouched beside the corpse, a flash of gold caught his eye. He reached for it. From beneath the gardener's rough linen tunic he drew a medallion bearing the royal crest. It was true. The assassin dropped the medallion and sat back on his heels, dizzy with elation. Through the most fortunate of errors, he had killed King Zaor!

A keening scream, anguished and female, interrupted his private celebration. In one quick motion the elven assassin leaped to his feet and whirled, twin swords in hand. He found himself facing his original quarry. So white and still she was, that for a moment she seemed carved from marble. No sculptor, however, could have captured the grief and guilt that twisted her pale face. The knuckles of one hand pressed against her mouth, and with her other hand she clung to the arm of the tall man at her side.

Ah, the fates were kind today, the elven assassin gloated. Swiftly and confidently he advanced on the pair, blades leading. To his surprise, the wench's oversized companion had the presence of mind to snatch a small hunting bow from his shoulder and let fly an arrow.

The elven assassin felt the stunning impact first, and then a burning flash of pain as the arrow pierced his leather armor and buried itself in his side, just below the rib cage. He looked down at the shaft and saw that arrow was neither deeply imbedded nor in a vital spot. Summoning all his austere self-discipline, he willed aside the pain and raised his swords. He could still kill the wench—kill them both—before making his escape. It would be a fine day's work, indeed.

"This way!"

A vibrant contralto voice rang out, very near. The female's scream had alerted the palace guard. The assassin could hear the rapidly approaching footsteps of at least a dozen guards. He must not be captured and questioned! Die for the cause he would do and do gladly, but the gray rulers would surely not grant him the dignity of death. The elven assassin hesitated for only a moment, then he turned and fled back toward the glade and the magic portal that stood there.

Breathing hard and feeling lightheaded from pain and loss of blood, the elf plunged through the circle of blue smoke that marked the magical doorway. Strong, slender arms caught him and eased him to the ground.

"Fenian! Tell me what happened!"

"The portal leads to Evermeet," the wounded elf gasped. "King Zaor lies dead."

A triumphant, ringing cry escaped the elf's companion, echoing over the mountains and startling a pair of songbirds into flight. "And the elf wench? The Harper?" he asked excitedly.

"They still live," the elf admitted. The effort of speaking brought a fresh spasm of agony. He grimaced and grasped with both hands at the arrow shaft.

"Take ease," his friend consoled him. "Amnestria and her human lover will soon follow Zaor into death." He gently moved the elf's hands aside and began to work the arrow out. "Were you seen?"

"Yes." The answer came from between gritted teeth.

The hands on the arrow stilled, then tensed. "Even so, you have done well." With a quick motion, he plunged the arrow up under the elf's rib cage and into his heart. When the flow of lifeblood stilled, he wrenched the arrow free and thrust it back into the elf's body at the original angle. He rose to his feet and gazed with a touch of regret at the dead elf. "But not well enough," he murmured.

One

The moon rose, and in its wake trailed the nine tiny stars known to bards and lovers as the Tears of Selune. Slowly the weeping moon washed the color from an autumn sunset. In the darkening garden the mists—the eerie, earthbound clouds for which the Greycloak Hills were named—began to gather, shrouding the garden and muting the final peals of elven funeral bells.

There were few places in Evereska more peaceful than the temple of Hannali Celanil, the elven goddess of beauty and romantic love. The temple, an enormous structure of white marble and moonstone, rested upon the city's highest hill, surrounded by gardens that even in late autumn bloomed with rare flowers and exotic fruits. On a low pedestal at the very center of the gardens stood a statue of Hannali Celanil, carved from rare white stone.

But the lone figure huddled at the foot of the statue cared little for her exquisite surroundings. Numb with grief and shock, a half-elf maiden wrapped her thin arms around her knees and stared with unseeing eyes over the city toward the distant hills. She didn't notice the lighting of Evereska's street lamps; she didn't draw her cloak against the chill of the gathering mists. The child had been drawn to the temple gardens as if by instinct, perhaps hoping that this place, which had been her mother's favorite haven, might hold some lingering echo of her mother's presence.

Less than fifteen winters of age, Arilyn of Evereska could not comprehend how her mother, Z'beryl—an elven warrior-mage of considerable skill—could have died at all, much less at the hands of common cutpurses. There could be no doubt. The pair of murderers had confessed, and even now their bodies swung from the walled city's battlements. Arilyn had attended the execution, watching the grim ceremony with a curious sense of detachment.

Too much had happened for Arilyn to absorb. The young half-elf hugged her legs closer to her chest and let her forehead drop to her knees. She was weary with the effort of making sense of it all. Z'beryl was the only family Arilyn had ever known; could she truly be gone? And then, treading in the shadow of her mother's death, had come a second shock: the sudden and secretive appearance of Z'beryl's kin.

Remote and aloof, the strange elves had barely acknowledged Arilyn's presence, preferring to grieve behind the veils of their silver mourning robes. Family without faces. Even now the memory chilled Arilyn, and she drew her old cloak tightly around her huddled body. Right after the funeral, Arilyn had shed her own mourning robes and sought the familiar comfort of her usual garb. She wore a simple tunic over a loose shirt, and her dark trousers were tucked into well-worn boots that were as comfortable as they were disreputable. Indeed, the only thing that distinguished her from a street waif was the ancient sword that was strapped to her side.

Arilyn's hand strayed to the sword, her only legacy from her mother, and her fingers absently traced the arcane runes that ran along the length of the scabbard. Already the sword felt a part of her. Her mother's relatives, however, had lingered after the funeral to hotly debate whether Z'beryl had the right to bequeath the sword to a half-elf. Strangely enough, no one had made a move to take the sword from Arilyn. When finally they had left, as mysteriously as they'd arrived, Arilyn had felt no more or less alone than she'd been before they showed up.

"Arilyn of Evereska? Excuse me, child. I do not wish to intrude upon your grief, but I must speak with you."

The softly spoken words jolted Arilyn from her reflection. She sat upright and squinted in the direction of the musical voice. A tall, slender elven male stood poised at the gate of the innermost garden as if awaiting her permission to enter.

Arilyn had the keen eyes of her mother's race, and even in the mist-shrouded twilight she quickly discerned the identity of her visitor. Her customary self-possession evaporated in the face of her childhood idol. To meet with Kymil Nimesin, and in such disarray! Both chagrined and excited, she scrambled to her feet and wiped her hands clean on the seat of her trousers.

Kymil Nimesin was a high elf, of a noble family who had once held a council seat in the long-lost elven kingdom of Myth Drannor. Currently swordsmaster at an arms academy, he was a renowned adventurer and a master of arcane battle magic. Rumors persisted that he was connected to the mysterious group known as the Harpers. Arilyn firmly believed these stories, for they supported the heroic image she had fashioned of Kymil Nimesin. Such stories also would explain his presence; Z'beryl had once told Arilyn that the elves of Evereska maintained a keen interest in the doings of the Harpers.

"Lord Nimesin." Arilyn pulled herself up to her full height and held out both hands, palms up, in the traditional gesture of respect.

The elf inclined his head in acknowledgement, then glided toward her with the grace of a dancer—or an incomparable warrior. A high elf, also known as a gold elf, was not a common sight in the moon elf colony of Evereska. Arilyn felt very drab and common as she compared her white skin and boyishly shorn black hair to the exotic coloring of the fey gold elf. He had the bronze complexion of his sub-race, long golden hair streaked with copper lights, and eyes like polished black marble. As the master approached, Arilyn marveled at the grace, the sheer physical beauty that enhanced his aura of nobility and power. Kymil Nimesin was truly a *quessir*, an honorable elven male. She took several paces toward him, then swept into a low bow.

"I am honored, Lord Nimesin," she repeated.

"You may call me Kymil," he corrected her gently. "It has been many centuries since my family have been lords." The elf studied Arilyn for a long moment, then turned his obsidian eyes to the statue behind her. "I thought I might find you here," he murmured.

"Sir?" Arilyn's brow furrowed in puzzlement.

Kymil glanced over at Arilyn. "The statue of the goddess of beauty bears a striking resemblance to your mother. Were I you, I would have come here tonight," he explained.

"You knew her? You knew Z'beryl?" Arilyn asked eagerly. In her excitement she took a step forward and clasped the elf's forearms. So few persons could tell her anything of her mother's early life, and in her hunger for information she forgot her awe of the famous *quessir*.

"We met briefly many years ago," Kymil replied. He gently disengaged himself from Arilyn's impulsive grasp and resumed his reflective study of the statue of Hannali Celanil. Once or twice he glanced at Arilyn, and it seemed to her that he was trying to come to a decision about something.

Arilyn shifted impatiently, but Kymil did not seem inclined to say more. After a moment's silence she tore her expectant gaze from the *quessir* and squinted dutifully at the statue of Hannali Celanil, trying to see something of her mother in the cold white beauty of the goddess.

Moonlight seemed to linger on the statue as if delighted with its loveliness. More slender and beautiful than any human woman, Hannali Celanil bore the angular, delicate features of the elven race. A small, knowing smile curved her exquisite lips as she surveyed her domain through almond-shaped eyes.

One long-fingered hand rested over her heart, the other touched a pointed ear. Thus was Hannali Celanil often portrayed, to show that she was ever receptive to the prayers of lovers.

On the canvas of her imagination, Arilyn painted the statue's cheekbones and ears with a touch of blue, and replaced the elaborate white stone coif with Z'beryl's long sapphire braids. Arilyn mentally strapped a sword to the goddess's side, and finally she imagined that the eyes were a gold-flecked blue, warmed with a mother's love.

"Yes," Arilyn agreed. "I suppose it is very like her."

The sound of her voice drew Kymil from his reflection, and his abstracted look disappeared. He rested a hand on Arilyn's shoulder, a brief and silent gesture of condolence that seemed oddly foreign to his austere nature. "I am sorry for your loss, child," he said. "If I may ask, what do you plan to do now?"

Startled, Arilyn drew back, staring blankly at the *quessir.* The question was reasonable enough, but it jolted her into a disturbing realization.

She had no idea what she would do next. She simply hadn't thought that far ahead.

The silence was broken by the brassy, nasal tone of crumhorns. Arilyn recognized the signal for the changing of the guard; the barracks of the Evereska Watch stood at the foot of the hill, and the sounds of their ritual evening maneuver drifted up to the temple gardens.

"I'll join the watch," Arilyn volunteered impulsively.

A smile flickered across Kymil Nimesin's face. "If the wind had blown from the west, we might have heard chanting from the College of Magic. Would you then have decided to become a mage?"

Arilyn hung her head, embarrassed by her childlike outburst. But her tone was stubborn as she insisted, "No. I've always wanted to be a warrior, like my mother." As she spoke, her chin came proudly up and her hand drifted to the hilt of her mother's sword.

Her sword.

"I see." Kymil's eyes followed the movement, narrowing as he studied Arilyn's weapon. "Your mother was a mage as well as a fighter. As an instructor at the College of Magic and Arms, she was highly regarded. Did she teach you much of the art?"

Arilyn shook her head. "No. I'm afraid I have no gift for magic." Her grin was fleeting. "Not much interest, either."

"She did not pass on the lore of the moonblade, I take it?"

"You mean this sword? If it has a story, I've never heard it," Arilyn replied. "My mother only said that it would be mine some day, and she promised to tell me about it when I came of age."

"Have you used the weapon?"

"Never," she said. "Neither did Mother, although she kept the sword with her. She wore it always until . . ." Arilyn's voice faltered.

"Until the funeral," Kymil finished gently.

Arilyn swallowed hard. "Yes. Until then. Mother's will was read, and the sword was given to me."

"Have you drawn it?"

The *quessir*'s question puzzled Arilyn, but she assumed he had his reasons for asking. She answered him with a simple shake of her head.

"Hmmm. You're quite certain Z'beryl told you nothing of the weapon?" Kymil pressed.

"Nothing at all," Arilyn confirmed sadly. She brightened and added, "Mother did teach me to fight, though. I'm very good." She stated the last comment with a child's artless candor.

"Are you indeed? We shall see."

Before Arilyn could draw another breath, a slender sword gleamed in the swordsmaster's hand. Almost of its own accord, her sword hissed free of its scabbard, and Arilyn met the elf's first lighting thrust with a two-handed parry.

An intense emotion flooded Kymil's black eyes, but before Arilyn could put a name to the *quessir*'s reaction, his angular face was again inscrutable.

"Your reflexes are good," he commented in an even tone. "That two-handed grip, however, has its limitations."

As if to prove his point, Kymil drew a second weapon from his belt, this one a long, slender dagger. He lunged toward Arilyn, feinting with the dagger as he brought his sword around and down in an overhead strike. With instinctive grace, Arilyn leaped aside, avoiding the dagger thrust as she easily turned aside Kymil's blade with her sword.

The *quessir*'s eyebrows rose, more in speculation than surprise. He spun his sword around once in a gleaming circle, and then again. Before the second cycle was completed, he thrust toward Arilyn with his dagger. Although the child seemed intrigued by the twirling sword, she was not distracted by it and her moonblade flashed forward to block the dagger. Kymil withdrew, dancing back several paces and lowering his weapons a bit, but Arilyn did not relax her defensive position. She remained in a partial crouch, eyes alert and both hands gripping the ancient sword.

Excellent, Kymil applauded silently. The child showed not only a natural instinct for fighting, but the beginnings of good judgment. Still testing, he advanced again and showered a flurry of blows upon her, alternating with sword and dagger in an intricate pattern that had confounded many a skilled and seasoned adversary. Arilyn met each strike, a feat made more remarkable by her persistent use of that two-handed grip.

Speed she certainly had, Kymil mused, but what of strength? The elf tucked his dagger back into his belt and raised his sword high, holding it firmly with both hands. He slashed down with considerable force, fully expecting the blow to knock Arilyn's sword from her hands. Her weapon flashed down in a semi-circle and came up to meet Kymil's strike. The blades clashed together hard enough to send sparks into the night, but the young half-elf's grip on her sword did not falter. Satisfied, Kymil stepped back from the fight.

Still holding his weapon at the ready, he slowly circled the child, studying her as if seeking some weakness. What he saw pleased him immeasurably.

Z'beryl's half-elf daughter stood about three inches short of six feet. That was tall for a moon elf female, but the child's gawky frame was slender and well-formed. Her strength and agility would have been exceptional even in a full elf. And she was, as she had said, very good. Yes, the child had unmistakable promise.

What was most important of all to the weapons master was that Arilyn had drawn the sword and lived, which meant that the magic weapon had chosen to honor Z'beryl's heir. As Kymil noted the extraordinary spirit that shone in the child's clear, gold-flecked eyes, it occurred to him that the sword had chosen well. Kymil Nimesin had come to the temple gardens expecting to find a pathetic halfbreed, but here before him, in raw and unlikely form, stood a fledgling hero.

Keenly aware of Kymil's scrutiny, Arilyn turned with the circling elf, always facing him as she held her sword in a defensive position. Exhilaration flowed through her veins, and a fierce joy lit her eyes as she anticipated renewed battle.

Although Arilyn had grown up with a sword in her hand, she had never faced such an opponent as this. Neither had she wielded such a sword. More than anything, she wanted the match to continue. Impulsively she lunged forward, trying to draw Kymil. He easily parried her strike, then he stepped back away from her and sheathed his weapon.

"No, that is enough for now. Your spirit is commendable, but unnecessary swordplay in the temple garden would be unseemly." He extended his hand. "May I see the moonblade now?"

Although disappointed by the *quessir*'s refusal to continue the match, Arilyn sensed that she had passed some sort of test. Swallowing a triumphant smile, she took the sword by its tip and offered it hilt-first to the master.

Kymil shook his head. "Sheath it first."

Puzzled, she did as she was told. She slid the sword into the scabbard, then removed her sword belt and passed it to the gold elf.

Kymil examined the weapon carefully. He studied the runes on the scabbard for a long moment before he turned his attention to the hilt of the sword, gently running his fingers over the large, empty oval indentation just below the blade's grip.

"It will need a new stone to replace the missing one." He raised an inquiring brow. "The balance is slightly off, I imagine?"

"Not that I noticed."

"You will, as your training progresses," he assured her.

"Training?" A score of questions tumbled through Arilyn's mind and flashed across her face, but Kymil waved her curiosity aside with an impatient hand.

"Later. First, tell me what you can about your father."

The elf's request shocked Arilyn into silence. It had been many years since she had allowed herself the luxury of thinking about her father. As a small child she had constructed elaborate fantasies, but in truth she knew virtually nothing about the circumstances of her birth. Although elves as a rule gave great importance to their heritage, Z'beryl had always stressed that family background was less important than individual merit. Arilyn accepted this unorthodox view as best she could, but at the moment she wished desperately for some grand paternal history to tell Kymil Nimesin. Arilyn knew how important such things were to the lineage-proud gold elves.

She replied carefully, "You may have noticed that I'm a half-elf. My father was human."

"Was?"

"Yes. When I was much younger, I used to ask my mother about him, but it always made her so sad that I stopped. I've always assumed that my father is dead."

"What about Z'beryl's family?" Kymil pressed. Arilyn's only response was a derisive sniff. The *quessir* raised one golden eyebrow. "I take it you know of them?"

"Very little." Arilyn's chin came up proudly. They had wanted no part of her, and she would claim no part of them. "I never saw any of them before Mother's funeral, and I never expect to see any of them again."

"Oh?"

Kymil's interest was obvious, but Arilyn merely shrugged aside his question. "The only thing they wanted of me was the sword. I still can't understand why they didn't just take it."

The gold elf permitted himself a sneer. "They couldn't. This is a moonblade, a hereditary sword that can be wielded by one person alone. Z'beryl left the moonblade to you, and it has honored her choice."

"It has? How do you know that?"

A wry expression settled about the elf's features. "You drew the sword and you still live," he said succinctly.

"Oh."

Kymil held the sheathed moonblade out to Arilyn with an almost deferential gesture. "The sword has chosen, and in choosing it has set you apart. No one but you can wield it or even handle the sheathed weapon without your consent. From this night until the moment of your death, you cannot be parted from the weapon."

"So the sword and I are a team?" she asked hesitantly, eyeing the weapon that Kymil held out to her.

"In a manner of speaking, yes. Its magic is yours alone."

"Magic?" Arilyn reclaimed the sword and belted it on gingerly, as if she expected the thing to shapechange at any moment. "What can it do?"

"Without knowing the specific history of this blade, I cannot tell," Kymil replied, watching with approval as Arilyn drew the sword and studied it with new interest, her momentary fear of the blade forgotten. "No two moonblades are alike."

She glanced up. "There are more of them?"

"Yes, but they are quite rare. Each blade has a unique and complex history, for the sword's magic develops and grows as each wielder invests their moonblade with a new power."

Excitement lit the half-elf's face. "So I can add a new magic power to the sword, too? Whatever I like?"

"I'm afraid not," Kymil said, pointing to the oval indentation beneath the blade's grip. "Your sword lacks the enspelled moonstone that acts as a conduit between wielder and weapon. All magical powers come from the wielder, pass through the stone, and are eventually absorbed by the sword itself."

"Oh."

The gold elf smiled faintly. "Do not be so disappointed, child. All the established powers of the moonblade are yours to command."

"Like what?" she demanded, intrigued.

Kymil's black eyes drifted shut. He shook his head and breathed a gentle sigh of resignation. "I can see that you will be a demanding pupil," he murmured. "Since you have no one else, I propose to train you myself, if this is what you wish."

Delighted, Arilyn blurted out, "Oh, yes!" The next instant her face fell. "But how? The Academy of Arms won't accept me."

"Nonsense." Suddenly brisk in manner, Kymil waved away that barrier with a flick of one long-fingered hand. "You already show more skill and promise than many of their finest students. The humans, in particular, are at best capable of learning no more than the rudiments of the fighting arts. It would be a welcome change to have a worthy student. And Z'beryl's daughter . . ." The elf's voice trailed off as he considered the possibilities.

Not completely reassured, Arilyn regarded the much scuffed toe of her boot. "It will be several years before I reach the age when half-elves can be accepted—"

"That will not be an issue," Kymil broke in, and his tone indicated that the matter was settled. "You are an *etriel* under my tutelage. That is all the academy will require."

Arilyn's head snapped up in surprise. Her eyes widened with awe at what Kymil had said and what the statement had implied. Then her shoulders squared, and with a quick decisive move she sheathed her magic weapon. She was no longer a half-elven orphan, child of an unknown father. She was an *etriel*, a noble elf-sister. Kymil Nimesin had said so.

"Very well, then," Kymil concluded brusquely, "it's settled. You need only take the pledge of apprenticeship. Draw your sword, if you will, and repeat after me the words I speak."

Overwhelmed but excited, Arilyn drew the moonblade. On a sudden whim, she stepped to one side of the statue and there sank to her knees; she would take this pledge at the foot of the elven goddess, as befitted an *etriel*. Grasping the moonblade with both hands, she extended the sword before her and raised her eyes to the master, waiting expectantly for the words of the pledge.

Kymil's only response was a sharp intake of breath. Filled with uncertainty, Arilyn rose to her feet, but the gold elf withdrew from her, his eyes locked on her moonblade.

Arilyn looked down. In her hands, the sword was beginning to glow with a faint blue light. The light grew brighter until, like a live thing, it wandered from the sword, touching the mists and setting them swirling, wraithlike, around the elves. As the stunned pair watched, the seeking mists turned here and there as if confused. The mists finally reached the statue, bringing an azure blush to the face of the goddess.

In the back of her mind, Arilyn began to separate a distinct note from the jangle of her emotions. Whether it felt more like cold energy or the presence of some strange entity she could not say, but it was a force that was both inside her and around her. The force grew until the garden shone blue with its light and her senses hummed with its power. Was this what magic felt like? It was frightening and foreign, yet it was as much a part of her as her sword arm. Shaken, Arilyn threw down the blade.

Instantly the garden was slammed into darkness, a darkness relieved only by the mist-veiled moon and the rapidly fading glow of the moonblade. "What was that?" Arilyn asked in an awed whisper. "Where did it go?"

Kymil returned to her side. "I do not know," he admitted. "There is much mystery about the moonblade."

Arilyn reached up with tentative fingers to touch the stone hand that lay over the goddess's heart. It seemed to her that a bit of the blue light lingered there.

"Come now," admonished Kymil, and his brisk tone banished the sense of awe that held Arilyn in thrall. "Do not let this incident frighten or distract you. I'm sure an explanation will come to both of us in due time. We will discover the moonblade's abilities together. You have talent and an extraordinary inheritance; I can give you skills and a worthy cause. Now, shall we proceed with the oath?"

To have Kymil Nimesin as teacher and mentor! Arilyn nodded eagerly took up her sword once more. The light in Arilyn's blue eyes outshone that of the fading moonblade as she repeated the words of the ritual.

Two

 "Oh, this is rich! This is one for my memoirs, that's sure and certain. The Harpers' pet assassin, coming to *me* for advice!" The old man cackled with delight, clinging to the edge of his writing table as he rocked back and forth in his chair, caught up in a delirium of wheezing mirth.

His enjoyment of the situation did not at all endear him to his visitor. Hands clenched at her side, Arilyn Moonblade gritted her teeth and waited for the retired Zhentarim agent to have done with his amusement. In her opinion, any encounter with the Zhentarim should be handled with a sword, not with diplomacy and bargaining. The Dark Network was devoted to the gods of evil as well as to the individual and collective greed of its members, and this man was a particularly unsavory specimen. The moonblade at Arilyn's side fairly hummed with silent indignation, echoing her opinion precisely. Besides, the man's taunt had struck her a little too close to home.

The half-elven adventurer had little choice but to endure

the cackling fool, since he possessed information that she was unlikely to get elsewhere. She waited calmly, eyeing the old man with a well-concealed revulsion. His wrinkled skin had an unhealthy grayish hue, and his gaunt limbs and bloated belly made him look very like an oversized spider. He was spiderlike in character, as well, and every time Arilyn looked at him, she was surprised anew to see that he did not possess the standard-issue eight legs of his kind. His lair was an appropriate setting, a low-beamed dark room over a tavern, festooned by dust webs and enlivened only by the dim light of a lantern and the rising odor of dinner cooking—liver and onions would be Arilyn's guess. Where the man spent his ill-gotten wealth was immediately apparent; he had literary pretensions and was engaged in writing a massive tome. Piles of expensive parchment littered his writing table, which shook under the assault of his laughter.

Finally the old man wound down to a chuckle and wiped his streaming eyes. Still beaming, he motioned to the chair next to his writing table. "Sit down, sit down. Make yourself comfortable, and let's talk shop."

Arilyn resented his cozy inference. The man had also been an assassin in his day, but she had nothing in common with this vile human. She perched on the edge of the offered chair and said in a formal tone, "You've received our communications, and I trust you understand the situation."

"More or less." The man raised one shaggy eyebrow. "Seems like a lot of trouble to go through for a bunch of religious trinkets."

"Priceless artifacts, sacred to the goddess Sune," she corrected.

"Suddenly the Harpers are overcome with devotion to the goddess of beauty, eh? When did this come about?"

"The artifacts were stolen from an envoy of Sune's church, and the clerics with him were murdered."

"So? These things happen." The man shrugged.

His attitude raised Arilyn's ready temper to dangerously near its boiling point. She had been in the search party that had discovered the twisted bodies, and the memory banished her halfhearted commitment to diplomacy. "Of course, the loss of innocent lives is a trivial matter," she said with venomous irony, "but the Church of Sune would very much like to get the artifacts back."

"Innocent lives or not, this isn't the type of pie Harpers generally poke their fingers into," the Zhentishman pointed out with sarcasm of his own. "Recovering stolen property? Come on, now. It's not lofty enough by half."

That much was true, Arilyn agreed silently. The Harpers sponsored noble causes seemingly at random, chosen through some mysterious process to which Arilyn was not privy. This time, however, she knew exactly what the Harpers' purpose was. The previous year, the kingdoms of the Heartlands had united in a crusade to stop a barbarian invasion. This crusade, although successful, had left the Heartlands politically unsettled and had, ironically, strengthened the position of the Zhentarim stationed at Darkhold, their mountain fortress. To these issues the Harpers now addressed themselves.

"As you no doubt know, the Zhentarim has a one-year treaty with the local government. The year's almost up, but for a time Darkhold's raiding parties can strike without fear of harassment or reprisal. Fortunately," Arilyn said wryly, "the Harpers don't answer to the local government. The Church of Sune has no recourse through the usual channels, so like many other victims of the raids, they turned to the Harpers for help."

The old Zhentishman grinned and leaned back in his chair. He tapped out a jaunty rhythm on his table with knotted, ink-stained fingers. "Of course. So the Harpers are sending a highly skilled assassin to infiltrate Darkhold, politely ask for Sune's property back, stay to share afternoon tea with the locals, and sneak back out. That sound about right?"

"I generally don't drink tea," Arilyn said with a touch of grim humor, "but you've got the basic idea."

"Aha. Now that the formalities are out of the way, why don't you tell me what you're really planning."

"To retrieve the stolen artifacts."

Another rheumy chuckle grated from the old man. "Stubborn wench, aren't you? All right, we'll play it your way. What unlucky bastard *has* these artifacts?"

Arilyn hesitated for a long moment before answering. There were rumors of bad blood between this man and the person she sought, and she'd been advised that this informant would relish an opportunity to even the score. Selling out a former comrade was inconceivable to her, yet she knew that it was a fairly routine practice among the Zhentarim. Indeed, the man before her looked as though he would gladly sell his own mother to an Ulgarthian harem.

"Well?" he prompted.

"Cherbill Nimmt," she said grudgingly.

The Zhentishman let out a slow whistle. "Now I'm beginning to see what's what. We used to run together some, Nimmt and me, when he was just starting out. If ever a man needed killing, it's him. Nasty piece of work. And coming from me, that's saying something," he noted with a perverse pride. The old assassin reflected for a moment on the pleasant prospect of his former friend's death before he concluded with a touch of regret, "Still and all, I don't suppose killing Nimmt's worth dying over."

"I don't intend to do either. I have been instructed to barter with him for the stolen items, no more."

The sarcastic look that the man threw Arilyn clearly stated that he didn't consider her denial worthy of comment. "Clerics of Sune are chosen for their beauty, aren't they? I imagine Nimmt and his men had a good time before they wiped out the envoy." A nostalgic look oozed onto the man's face. "Nimmt could be good company on a raid. I remember the time we—"

Arilyn raised her hand, cutting the man off before he could journey too deeply into the swamp of his memories. "You were about to sell me some information about the fortress."

"For the right price, I'll sell anything."

Arilyn took the cue. She produced a bag of gold from the folds of her cloak and tossed it to him. The informant caught the bag with amazing dexterity and hefted it in a practiced hand. "This is about half the agreed-upon price," he noted.

"It's exactly half," she told him. "You'll get the rest upon my safe return."

"Safe," he repeated with scathing emphasis. "Sneaking into Darkhold and facing down a man like Nimmt is no way to insure your old age. No, I want the rest of the gold upon the conclusion of your mission, whether you're dead or alive."

"If I agree, what will stop you from contacting your old friends at Darkhold?" Arilyn shook her head. "No, the original deal stands. I risk my life on your information, and you risk half your fee on my chance of success."

The old Zhentish assassin considered this, then shrugged. "All right. There's not much call for this information, so I might as well take what I can get for it. Let's get down to work." He fumbled through a stack of papers on his desk and drew out several hand-drawn maps.

Maps! Arilyn leaned closer for a better look, taking care to keep her face impassive. Any sign of excitement would surely raise the man's price. She had not expected to find maps of the fortress. Her secret elation mounted as the man talked. She could see why he commanded such enormous fees. Carefully and in great detail he discussed the layout of the fortress, outlined its defenses, discussed the habits and the timetables of the various factions and leaders. As he talked, Arilyn began to formulate a plan. After an hour with the old man, all that remained to her was figuring a way into the keep's parameters.

As if he read her mind, the informant stopped talking and looked up at her. "Here's your first big problem," he said, tracing a broad oval around the edge of the map with one gnarled finger. "This line here represents the cliffs that surround the Vale of Darkhold. Solid granite, anywhere from sixty to one hundred feet high, and sheer as a city wall. Not an easy climb. To make it worse, slaves keep the cliffs completely clear of bushes, grass, you name it. There's no cover at all.

"Now this," he continued, pointing to a straight line at the western end of the cliffs, "is the perimeter wall, and this mark here is the gate. It's the only safe way into the valley, but don't even bother thinking about it. It's too well-guarded. No one comes over or through that wall unless Sememmon, Master of Darkhold, wants them to. Got that?" He looked at her expectantly.

Arilyn nodded. "Go on."

"The fortress itself sits in the middle of this valley. Nothing much on the valley floor except a few acres of trees over here. There's a stream, but it's full of rocks and none too deep. Can't swim up without getting shredded or spotted. It's not going to be easy to sneak up to the castle." He paused to let his words sink in, then added slyly, "As it turns out, though, I have just the thing. For the right price, of course."

Without waiting for her reply, he hauled himself out of his chair and hunched over a brass-banded chest. He flipped open the lid and, after a few moments of rummaging, he pulled out a glittering black cape. Arilyn caught her breath. It was a *piwafwi*, a magic cape of invisibility created by the evil drow elves. How did this man get hold of such a rare and ferociously guarded treasure?

"Nice, isn't it?" he said, turning the cape this way and that to catch and reflect the dim lamplight. "Wear this, and you'll have clear sailing right up to the fortress."

"Isn't Darkhold protected by spells that alert the guards to such magic?" she hedged, eyeing the dark cape with a mixture of fascination and repugnance.

The old assassin resumed his seat, draping the cape over his lap. "They have some wards, but nothing that'll spot this. Lord Sememmon doesn't expect any trouble from the drow. This beauty here will get you into the fortress." He smiled evilly. "It got the original owner in, right enough. A drow female. The cape's magic doesn't seem to work *inside* Darkhold, though. I caught her sneaking around in the arsenal. Whether she was a spy or a thief I didn't bother to ask, but I kept her around for a bit. Hard to kill, those drow. I like an elf, now and then, and this one had real spice to her."

He paused, reflected, then reached across the table for his

lantern and turned up the flame to get a better look at his visitor. Twenty five years of adventuring lay lightly upon the half-elven woman, and her lack of battle scars gave testament to her uncanny skill with a sword. Arilyn Moonblade possessed the fresh beauty of a woman still south of her twentieth winter, but the informant knew her age to be almost twice that. Her angular elven features were softened by her human blood, and her slender form looked deceptively fragile. Delicate and deadly, she was; a combination that would make her a favorite in any brothel in Faerun. His familiarity with such establishments lent authority to his judgment. Old as he was, his gaze swept over Arilyn and took in every detail with lascivious precision.

"Hmmm. You're a gray, aren't you?" he asked, noting that her pale, almost white skin was touched with blue along her high sharp cheekbones and pointed ears.

"I am a moon elf, yes," Arilyn corrected.

"Gray elf" was a derogatory term when used by a human or a dwarf, and a deadly insult from the lips of another elf. Oblivious to the slight he had just given her, the man continued to examine Arilyn. "A half-gray at that. Oh, well. Half an elf is better than none, I always say," he noted with a leer. "After we're done here, maybe you'd like to—"

"No," Arilyn said quickly. The lecherous expression on the man's loathsome face raised her bile. After his comment about her lineage, she wouldn't have had anything do to with him even if he'd been as handsome and virtuous as the elflord Erlan Duirsar.

"Your loss." He shrugged, then held up the *piwafwi* again. "Do you want the cape, or not?"

Arilyn hesitated. She had assumed many identities in her career, and on one occasion she'd had to disguise herself as a dark elf to join a renegade band of drow mercenaries. It was not a pleasant memory. The drow, if possible, were worse than the Zhentarim. Once the assignment was over, it had taken her hours to wash the ebony stain from her skin and days to banish the pervasive sense of evil from her soul.

"Squeamish?" he taunted.

"Not really. I'm just wondering how you can part with such a sentimental token," she said coldly.

The Zhentishman responded with a grin. "Why not? I've got some real interesting battle scars to remember her by."

"Ten gold pieces for the cape?" Arilyn asked, cutting off the old man before he could regale her with more of his vile anecdotes. The mention of money brought him right around.

"Ten? Huh! Not likely. Twenty pieces, and make it platinum."

"Five platinum," Arilyn counteroffered.

"Ten."

"Done." The money and the cape changed hands, and Arilyn quickly tucked the garment into her bag before the lantern's light could further erode it. She noted that the *piwafwi*'s luster had already dimmed in the short time it had been out of the dark trunk. The cape would probably disintegrate completely with the coming of dawn, and its magic had waned long before the death of the dark elf who once wore it. Arilyn had learned that drow magical items faded outside of the Underdark, their subterranean world. She suspected that the informant knew this as well, judging from his small sly smile as he pocketed the ten platinum coins. He looked immensely pleased with himself, probably picturing the look her face would likely hold when the expensive cape dissolved into gray smoke.

Arilyn intentionally allowed the old man this small triumph. He took pride in the quality of the information he sold, but he also felt a compulsion to cheat his clients.

"By the way," he said expansively, "how do you plan to get into the fortress?" Arilyn raised a skeptical eyebrow, and he cackled again and waved a wizened hand. "You're right, you're right. If I were you, I wouldn't tell me, either. I suppose that concludes our business, unless, of course . . ." He let his words trail off suggestively.

Arilyn ignored him and pointed to one of the maps. "I need more information about this area. Can you list all the ways out of the basement level?"

"Sure, but why bother? I doubt you'll get that far."

Arilyn held her temper with difficulty. "Any secret doors? Passages? Or do I have to swim out through the midden?"

The Zhentishman scratched his chin thoughtfully. "Now that you mention it, I believe there *is* something that could be of use. It will cost you extra, of course." He picked up a pile of parchment and rifled through it until something caught his eye. He scanned a few pages of his manuscript, then nodded in satisfaction. "Ah, good. Very few people know about this door. I'd almost forgotten about it, myself."

"Well?"

He handed her a page of manuscript, and after she'd scanned it they discussed the escape route in detail. When she was satisfied, she handed him a few more coins and stood to leave. "Remember, you won't get the second half of your original fee until I return from Darkhold. Are you still confident of your advice?"

"I'll stand by my information," he proclaimed stoutly. He gave his last word a slight emphasis, barely stifling a grin as he glanced at the bag holding the doomed *piwafwi*.

He believes he's bested me, Arilyn noted, though she was pleased with that. Such a belief would enable him to save face in the light of her next move. She drew a rolled parchment from her belt and tossed it onto the table. "This is a letter describing our deal. My associates hold copies. If you sell me out, you die."

The Zhentishman laughed, albeit uneasily. "Harpers don't work that way."

Arilyn placed both hands on the writing table and leaned forward. "Remember, I'm not really a Harper," she said.

The threat was a bluff, but the old man appeared to give her words serious consideration. He picked up the bag of gold again, balancing it in his hand as if he were weighing the risk along with the promise of future payment.

In truth, Arilyn was an independent adventurer. She had been an oft-used agent for the Harpers for several years, but she had never been invited to join the Harpers' ranks. Many of her assignments came to her secondhand, through her mentor, Kymil Nimesin, for there were those in the secret organization who looked askance at the half-elf and her deadly reputation. As both Harper-friend and assassin she was an odd hybrid, but in encounters like the one in which she was presently involved, the combination gave her an edge. The informant eyed her warily, completely convinced that she would carry out her threat against him.

Finally he glanced again at the bag holding the drow cape, and broke into a grin. "Half-elf, half-Harper, eh? Nice title for a chapter of my memoirs."

The comment stung Arilyn, even coming from such as he. "If you keep our bargain, you just might live long enough to finish that chapter," she said. Not wanting to cast any shadow upon the Harpers, she clarified her original threat. "If I die through my own error, you merely lose your fee. If I am betrayed, copies of the letter will be sent to Cherbill Nimmt as well as the elven mage who rules as Darkhold's second-in-command. I understand that Lady Ashemmi is no friend of yours, and I imagine that neither she nor Nimmt will be amused to learn of this transaction."

The informant shook his head and wheezed out another chuckle. "Not bad, not bad," he admitted. "With a mind like that, you might just make it through Darkhold after all. I must say it's refreshing to see the Harpers develop a devious streak."

"The cause is the Harpers', but my methods are my own," Arilyn said firmly.

"Whatever." He waved a hand in dismissal. "Don't worry about the information I gave you. It's good. Go along, and have fun infiltrating the fortress."

Since Arilyn could think of no appropriate response, she gathered up the maps and with a deep sense of relief left the old Zhentish spider alone in his lair.

The informant gazed after her for a long silent moment. "Half-elf, half-Harper," he murmured into the empty room, enjoying the sound of his phrase. He nibbled reflectively on a hangnail for several moments, then with a flourish he drew his quill from the ink pot and began to write. This would be one of the finest chapters in his memoirs, even if he did have to improvise a bit to come up with a satisfying ending.

Deep into the night the old man wrote, caught up in his own salacious imaginings. His lantern ran out of oil, but he lit the first of many candles and kept writing. It was nearly daybreak when his door swung open, noiselessly and unexpectedly. He looked up, startled, then his face relaxed into a leer. He lay down his quill and flexed his stiff fingers in anticipation.

"Welcome, welcome," he said to the approaching figure. "Changed your mind, I suppose? Well, that's fine. Come right on over to old Sratish, and I'll—"

The old man's invitation ended in a strangled gulp as two slender feminine hands closed around his neck. Frantically he tried to pry the hands loose, but his attacker was inhumanly strong. He threw himself back and forth, but the intruder hung on, her grip tightening. Within moments the informant's rheumy eyes bulged, and his mouth opened and closed like that of a fish gasping on the sand. Finally his spidery body slumped, lifeless, onto piles of parchment.

The intruder casually pushed the body to the floor and sat down at the writing table. She picked up the smudged page, quickly scanning the still-damp writing by the light of a single, rapidly diminishing candle. Quiet as a shadow, she rose and carried the candle and several pages of parchment to the room's fireplace. The manuscript fluttered onto the hearth, and she stooped and held out the stub of burning candle. The edges of one page turned brown, then curled in upon itself as the flame caught and spread. The shadowy figure stood and watched as the final chapter of the old man's memoirs turned to ash.

Three

The merchant caravan made camp for the night, but underlying the usual bustle of activity was a deep spirit of unease. On route from Waterdeep to Cormyr, the caravan was camping in the shadow of Darkhold.

It was not unheard of for lawful merchant trains to stop at the Zhentarim stronghold; after all, business was business. Openly trading with the Dark Network was vastly preferable to defending a caravan against it. Since raiding was a random business and supplies had to be maintained, the outpost fortress routinely traded for whatever items they could not steal.

The merchants had been given every assurance of safety and fair trade, but no one in the caravan would rest easily that night. Peace of mind was impossible; surrounded on all sides by sheer rock cliffs and a heavily fortified wall, they were effectively trapped inside the Vale of Darkhold with the thousand or so members of the Zhentarim-sponsored contingent. The caravan's watch had been tripled, but so apparently had the guard on the perimeter wall above them.

Members of the merchant caravan who did not draw watch also stayed awake long into the night. Tensions were channeled into games of chance, hard drinking punctuated by loudly told tales of bravado, and furtive, frantic trysts.

In a small tent at the very edge of the camp, a lone figure waited impatiently for the others to sleep. Hours of noisy revelry passed, and after a time she could delay no longer. Arilyn Moonblade gathered her supplies and slipped away into the night.

Years of practice and an innate elven grace enabled Arilyn to move without sound, and the moonless night cloaked her in darkness. The half-elf slowly made her way toward the fortress, using the route she had painstakingly mapped. Except for a few acres of trees, the valley floor had little natural cover. Arilyn used whatever was available, darting between heaps of boulders and crawling through scrubby brush. Finally she reached the copse of trees just west of the Postern Gate Tower. Before her lay a moat, and beyond that the massive outer wall of the fortress.

The old Zhentish informant had told her most emphatically that she should not attempt to swim the moat. It was full of dangerous creatures, including small fish with razor-sharp teeth. A school of these fish could strip the flesh from a horse in a matter of minutes. Across the deceptively still waters of the moat, the fortress loomed against the starless night, its black towers thrusting upward. Crouched in the shadow of the trees, Arilyn took several items from her bag and prepared to enter Darkhold.

Several weeks of hectic planning had gone into this assignment. By now Arilyn knew so much about the fortress that she felt somehow sullied by the knowledge. Built by evil giants centuries before, the castle had in turn housed dragons and an undead mage before being conquered and inhabited by the Zhentarim. Evil seemed to permeate the very structure, as if it had been mixed into the mortar.

Arilyn assembled a small crossbow, then fitted to it a most

unusual arrow. Specially designed for this assignment, the arrow was very much like a child's toy, ending in a cup rather than a point. Filling the cup was spider-sap, a powerful adhesive alchemically derived from the coating of giant spider webs. She took careful aim at the Visitors' Tower. Her arrow flew, trailing behind it a length of gossamer rope, and found its mark just below the roof of the tower. Arilyn pulled hard on the rope, a lightweight but unbreakable cord spun from silk. Satisfied that it would hold, she swung over the moat, released the rope, and landed lightly at the base of the wall.

The Visitors' Tower was part of the outer wall and often was used, as it was tonight, to house guests considered too dangerous to allow in the castle proper. There were guards, of course, but they were stationed inside the fortress and were concerned with monitoring the visitors' passage between the tower and the courtyard. Arilyn again grasped the rope and began to climb the tower, hauling herself up hand over hand.

Near the third and top level of the tower was her goal: a window covered with rusted iron bars. Arilyn reached it, pulled herself up onto the stone sill, and took out a small flask. Working carefully, she daubed a bit of distilled black dragon venom on the tops and bottoms of two of the bars. A faint, corrosive hiss filled the air as the powerful acid ate away the rusted metal. Arilyn wiggled the bars free and carefully wiped the remaining acid from the edges, then she squeezed in through the window. She stuck a bit of acacia tree gum on each end of the bars and replaced them in the window.

As she had anticipated, she was in a narrow corridor that circled the entire tower. This level housed the dining quarters, and at this hour the only sounds were a few random clangs from the kitchen. With a shudder of distaste, Arilyn shrugged on her disguise: the dark purple clerical robes belonging to devotees of the evil god, Cyric. She pulled up the cowl of the robe to obscure her face and headed for the tower's spiral staircase that led down and out to the courtyard.

According to her maps, the floor below held the visitors' quarters. Arilyn made her way downward as swiftly as she dared, hoping to avoid confrontation with any of her "fellow clerics." Her luck held until she reached the lowest level. A short, stubby man stood at the foot of the stairs, scowling up at her. His purple cowl was thrown back, and on his forehead was painted a dark sun with a glowering skull in the center.

"Simeon! It's about time. Hurry up or we'll miss the procession," he snapped.

Arilyn only nodded, keeping her head low as she motioned for him to proceed her into the courtyard. The cleric's eyes narrowed.

"Simeon?" A note of suspicion had crept into his voice, and one hand inched toward the clerical symbol that rested over his heart. Arilyn recognized the beginning of a spell. She leaped down the last few steps, kicking out with one booted foot.

Her foot connected hard with the man's midsection, and they both fell to the floor in a tangle of purple robes. Arilyn rose to her feet, but the cleric stayed down, bent double and completely winded. She delivered a second well-placed kick to the side of his neck, and the cleric went completely limp.

With a sigh of frustration, Arilyn considered her situation. She could hardly leave the unconscious man there for others to trip over, yet, as he had said, she would be late for the procession if she tarried long. Three wooden doors led out of the stairwell; quickly she cracked one open. Beyond lay a storage chamber filled with large traveling chests. Arilyn slipped inside, and with the tip of a knife she broke open the lock on the nearest chest. It was full of robes, and she tossed some out to make room for the cleric. She returned to the stairwell and, grabbing the fallen man under the arms, dragged him into the storage room. She dumped him into the chest and lowered the heavy lid. Readjusting her cowl low over her face, she returned to the stairwell and opened the door to the courtyard.

The rhythm of a dark and unholy chant greeted her. Just beyond the door, a vast column of priests passed by the tower on their way to the castle's main entrance. Arilyn folded her hands into her sleeves and lowered her head, assuming the posture of a novitiate and falling in behind the chanting, swaying company.

The clerics gathered to celebrate the Sacrifice of Moondark, a ceremony honoring Cyric, God of Death, Destruction, and Assassination. A powerful new deity, Cyric had been an evil and ambitious mortal. He'd received godhood, taking the place of Bane, Bhaal, and Myrkul, three foul gods who were destroyed during the Time of Troubles. Although he was not universally worshiped by the followers of the three defunct gods, Cyric worship was rapidly gaining ground among the Zhentarim and their allied priesthoods. Since Cyric had few supporters outside the Zhentarim, his priests had elected to meet within the protection of Darkhold. A large gathering of such clerics in any other setting would have been about as welcome as a barbarian invasion.

Arilyn had learned of the Moondark Ceremony months earlier, and it provided her the ideal time and method for infiltrating Darkhold. Most people—even the Zhentarim—feared the priesthood of Cyric and tended to give the priests a wide berth.

The half-elf had worn many disguises and she had become reconciled to appearing to be what she was not, but her skin crawled under the dark purple robes of an unholy priesthood. Nevertheless she moved smoothly along with the formation, pretending to join in the chanting that signaled the beginning of the profane service.

Through the front gate they marched, into the vast entrance hall and toward an ancient shrine. Caught up in the chant and overawed by their first glimpse of the famous temple, the clerics did not notice that one figure broke away from the formation and slipped toward the basement stairway.

* * * * *

Captain Cherbill Nimmt considered himself a reasonable man, but there were limits to his patience. "You came here expecting to just walk away with this treasure?" he growled, brandishing the large leather sack he clutched in one fist.

The "priest" raised an eyebrow, a gesture that was barely perceptible under the deep cowl of the dark purple robe. "Hardly. You set a price on these items; I agreed to meet it," Arilyn said in a husky whisper, doing her best to make herself sound like a young man. She reached into a pocket of her robe for a small bag, which she tossed onto the stone floor.

It landed in front of Cherbill Nimmt with a satisfying chink, and he licked his lips in anticipation of his long-awaited reward. Several months earlier he had been heading a patrol in the Sunrise Mountains north of Darkhold when he'd acquired the goods he now hoped to sell: sacred vessels encrusted with gems, a perfect rose that could not die, and a crystal figurine that greeted every dawn with songs of praise to Sune, goddess of beauty. The last item was, to say the least, a damned nuisance.

"That's filled with gold coins, I hope," Cherbill said. He nudged the sack with his foot and let out a studied yawn of boredom.

"Better," Arilyn answered. "The bag is half full of gold coins, half of Dragonsmere amber."

Surprise and greed washed over the soldier's florid face. He snatched up the bag and dumped the contents onto a large wooden packing crate. Bright coins skittered across the wood, some spilling unheeded onto the floor of the basement chamber. Cherbill dropped the sack of artifacts and gathered up the five pieces of amber, cradling them in his meaty fingers. They were large pieces, the rare dark color of sandflower honey, and artfully cut. Alone, each piece would ransom a Cormyrian lord.

Cherbill slipped the gems into his pocket and stooped to pick up the leather sack that lay beside him. A crafty smile split the soldier's face, and he jerked his head toward the heavy oak door. "Thank you very much. Now get out," he ordered.

"Not until I get what I came for."

"Like all priests, you're a fool," Cherbill said scornfully. "You should have gone when I gave you the chance. What's to stop me from killing you and keeping everything?"

Arilyn reached into a slit in the side of her purple robe and drew out the moonblade. "This?"

A hoot of derisive laughter broke from the man, and his own sword hissed from its scabbard. Wearing a confident sneer, he attacked.

Arilyn sidestepped Cherbill's lunge with contemptuous ease and parried the next several attacks. The soldier changed his strategy. At least five inches taller and one hundred pounds heavier than his opponent, Cherbill tried to overwhelm his slender foe with sheer physical strength. His heaviest blows were turned aside, and soon the soldier's face began to betray exhaustion as well as the first icy touches of doubt.

"Who are you?" he gasped.

"Arilyn Moonblade," the half-elf declared firmly, abandoning the dry whisper of the cleric for her own clear, resonant alto. She pushed back the purple cowl and let Cherbill Nimmt see the battle gleam in her elven eyes.

"I was sent to recover the stolen artifacts. I was to *barter* for them," she said in a contemptuous voice. "Or do you prefer battle?" Using the two-handed grip that five years of study at the Academy of Arms had not changed, Arilyn raised the moonblade in challenge.

Cherbill seemed to recognize the name. He gulped audibly and let his sword clatter to the floor. "I have no interest in dying." He held up his hands in surrender, then nodded at the bag of artifacts. "Take what you came for and leave."

Arilyn studied him for a moment, her expression dubious. Honor prevented her from attacking an unarmed man, but neither did she trust him to let her go.

"Go ahead," he urged.

She slid her sword into its scabbard, then turned to pick up the bag. Cherbill Nimmt apparently did not know about an elf's peripheral vision, for he grinned in triumph and pulled a long, slender dagger from his belt. His expression said clearer than words that, yes, perhaps the stupid elf-wench could fight, but she was still no match for him. He lunged for her back.

Arilyn whirled and knocked the dagger out of Cherbill's hand in a lightning-quick movement. His jaw hung slack for an astonished moment, then firmed as he closed his eyes and prepared himself to receive the killing stroke.

"Arm yourself."

Her command stunned Cherbill into compliance. He stooped to retrieve his sword, then faced her warily.

"Why?" he asked simply. "If you're going to kill me, why not have done with it?"

"Why not indeed?" Arilyn said dryly. For a moment she wished that the Harpers were not quite so picky about certain matters. As her Zhentish informer had observed, if ever a man needed killing, it was this one. The Harpers were willing to discount her past adventures, but they'd made it clear that assassins—however noble their causes or honorable their methods—were frowned upon. For the most part, Arilyn honored the Harpers' wishes, but at the moment she did not regret that circumstances had again cast her in the role of honorable assassin.

"I did not choose to fight this battle," she told him. "But know this, Cherbill Nimmt of Darkhold: I intend to kill you in honor-bound combat. It is more than you deserve." She raised her sword to her forehead in a gesture of challenge.

Her words held the chilling quality of ritual. Trying to summon a defiant sneer, the soldier returned the salute and assumed a defensive position.

Her first attack was low. Cherbill parried it easily, and his confident grin returned. He beat at her blade, trying to back her against the wall, but Arilyn held her ground and turned aside his blows.

So intent was the soldier upon the battle that he did not see the faint blue light lining his opponent's sword. Arilyn, however, recognized the moonblade's danger warning and knew that she must end the fight. With her next stroke the sword opened Cherbill Nimmt's throat, and the man fell heavily to the floor.

Arilyn cleaned the glowing moonblade on the empty money sack, then sheathed it. Looking down at the dead soldier, she shook her head and muttered, "That's the way it should have been handled in the first place."

Her keen ears caught the ominous chink of armor in the hallway. Moving swiftly, Arilyn gathered up the fallen coins and retrieved the gemstones from the dead man's pockets. It did not occur to her to steal the money and jewels; since they were not needed to complete the deal, she would simply return them to the priesthood of Sune. Tying the heavy sack of magical items around her waist, she began to search for the secret door.

She and Cherbill Nimmt had agreed in advance to meet in this small storage chamber in the most remote corner of Darkhold's basement. Arilyn had suggested it because it boasted the little-known escape tunnel revealed to her by the retired Zhentish soldier. Cherbill had agreed to the location because it was as far from the guard post as possible.

"Over there! I heard something over this way," a guttural voice called. The heavy footsteps—ten men, Arilyn guessed—were very close.

Although Arilyn was half-elven, she had in full measure the elven ability to locate hidden doors. A faint outline surrounded several of the large moldy stones that formed the chamber wall. Falling to her knees, Arilyn ran her fingers around the irregularly shaped door. She found a minuscule latch in the cranny of a rock and pressed it. The door slid open.

Arilyn slipped into the darkness of the tunnel, pushing the stone door back into place. Behind her, she heard the puzzled oaths of the guard as they burst into the room and stumbled upon the body of Cherbill Nimmt. Turning her back on Darkhold, Arilyn started down the tunnel.

For several hundred feet, the grade sloped sharply down. It became so dark that even Arilyn's exceptional night vision could not penetrate the gloom. Aware that her infravision could discern only heat patterns, not the strange traps that her informant had promised, she reluctantly removed a small torch from her belt and struck tinder to it. As she'd expected, a flurry of tiny wings and high-pitched squeaks greeted the light.

"Bats," she muttered, waving the torch around her head to ward off the spooked creatures. Arilyn hated bats, but she would count herself fortunate if they were the only creatures with which she had to contend. The Zhentish informer had gleefully warned her to watch out for carrion crawlers. Twice the length of a man, these monsters looked like overgrown green cutworms. They generally fed upon carrion, but if food were scarce—and in this tunnel it probably would be—the crawler would attack live prey. Its armored body, clawed feet, and poisonous tentacles made it a fearsome foe. Come to think of it, Arilyn thought, bats really weren't all that bad.

She pressed on, brushing aside thick cobwebs as she went. The foul odors of mold and bat droppings surrounded her, and her feet crunched along on a moving carpet of small, hard-shelled creatures. Holding the torch high, Arilyn quickened her pace. She did not care to investigate the floor too closely.

Finally the grade began to slant upward. The tunnel curved sharply to the right, and Arilyn stopped short. Before her was a peculiar, vaguely familiar gate. The gate was shaped like a cone lying on its side with the wide end toward her, formed of many long strips of metal, each of which ended in a sharp point. Arilyn ran an experimental finger over the edge of one strip. When she drew her hand away, her finger dripped blood. So sharp was the edge that the cut had been completely painless.

Tentatively she put a foot on the bottommost strip. It bent under her weight, but sprang back into place the moment she removed her foot. Suddenly Arilyn understood the nature of the gate. It was a one-way door, functioning like one of the lobster traps she'd seen used off the coast of Neverwinter. That would explain why the only creatures in the tunnel were bats and insects. Nothing else could get through that lethal portal.

As she again tested the cone with her foot, Arilyn felt a flash of admiration for the simple effectiveness of the design. It kept intruders out of Darkhold, while providing an escape route for those careful enough to avoid being sliced into strings.

Holding the torch carefully to one side, she stepped into the oversized lobster trap, moving sideways with her feet set apart to depress enough razor-sharp strips to ensure safe passage. The trap bent with her as she inched carefully forward. Finally she ducked her head to avoid the tip of the cone and leaped free. The trap sprang back into place behind her with a vicious metallic snap.

From that point on the tunnel sloped upward. Arilyn encountered two more such gates, then the tunnel ended abruptly with a stone door of massive proportions. From the old informer's maps, Arilyn knew that the tunnel was part of the ancient stone quarry that lay to the southeast of Darkhold. From here giants had mined the original stone for the castle, and a few giants still inhabited parts of the quarry. The door before Arilyn was giant-built and giant-sized, far beyond her strength.

Unconcerned, Arilyn placed her flickering torch into a holder on the wall and ran her fingers over the stone door until she found what she sought. According to her sources, a series of coded runes was carved into the stone, giving the location of the hidden lock. The runes yielded a combination of numbers: four down, two to the right, three down, seven left. Arilyn's nimble fingers found a pattern of tiny holes on the doorjamb. Carefully counting to the correct one, she inserted a long, slender pick. The door swung open with the grating shriek of stone upon stone.

Arilyn stepped out, relieved to feel once again the open sky above her. She blinked several times to help her eyes adjust to the light. Although the night was moonless and overcast, it seemed bright after the blackness of the tunnel. She slipped her pick into a second hidden lock, and the massive door swung shut. So well constructed was the door that it blended perfectly with the rough granite cliffs surrounding the vale. Even with her elven ability to locate hidden doors, Arilyn was not sure she could find it again. With luck, she'd never have to try.

Content with her victory she headed back to her camp. She had no fear of pursuit from within the fortress, for the Zhentarim's mercenaries would surely assume that Cherbill Nimmt had fallen victim to some internal power struggle. It would probably not occur to them to look outside the fortress for the cause of the soldier's death.

Arilyn slipped into her tent shortly before daybreak, undetected by the restless watch. She barely managed to crawl into her bedroll before she fell into a dream-haunted slumber.

In another part of the merchant camp, Rafe Silverspur stirred in his sleep. A half-elven ranger and a fearless adventurer, Rafe had been hired to scout and to help protect the caravan. At his side slept a buxom woman, a smile still lighting her sleeping face and an empty mead jug lying on its side near her bedroll. Despite the prior evening's indulgences, the young ranger slept lightly, and Darkhold's unholy chanting echoed through his dreams.

Rafe muttered in his sleep and turned over. As he did, a slender figure entered the tent, moving silently as a shadow. Removing something from the depths of a dark cloak, the intruder took up the sleeping ranger's left hand, turned it, and pressed the small object into the palm.

A faint hiss filled the tent. Rafe's body stiffened, and his eyes flew open. The ranger's gaze fastened on his assailant. Even through the pain his eyes registered recognition. His lips moved as if to frame a desperate question, but no sound emerged.

The shadowy assailant held Rafe Silverspur fast as his body jerked convulsively. Finally Rafe's eyes rolled upward and he lay still. Amazingly the woman next to him slept undisturbed. Sparing her no more than a glance, the killer raised a hand to the victim's throat seeking a pulse. Satisfied that there was none, the dark figure checked one last detail of its handiwork.

In the palm of the dead ranger's hand, a brand glowed with faint blue light. Worked into the intricate design of the brand was a small harp and a crescent moon.

The symbol of the Harpers.

* * * * *

Night had fallen some time ago, and only the stars and an adventurer's finely honed sense of direction guided the solitary rider toward Evereska. The moon was high when the rider finally paused, dismounting at the bank of the River Reaching.

Arilyn Moonblade would have preferred to keep moving, but there was no question of fording the rapids at night. Since the morning of the previous day, the half-elf had put many miles between herself and the fortress of Darkhold. At this rate she could reach Evereska in a matter of days. In her eagerness to be home, she had pressed both herself and her horse, a gray mare of great speed and stamina, to the border of exhaustion.

Feeling a surge of guilt, Arilyn led her horse to the river for a drink. She spent a long time rubbing down the animal, then tethered it in the best grazing spot she could find.

Once the mare was comfortably settled, Arilyn built a fire and sat crosslegged in front of it. She had ridden like a demon throughout the day, as much to escape her own thoughts as to elude possible pursuit. Now, in the quiet of the starlit night, she could no longer avoid thinking about Rafe Silverspur's death.

After the ranger's body had been discovered, the merchant captain agreed with Arilyn that she and the caravan should part company. Since the half-elf was a known Harper agent, she was considered a target for the mysterious assassin and therefore a risk to the entire company. No one questioned her innocence. She and Rafe had spent much time together during the trip, and it was widely assumed that the two half-elves were lovers.

Sighing, Arilyn poked restlessly at the fire. She had done nothing to squelch those rumors, for they tended to discourage unwanted advances from other members of the merchant caravan. In truth, she and Rafe had shared only friendship. To the solitary half-elf, friendship was a rare gift indeed.

Arilyn glanced down at the only ring on her left hand. It gleamed faintly in the firelight, and she spread her fingers to look at it more closely. It was a simple ring, just a silver band engraved with the unicorn symbol of the goddess Mielikki, patron of rangers. She'd won the ring from Rafe in a game of dice, and she wore it now in his honor. It was symbolic of the friendship they'd shared, a camaraderie born of a shared road and the good-natured competition of a worthy opponent.

Dismayed at the unaccustomed sense of loneliness that plagued her, Arilyn busied herself with the tasks of setting up her simple camp. She unrolled her blanket and spread it before the fire, then took some dried fruit and travel biscuits from her bag and settled down to eat. As much as she disliked cooking, Arilyn usually ended a day of travel with a hot meal. Tonight, cooking for just one person didn't seem worth the trouble.

For almost a quarter of a century Arilyn had walked alone, well aware that an adventurer should have few ties. It had always seemed unfair to her to encourage someone to care, only to expose them to the dangers and potential heartache inherent in the life she had chosen. Even her friendships were few and cautious.

As Arilyn settled into her bedroll, she considered swearing an oath of solitude and chastity at the foot of Hannali Celanil's statue in Evereska. Or would such an oath be an affront to the elven goddess of beauty and romantic love? In her case, Arilyn noted with a wry grimace, the oath would be redundant. Perhaps she had no business at all being a devotee of that particular goddess.

Arilyn rolled over onto her back, lacing her fingers beneath her head as she pondered the matter.

Close relationships of any kind did not come easily to the half-elven. Their life cycles were out of sync with both humans and elves. Arilyn was nearing her fortieth winter. If she were human, she'd be approaching midlife. A moon elf her age would be barely out of childhood. It seemed to Arilyn that she'd spent her life being neither one thing nor the other, and even her alliance with the Harpers bore this out. Her services were valued, but her past as an "honorable assassin" had kept the secret organization from accepting her as a full-fledged member.

It would seem, however, that the Harper Assassin was not concerned with her lack of credentials. For some time Arilyn had suspected that she was a target. Wherever she turned, she felt unseen eyes upon her. She was skilled in tracking, but she had not been able to discern a trace of her foe. The Harper Assassin constantly dogged her path, and for months she had steeled herself for the confrontation that was sure to come.

As time went on, she'd changed her mind about the assassin's purpose. There had been so many deaths, each one coming closer to her. Arilyn had often expected that the assassin was deliberately and cruelly taunting her. The death of her friend Rafe left no doubt in her mind.

Gritting her teeth, Arilyn let out a long, hissing breath. She'd spent her life settling matters with a sword, and she hated to wait for this invisible assassin to play out his hand. Months of enforced inactivity had left her perpetually on edge. Whoever her foe was, he knew her well.

But who could this assassin be? She'd crossed swords with many over the past twenty-five years, and she had made her share of enemies. Those who had openly come out against her were dead, and although Arilyn racked her brain, she could not think of a live adversary who had the wit or skill to carry out such a drawn-out and devious revenge.

The night passed, and the moon sank toward the horizon, yet no answers came to the weary half-elf. In an effort to court sleep, Arilyn edged her thoughts toward more pleasant things. Soon she would reach Evereska, and home. There she could rest. Rest she needed badly, and not just from the rigors of travel. She was truly exhausted from grief, from the knowledge that a shadowy trail of death lay behind her, from the hidden eyes that watched her every move.

Even now she felt them upon her. There was no sound, no shadow, no indication that someone was watching her camp, but Arilyn felt a presence lurking beyond the reach of the campfire's embers. Her eyes flashed to her moonblade that lay beside her like a constant, vigilant companion. It gave her no sign of warning.

Arilyn had learned early in her career that the magic sword could alert her to danger. Working with her teacher, Kymil Nimesin, she had discovered that the moonblade could warn her in three different ways. It glowed with blue light when danger approached, and when danger was close-at-hand it hummed with a silent energy only she could sense. Even as she slept the sword kept guard. Many times she had awakened from a dream about approaching orcs or trolls to find her dream made reality. The dreamwarning was particularly handy, since she so often traveled alone.

Tonight, however, the sword was dark and silent. There was no danger on the riverbanks. Why, then, did she have such a persistent feeling of eyes upon her?

Four

The festival of Higharvestide was the social highlight of the month of Eleint. Known as The Fading, Eleint was nonetheless far from dull. As summer drew to a close and the days grew short and chill, autumn paid its dividend in the form of longer, revel-filled nights. Harvest festivals crowded the calendar; Waterdeep's economy was based on commerce rather than agriculture, but the wealthy Waterdhavians never overlooked any opportunity to throw a party.

They came out in full force, the noble merchants of Waterdeep. The members of the older generation considered the festival serious business. It was a time to assert their position in society, to upstage business competitors, to gather useful information and start potentially beneficial rumors, and to generally move from deal to deal. The younger set merely gathered to enjoy their unearned wealth with smug high spirits.

The joint effort of several noble families, the Higharvestide Ball was always a lavish affair. It was held in the House of Purple Silks, one of the city's largest and finest festhalls. Several hundred guests gathered in the vast main room, which was ablaze with the light of a thousand tiny lanterns that magically changed colors to match the tempo and mood of the dance music. In the center of the marble floor a large circle of dancers moved through the intricate patterns of a rondellere, and as they laughed and spun, their glittering jewels and silks reflected the colorshifting light like a vast kaleidoscope.

Other revelers enjoyed the buffet tables or helped themselves to the trays of delicacies circulated by a small horde of servants. No expense had been spared; tonight everything was of the finest quality available to the City of Splendors. Vases of rare hothouse flowers scented the air. The musicians were among the best in Faerun, and several small concerts were planned for the evening's entertainment. At the moment a consort of viols and woodwinds played for those who wished to dance, but lutanists and harpists were also scattered in remote corners and alcoves to set the proper mood for trysts.

One corner of the room—a corner very near a well-stocked bar—echoed with peal after peal of laughter. A merry group had gathered there around Danilo Thann, a favorite with the younger Waterdeep set.

The young man holding court in the center of the circle was dressed to the nines in an outfit designed to enhance his recently acquired image as a far-traveled man. He sported a broad-brimmed hat of green velvet, deliberately styled after the trademark hat of a famous Ruathym pirate, right down to the sweeping plumes. The dandy's soft, slouchy boots were like those favored by Sembian adventurers, but they were made of rare chimera leather, also dyed green. Finely embroidered dragons and griffons cavorted on his shirt of pale green Shou silk. There, however, the world-trotting theme ended. His jade green coat and trousers were of the latest local style, and a velvet cape in a matching shade swept dramatically to the floor. Several rings decorated his gesticulating hands, and a pendant with a large, square-cut emerald gleamed from his chest. Blond hair flowed over his shoulders, framing his animated face with shining, lovingly maintained waves.

Danilo Thann was a devoted dilettante as well as a fashion plate, renowned for his amusing but half-honed talents in music and magic. At the moment, he entertained his friends with a new magic trick.

"Dan, what ho! The wanderer has returned at last," called a voice behind Danilo, interrupting the would-be mage in midspell.

A chorus of cries met the new arrival. Splendidly attired in his family colors of red, silver, and blue, Regnet Amcathra strode into the circle of nobles. He and Danilo clasped hands with the gravity of warriors, then fell laughing into a backthumping hug.

"By Helm's eyes, you're a welcome sight," swore Regnet heartily when the pair broke apart. A boyhood friend as well as Danilo's competitor in matters of sartorial excess, Regnet scanned the dandy's green ensemble from top to toe and drawled, "But tell me, Dan, will you turn another color as you ripen?"

The group burst into laughter. Before Danilo could respond in kind, Myrna Callahanter spoke up. "Yes, well, speaking of green, did you hear that our good friend Rhys Brossfeather was spotted entering the Smiling Siren?"

The young nobles joined in a collective smirk. A flighty and casually malicious gossip, Myrna was ever on the alert for an opening, however small, for one of her tattling tales.

"Really? I've heard some wonderful stories about that place," Danilo said, grinning broadly at the thought of the shy young cleric in that notoriously bawdy tavern. "Is the entertainment there every bit as wicked as they say?"

"Well . . . So I've heard," responded Myrna, eyes demurely downcast.

The group hooted with laughter at her evasion. "Myrna was probably on stage that night," Regnet suggested, bringing about another chorus of mirth.

Not insulted in the least, Lady Callahanter responded with an evil grin that would have shamed a red dragon. She was always delighted to be the center of attention, and with a practiced gesture she reached up to pat her bright red hair. As she did, her outer robe fell conveniently open, revealing a translucent gown and a good deal more. Several jaws fell at the sudden display, and one guest noisily dropped his goblet.

Wearing a droll expression, Danilo leaned closer to Regnet. "Her timing rivals that of a bard, but can she sing?"

"Does it matter?" his crony responded dryly.

As were most of the guests, Myrna Callahanter was dressed to dazzle. Her blue-green gown was almost sheer, with clusters of sequins cleverly located to create an illusion of decency. The dress was cut low enough to reveal a lavish expanse of flesh. Multi-colored glitter had been glued in artful patterns to the skin of her arms, throat, and impressive curves. Even her hair—the raucous scarlet hue of Calimshite henna—was elaborately woven with gems and gilded ribbons. Nothing about Myrna was subtle; she had the reputation of devouring men with the speed and appetite of trolls in a butcher shop.

Making the most of the attention, Myrna heaved a theatrical sigh. Glancing around the circle through lowered lashes, she continued her litany of gossip. "And then there's that terrible scandal involving Jhessoba, the poor dear—"

"Myrna, love, I know rumor-mongering is your family trade, but *must* you talk shop at a party?"

Again the young nobles grinned in unison. The speaker was Galinda Raventree. She and Myrna were sworn foes, and their catty warfare could always be counted on to liven up things.

This evening, however, Galinda had another motive for curbing Myrna's tongue: Jhessoba's latest misfortune had political implications, which could lead—the gods forbid—to serious debate upon substantive issues. A devoted party-goer, Galinda had seen to catering this affair, and she was determined that it remain appropriately frivolous.

Danilo draped an arm around Myrna's shoulders, coming valiantly to her defense. "Really, Galinda, you must let Myrna talk. After two months with that dreary merchant train, I for one am longing for a bit of local gossip."

He gave Myrna a squeeze of encouragement. "Do go on."

"My hero," the gossip purred. She snuggled a bit closer, and one scarlet-tipped hand snaked up Danilo's chest to toy with his emerald pendant.

Noting the familiar, predatory expression in the noblewoman's eyes, Danilo wisely retreated. His arm came away faintly dusted with glitter, though, and he regarded his defiled garment with dismay. "I say, Myrna, you've got that damnable stuff all over me."

Several women in the group surreptitiously checked their escorts for similar telltale sparkles. Galinda Raventree took note of their suspicious scrutiny, and with great satisfaction she smirked into her wine goblet.

Incapable of being insulted, Myrna draped herself over Danilo again. "Do another trick," she begged him.

"Love to, but I've cast all the spells I've got for the day."

"Oh, no," she cooed, pouting up at him. "Not every one?"

"Well . . ." Danilo hesitated. "I *have* been working on some interesting spell modifications."

Regnet guffawed. "Another Snilloc's Snowball?"

"Now, there's gratitude for you," Danilo huffed in mock pique. He turned to the group, and with one ringed hand he languidly gestured toward Regnet. "About three months ago our over-dressed friend here managed to insult some very large, very drunk gentlemen in a tavern down in the Dock Ward. A small fight ensued, and of course I leapt to his aid. Using the Snilloc's Snowball spell, I conjured a magic missile—"

"A snowball?" sneered Wardon Agundar. His family dealt in the forging of swords, and he had little regard for lesser weapons.

"Well, not exactly," Danilo confessed. "I tried a variation on the spell and came up with a slightly, um, more exotic weapon."

"Thus creating the spell for Snilloc's Cream Pie," put in Regnet with a broad grin. The nobles shouted with laughter over the image this conjured, and Danilo bowed in acknowledgement.

"My claim to immortality," he replied, laying a hand over his heart and striking a heroic pose.

"What happened?" demanded Myrna breathlessly. "Did you have to fight those men or did the watch step in?"

"Nothing so dramatic as that," admitted Danilo. "We settled our differences like gentlemen. Regnet bought a round of drinks for our erstwhile opponents. Dessert, of course, was on them."

A universal groan greeted Danilo's pun. "You'd better do another trick now, to redeem yourself," Regnet advised.

His friends joined in coaxing Danilo to casting another of his illusions. After modestly disclaiming that he hadn't quite worked all the bugs out of this one, he agreed to try.

"Hmmmm. I'll need something truly vulgar to use as a spell component," Danilo mused. His gaze fastened on Regnet's pendant, a rendering of the Amcathra crest in sparkling red and blue stones. "Oh, I say, Regnet, that will do splendidly."

Regnet pretended to wince at the good-natured insult, but he handed over the bauble. His friend began the spell, chanting the arcane words and gesturing broadly. Finally Danilo tossed the pendant into the air, and the show climaxed in a loud pop and a puff of multi-colored smoke.

When the smoke cleared, the young nobles stared at Regnet in a moment of stunned disbelief. Then their laughter echoed throughout the hall. The spell had turned his colorful finery into the drab brown robes of a druid.

Danilo's eyes widened in mock dismay. He rocked back a pace and folded his arms across his chest. "Hmm. Now, how did *that* happen?" he murmured, raising one hand to tap reflectively at the highly decorative cleft in his chin.

Regnet's face was a study of astonishment as he regarded his unfashionable ensemble, and his chagrin sent his friends into new peals of mirth. Suddenly the laughter died, and a nervous silence fell over the merry group.

A tall, burly man approached their corner. Unlike most of the party-goers, this man was dressed in solemn black, his only ornaments a silver torque and a cape lined with fine gray fur. His black hair was streaked with gray, and his brow was knit in disapproval.

"Uh-oh," murmured Myrna, her eyes brightening with glee at the thought of impending disaster. Another of their number, a young nobleman deeply into his cups, blanched at the sight of the stern newcomer and edged out of range.

Danilo, however, raised a hand in delighted greeting. "Uncle Khelben! Just the person we need. That last bit of magic went awry. Can you show me where I went wrong?"

"I wouldn't presume," Uncle Khelben said dryly. "It would seem, Danilo, that we need to have another little talk." He took a firm hold of the dandy's glitter-speckled arm and glared around the circle of nobles.

The gay assemblage took the hint and scattered like a flock of startled birds, muttering excuses as they went. This would not be the first time that Khelben "Blackstaff" Arunsun, archmage and reputed member of the secret circle that ruled Waterdeep, had chastised his frivolous nephew over the irresponsible use of magic, and Danilo's friends did not care to witness the coming lecture.

"Cowards, all of them," Danilo mused as he watched the rapid retreat of his friends.

"Forget them. We have more important matters to discuss."

Danilo grimaced and captured two goblets of Sparkling Evermead from the tray of a passing waiter. He thrust one of the goblets into his uncle's hand. "Here, take this. I suppose it's safe to assume that you'll be as dry as usual."

Khelben's dour response was drowned out by a delighted squeal.

"Danilo, you're back!" A tipsy young noblewoman, dressed in an incongruous mixture of sheer lace and white furs, launched herself at the green-clad dandy.

Adept at avoiding wine stains on his finery, Danilo held his goblet out at arm's length as he caught the attractive missile in a careful, one-armed embrace. "I've counted the minutes, Sheabba." He smiled into her upturned face.

The blond woman wrapped her arms around his waist and giggled up at him. "Of course you have. I suppose you've been charming all the women from here to Suzail?"

"Fertilizing the fields, more likely," interjected Khelben in a sour tone.

"Bray elsewhere, old donkey," Sheabba snapped. She threw a withering look at the mage, then recoiled in mortification as she realized whom she had insulted.

Danilo noted her dismay and came quickly to her rescue. "You'll be at the festival games tomorrow, Shea, won't you? Oh, marvelous. I'll have to ride in one or two events, but a group of us are getting together at the Broken Lance afterward for drinks. My treat. Meet me there?"

The young woman managed a weak nod of agreement, then she took flight, weaving unsteadily through the crowd.

Danilo sighed noisily and shook his head. "Really, Uncle, the effect you have on women is beyond belief. Don't despair. I've been working on this new spell, don't you know, that might do your social life a world of—Hey, mind the silk!"

Khelben had once again seized Danilo's arm. Ignoring the young man's sputtering protests, the mage drew his nephew out of the room and into a secluded alcove.

Once released, Danilo leaned against a marble bust of Mielikki, Goddess of the Forest, and arranged his cape in artful folds before addressing himself to his glowering uncle. "To what do I owe the honor of this abduction?"

"You've heard about Rafe Silverspur." Khelben was not given to lengthy preambles.

Danilo took a sip of his wine. "No, can't say that I have. What's the good ranger doing these days?"

"Very little. He's dead."

Danilo paled, and a look of remorse washed over Khelben's face. The wizard continued in a gentler tone, "I'm sorry, Dan. I'd forgotten that Rafe and you had become good friends."

The young man nodded acknowledgement. His face was without expression, but he studied the bubbles in his glass for a long moment before he looked up.

"Branded, I suppose?" Danilo's voice was flat, all hint of the lazy drawl gone.

"Yes."

"Rafe Silverspur," Danilo repeated in a distant voice. "Your death will be avenged, my friend."

The vow was spoken quietly, yet no one could hear it and doubt that it would come to pass. Danilo's voice rang with quiet strength and stubborn resolve. Anyone who saw the young noble at this moment would have had a hard time equating him with the smug dandy known to Waterdeep society. His handsome face was dark with fury as he turned to the mage, but his rage was held in check by a control as remarkable as it was unexpected.

"How did he die?"

"Same as all the others—in his sleep, for all we can tell," Khelben responded. "If a ranger as good as young Silverspur could be taken unaware, it's no wonder the Harpers are running around in circles after this assassin."

"The search, I take it, is not going well."

"No," the mage admitted. "That's where you come in."

Dropping back into his foppish persona, Danilo crossed his arms and quirked one eyebrow. "Somehow I knew you'd get around to saying that."

"Indeed," Khelben agreed dryly, recognizing that his nephew's manner covered strong emotion.

"Naturally, you have a plan," Danilo prompted.

"Yes. I've been following the assassin's route, and a pattern is starting to emerge. It leads here." Khelben reached into a pocket and drew out a pewter-framed miniature.

Danilo accepted the portrait and studied it, then whistled in appreciation. "You did this? By the gods, Uncle, there may yet be some hope for you as an artist."

The young man's teasing brought a faint smile to Khelben's face. "I did not know you were a connoisseur of art."

"Art, no. Women, definitely," Danilo said fervently, his eyes still fixed upon the portrait. The subject was a woman of rare and exceptional beauty. Curly raven-black hair framed the perfect oval face and contrasted with her creamy white skin. Her cheekbones were sharp and high, her features sculpted by a delicate hand. Most extraordinary were her eyes, almond shaped and vividly green. Danilo was highly partial to green.

"Does she really look like this, or did you take artistic license?" Danilo asked.

"She really looks like that," Khelben confirmed. He cocked his head and amended cryptically, "Well, sometimes she looks like that."

Danilo glanced up, his brow furrowed. He shook his head to rid himself of the temptation to pursue the subject and got back to the business at hand. "Besides being the future mother of my children, who is this beauty?"

"The assassin's target."

"Ah. You want me to warn her?"

"No," Khelben continued, "I want you to protect her. And, in a manner of speaking, spy on her. If I'm right, you'll need to do both in order to catch the Harper Assassin."

Danilo sank onto the stone bench beside the statue. The vague, charming smile had disappeared from his face, and once again his tone was grim. "I'm supposed to catch this Harper Assassin, am I? Perhaps you'd better start at the beginning."

"Very well." Khelben seated himself beside his nephew. He stabbed a finger at the portrait that still lay cradled in Danilo's hand. "During most of the assassinations, perhaps all of them, this woman has been near at hand."

"Sounds to me as if you have a suspect, not a target." Danilo's tone was laced with regret as he eyed the portrait.

"No."

"No?" Danilo's tone was both surprised and hopeful.

"No," reiterated Khelben firmly. "And I say this for several reasons. She's a Harper agent. One of the best. In my opinion, the assassin has been after her for some time. When he can't get close enough to strike and still avoid detection, he settles for a less challenging target."

"I'm sorry, but considering some of the Harpers who have

fallen to this assassin, I find your theory difficult to swallow," Danilo protested. To support his argument, he ticked off a list on the fingers of one hand. "Sybil Evensong, Kernigan of Soubar, the mage Perendra, Rathan Thorilander, Rafe Silverspur . . ." Danilo's voice trailed off, and he had to clear his throat before he continued. "This woman couldn't be more capable than any of those."

"Yes, she could."

"Really? Hmm. Why does your pretty Harper agent draw this assassin? Apart from the obvious reasons, naturally."

"She has a moonblade," Khelben explained tersely. "It's a magic elven sword, very powerful. It is possible that the assassin, whoever he is, is after Arilyn's sword."

"Arilyn," Danilo repeated the name absently, looking down at the picture once more. "It suits her. Arilyn what?"

"Moonblade. She has taken the sword's name as her own. But we digress."

"Indeed. So, what can this magic sword do?"

Khelben took his time before answering. "I'm not aware of all its powers," he said carefully. "That's where you come in."

"You said that already," Danilo observed.

The mage's face darkened with exasperation. "Apart from you and me, do you see anyone in this room?" he snapped. "There's no need to continue playing the fool."

Danilo smiled apologetically. "Sorry. Habit, you know."

"Yes, well, please attend to the matter at hand. The possibility exists that Arilyn Moonblade has been targeted for her sword as well as her talents. If we find out who has an interest in the moonblade and why, we have a better chance of finding this assassin."

Danilo sat quietly for a long moment. "One question."

"Go ahead."

"Why me?"

"Secrecy is vital. We can't send someone obvious."

"Oh," Danilo crossed one knee over the other and flicked a lock of hair over his shoulder in an exaggerated, effeminate gesture. "Is it my imagination, or was I just insulted?"

Khelben scowled. "Don't belittle yourself, boy. You've proven to be a more than capable agent, and you're perfect for this job."

"Indeed," Danilo agreed wryly. "Protecting a woman who doesn't seem to require my protection."

"There's more. We need information about the moonblade. You have proven to be very successful at separating women from their secrets."

"It's a gift," Danilo modestly agreed. He tapped the portrait and added, "Not that I'm trying to get out of this assignment, mind you, but someone's got to point out the obvious: why don't we just ask her about the sword?"

Khelben faced the young nobleman, his expression grim and earnest. "There's more to this than meets the eye, although an assassin of this skill, systematically wiping out Harpers, is trouble enough. No one must suspect that you work with me—not the assassin, not the other Harpers, and especially not Arilyn."

"Intrigue within the ranks?" Danilo asked mockingly.

"It is possible," Khelben answered cryptically.

"Marvelous," Danilo muttered, looking genuinely appalled by Khelben's unexpected response to his jest. "Even so, I don't see why we need to keep this from Arilyn. If the assassin is after her, shouldn't she be forewarned? Once she knows I've been sent to help her, she may be more prone to work with me."

Khelben snorted. "Far from it. For all her talents, Arilyn Moonblade is one of the most stubborn, hotheaded, and unreasonable persons I've ever met. She wouldn't agree to protection, and she wouldn't take kindly to the notion that she couldn't handle the assassin alone." Khelben paused, and a grimace tugged the corners of his mouth down. "She reminds me of her father, come to think of it."

Danilo regarded the mage with a skeptical expression. "This is all very interesting, but I sense that you're skirting the real issue. It's the sword, isn't it? You know something about it that you're not telling me."

"Yes," Khelben agreed simply.

"Well?" Danilo prompted.

Khelben shook his head. "I'm sorry, but you'll have to trust me. The fewer people who know, the better. I doubt even Arilyn herself knows the full extent of the sword's power. We need to find out what she knows about the sword, and that's—"

"Where I come in," Danilo finished glumly.

"Indeed. You have a knack for getting people to talk. A word of caution, however. Until the assassin is identified and captured, you must never let down your facade."

"Surely, after she becomes accustomed to my presence, she would—"

"No," Khelben broke in. He raised a cautioning finger and paused for emphasis. "There is something you should know. Arilyn Moonblade is very good. She is not easy to follow, yet the assassin keeps cropping up near her. She is obviously being closely observed, probably through magical means. As a charming but ineffectual dandy, you may not seem a threat to whomever is watching Arilyn. If you should ever step out of your role . . ."

"Don't worry," Danilo said with an insouciant shrug. "I always did perform best for an audience."

"I hope so. It could be a long performance. Arilyn is no fool, and you've got to stay with her until she leads you to the Harper Assassin."

An expression of intense distaste crossed the young nobleman's face. "I don't like the idea of using this woman as bait for a trap."

"Neither do I, " growled Khelben. "But can you think of a better alternative?"

"No," Danilo admitted.

"Exactly." Khelben rose abruptly, indicating that the interview was over. "I suggest that you make your apologies to Lady Sheabba. You leave for Evereska in the morning."

Five

 The tavern hall of the Halfway Inn was bustling with activity when Arilyn came down from her room. Near the northwestern border of the mountain range that surrounded Evereska, the Halfway Inn was a stopping place for both human and elven trade caravans. There were few inns in the Greycloak Hills, and this one boasted comfortable rooms, vast stables, and warehouses for temporary secure storage of goods. Elves and humans, halflings and dwarves, and an occasional member of one of the other civilized races all commingled in a relaxed, congenial atmosphere.

The Halfway Inn was much more than an inn. Among other things, it was a trading center for the elven colony of Evereska. Set in a valley of fertile farmland and surrounded on all sides by mountains, Evereska was a beautiful and heavily fortified elven city. It was protected by an impressive arsenal of elven magic and military might. The Evereska Valley had been inhabited by elves longer than anyone could reckon, but the city itself was young by elven standards. As was the case with most elven settlements, little was known about Evereska other than its reputation for impregnability and the calibre of elven mages and fighters trained at its College of Magic and Arms. To most of those who traveled through the Greycloak Hills, the Halfway Inn *was* Evereska. Few persons got any closer to the city.

Myrin Silverspear, the inn's proprietor, was a dour, silent moon elf whose silver eyes missed nothing. He kept his own council better than anyone Arilyn had ever met, and his cozy establishment seemed designed especially with discretion in mind. As a result, the Halfway Inn was ever abuzz with intrigue, dealmaking, and clandestine meetings.

Arilyn always stopped here on her way into Evereska, to receive assignments or to meet contacts. For no reason that she could fathom, Myrin Silverspear had taken a special interest in her and her career. Whenever she stayed at the inn, he looked after her as if she were elven royalty.

As usual, he met her at the foot of the stairs with a low bow. "Your presence honors this house, Arilyn Moonblade. Is there anything that you require this evening, *quex etriel?*"

As usual, Arilyn winced at the extreme deference of his greeting. "Just to be seen."

"I beg your pardon?"

Arilyn grinned. "Let's just say that I'd like to be seen coming into the inn, but not going out."

"Ah. Of course." As usual, that was explanation enough for the discrete innkeeper. He took her arm and escorted her with grave ceremony to the large bar. She took one of the most conspicuous barstools, and Myrin made a show of going behind the bar and serving her himself.

Arilyn sipped at the elven spirits he'd poured her and fought back a surge of laughter. "Thank you, Myrin. I've definitely been seen."

"Not at all. Anything else?"

"Do I have any messages?"

Myrin produced a small scroll and handed it to her. "This came just this afternoon."

She glanced at the seal, and her mood darkened. With a sigh, she took the scroll from the innkeeper, opened it, and scanned the fine, precise elven runes. Kymil wanted to meet her here, tonight. That would most likely mean that the Harpers had given him another assignment for her, just when she was so looking forward to getting back home to Evereska. Another unconscious sigh escaped her.

"Good news, I trust?"

Arilyn looked up into Myrin's concerned silver eyes. "You might not think so. Kymil Nimesin is meeting me here tonight, at the usual place."

The moon elf received her announcement without blinking. "I'll see that your usual booth is cleared."

"You're a diplomat, Myrin," Arilyn murmured. Little love was lost between the proud innkeeper and the patrician arms-master, but Myrin Silverspear always received Kymil with the utmost courtesy. To Arilyn's puzzlement, Kymil treated the innkeeper with considerably less respect.

"So I have been told," Myrin said. With another bow, he excused himself to see to Arilyn's booth. She went upstairs to get the artifacts she'd retrieved from Darkhold, then returned to the tavern and made her way to the back of the large room where she slipped inside a heavily curtained booth.

Almost immediately tiny motes of light flickered over the bench opposite her. The golden pinpricks broadened, expanded, and finally coalesced into the form of her longtime friend and mentor, Kymil Nimesin.

"Your mode of entering a room never ceases to unnerve me," Arilyn murmured with a smile of welcome for her teacher.

The elf dismissed her comment absently. "A simple matter. Your last venture went well, I trust?"

"If it didn't, I wouldn't be sitting here." She handed him the sack containing the artifacts. "Will you return these to Sune's people and see that our informant gets the rest of his money?"

"Of course." After a brief silence Kymil attended to the amenities. "I heard of Rafe Silverspur's death. A shame. He was a good ranger, and the Harpers' cause will miss him."

"As will I," she replied softly. Kymil's words were a polite formula required by convention; hers revealed genuine emotion. She looked up sharply. "How did you hear about Rafe's death so quickly?"

"I was concerned about you, so I made inquiries."

"Oh?"

Kymil regarded his pupil keenly. "You know, of course, that the assassin was looking for you."

Arilyn stared down at her clenched hands. "I've come to that conclusion, yes," she said evenly. "Now, if you don't mind, could we please speak of other matters? Have you another assignment for me?"

"No, I called the meeting to discuss the assassinations," Kymil said. He leaned forward to emphasize his words. "I'm concerned about your safety, child. You must take steps to protect yourself from this assassin."

Her head jerked up, and anger flooded her face. "What would you have me do? Hide?"

"Far from it," Kymil corrected her sternly. "You must seek out this assassin."

"Many seek him."

"Ah, but perhaps they are looking in the wrong places. As a Harper agent, you can succeed where others fail. In my opinion, the assassin hides within the ranks of the Harpers."

Arilyn drew in a sharp breath. "The assassin, a Harper?" she demanded, incredulous.

"Yes," Kymil noted. "Or a Harper agent."

She considered her teacher's words and nodded slowly. It was an appalling possibility, but it made sense. The Harpers were a confederation of individuals, not a highly structured organization. Harper agents—those like Arilyn who were not official members of the group, but worked on particular assignments—tended to operate alone, and many of the members kept their affiliation secret. It seemed incredible to Arilyn that this veil of secrecy could be turned against the Harpers, cloaking an assassin in their very midst. On the other hand, she had grown to trust Kymil Nimesin's judgment. He had been allied with the Harpers since she was an infant, and if he thought that the Harper Assassin was within the ranks she was inclined to believe him.

Kymil's urgent voice broke into her reflections. "You must find this assassin, and soon. The common people hold Harpers in high regard. If we cannot find and stop the murderer, it will damage the Harpers' honor and reputation."

The gold elf paused. "Have you any idea of the implications of this? Why, the Balance itself could be disrupted! The Harpers serve a vital function in fighting against evil, in particular the encroachments of the Zhentarim—"

"I know what the Harpers stand for," Arilyn said with a touch of impatience. Kymil had lectured her on the need for Balance since she was fifteen, and she knew his arguments by heart. "Have you a plan?"

"Yes. I would suggest that you go among the Harpers, in disguise if necessary, to ferret out the assassin."

Arilyn nodded. "Yes, you might be right." A slight, humorless smile flickered across her face. "At any rate, it is better than doing nothing. Just waiting for the assassin to strike is intolerable. I can't keep at it much longer."

"Why is it that you seem so unnerved by this threat? Your life has been in danger many times." Kymil paused and eyed her keenly. "Or is there something else?"

"There is," she admitted reluctantly. "For some time now—several months, actually—I've had the sense that I'm being followed. Try as I might, I can find no trace of pursuit."

"Yes?"

She'd expected him to reproach her, or at least to question her regarding her inability to lay hands upon her shadowy pursuer. "You don't seem surprised by this," she ventured.

"Many Harpers are highly accomplished rangers and trackers," Kymil responded evenly. "It's not inconceivable that this assassin, especially if he or she is from the Harper ranks, is skilled enough to avoid detection—even by someone as skilled as you. All the more reason, I believe, for you to take the offensive. Agreed?"

"Agreed."

"That is all I have to say this evening. I would be happy to teleport you to Waterdeep—"

"No, thank you," Arilyn cut in hastily.

Kymil's eyebrows rose. "You do not intend to go to Waterdeep? It would seem a likely place to begin your search."

"I agree, and I do plan to go to Waterdeep. I just prefer to get there on horseback."

Exasperation flooded Kymil's face. "My dear *etriel*, I will never understand your aversion to magic, especially considering that you've been carrying a magic sword since childhood."

"That's bad enough," Arilyn said with a rare hint of bitterness. "Where magic is concerned, I draw the line where the moonblade ends."

"I don't understand you." Kymil shook his head. "Granted, there was an unfortunate incident during the Time of Troubles—"

"*Unfortunate?*" Arilyn broke in, her voice incredulous. "I wouldn't exactly call the accidental disintegration of an entire adventuring party a 'misfortune.' "

"The Hammerfell Seven," Kymil said, his tone dismissing the human adventurers as inconsequential. "You yourself had little need for concern from magic fire."

"Oh? Why not?"

For an instant Kymil looked disconcerted, then he smiled faintly. "Ever the demanding student. Elves and elven magic were not as severely affected as humans by that interlude."

He settled back and steepled his fingers, the very picture of an erudite professor. Knowing what was coming, Arilyn groaned silently. Kymil was currently guest-teaching a seminar at the Evereska College of Magic and Arms on the effect on elven magic by the Time of Troubles. Not a scholar in the best of times, Arilyn was of no mind to sit through the inevitable lecture. And she did not care to relive the Time of Troubles, the disastrous interlude when gods walked Faerun in the form of mortal avatars, creating havoc and immense destruction.

"It is thus," Kymil began, his voice taking on a pedantic tone. "In layman's terms, humans use the weave to work magic. Elves are, in a sense, part of the weave. Tel'Quessir are inherently magic, by our very nature, and . . ."

Arilyn abruptly lifted one hand, again cutting him off. "Many would consider me N'Tel'Quess: not-people. I am half-human, remember? I have little inherent magical ability."

Kymil paused, then inclined his head in a gesture of apology. "Forgive me, child. Your superior gifts often lead me to forget the unfortunate circumstances of your birth."

Arilyn had known Kymil for too long to be insulted by his patrician airs. "Unfortunate circumstances? I am a half-elf, Kymil, not a bastard." She grinned fleetingly. "Of course, there are those who would disagree."

As if on cue, a hoarse voice roared her name. Arilyn edged aside the curtain for a look. She shook her head and swore softly in a mixture of Elvish and Common.

Arilyn's bilingual curse brought a startled gasp from Kymil Nimesin. She shot a quick glance at him and bit her lip to keep from laughing at his outraged expression. "Sorry."

He started to speak, undoubtedly to chide her about her undignified use of Elvish. His words were drowned out by a racket that sounded like a minor barbarian invasion.

A small horde of ruffians had stormed into the tavern. They stomped around in a rather aimless fashion, overturning empty tables, emitting an assortment of whoops and shouts. The leader of the band was a uncouth giant of a man, an almost comic caricature of a thug. The man's appearance was sinister enough: an eyepatch covered one eye, a mace studded with iron spikes hung from his belt, and a shirt of rusty chain mail more or less covered his belly. Yet something about him tended to inspire covert smiles. Perhaps it was a pate as bald as a new-laid egg, framed by a wispy blond fringe that had been gathered into two long, skinny yellow braids.

The blond-and-bald man stalked over to Myrin Silverspear. Grabbing the slender innkeeper, the lout hoisted him up to eye level.

"Maybe you didn't hear me, elf. I asked if Arilyn Moonblade was here tonight. If you don't answer me, my men here—" He jerked his head at the group of toughs clustered behind him. "My men will take to questioning your patrons. Not good for business."

Not many men, human or elven, could maintain dignity while their feet dangled several inches from the floor, but Myrin Silverspear returned the huge oaf's threatening glare with a calm, measured look. Something in the innkeeper's expression took the bluster out of the ruffian's face, and he lowered the elf to the floor.

"Wasting my time," he announced to his men, his voice loud enough to carry throughout the room. It was an obvious and transparent exercise at saving face. "This elf don't know anything. Spread out. If that gray wench is within a mile, we'll find her!"

Kymil dropped the curtain and turned to Arilyn. "Do you know this man?"

"Oh, yes," she said wryly, still watching the drama unfold in the main tavern area. "That's Harvid Beornigarth, a third-rate adventurer. Some months ago we sought the same prize. He lost."

"Ah. Not a gracious loser, I take it," Kymil concluded.

"Hardly." Arilyn parted the curtain another fraction of an inch, watching as Harvid's thugs spread out and started working the room. "Neither is he much of a challenge, but at the moment I have enough to think about."

So much for my plan to slip away from my mysterious shadow, Arilyn thought. With Harvid Beornigarth creating such a stir, she might as well stay right in the booth where she was and hang out a sign: "Arilyn Moonblade. Assassins Inquire Within." On the other hand, she mused, all that racket might create enough of a diversion . . .

Arilyn abruptly let the curtain fall. She reached into the small bag that hung from her belt and drew from it a tiny mirror, a handful of gold mesh, and some tiny gilded pots engraved with the bright pink runes that identified the cosmetic unguents of "Faereen the Far-Traveled."

Deftly she spread a pale ivory cosmetic over her face, concealing the hint of blue that highlighted the fine bones. The second pot yielded a rose-colored cream. With this she touched her lips and cheeks. She shook the gold mesh, a quaint ornamental headpiece made of tiny metal rings linked in intricate patterns and studded with green stones. After smoothing her hair over her pointed ears, she covered the ebony waves with the headpiece.

Now that her part was completed, Arilyn closed one hand around the moonblade's grip and shut her eyes, forming a mental picture of a Sembian courtesan. When she looked down at herself a moment later, she saw that the moonblade's work was complete. Her travel leathers were replaced by a filmy, multi-tiered gown of jade and sapphire silk, and her loose shirt was now a bodice laced tight and low. The moonblade itself appeared to be a small, jeweled dagger. Arilyn held out the tiny mirror at arm's length and considered the effect. Even after twenty years, she felt a bit unnerved by the transformation. The half-elven fighter had disappeared, and in her place sat an exotically beautiful human woman.

One final touch was needed: Arilyn drew a tiny carved box from her bag and removed from it a pair of delicate lenses. She placed them directly over her eyes, and the distinctively elven gold-flecked blue became a startling—but very human—shade of green.

The entire transformation had taken place within minutes. Ready to go, Arilyn glanced up at Kymil. For once, his inscrutable demeanor had slipped, and a look of obvious distaste twisted his features. Early in Arilyn's training, Kymil had discovered the moonblade's ability to create disguises for its wielder. Arilyn and the moonblade had developed a repertoire of several practical facades, but Kymil had never become reconciled to what he considered an undignified manner of doing business.

"Dressed this way, I can leave without attracting notice," she explained a trifle defensively. Even after all the years she'd known Kymil, she was stung by any sign of disapproval from her mentor.

Kymil recovered his composure and harumphed. "Hardly. Dressed in that manner, you cannot possibly escape notice. A courtesan without a patron? It is unusual, and you will be a matter of much speculation. Many will remember you."

"True," Arilyn agreed. "They will see and remember a human courtesan. An illusion."

The noise of the approaching ruffians came closer, cutting short any argument Kymil might have had. "Your methods are highly successful," he conceded. "Go then, and the gods speed your quest. Sweet water and light laughter until next," he concluded, in the traditional elven form of leave-taking.

Having dismissed Arilyn, Kymil's eyes became distant as he focused on some faraway destination. He murmured, "Silver path. Evereska College of Magic."

His body became translucent, then the outline of his form wavered and filled with golden pinpricks of light. These in turn flickered briefly, then disappeared.

Arilyn shuddered. As the wielder of a moonblade, she had of necessity become reconciled to using magic, although she still bore a fighter's distrust of the art. Magic fire and dimensional travel appalled her. Her earliest experiences with teleportation at Kymil's side had left her sick and shaken, and her strong bias against magical travel had been strengthened during the Time of Trouble; she'd seen one mage too many teleport himself into a solid wall. Kymil might not like her attitude, but she simply couldn't change the way she felt. With the elf gone, Arilyn returned her thoughts to the matter at hand. Again she drew the curtain aside, searching for the final piece of her disguise.

She needed a man.

Kymil was right about that much: a courtesan needed a patron. So accustomed was she to traveling alone that she had forgotten this. To properly play her sultry role, she needed to borrow a man as a prop. Arilyn scanned the tavern for a likely prospect. A burst of laughter drew her eye toward the front door.

Several merchants slouched around a table littered with empty ale mugs. One of their number, a young man in bright green finery, was openly flirting with an elven barmaid. Arilyn couldn't hear his words, but they brought a roar of approving, tipsy laughter from his comrades and made the smiling young moon elf blush a bright shade of blue.

Perfect, Arilyn thought, her mouth twisting in a faint smile of derision. She could not have produced a better prospect if she had been capable of conjuring one from thin air. The man was young, less than thirty winters. His flaxen hair was meticulously styled, his richly embroidered cloak was draped over his shoulders with consummate artistry. He lounged indolently in his chair as he ogled the swaying walk of the departing barmaid. His clothes and lazy elegance bespoke wealth and privilege, and his smile indicated supreme self-satisfaction. By all appearances, he was spoiled and shallow and selfish. In short, he was perfect.

She disliked his type, those who were content with a path of ease and luxury. On the other hand, the services of a Sembian courtesan didn't come cheap, and of all the men in the tavern he seemed the most credible—and the most receptive—target for her advances.

Blissfully unaware of Arilyn's scrutiny, the young man made another, presumably witty observation. One of his companions, a rough-looking man in the garb of a mercenary, roared with laughter and swatted the humorist's shoulder with a large, grimy paw. The young man did not seem affronted by the mercenary's familiarity; rather, he winced and clutched at his shoulder, making another remark that set the table to laughter.

Probably not a nobleman, Arilyn concluded, but a wealthy merchant. The men at the table did not appear drunk enough to take such liberties with a noble. The pale-haired dandy did not seem to have been drinking heavily, which was also good. He appeared to have his wits about him.

Arilyn rose and slipped quietly into the room. The back half of the tavern was kept deliberately dark, and she hugged the

wall and stayed within the convenient shadows. She wanted no
one to connect the airy courtesan with the travel-worn *etriel*
who had entered the tavern earlier. A sudden lull in the various
conversations about the room greeted her as she moved into
the lighted area. Men and women alike cast speculative
glances at Arilyn. She tilted her head at a coquettish angle and
moved purposely toward her target.

One of the fop's companions stopped gaping at Arilyn long
enough to elbow her intended quarry in his ribs. The young
dandy looked up at her, his eyebrows raising in a lazy expression of appreciation. He rose politely as she reached his table,
and Arilyn was surprised to note that he was taller than she by
several inches.

"Well met, indeed. I must be living right," he marveled,
claiming her hand and bowing low over it.

Arilyn doubted it, but she answered him only with a soft
smile. The fool could take that as he would.

"Would you care to join me? I'm Danilo, by the way. Danilo
Thann."

With effort, Arilyn held back a groan. She knew that name:
the Thann family had far-flung merchant concerns, as well as
vast lands north of Waterdeep. The dandy was a Waterdhavian
nobleman. It was too late to withdraw, so she held her seduc-
tive smile in place as Danilo Thann elbowed aside a comrade
and ushered her into the vacant seat. He slid comfortably into
the chair next to her.

"And you are . . . ?" His voice trailed off, inviting her to
finish.

"Drinking Elquesstria, please," she purred, deliberately
misunderstanding him.

His eyes lit up. "Ah! No name. A lady of mystery. And
drinking elven spirits. That makes you a lady of taste, as well."
He smirked around the table at his audience. "Although your
choice in companions has already established that fact beyond
question." His cronies chuckled in agreement, apparently
sharing young Thann's comfortable opinion of himself.

The clank of an ill-kept chain mail shell interrupted the

groups' merriment, and Arilyn stiffened involuntarily. She didn't have to look up to know it was Harvid Beornigarth himself. Arilyn's hands itched to grab the moonblade and cleave the pesky human crustacean in two, but she willed herself to maintain the languid posture of a courtesan.

"Pardon, my lord, but have you seen this elf-wench about?"

Harvid thrust a roughly-drawn sketch of Arilyn at the young noble. Danilo took it, gave it a quick glance, and handed it back.

"No, can't say that I have."

"You're sure?"

Danilo draped an arm around Arilyn's shoulders, smiling up at Harvid Beornigarth as if he and the adventurer were old friends. "Frankly, no. If you were in my position," he drawled, squeezing the woman beside him, "would you have eyes for another?"

The lout's approving leer swept over Arilyn, and in response she forced herself to raise her eyes to his face. Harvid showed no sign of recognizing her. He grinned, revealing several rotting teeth.

"I wouldn't be looking, either," he admitted. He moved on to the next table, where he began to question the patrons with considerably less courtesy.

Arilyn relaxed. Now to get out of the inn and away. She would definitely have to take Danilo with her; the respect Harvid had shown the young noblemen indicated that she would probably not be approached by any of the other thugs as long as she was in the dandy's presence. Resisting the urge to peel the noble's arm from her shoulder, she glanced up at her future hostage.

Danilo Thann was leaning back in his chair, eyes narrowed and fixed intently upon something. Arilyn followed the line of his gaze. From his angle, he could see her hands, resting on her lap and tightly clenched. He appeared to be noting her whitened knuckles, and there was a speculative expression on his face.

She glanced sharply at him. What had he guessed?

He looked up and met her eyes, and her suspicions faded away. The young fool's face was as bland as porridge, and he flashed the charming smile that she was beginning to find irritating.

"Lovely ring. Very popular style in Waterdeep," he commented lightly. He picked up Arilyn's hand and surveyed it with the grave expression of a connoisseur, several of his own rings catching the light as he turned her hand this way and that. "They were selling these at the open-air market last summer festival. Did you get it then?"

His question seemed innocent enough, but Arilyn answered evasively. "My business hasn't taken me to Waterdeep in some time."

"What business are you in?" A huge man with black hair and rust-colored whiskers addressed the neckline of Arilyn's gown, leaning forward for a better view as he spoke. "A fellow merchant, perhaps?"

"No, not a merchant," Arilyn answered sweetly. Out of the corner of her eye, she saw the last of Harvid's men leave the tavern. The inn's patrons relaxed, and renewed conversation and calls for ale filled the tavern. It was the perfect moment to slip away. "My 'business,' such as it is, is best conducted in private." She rose, extending a hand and a smile of invitation to Danilo.

The red-whiskered man guffawed and clapped Danilo on the back. "Well, lad, you're set for the evening."

"If I don't return for a while, don't bother looking for me," he told the men with mock sternness. He took Arilyn's hand and let her lead him to the rear of the tavern. There was a door there, an exit that could lead upstairs or outside. She'd have to persuade him to take the latter option.

"Perhaps a short stroll?" Danilo suggested when they reached the doorway. "The night is lovely. Cool, but I do love autumn weather."

That's one problem solved, Arilyn noted, and she readily agreed. A pair of lovers out for a moonlight stroll would not draw a second glance. Then, once they were safely in the forest, she could conveniently lose him. Let him wander back on his own and explain her absence to his cronies.

Danilo tucked her arm cozily into his. He chattered merrily as they walked down the street behind the tavern, regaling her with a version of Waterdhavian gossip that would have been highly amusing if Arilyn had been in the mood to be entertained.

Arilyn encouraged the young nobleman's cheerful talk with appropriate inane noises, subtly guiding their path out of the bustle of arriving merchant caravans and toward the forest. The trading center at the Halfway Inn was as large as some towns, and at their leisurely pace it was almost an hour before they neared the path that followed the forest edge. The fickle autumn weather changed as they walked, and a damp wind began to hint at rain.

As Danilo Thann talked, Arilyn listened carefully to the night sounds. Voices drifted toward them from the inn, and horses nickered contentedly in the nearby stables. Once, she noticed that the shadow of a bush seemed disproportionately long. Later, a partridge flew up as if something had come too close to her nest. Never was there a suspicious sound, but Arilyn slowly became convinced that someone was following her still.

Damn! she thought vehemently. And after all the trouble she had gone through in the tavern to leave her shadow behind. Harvid's men were still stomping around the inn's grounds, and sounds of a fight would draw them like vultures to carrion.

A twig snapped a few feet away. Keeping her face expressionless, Arilyn slid one hand between the folds of her bright skirt and drew a dagger from its hiding place. As she and Danilo passed a large elm, Arilyn burst into motion. Wrenching her arm free from the nobleman's grasp, she reached behind the tree and dragged out a man by a handful of his hair. She threw the man against the trunk of the tree and pressed her dagger firmly against his neck. Immediately she recognized him as one of the ruffians who'd been with Harvid Beornigarth in the tavern, although she had not seen him in Harvid's crew before tonight. His face would be hard to forget; a jagged purple scar cut across one cheek, his nose had been broken at least once, and he was minus an ear.

"Why are you following me?" she demanded.

The man licked his lips nervously. "I saw you in the tavern. You came out alone, so I thought I'd . . . you know."

"The lady is *not* alone," Danilo Thann broke in haughtily. "Most certainly not. She is with me."

"Stay out of this," growled the lady in question. The noble-man fell back a step, raising his hands obligingly.

"You've been following me since I left the tavern? Not before?" It seemed unlikely to Arilyn that this ruffian could be her mysterious shadow, but she planned to find out for sure. The man hesitated just a shade too long before answering.

"No, just since the tavern. I've never seen you before."

Arilyn's blade slid along the man's jawline, removing a good deal of dark stubble as well as a bit of skin. "I'm not sure I believe you. Who are you working for?"

"Harvid Beornigarth. The big man with the yellow braids."

"No one else?"

"No!"

In spite of his guilty, furtive eyes, Arilyn was inclined to believe him. This was no canny assassin. She started to ease the dagger away when a dull flash of gold caught her eye. Her free hand darted into the open sack that was tied around the man's waist, and she drew out a golden snuff box with a curling rune engraved on the lid. It was a familiar rune. Arilyn caught her breath.

"Where did you get this?" she rasped, thrusting the box close to the man's face. The rune on it was the sigil of the mage Perendra of Waterdeep. She had been one of the first to fall to the Harper Assassin.

The man's eyes filled with panic and flickered back and forth as if seeking a means of escape. "Waterdeep," he croaked. "I got it in Waterdeep."

"I *know* that. Tell me more."

"From an elf. In Waterdeep. That's all I know, I swear."

"Does this elf have a name?"

Beads of sweat broke out on the man's face. "No, please! If I tell you his name he'll kill me."

"If you don't, *I'll* kill you."

"Life is just full of difficult decisions," Danilo Thann noted behind her. The unexpected sound startled Arilyn.

"Are *you* still here?" She threw a glance over her shoulder. The nobleman was leaning casually against a tree, arms crossed.

"Well, naturally," he replied. "It's dangerous out here. Who knows, there could be more of these men lying in wait."

"I don't need protection," she said emphatically.

"My point precisely," he said. "If it's all the same to you, I don't mind remaining in the company of a lady who knows her way around a dagger."

"Suit yourself." Arilyn turned her full attention back to her captive. "The elf's name?"

"I can't tell you!" he said in desperation. The dagger began its path along his jaw again. "All right! All right."

"Well?"

"His name is—"

The ruffian's voice snapped off as if he'd been throttled. Slowly Arilyn lowered the dagger, watching in disbelief as the man's face blackened and his tongue bulged out of his mouth. She backed away, unable to take her eyes from the horribly distorted face. A low, rattling gurgle burst from the man, and he slid, lifeless, down the length of the tree trunk.

"Merciful Mystra!" exclaimed Danilo Thann. "You've killed him!"

Six

Arilyn spun around to face the horrified nobleman. "I did not kill this man," she said.

"Well, *I* certainly didn't," retorted Danilo Thann. "I might not know much, but I do know dead. And he's it. How do you explain that?"

"I can't."

"Me either. We'd better go back to the tavern and alert the local authorities. Let them figure it out."

"No!"

Her vehemence seemed to surprise the young dandy. "If you didn't kill him, what do you have to worry about?" he asked reasonably.

Plenty, Arilyn thought. The last thing she needed right now was to leave another body in her wake. Her past invited speculation, and sooner or later someone would put the pieces together and label her the Harper Assassin. That day seemed close at hand, for the news of Rafe's death was spreading far too quickly. Kymil already knew, so it was possible that the Evereska authorities had also learned of the young Harper's death.

"Come on," she said abruptly. She tucked the gold snuff box into her sleeve and set a brisk pace back to the stables. The noblemen fell in beside her.

"Where are we going?"

"The stables."

"Oh? Why's that, I wonder?"

Arilyn was in no mood to banter. Under the guise of reclaiming Danilo's arm she pressed the tip of her dagger to his side. It pierced his silken tunic, but the fool's slightly amused expression never faltered.

"Do be careful of the fabric, will you?" he admonished her.

Arilyn looked at his vague smile, wondering for the first time if the man were simple. "You're coming with me."

"Yes," he agreed calmly, pausing as Arilyn swung open the door to the stable. "So it would appear."

Irritated, she prodded him inside. "Just keep walking."

"Well, really," he huffed. "There's no need to be so grim about this. Believe me, I'm a willing victim," he said, looking her over and smiling.

His calm acceptance of the situation temporarily disconcerted Arilyn. Danilo smirked at the bewildered expression on her face.

"Don't look so surprised, my dear lady. I will admit that the dagger is a new approach, but I often encounter women who are most eager for my company."

Arilyn snorted. "We're here for horses, not a pile of hay."

Danilo cocked his head and considered the possibilities. "My, my. You are full of innovative ideas, aren't you?"

Gritting her teeth in annoyance, Arilyn dropped his arm and threw open the door of the first stall. A matched pair of chestnut mares, fine-boned and high-spirited, tossed their heads and whinnied. The horses looked fit and, most important, fast.

"These will do," Arilyn announced.

"I should say," he murmured in reply.

She tucked the dagger back into her belt, grabbed a finely wrought saddle from a hook, and thrust it at Danilo. "I assume you can ride."

He took the saddle from her outstretched hands. "Please! You wound me," he protested.

"Don't tempt me."

Danilo sighed and shook his head. "I can see that setting the proper tone for this moonlight ride will be my responsibility entirely."

It was time to convince this grinning idiot that matters were serious. In one quick fluid movement, Arilyn drew the dagger and hurled it at him. The weapon streaked past Danilo, sweeping off his hat before imbedding itself in the wooden beam behind him. Arilyn strode past him and plucked the dagger and the hat from the beam, then thrust his hat at him.

He fingered the hole in disbelief. "Really! This was a new hat," he protested.

"Consider the alternative," she pointed out with grim humor. "Saddle up."

Sighing lustily, the dandy stuck the mutilated hat back on his head and did as he was told. To his credit, he worked quickly. Arilyn watched the stable door, but she could detect neither sound or movement. Perhaps she *had* shaken her shadow, after all.

After years of stopping at the Halfway Inn, Arilyn knew its secrets very well. Although the front of the stable opened on to a busy, well-lit street, a door at the rear of the building would put them directly onto a wooded path that would take them northward through the forest. She'd used that exit on more than one occasion. When both mares were saddled, she motioned for Danilo Thann to follow her. Obligingly he led his horse after her.

On the way out Arilyn stopped by her own horse's stall. She retrieved her saddle bags, and for a moment she looked with longing eyes at the gray mare. It pained Arilyn to leave her horse behind, but the mare needed rest badly. Arilyn took a bit of parchment from her saddlebags and scribbled a note to Myrin Silverspear, asking him to care for her horse and to reimburse the owner of the paired chestnuts for their loss. The innkeeper had handled such a transaction for her once before, and he would trust her to pay him back as soon as she returned. Theirs was a strange friendship, but she knew she could rely on him for anything. Arilyn placed the note between two of the boards that formed the wall—the stableboy would know to check there for messages—and then gave her horse a farewell pat.

As she turned to go, Arilyn looked up at the nobleman. His expression was sympathetic, and she felt a wave of irritation. Many killers were tender of their horses, so why did the fool regard her as if she were a new mother cooing over an infant?

"Come on," she snapped. After leading the way out of the stables and onto the path, she hiked up her flowing skirts and mounted her borrowed horse. When they reached the edge of the forest Arilyn drew a knife from her boot and held it up for Danilo to see.

"If you run, this will find your heart before your horse takes ten paces."

Danilo smiled and raised his hands in a gesture of surrender. "I wouldn't dream of running. Now that you have well and thoroughly captured my attention, I can't wait to find out what all this is about. What a story I'll have to tell once we get home! We are going to Waterdeep, aren't we? I mean, eventually? Just imagine, I'll dine out for a month of tendays on this adventure and . . ."

The rest of his words drifted mercifully into the winds. Arilyn smacked the rump of his horse, sending it running into the night.

They rode hard, but Arilyn could discern no sign that they were being followed. Dark clouds scuttled across the sky, and the trees twisted and writhed in the rising wind. Finally the storm began, and huge raindrops pelted the travelers. The presence of the garrulous hostage made Arilyn almost grateful for the foul weather. The wind and driving rain made conversation impossible, and their situation worsened when they left the relative shelter of the forest. Arilyn pressed on, following the swiftly flowing river known as Winding Water. A travelers' hut on the lower branch promised shelter.

Finally she sighted the small barnlike building and urged her horse toward it. She dismounted and lifted the bar from the double door. A gust of wind blew the doors inward, and the travelers led their horses inside. Arilyn swung the doors shut and threw her weight against them, struggling to close them against the wind. At last she succeeded and slid the inside bolt.

Danilo stood with his hands in his pockets, oblivious to her difficulties with the door. Arilyn was annoyed with him for a moment, until she remembered that the human probably could not see in the darkness of the room.

"What is this place?" he asked.

"A clerical outpost, not far from a monastery where priests of Torm train."

"Oh. Will they mind us using it?"

"No. The students maintain it as a travelers' shelter. We can leave an offering to Torm in the big stone box over there."

"Over where? I can't see a thing. It's as dark as Cyric's shorts in here."

"Right." Arilyn took flint from her saddlebags and lit a tiny wall lamp to dispel a bit of the blackness. The flickering light revealed a large, square room, divided to accommodate travelers and their mounts. There was little by way of comfort: a wooden floor, a few bales of dusty hay for the horses, and three benches in front of a rough stone fireplace.

"All the comforts of home," Danilo Thann remarked lightly, "provided one is accustomed to living in a cave."

"See to the horses, then we'll eat," Arilyn said absently, more concerned with the practical details of their journey than with the dandy's opinions of their accommodations. She had a little hardtack and a few travel biscuits left in her saddlebags. That would do for tonight, but tomorrow she would have to hunt.

While Danilo stumbled around in the dim light caring for the horses, Arilyn gratefully shed the persona of the Sembian courtesan. Calling upon the moonblade, she dispelled the disguise. After tucking her wet black curls behind her ears, she took a linen square and scrubbed her face clean of the cosmetic unguents. Finally she slipped the green lenses from her eyes and returned them to her bag of disguises. Feeling like herself again, she shook a little of the hay loose from a bale and fashioned a couple of sleeping pallets. She got one of her saddlebags and sank down with it onto her bed, rummaging in the bag for food.

"Those are two happy little horses," Danilo announced as he joined her. "The way they tore into that hay, they actually made it look good."

Without speaking, Arilyn handed Danilo a ration of dried meat and hard biscuits. He took it, sniffed it, and held it close to his eyes for inspection. "*This* makes the hay look good, for that matter."

Nevertheless, he took a hearty bite of the meat and chewed vigorously. "Puts up a fight, doesn't it?" he observed cheerfully. After another bite, he took a flask from the bag that hung from his belt and took a deep swallow. He offered it to Arilyn, but she shook her head. Danilo shrugged and tipped up the flask again.

"Is there any way we could get more light in here?" he asked. "I can barely see my hand in front of my face."

"As long as you know it's there, what's your worry?"

"Well, I suppose that covers *that* topic," he said with a touch of humor. "I suppose we could talk about something else."

"Must we?"

Her tone quelled him for perhaps two minutes. They ate in a silence interrupted only by the sound of rain pounding at the wooden structure. Just as Arilyn was beginning to relax, the nobleman started in again.

"So," he said briskly. "What are we running from? From the timing of our exit, my guess would be that pot-bellied giant and his crew. Never overlook the obvious, I always say."

"No," she said, her tone curt.

"No, what?"

"No, we're not running from him."

"Who, then?"

Arilyn merely took another bite of her travel biscuit. Danilo shrugged and tried again. "I have a friend who makes and trades fine weapons. Nord Gundwynd. Do you know him, by any chance? No? Well, he collects antique weapons. He'd love to get his hands on that dagger you were using earlier."

"It's not for sale." Her tone held little encouragement.

And so it went. Danilo continued undeterred in his efforts to draw Arilyn into conversation. She ate her meal in silence. He downed his between bits of gossip and nosey questions.

Finally he stretched. "Well, that was delightful. I feel positively refreshed. Shall I take the first watch? Not that I could see anything, mind you."

Arilyn stared at him in open disbelief. "The first *watch*? You're a hostage."

"Well, yes," he admitted as if that were a matter of small consequence, "but we've got a long road ahead, and you'll have to sleep sometime."

Arilyn was silent for a long moment as she considered his statement. "Was that a warning?" she asked quietly.

Danilo threw back his head and laughed. "Hardly. No, from where I sit it sounds like a simple statement of reality."

That was no more than the truth, but it reminded Arilyn that certain precautions were in order. She glanced down at Danilo's sword, bound to its elaborate scabbard by a peace knot. Many cities required that swords be so bound. It was a precaution that prevented many furtive attacks and impulsive fights, but the law seemed pointless when applied to the dandy beside her. Arilyn had a hard time imagining him becoming carried away by battle lust.

Nevertheless, she insisted, "Your sword, please, as well as any other weapons."

Danilo shrugged agreeably. He worked the peace knot loose and handed over the sword and scabbard. He then drew a jeweled dagger from one of his boots. "Have a care with the dagger," he advised her. "Apart from the gems—which really are rather nice, aren't they?—the weapon has a good deal of sentimental value. I acquired it rather by accident last winter. Actually, it's quite an interesting story."

"I don't doubt it," she cut in dryly. "What's in there?" she asked, pointing to the green leather bag that hung at his waist.

Danilo grinned. "Clothing. Jewelry. Dice. Brandy. Rivengut. Even Moonshae Moonshine—and I dare you to say that three times fast. You know," he concluded, "the essentials."

"All that?" Arilyn eyed the sack skeptically. It looked big enough to hold a tunic and two changes of wool stockings, no more.

"Ah, but this is a magic bag," Danilo advised her in a smug tone. "It holds much more than appearances would indicate."

"Empty it."

"If you insist."

Danilo reached into the sack and drew out a neatly rolled shirt of white silk. He placed it lovingly on the hay, then lay several colored shirts beside it. Next came a velvet tunic and some soft, fur-lined gloves. Three pair of trousers followed, then some undergarments and stockings. There was enough jewelry to bedeck the occupants of a brothel, as well as several pair of dice and three ornate silver flasks. He drew out no less than three hats, one with nodding peacock plumes. The pile grew until the place resembled an open-air market.

"That's enough!" Arilyn finally insisted.

"I'm almost done," he said, rummaging in the bottom of the sack. "Best for last, and all that. Ah! Here it is." He fished out a large flat object and waved it triumphantly.

Arilyn groaned. The fool had produced a spellbook from the bowels of that Beshaba-blasted sack. Of all the things the goddess of bad luck could have sent to torment her! She'd abducted a would-be mage.

"Please tell me you don't casts spells," she pleaded.

"I dabble," he admitted modestly.

Before Arilyn could discern his intent, he took a bit of flint and pointed it at the wood neatly stacked in the fireplace. "Dragonbreath," he muttered.

There was a spark. The flint disappeared from his hand, and a cozy fire filled the room with warmth and light. He turned to Arilyn with a triumphant smirk, then froze. "Nine hells!" he blurted out. "You're an elf."

She banked down the rising flame of her anger. "So I've been told. Put out that fire."

"Why?" he argued in a reasonable tone. "It's dark, and it's cold, and that's a particularly lovely fire, if I may say so."

How could she explain to this pampered dandy her aversion to magical fire? He hadn't seen the miscast fireball; he hadn't heard the screams of his comrades, or smelled their burning flesh as they died in flames that refused to consume *him*. As she formulated a half-truth, Arilyn struggled to push away the memory of the Hammerfell Seven's death. With great effort, she kept her voice calm, her words objective.

"As you guessed earlier, we were being followed. I believe we've eluded pursuit, but I don't wish to risk making a fire while we're still so close to Evereska."

Danilo studied her, then as if he hadn't heard anything she'd just said, he repeated, "An elf. You're an elf. And your eyes aren't really green, after all."

He made the last observation in such a mournful tone that Arilyn blinked in surprise. "Is that going to be a problem?"

"No," he said slowly. "It's just that, well, I *am* highly partial to green. By Mystra, you're definitely not what you appeared to be at first glance."

"Who is?" she asked with asperity. She glanced at Danilo's waterlogged finery and added in an arch tone, "Except perhaps you."

"Thanks," he murmured absently.

Arilyn cast her eyes upward in disbelief. Still absorbed in his intent study of her, Danilo was oblivious to the insult.

"Wait! I've got it!" he crowed triumphantly, jabbing a finger in Arilyn's direction. "I knew you looked familiar. You're the person that the oaf in the bar was seeking. Ariel Moonsomething, right?"

So he wasn't a complete fool. "Close enough," she admitted

grudgingly. She rose, feeling a need to walk about.

"How interesting! So what's your story?" Danilo asked, settling comfortably down for the evening's entertainment. He lay on his side, crossing his ankles and propping himself up on one elbow. Arilyn cast him a dismissing look and walked to the fireplace.

"No, leave it alone," he insisted, as Arilyn began to poke at the burning logs with a stick. "We're both wet and cold, and the fire will do us good. Just forget about it and sit down." He noisily patted the straw beside him in invitation. "Come on. Relax. You had them moonswaggled back at the inn with that fancy getup. That thug didn't follow us."

"I told you, I'm not worried about him," she said.

"If not him, who? We *are* being followed, you said."

"*Were*," she stressed, looking over her shoulder at him with a quelling glance.

Danilo Thann was not easily quelled. He rolled his eyes in comic disgust. "*Were*. Well, that clears everything right up."

Arilyn turned away, ignoring his friendly sarcasm.

"Look," Danilo said to the back of her head, "since I'm along for the ride, so to speak, don't you think I should have some idea who or what I'm up against? And where we're going, for that matter?"

Why not? Arilyn thought. Maybe the truth would frighten him into holding his tongue. She sank down in the straw beside Danilo, drawing her knees up tight against her chest.

"All right, then, here it is. Since you seem to be current on most of the gossip in the area, you may have heard that someone is systematically assassinating Harpers."

"Ghastly business," Danilo said with a shudder. His eyes widened. "Oh gods. I'm not sure I like where this is leading. You're saying that the Harper Assassin is after *you*?"

"You're sharper than you appear," she said dryly.

"Thank you, but how do you know? About the assassin, I mean."

Arilyn shrugged, trying to appear matter-of-fact. "For some time now, I've been followed everywhere I go. Several of my friends have been killed. I was usually nearby when it happened."

"Oh, my dear. How awful for you."

The genuine warmth and concern in the young noble's voice temporarily disconcerted Arilyn. Her eyes flew to the fire, and she stared fixedly into the magically conjured flames that had ignited such bitter memories. At the moment anything was better than meeting Danilo Thann's kind, gray eyes. She had put this young man's life in danger, and fool though he might be, he'd done nothing to deserve the treatment she'd dealt him.

"I regret involving you in this," she murmured. "Believe me, I had not planned to bring you this far."

"So far, no problem," he replied, cheerfully accepting her apology. "Anyway, it's a rare honor for a humble fashion plate such as myself to be of service to the Harpers. You are one of them, I take it?"

"No," she said slowly. "I'm no Harper."

"Oh? Then why is the Harper Assassin after you?"

"I work for the Harpers on occasion."

"Ah. And what is it that you do?" Danilo drawled, eyeing her and waggling his eyebrows in a broad parody of a leer.

Arilyn glared at him, and he grinned in return. The fool enjoyed baiting her! she realized suddenly. It was a game. His scrutiny was not lascivious, but boyishly mischievous. All of her irritation with Danilo Thann flooded back, pushing aside the guilt of a moment before. An unworthy but irresistible impulse urged her to make him squirm a bit.

"I am an assassin," she intoned in a threatening voice.

A droll expression crossed Danilo's face. "Do tell. And you've got some lakefront property in the Anauroch Desert to sell me as well, I suppose?"

Arilyn grinned despite herself. "Remember, appearances can be deceiving. In some cases," she added with a touch of sarcasm.

Her gibe went over Danilo's head with a foot to spare. He waved away her comment. "No, no, it's not that. I could buy you as an assassin, although I imagine you're prettier than most. It's just that, well, since when do Harpers have people assassinated?"

"They don't," she admitted. "I haven't done that sort of work for years, and never in the employ of the Harpers. Now I recover lost items, lead quick-strike parties, guard travelers. I'm a ranger, spy, or sell-sword as the need arises."

Danilo rolled onto his stomach and propped up his chin with his hands. "Your versatility is astounding, but for my own peace of mind, let's get back to this assassin thing. Do you— oops! excuse me—*did* you really sneak up on people and kill them?"

Arilyn's chin lifted. "No, never. I challenged armed and capable fighters and overcame them in single combat."

"I see." Danilo nodded knowingly. "No wonder the Harper Assassin is after you." She raised her eyebrows in inquiry, and he grinned. "You know, for trying to raise the standards of the trade. Against the guild laws, and all that."

A bubble of laughter welled up in Arilyn, but she held it under control. "I never actually belonged to the Assassin's Guild."

"You see? There's yet another motive. They want to collect their back guild fees out of your estate."

Arilyn finally succumbed to a chuckle. "I'm not sure the Assassin's Guild would want to claim me as a member."

"Really. There is a tale here, perhaps?"

She shrugged. "Not really. Very early in my career, 'assassin' became a sort of nickname. If someone crossed swords with me, they died," she said simply, in answer to Danilo's inquiring look.

"Hmmm. I'll bear that in mind. And then?"

"The name stuck. In time I was truly considered an assassin, and I began to think of myself as one, albeit an honorable assassin. For years I was an independent adventurer, hired to fight and therefore to kill."

"That sounds like an assassin to me," Danilo murmured.

"Yes, but never did I fight one who was unarmed, never did

I shed innocent blood."

"You know that for a fact, do you? It must be nice to be so confident of one's judgment," he said, a little wistfully.

"For good or ill, I do not have to rely upon *my* judgment," she said. Even to her own ears, her voice sounded a little bitter. She lay her hand on the sword at her side. "The sword I carry cannot shed innocent blood. It *will* not. I learned that while I was little more than a child, training at the Academy of Arms. One of the older students, Tintagel Ni'Tessine, used to taunt me about my race. I lost my temper one day and drew on him."

"What happened?" Danilo encouraged her.

A small smile tightened Arilyn's lips. "My sword arm went numb, and the moonblade dropped from my hand. Tintagel took the opportunity to beat me senseless."

"That's terrible!"

She shrugged. "It happens."

"That's hardly an innocent man's behavior," Danilo said heatedly. "I had not realized there was such prejudice against elves."

Arilyn looked at him strangely. "Tintagel Ni'Tessine is an elf."

"Wait a minute." Danilo held up one hand, and he appeared to be thoroughly puzzled. "Did I miss something?"

"He's a gold elf. I'm a moon elf, and a half-elf at that," she admitted grudgingly. "You didn't know that there are several races of elves?"

"Well, yes. I've just never realized that there might be significant differences."

That remark, so typical from humans, jolted Arilyn. "Why am I not surprised?" she said so harshly that Danilo blinked in surprise.

Her hostage could not know that her manner covered her own chagrin. When was the last time she had chattered like such a magpie? Had she *ever* told anyone about that incident with Tintagel? Or admitted even to herself that she sometimes felt belittled by the power of her own sword? Damn it, something about the young man seemed to break down the defenses of her natural reserve, and she resented him for it.

Danilo, however, did not seem to be put out by her abrupt change of mood. "You share my passion for fine gems, I see."

"How did you come to that conclusion?"

With a smug little smile, he pointed to her sword. "That stone in the hilt. It's a topaz, isn't it?"

"I suppose so. Why?"

"Oh, I'm just curious. The sword itself looks quite old, but the stone is cut in a modern fashion."

Arilyn gaped at him for a moment. "That's a remarkable observation."

"Not at all," he disclaimed modestly. "As I mentioned, I have a passion for precious stones, and I know a few things about them. See the way the tiny facets curl around the base of the gem, leading up like a honeycomb to a large flat surface? That style started becoming popular only about, say, fifty years ago."

"I'll have to take your word on that," she said. "But you're right: the stone is fairly new."

"The original was lost, I take it? What kind of stone was it?"

"A moonstone."

"Semi-precious white stone, often flecked with blue. Natural conduits for magic," Danilo recited in a learned tone. "Why was it replaced with a topaz?"

Arilyn shrugged. "When I started training, my teacher had the new stone made to balance the hilt."

"Not many teachers give that much attention to detail . . . or to their students for that matter." He grinned. "Mine generally tried to avoid me as much as they could. You must have been fortunate in your choice of teacher."

"I was," Arilyn said warmly. "To study with Kymil Nimesin was a great opportunity, and—" She broke off suddenly.

"And?"

Arilyn just shrugged. Damn it all, she thought angrily, I'm doing it again. This man would have her life history from her before she could be rid of him.

Most distressing to her was the inexplicable tug of camaraderie, the tiny seedling of friendship that was growing between her and this stranger—this shallow, foolish, overdressed human. Like a talisman, she deliberately brought to mind an image of Rafe Silverspur. The reminder of what could happen to those close to her strengthened her resolve to keep herself firmly apart.

Again Danilo Thann's cheerful voice broke into her thoughts. "You know, I just realized that you never told me your name. What was it that the comical barbarian in the inn called you? Arilyn, wasn't it? Arilyn Moonsinger. No, that's not quite right. Moonblade. Yes, that's it!"

Arilyn rose and kicked the bright embers of Danilo's fire into ash. "Get some sleep," she said curtly, keeping her back to the man. "We leave before daybreak."

Seven

Arilyn shook her hostage awake while it was still dark.

"Whazzat?" Danilo sat up abruptly, staring bleary-eyed into the grim face of the half-elf until his vision focused. "Oh. Hello there. I suppose it's time for my watch?"

"Time to leave," she said flatly.

"Oh. If you say so." Danilo struggled to his feet and stretched, shifting this way and that and wincing as he worked out some stiff spots. "Where are we going?"

"Waterdeep."

"Oh, marvelous," he said, brightening. "We can probably catch up with one of the merchant trains within a few days and—"

"No," she broke in quietly.

"No?" Danilo looked puzzled, stopping in mid-stretch. "Whyever not?"

Arilyn explained with the patience usually afforded a rather slow child. "A very skillful tracker has been following me. I was headed west when he lost me. I'm assuming

92

he knows my routes and habits well enough to consider Waterdeep my logical destination. He is likely to take the most common route, the trade route. If we were to travel with a merchant train, he could easily catch up."

"Ah. Never overlook the obvious," Danilo commented, nodding sagely.

"Something like that," Arilyn admitted. "So we'll take the northern route."

The dandy shook his head and sputtered in disbelief, "Surely you jest. The northern route? As in, troll country? I'll have you know I detest trolls. Utterly."

"Don't worry. We'll skirt the High Moors."

"No trolls?"

"No trolls." Danilo still looked distressed, so Arilyn elaborated. "It's riskier than the southern trade route, but we'll get to Waterdeep faster. Also, we pass through open country. If my guess is wrong and someone is still trying to track us, we'll see them as soon as they see us." She thought it best not to tell the nervous dandy that she would actually prefer such a confrontation, and she paused before dropping the other boot. "And another thing. We'll save more time if we cut through the bottom lip of the marsh."

Danilo caught his breath and held up both hands in a gesture of protest. "The marsh? We're talking about the Marsh of Chelimber, I assume? We are. Well, no thank you. I think I'll just take my horse and head south, if it's all the same to you."

Arilyn had anticipated this reaction. "I'm sorry," she told him firmly, "but you're going to come with me."

He sighed with resignation, then smirked. "I do grow on people, don't I?"

"Hardly. I need to reach Waterdeep and disappear without alerting the assassin. But," she added pointedly, "if I let you loose along the merchant route, you would sing this song to anyone who would listen, and I'll be back where I started."

Danilo considered her argument for a brief moment, then nodded. "All right," he said agreeably. He started to stuff his belongings back into his magic sack.

His ready compliance surprised Arilyn. "You agree? Just like that?"

Still packing, he arched an eyebrow at her. "Do I have much choice in the matter?"

"No."

"Well then, no sense in whining about things you can't change, is there?" he concluded cheerfully. He picked up the last item—a silver flask—and took a bracing pull at it before he slipped it into the sack. Thus fortified, he rose and faced Arilyn.

"There. Packing's done. I say, do you think you could catch us something for breakfast? Anything at all? At this point I could eat a pickled wyvern. And while you hunt, I'll just freshen up a tad. Not that we're likely to meet anyone from polite society along the route you've chosen, but one can't travel looking like leftovers from a gnoll's feast, can one?"

Danilo's gaze swept over Arilyn, who was clad for travel in boots and trousers, a simple blue tunic over her loose shirt, and her dark cloak. "By the way," he added casually, with an obvious and exaggerated attempt at diplomacy, "that outfit is very . . . well, it's certainly very practical. It looks comfortable, really! For whatever it's worth, I vastly prefer the clothes you wore at the inn. Maybe all those veils would be a bit much for the road, but at least let me lend you a few pieces of jewelry to brighten up your ensemble?"

Arilyn stifled a sigh. It was going to be a very long trip to Waterdeep.

The sun was edging above the horizon when the half-elf finally nudged her well-fed and immaculately groomed hostage into his saddle. Worried by even a brief delay, Arilyn set as brisk a pace as she felt the horses could handle: it was important that they cross the Marsh of Chelimber before nightfall.

As they left the rolling foothills of the Greycloak Mountains behind, the friendly, autumn-tinted woodlands gave way to a flat, grim valley littered with jagged boulders and scrubby brush. As the ground beneath their horses' hooves became increasingly soggy, even those pitiful bushes disappeared, and the only vegetation in sight were the rushes and cattails that ringed small pools of tea-colored water. The happy twitter of the forest birds had long ago faded, to be replaced by the incurious stare of an occasional heron.

Arilyn was not unhappy to note that the repressive ugliness of the landscape had curbed the nobleman's tongue, for his chatter had dwindled to an occasional question. He rode well, she was relieved to see, and as he rode he took in the sights like some slightly distressed pleasure-traveler.

"What's that?" he demanded, pointing to a large square depression in the bog. Arilyn looked, and her heart sank.

"Someone's been cutting peat," she said tersely.

"Whatever for?"

"Fuel. It burns well."

Danilo considered her words. "Why would someone want to come all the way into this flattened-out version of the Abyss for fuel? There are perfectly good woodlands between here and the nearest civilized area." When Arilyn didn't comment on his observation, Danilo puzzled it over. He finally snapped his fingers and smiled in triumph. "Wait a minute! I've got it! Our peat-cutting friends must be from one of the uncivilized races. Orcs, maybe? More likely goblins, given the terrain. Am I right?"

Arilyn cast him a sour look. "You needn't look so pleased about it. Listen, that peat was recently cut. Whatever did it is probably nearby."

"You jest," Danilo said, a hopeful note in his voice.

"Not very often. We're nearing the marsh. Hold your tongue until we're through it."

The dandy subsided. Soon the spongy texture of the peat bog gave way to open wetlands, and the air took on a repressive, swampy tang. Before highsun they had reached the edge of Chelimber Marsh.

"I say, this is a dismal place," Danilo noted with dismay.

Arilyn silently agreed. In her opinion, the Marsh of Chelimber could easily be mistaken for one of the lower levels of the Nine Hells.

There was no sign of animal life, yet an eerie, insectlike chirruping came from everywhere and nowhere. Bare, rock-covered ground alternated with soggy patches of waist-high marsh grasses, which swayed and beckoned despite an utter lack of wind. Many of the small pools that dotted the ground bubbled and seethed, sending up gushes of sulphur-scented steam. Even the air seemed heavy and oppressive beneath a slate-colored sky.

"Let's get it over with," Arilyn whispered, resolutely guiding her horse forward. Danilo followed, looking none too happy.

Despite the known and rumored dangers of the marsh, their ride was uneventful. Arilyn did not relax her guard, but listened alertly to the strange sounds of the marsh. From no discernable source, Chelimber emitted a continuous spate of chirps, pops, groans, and belches. The noise was unnerving, and Arilyn noted the toll it took on the high-strung mares. Yet there was no sign of danger, and by late afternoon it began to appear that the trip would pass without incident. Even Danilo managed to hold his tongue until, by Arilyn's reckoning, they neared the western border of the marsh. The mist-shrouded sun hung just above the marsh grass. Tension began to drain from Arilyn's taut body as the horses picked their way toward relative safety. They would escape Chelimber before nightfall, despite the morning's delay.

That hope was premature. Almost lost in the swamp's music was a new note, a faint, grating sound that brought to Arilyn's mind the image of a dragon with hiccoughs. She hoped that the bizarre noise was just another of the marsh's aural tricks, but just to check she held up a hand to halt Danilo's progress. "Did you hear that?" she mouthed at him.

The nobleman's attention was elsewhere. Arilyn followed the direction of his gaze, and her throat tightened in foreboding: at her side, the moonblade glowed with an ominous blue light.

"What's that all about?" he asked, pointing to her sword.

"Lower your voice."

"Why is your sword blue?" he asked softly.

"Magic," she explained tersely, looking about for whatever the moonblade sensed. "A danger warning."

"Quaint. Very quaint," he drawled, regarding the pale blue light of the sword with casual interest. "A glowing sword. Tell me, does it come in green? If so, where can I get one?"

The lack of concern in his voice infuriated Arilyn. She glared at him, incredulous. "Goblins," she stressed in a quiet voice. "Remember your peat-cutting goblins? Surely not even you could find such creatures amusing."

Danilo pursed his lips and considered this. "Actually, there *was* this little fellow down in Cormyr . . ."

"Oh, be still," Arilyn hissed. Her fingers curved around the moonblade's grip, and she dismissed Danilo and his foolishness to concentrate on the battle that was sure to come. She eased her horse westward and gestured for the dandy to follow her. The ground was less flat here, and a small hill some hundred yards away bore the ruins of what appeared to be an ancient keep. The setting sun would be at their back, providing a disadvantage to any attackers. There they could take a stand.

No, there *I* can take a stand, Arilyn corrected silently, casting a derisive glance at the man beside her. Even if Danilo Thann were capable of holding his own in a fight—which she doubted—he would never risk getting blood on his big-city finery.

For the hundredth time since sunrise Arilyn cursed herself over her unfortunate choice of a hostage. She had fought goblinkind many times, and she knew better than to be too confident about the outcome of such a battle. Even the horses, pampered fancy mounts that they were, sensed that danger lay before them; their ears lay back against their heads and they whickered uneasily. Granted, Danilo Thann was not traveling with her of his own choice, therefore she was honorbound to give him what protection she could. But by all the gods, she would much rather turn him over to the goblins. Perhaps *they* could wipe that complacent look off his foolish face!

Arilyn's angry thoughts were interrupted by an unearthly screech. The sound split the air and hung, reverberating, over the marsh. That was the final straw for her temperamental horse, who reared up violently and unexpectedly. Arilyn grabbed at the pommel of her saddle with both hands to keep from being thrown. Before she could reclaim the reins, the horse bolted.

"Hang on," Danilo yelled, urging his own horse close to Arilyn's panicked mount. What was he trying to do? she wondered. His horse looked no calmer than hers. It careened along with teeth bared, its ears flat back against its mane and the whites of its terrified eyes gleaming. Danilo seized Arilyn's reins, struggling to control his own mount with one hand.

That's it, Arilyn thought with a flash of resignation. We're both down. Before their spooked mounts had gone a dozen paces, by sheer strength of arm and will Danilo brought both horses to a halt.

Arilyn gaped at the noble in disbelief, earning one of his charming, infuriating smiles. He tossed her reins back to her. "Nice trick, eh? Luck is with you. You abducted the captain of Waterdeep's champion polo team. Next time, my dear, do try to steal battle-seasoned horses, hmmm?"

Before she could respond to his gibe, a second roar rolled across the marsh. Arilyn drew the moonblade and readied herself for the attack. One of the dangers of the marsh lay in the weird way in which it warped sound. The taunts of their unseen enemy seemed to come from everywhere at once. Where, then, could she and Danilo run?

From behind the ridge of a nearby hillock rose half a score of enormous, scale-covered nightmares. Arilyn had heard tales of the lizard men of Chelimber Marsh, but the reality brought a quick lump of horror to her throat.

Tall as men, the scaly gray-green creatures lurched toward them through the mist and the marsh grass on heavily muscled legs, shrieking and roaring with bloodlust as they brandished blades and battlehammers in their massive, taloned hands.

"Wait a minute! You said there'd be goblins. Those don't

look like goblins to me," Danilo protested. "I could be wrong, of course."

"Lizard men," Arilyn snapped, struggling to control her terrified horse as she formulated a battle plan. Outnumbered as they were, five-to-one, flight seemed the best course. As she flashed a look over her shoulder, she saw a small band of goblins—a hunting party, most likely—rising from the marsh grass, effectively cutting off the chance of a southward retreat.

"So. Do we fight or run?" Danilo asked.

The half-elf spun back around. The lizard men had fanned out into a line, blocking escape to the north or east. "I'll fight. You run," she shouted, pointing with the moonblade toward the ruined keep.

Danilo extended his hand. "My sword?"

Arilyn had forgotten. She reached behind her saddle, snatched his blade from its scabbard, and tossed it to him. Danilo deftly caught the weapon, then squinted toward the setting sun. "Now *those*," he remarked, "are goblins."

The half-elf groaned. Three more of the creatures had sprung from behind the piles of stone and rubble, their weapons drawn. Gibbering and snarling, they rushed forward, and Arilyn caught a whiff of the stench that rose from their dark orange skin and filthy leather armor. All three goblins waved rusted swords, and their snarls bared rows of short, sharp fangs. Lemon-colored eyes gleamed with eagerness for battle.

"I'll take those little ones," the dandy volunteered.

"Go, you half-witted troll," she shouted.

Danilo saluted her and wheeled his horse around, galloping toward the ruins and the onrushing goblins. On horseback, Arilyn reasoned, even Danilo should be able to handle three unmounted goblins. To her surprise, he slashed at the western-most lizard man as he rushed past it, as if daring the creatures to follow him.

Good tactics, she acknowledged briefly. If we divide them, they can't surround us as easily. Then there was no more time for thought. The lizard men were almost upon her.

All of the lizard men.

A moment's surprise, and then Arilyn understood. The
creatures might hunt in a band, but they had little intelligence.
Their instincts were for survival, not strategy. Thus, each individual lizard man chose to attack the smaller, seemingly
weaker member of the pair. Their mistake, she thought with a
thin smile. Raising the glowing moonblade aloft, she forced her
horse into a charge.

The first of the lizard men lumbered into range, swinging a
curved scimitar in a wicked arc. With a lightning combination,
Arilyn parried its first blow and then ran the creature
through. The next lizard she disarmed by lopping off its taloned hand. Its shrieks of rage and pain set the rest of the
pack rocking back a step, buying Arilyn an instant's respite.
She struggled to control her horse as she flashed a glance in
Danilo's direction.

He was faring far better than she'd dared to hope. Somehow he had managed to fell two of the goblins. Still on horseback, he was making short work of the third. The lizard men,
having decided on Arilyn, were paying him no heed whatso-
ever. For the span of one heartbeat, Arilyn knew despair.
Her hostage would surely take the opportunity handed him
and flee, leaving her to face the monsters alone. Well then,
she would give them a fight. With a fierce battle cry, she
raised the sword in challenge and dared the lizard men to
come within its range.

The creatures halted, uncertain. Long, reptilian tongues
flickered in and out between daggerlike fangs as the lizard
men weighed their hunger and the encouraging shouts of the
goblin band against the glowing sword and half-elf's unexpectedly strong resistance. Arilyn's prancing mare whinnied
in terror, and the sound seemed to shatter the lizard men's
momentary reluctance. Sensing a weakness, they shrieked
anew and pressed forward, almost climbing over each other
in their eagerness.

The moonblade danced and twinkled as Arilyn slashed at her
attackers. Three more lizard men fell, clutching at sliced
throats or severed limbs. One of the remaining creatures

came in low with a large, upturned knife and a bright idea: attack the horse. Perceiving the monster's intent, Arilyn viciously dug her heels into her horse's side and jerked back the reins. The terrified mare reared, just barely avoiding a slash that would have gutted it.

Arilyn used the momentum of the horse's movement to dismount. Throwing herself backward in a somersault, the agile half-elf rolled out of the saddle and landed on her feet, moonblade in hand. With the flat of her blade she smacked the mare's flanks, hard. The horse fled, dodging the clutching talons of the five still-standing, hungry lizards. The lizard men, robbed of the promise of horseflesh, surrounded Arilyn and closed in.

The half-elf could hear excited squeaks and harsh, high-pitched chattering just outside the tight circle of scales and blades. Wonderful, Arilyn thought with dismay. The goblin hunting party had finally decided to join in. As if she didn't have enough to deal with.

One of the lizard men got through her guard, and the tip of its sword slashed a burning line across her left shoulder. With her next swing Arilyn cut the lizard across the face. Blinded and roaring, the creature pawed at its eyes and reeled away, knocking one of its brothers to the ground in its frenzy. The fallen lizard man thrashed about, struggling to regain its footing on the marshy, blood-slick ground. With a quick jab, the moonblade found its heart, and the monster lay still. Arilyn leaped over it toward the blinded lizard, and quickly ended that beast's suffering.

Now there were but three of the lizard men left. Even tired and wounded, Arilyn felt confident of winning against those odds. She doubted, however, whether she would have the strength at battle's end to wade through a band of goblins.

As she fought, Arilyn heard a strange battle hymn drifting from somewhere on the marsh. It was a bawdy ballad, set to a well-known drinking song, and it was rendered triply incongruous by the refined tone of a well-trained tenor voice:

> They're far from staid after a raid
> Those men of Zhentil Keep:
> They kill off all the women
> For they much prefer the sheep.
>
> The Zhents don't eat their ill-got treat;
> Not one of them's a glutton.
> So isn't it a marvel
> That they always smell of mutton?

Blasted human! Arilyn ducked a battle axe and gritted her teeth in annoyance. To her surprise, she found that the foolish song rallied her more effectively than the battle skirl of Moonshae pipes. She fought on, buoyed up by a mixture of relief and irritation. Danilo would get away, and in his own flamboyant fashion.

Unimpressed by the music, the three lizard men pressed in. One of them lunged at her with a dagger. Arilyn knocked the weapon from its claws and darted forward, thrusting the moonblade deep into its reptilian eye and immediately killing it. The creature fell heavily forward, and the half-elf tore her sword free and leaped clear of the toppling corpse.

With a triumphant roar, a huge, brown-scaled lizard man hefted his battle axe and took a mighty swipe at the half-elf's knees. She leaped high to avoid the blade, but on the backswing the axe's handle caught her and knocked her sideways. Thrown off balance, she flew several feet before she hit the ground hard. She stopped face down beside a steaming, sulphur-scented pool. Arilyn scrambled to her feet. If she had been hurt by the fall, the pain would come later.

The remaining pair of lizards, smelling blood, closed in. Arilyn faced them and crouched in a defensive stance, holding the moonblade before her in a two-handed grip. The sword glowed a brilliant blue in the gathering darkness, lighting the half-elf's grim face and reflecting the cold fire of her eyes. The monsters, expecting a wounded half-elf and an easy kill, fell back in surprise and fear. Taking advantage of their reaction,

Arilyn advanced, raising the magic sword high.

A clatter of hooves distracted the lizard men. Brandishing his sword, Danilo Thann rode his dainty chestnut mare in tight circles around the creatures and the half-elf, his blade prodding and teasing as he harried the monsters, as if trying to draw their attention away from Arilyn.

What now? she thought in exasperation. The fool would get dizzy and fall off his horse before he managed to accomplish anything of value.

Roaring its annoyance, one of the creatures raised a length of rusty chain and tried to swat away the pesky human. Its first blow knocked the sword from Danilo's hand, and with a triumphant snarl the creature started whirling the chain, preparing to launch the weapon at the nobleman.

Arilyn pulled a knife from her boot and hurled it into the creature's open, snarling mouth. With a strangled gurgle, the beast stopped dead. The chain kept whirling, however, wrapping itself around the lizard man's arm with a cracking of bone. To Arilyn's surprise the monster merely spat blood and switched its weapon to its other hand.

Danilo's wild ride brought him too close to the axe-wielding brown lizard. The monster hoisted his weapon and swung, slashing the nobleman's silk sleeve from elbow to wrist and drawing blood.

Danilo galloped several yards away, then reined in his horse and regarded his ruined garment with dismay. He jabbed a finger at the lizards. "That's it. Now I'm angry," he informed them. The lizard men roared and continued to lumber toward Danilo, chain and axe raised for the kill.

"When in doubt, run," Danilo announced to the marsh at large. He wheeled his horse around and headed to the north. The lizard men fell in behind him.

"Oh, no you don't," Arilyn shouted at the monsters. For lack of another weapon to hurl, she snatched up a stone and threw it. "Stand and fight, you overgrown sacks of shoe leather!"

The missile struck the axe-wielding lizard man in the back of the head. Bellowing its fury, it threw its weapon aside and thundered back toward Arilyn. The beast lunged forward in an elemental frenzy, its fangs bared. Arilyn stood her ground until the last moment, then she dove to one side and rolled safely away. The charging lizard's jaws closed on air, and the monster skidded to a stop, arms windmilling wildly as it struggled to maintain its balance.

Arilyn came in low and sliced the lizard man cleanly across its throat. The beast crashed nose-first into the ground. With a brief nod of satisfaction, the half-elf headed off at a run in the direction of Danilo and the final foe. She easily overtook the wounded and slow-moving beast, and stomped hard on its tail to distract it from its overdressed prey.

With an incongruous squeak, the lizard spun around. Ignoring Arilyn, it dropped its chain weapon and gathered up its tail and draped it over its wounded arm, gazing mournfully down at the tip and emitting pitiful, chirruping whimpers. Involuntarily, Arilyn's sword arm lowered.

Suddenly the beast stiffened. It hissed, gurgled, and slumped twitching to the earth. A sword protruded from its neck at a hideous angle.

Behind the fallen lizard man stood Danilo Thann. Not bothering to advertise his intent, the dandy had quietly skewered the monster through the back of the neck. Arilyn felt a sudden and unreasonable flash of anger. "Where are the goblins?" she demanded, thinking it better to vent her rage on them than on her hostage.

Danilo pointed. To Arilyn's surprise, all six members of the goblin hunting party lay in a bloody pile.

Breathing heavily, she held the moonblade up before her. Its light was almost gone, a sure sign that the danger was past and the battle over. She sheathed the weapon and turned to the nobleman. For a long moment they regarded each other silently over the dead body of the brown lizard man. "You had to kill him like that?"

Danilo recoiled, blinking in surprise. "Whatever are you talking about? Him who? There's a lot of dead 'hims' out here to choose from, you know. A few 'hers' too, I would imagine, although I'm no expert on lizard anatomy."

Arilyn raked one hand through her sweat-soaked black curls. "Forget it. Where's my horse?"

"She won't be far away," Danilo said. He placed one boot gingerly on the brown scales of the lizard man and yanked out his sword. After fastidiously wiping it clean on a clump of marsh grass, Danilo took the reins of his mare and went in search of the other mount. Arilyn trudged after him.

They hadn't far to go, for Arilyn's horse milled just inside the walls of the ruined keep. Danilo produced some sugar lumps from his magic sack, and coaxed the mare to him. The horse sniffed, then its rubbery lips folded around the sugar in Danilo's outstretched palm. The dandy smiled and scratched the white star on the horse's forehead. "The sugar should sweeten your temper a tad, my pretty," he said. The horse nickered softly and nudged at Danilo with her muzzle.

"It worked!" he said. He cast a speculative look at Arilyn, then with a sly smile he offered her a sugar lump.

Arilyn blinked, her mouth dropping open in astonishment. Then her worn face lit up unexpectedly and she laughed.

"I shall accept that as an apology," Danilo stated, an expression of delight flooding his face as he surveyed the loveliness of her usually stern visage. "Quite a fight, eh?"

His frank admiration disconcerted her, and his casual approach to battle defied her perception of him. Danilo Thann was not quite the helpless, shallow dandy he appeared. He was dangerous, in more ways than one. Arilyn's smile faded, and her eyes narrowed in suspicion.

"The goblins are dead," she observed.

Danilo quirked an eyebrow as he surveyed the carnage around them. "You have a firm grasp on the obvious."

"How?" she persisted, ignoring his teasing.

He shrugged lightly. "You know goblins. They're always fighting among themselves and . . ."

"Enough!" Arilyn snapped, rounding on him. "I am not a fool. I do not enjoy being treated like one."

"You get used to it," Danilo interjected mildly as he adjusted the angle of his hat.

"To which, no doubt, you can attest," she noted with asperity. "Whatever else you may be, though, you can fight. Where did you learn to fight goblins?"

He grinned disarmingly. "I have five older brothers."

"Very amusing," she said dryly, crossing her arms over her chest as she studied the man. "That is not enough to explain your skill or your confidence in battle."

"All right then, would you believe *six* brothers?"

Arilyn's shoulders sagged in defeat. "This isn't getting me anywhere," she muttered to herself. She straightened and addressed the young man in a brisk tone. "All right. Your secrets are your own. You saved my life, and I owe you. You have more than earned your freedom."

From beneath the brim of his hat, Danilo gazed pointedly around the forbidding landscape. "How lovely," he drawled. "Now that I'm no longer strictly necessary to you, you no longer require my company. In compensation, I get to pass some time in the Marsh of Chelimber, taking in the sights, conversing with the natives. A bargain, by my eyes. Tell me, am I to undertake this suicidal journey on foot?"

"Of course not," she retorted. "You'll ride."

Danilo lay one hand on his chest, a dramatic gesture of gratitude. "Ah, the lady gifts me indeed—freedom that I could have taken for myself and one of my own steeds. They *are* my horses, by the way. Truly, I'm overwhelmed."

Arilyn gritted her teeth and silently counted to ten. With sorely tested patience she spelled out her intent: "At daybreak, we head south. Both of us. Once we find a merchant train, I'll leave you in their care. Now do you understand?"

"Ah. Thank you for the kind thought, but no."

Exasperated, the half-elf sank onto the ground and dropped her weary head into her hands. It would seem that the fop had something of the merchant in him after all; judging from his tone, he was prepared to barter like a Calimshite peddlar.

"I take it you have something else in mind?" she observed.

He sat down on a rock facing her, grimacing as he held his

richly embroidered robe clear of the lizard blood that pooled on the ground near his feet. "As it happens, I do," he said lightly. "You."

Startled, she sat upright and eyed him with suspicion. "I beg your pardon?"

"Your company," he clarified. "From now on, we shall be partners and travel-mates."

Arilyn stared at the nobleman. Remarkable though it seemed, Danilo appeared to be serious. "That's impossible."

"Why?"

Leveling a stern look at Danilo, she said, "I work alone. I walk alone."

"Or so it is written in the stars," he intoned, gently mocking the stiffness of her tone.

Arilyn flushed and looked away. "I didn't mean to sound so pompous," she continued quietly. "I simply do not wish to travel with another."

"What have we been doing for the better part of two days?" he asked, then raised one hand to cut off the argument she had ready. "Yes, yes. I know. Escape, hostage, secrecy, that sort of thing. All that aside, you said you would keep me with you until you reached Waterdeep. Is the word of Arilyn Moonblade given with such fervor, but taken back so lightly?" He smiled at the angry flash that came to her eyes. "No, I thought not. Here it is, then: by your own words, you owe me. As payment for your life, I choose to stay with you, to Waterdeep and perhaps a while longer."

Arilyn massaged her aching temples as she tried to sort this through. "Why?"

"Why not?"

Arilyn's patience was thinning rapidly. "Why?" she demanded through clenched teeth.

"If the truth must be told, I'm a bit of an amateur bard. Well thought of in some circles, too, if I may say so."

"Eventually, this will have a point?" she asked wearily.

"Naturally. You heard me sing the Ballad of the Zhentish Raiders?" Danilo waited, his expression obviously courting praise. Arilyn's only response was a continued glare, so after a moment the dandy shrugged and continued.

"Yes. Well. This journey is turning out to be quite the adventure, isn't it? I've decided to seize the opportunity and write an original ballad about the Harper Assassin. The first! My fame will be assured! You'll feature largely in the tale, of course," he noted hastily and magnanimously. "Part of it is written already. Would you like to hear what I've got so far?" Without waiting for encouragement, Danilo cleared his throat and began to sing in his fine tenor voice some of the most strained verse Arilyn had ever heard.

Arilyn sat through two stanzas before drawing a knife and placing the tip at Danilo's larynx. "Sing another note," she said calmly, "and I'll carve that song from your throat."

Grimacing, Danilo took the blade between his thumb and forefinger and eased it away. "Merciful Milil! And I thought the critics in Waterdeep were harsh! What do you expect from someone who's merely a gifted amateur?"

"A straight answer would be nice," she suggested.

"All right then," he said bluntly, "I'm concerned about survival, plain and simple. I have no desire to be on my own, and you're as good a bodyguard as any I've seen. Frankly I doubt I'd be any safer traveling with a merchant caravan, so my present lot suits me just fine."

Arilyn considered the statement for a moment. His words rang true, and he looked as serious as his foolish countenance would probably allow. If he wanted protection, Arilyn acknowledged, she owed him that much. She thrust the blade back into her boot and gave in to the inevitable.

"All right," she conceded. "We ride hard and split the watch, the hunting, and the cooking. There'll be no chatter, no magic, and no singing."

"Anything," he agreed readily. "Get me safely to Waterdeep, my dear, and I'll even polish your weapons for you. By Tempus, they could use a good once-over." As he spoke, Danilo reached out to stroke the moonblade's ancient, tarnished sheath.

Immediately a spark of blue light lit the marsh. With a sharp oath, Danilo recoiled, jerking back his hand. He held up his index finger, regarding it with disbelief. The skin at the tip was blackened, blasted by the sword's magic.

"What did I do wrong? What prompted that thing to attack me?" he demanded. "Didn't you say it couldn't draw innocent blood? Oh, wait a minute—no blood. Forget the last question."

Keeping her eyes steady on Danilo and her voice level, she added, "There will be one more condition to this 'partnership.' You must never touch that sword again."

Sucking on the offended digit, Danilo nodded avidly. "That goes without saying."

The half-elf abruptly rose to her feet and swung herself up into the saddle. "Let's go."

"Shouldn't we tend to our wounds first?" Danilo asked, eyeing Arilyn's torn and bloodied shirt with concern.

She looked down at him with disbelief and disdain, assuming he referred to his finger. "You'll live," she said flatly. "Just be thankful you didn't try to draw the sword."

"Oh? What would have happened? And how do you keep it from doing that to you?" he asked as he rose to his feet.

Arilyn swore silently. No one had ever touched the moonblade without her permission. Why had she let her guard down now?

"Well?" he prompted.

"Night has fallen," she said in a tight voice. "You may have noticed that we are still in the Marsh of Chelimber. Would you rather ride out of here, or talk?"

"Can't we do both?"

"No."

The dandy gave a resigned shrug and mounted his horse. "I suppose we'll hunt for supper sometime soon?"

"Your turn to hunt." Arilyn pressed her heels to her horse's sides and headed westward out of Chelimber.

Danilo fell in beside her. He cocked his head and asked in a tentative voice, "Have you ever eaten lizard? I hear it tastes a little like chicken."

Thoroughly appalled, Arilyn twisted in her saddle to level an icy glare at the dandy. "If I thought you were serious, I'd leave you in the marsh."

"I'll hunt!" he said hastily. "Really!"

The pair rode in silence until they'd left the marsh behind. As the foul-smelling mists faded, the ground firmed beneath the horses' hooves. Stars began to twinkle, forming the autumn constellations that had been Arilyn's friends since childhood: Correlian, Esetar, and the Shard of Selune. Still far in the distance, a few trees formed dim silhouettes against the night sky. Trees, Arilyn thought with a silent sigh of relief. Trees were a sure sign that Chelimber was no more than a memory. Never had she been so glad to see trees. From deep within her elven soul welled a prayer of thanks, a silent song of welcome to the stars and the forest.

"I say," Danilo blurted out, "how far is it to Waterdeep?"

Arilyn's private joy evaporated like dew at highsun. "Too far."

Dark though the night was, Arilyn's elven vision took in the dandy's uncertain smile. "Have I been insulted, or is it just my imagination?"

"Yes."

"Yes, it's just my imagination?"

"No."

"Oh."

The exchange silenced Danilo. Arilyn urged her horse forward, intending to make camp at the stream that lay just beyond the far bank of trees.

They ate well that night, for a couple of plump rabbits inexplicably wandered into Danilo's snares. He swore roundly that skill, not magic, had been employed in the hunt. Arilyn did not believe him for a moment, but she was too tired and hungry to argue. Danilo even dressed and roasted the rabbits, seasoning them with the herbs and wine his magic sack yielded. The result was surprisingly good, and the travelers ate the greasy, savory meat in silence. Finally they slept, watched over by the vigilant magic of the moonblade. When daybreak came, Arilyn set their course for Waterdeep.

* * * * *

Sunrise colors still stained the sky when a large, shadowy figure slipped from his hiding place among the trees. He watched as the unlikely pair mounted and headed westward. To his way of thinking, with the High Moor to the south and the rugged Greypeak Mountains to the north, the half-elf had only one logical path to Waterdeep. She had surprised him before, of course, in choosing to brave the dangers of Chelimber.

The dark figure doubted that Arilyn Moonblade would take on the moor's trolls, or the orc tribes and black dragons that roamed the craggy Greypeak range. He'd followed and watched her since she'd left the Vale of Darkhold, and she seemed to know this area as well as he himself did. She must know that only one route offered relative safety. So he waited, allowing the adventurer and her companion a good lead. There had been several times when she had almost seen him, and he would not take any more chances, not until he was ready to make his move.

The morning was half spent when finally he urged his mount forward. Effortlessly he picked up the trail of the two pampered polo horses, and with a sense of reluctance he followed his latest quarry.

Eight

The east wind blew in strongly from the sea, carrying with it a chill drizzle. Every now and then a capricious gust extinguished one of the lanterns that lit the Trade Way to Waterdeep.

Despite the weather, the travelers waiting outside of Waterdeep's South Gate were in a merry mood. The Feast of the Moon would begin early the next morning, and the crowd looked forward to days of revelry and commerce. For the next tenday the streets of Waterdeep would be lined with vendors and enlivened by wandering entertainers. Most of the trade would center around the Market and the adjacent Bazaar Street, but the whole city was prepared for festivity.

It was a mixed group that gathered outside the South Gate. There were the usual market caravans carrying goods from the east and from the southern land routes. Artisans brought carts and wagons laden with goods for the open air markets. Travelers from all walks of life came to Waterdeep to lay in supplies for the winter and to enjoy one last outing before the cold weather settled in and rendered them virtually housebound.

Itinerant musicians and entertainers made good use of the delay to perform, displaying their money pots prominently and taking advantage of their captive audience. A large group gathered to watch a beautiful dancer, who was garbed only in the filmy draperies of a Calimshite harem, sway sinuously to the plaintive music of a wooden horn. The crowd around her grew larger as the rain rendered her costume more and more transparent. Not far away, four male dancers from the jungle of Chult whirled and circled. Their garments were embroidered with exotic flowers, and the bells attached to their bare ankles jingled emphatically as they stamped out a counterpoint to the flowing rhythm of their tawny arms and bodies. Several paces away, a dexterous halfling juggled an assortment of small weapons. A few of the food vendors were doing a brisk, impromptu business, and the clinking of exchanged coins threatened to drown out the sound of the autumn rain.

The South Gate guard had been doubled to deal with the expected crowds, and the officials checked papers and hustled people through the gates with brisk efficiency. The rain picked up, and the chilled and weary guard began to speed up the process even further. One of them, recognizing Lord Thann's youngest son, merely touched his forehead in respect and waved the young man through, sparing hardly a glance to the slight, dark-cloaked figure that rode beside him.

"Notoriety has its advantages," Danilo cheerfully told his companion. If Arilyn heard him she made no sign. She followed his horse north onto the High Road, a broad, cobblestoned street that was the main thoroughfare of the South Ward. This area was the point of entry for most of Waterdeep's inland trade, and it was lined with tidy stables and warehouses, as well as a number of inviting inns and taverns.

Waterdeep was indeed prepared to welcome an influx of travelers. Buildings blazed with light. Stablehands and porters bustled about, taking care of goods and beasts. Innkeepers welcomed their guests with cheery alacrity.

Danilo and Arilyn passed by the first few inns without stopping, for swarms of travelers were already being turned away. As they headed north the housing situation did not improve, and the storm worsened. The once-pampered mares sloshed resignedly through the puddles, their heads lowered against the driving rain. Danilo motioned for Arilyn to follow him, and he steered his mare out of the crowd and onto the first of a series of small, winding side streets.

They passed a string of warehouses, then a small trade district where tidy shops crowded companionably together on either side of the street. Dwellings had been built over most of these shops, and they jutted out into the narrow way so far that the occupants on either side of the street could lean out of their windows and shake hands if they were so inclined. The owners were obviously poor, but hardworking; the humble buildings were without exception meticulously kept. The streets were swept clean, and even in late autumn window boxes boasted gardens of kitchen herbs. A few stubborn, fragrant plants scented the falling rain.

Danilo led the way up a small hill onto a road appropriately named the Rising Way. Before them lay a sprawling building, framed with ancient timber and finished with wattle and daub. Long windows glowed with cheery light, and at them hung purple and white curtains embroidered with some guild's mark. A huge carved sign bearing the same mark hung over the front door and proclaimed the establishment to be the House of Good Spirits.

"Let's see to the horses," Danilo shouted about the rising wind. Arilyn gave him a curt nod and followed him around a series of connected buildings set on a street shaped like a horseshoe. They first passed a large wooden structure whose yeasty smell suggested a small brewery. From the next building, a stone warehouse, wafted the vanilla-and-butter scent of white wine aging in fine oaken barrels. A larger building next door was apparently dedicated to the storage of zzar, the fortified wine for which Waterdeep was famed. Arilyn wrinkled her nose in distaste; nothing but that fiery orange liquid could have that distinctive almond scent. Like many elves, she heartily disdained the vulgar beverage, but zzar was considered the quintessential drink of Waterdhavian society. There was a statement there, Arilyn thought.

Finally they rounded the curved street and came to the last buildings, the stables. Arilyn was pleased to note that the stables appeared warm and clean; the horses had endured a long and difficult journey and they deserved a good rest.

The young stableboy who ran out to take their reins recognized Danilo. He greeted the nobleman with great deference and solemn promises of special treatment for the horses. By the gods, Arilyn thought with irritation, is there any tavern or official in this city who isn't acquainted with Danilo Thann?

After leaving the horses and a generous number of coins with the grinning stableboy, Danilo grabbed Arilyn's hand and sprinted across the small courtyard that lay between the stables and the inn's back door, dragging her behind him. They burst into a small entrance hall, and Arilyn jerked her hand from the dandy's grasp. Not seeming to notice anything unusual about her mood, Danilo removed his rain-drenched cape and hung it on a hook. With a gallant flourish, he helped Arilyn off with her cloak and hung it beside his.

"Nice and warm in here," he noted. He added his broadbrimmed hat to the pegs, then smoothed his hair and alternately chafed and blew on his hands as he waited patiently for Arilyn to ready herself.

Even without the benefit of a mirror, Arilyn knew that her face was literally blue with cold. She slicked her wet black curls behind her ears and tied a blue scarf over her hair so that she would not look quite so bedraggled. Danilo pursed his lips but judiciously avoided comment. When she was ready, he placed a hand at the small of her back and ushered her through another door into the tavern.

"It's not the Jade Jug," Danilo apologized, naming Waterdeep's plushest inn, "but it's habitable, and—most important—it's the headquarters for the Vintners, Brewers, and Distillers Guild. I've been here many times. It has no ambiance or style, but it boasts the best selection of spirits in all of Waterdeep."

Arilyn bristled at Danilo's evaluation of the inn's merits. Perhaps the House of Good Spirits was not up to the pampered nobleman's standards, but after many days of hard travel, she found it an inviting haven. The tavern room was warm and dimly lit, with a low ceiling and scattered small nooks that created a cozy feeling. The air was redolent of roasting meat, pleasantly bitter ales, and the pitchy scent of the northern pine logs that crackled in a huge open fireplace. Whatever the inn's supposed limitations, it certainly did a brisk trade. Cheery barmaids and stout young men wielded large trays of drinks and simple, well-prepared food.

"I've seen worse," Arilyn responded curtly.

Danilo recoiled in mock surprise. "Praise Lady Midnight! It's a miracle! She speaks!"

Arilyn cast Danilo a withering glance and swept past him into the tavern. She'd tried unsuccessfully to ignore the fop for almost two tendays, speaking no more than necessary. Yet Danilo did not seem the least insulted by her silences, and he continued to chat and tease as if they had been friends from the cradle.

"If you'll find a good table, I'll get us some rooms," offered Danilo, trailing along behind her.

Arilyn spun around to face him. "This is Waterdeep. We part company here, tonight. Your most pressing goal may be getting drunk, but I'm here to search for an assassin, remember?" she said in a low voice.

Unperturbed, Danilo gave her his most winning smile. "Do be reasonable, my dear. Just because we've arrived in Waterdeep, I see no cause to pretend we don't know each other. In fact, since this is a rather small inn, such pretense might prove difficult. Look at this place."

He gestured around the tavern room. It was full nearly to capacity, a mixed clientele made up of hardworking Waterdhavian craftspeople with a scattering of wealthy merchants and nobles—all dedicated drinkers who knew the inn's merits. The

exotic clothing and road-weary appearance of many of the
guests marked them as travelers in for the festival. Conversation was low and leisurely, and the patrons savored their food
and drink with an air of contentment. Judging from their mug-
littered tables and blurred smiles, many of the patrons appeared to have hunkered down for a long evening of serious
imbibing. Few empty seats remained in the house.

"You see?" Danilo concluded. "You're stuck with me for one
more evening. Dinner hour is nearly past, and it would be foolish for one of us to go into that storm to seek another inn, just
to make a point. Truth be told, I doubt there are many rooms
left in the whole of Waterdeep. Since I'm a regular and, if I may
say so, a valued customer here, we'll be well taken care of."

Seeing her hesitation, he pressed on. "Come, now. We're
both cold and wet and in need of a good night's sleep, and I for
one would like to eat something for which we did not have to
hunt."

He has a point there, Arilyn admitted silently. "All right,"
she conceded rather ungraciously.

"It's decided." Danilo's attention drifted off to a point past
Arilyn's shoulder. "Ah! There's the innkeeper. What ho! Simon!" he called as he headed off toward a pudgy, apron-
draped man.

Will I never be rid of the fool? Arilyn stalked off toward the
fireplace in search of an empty seat. A number of small tables
were scattered there in the shadows, drawing her with their
isolation. Perhaps one of the nooks would be unoccupied.

"Amnestria! *Quefirre soora kan izzt?*"

The melodious voiced stopped Arilyn in midstride, and all
thoughts of weariness and hunger were washed away on a
flood of memories. When was the last time she had heard that
language?

She turned to find herself face to face with a tall, silver-
haired moon elf. Dressed in dignified black, the elf had the
graceful carriage—and the well-kept weapons—that marked
him as an experienced fighter. He spoke the formal language of
the moon elven court, a language that Arilyn had never quite

mastered. With a pang the half-elf recalled herself as a restless child squirming at her mother's side, impatient with Z'beryl's efforts to school her in anything other than swordplay.

"I'm sorry," she said with regret, "but it's been many years since I've heard that dialect."

"Of course," the handsome *quessir* replied, switching smoothly to Common. "An old tongue, and spoken all too seldom. Forgive me, but there are too few of our race in these parts, and I was momentarily overcome by nostalgia." The elf's smile was both wistful and charming.

Arilyn accepted his explanation with a nod. "What did you call me just then?"

The elf responded with a short bow. "Again, I must apologize. For a moment, you reminded me of someone I once knew."

"I'm sorry to disappoint you."

"Oh, I am certain you could never do that," he swore. "Even as we speak, I've grown to realize how fortunate an error I made."

Arilyn's rarely seen dimples flashed briefly. "Are you always this gallant with chance-met strangers?"

"Always," he responded in kind. "Seldom, however, does chance deliver me such lovely strangers. Would you do me the honor of joining me? This is one of the few places in Waterdeep were one can find Elverquisst, and I've just ordered a bottle. Not many can appreciate the nuances or the tradition."

Arilyn's face relaxed in a genuine smile. The surprise of meeting a moon elf in this place—and of hearing him speak the language Arilyn associated with her mother—had lowered her natural reserve. The elf's avowed homesickness reminded her that it had indeed been too long since she'd been to Evereska.

"A gracious offer, most gratefully accepted," she replied, using the formal polite response. She extended her left hand, palm up. "I am Arilyn Moonblade of Evereska."

The *quessir* placed his palm over hers and bowed low over their joined hands. "Your name is known to me. I am indeed honored," he murmured in a respectful tone.

The tread of approaching footsteps interrupted the elves.

"I've got good news and bad news, Arilyn," Danilo announced gaily as he sauntered up. "Hello! Who's your fr—" The young man stopped abruptly, his eyes narrowing as he focused on the moon elf.

Danilo's face darkened, and, to Arilyn's horror, his hand strayed to the hilt of his sword in unmistakable challenge. What was the fool doing? she thought with dismay.

The patrons of the House of Good Spirits were, for the most part, hard-drinking folk, many of them veterans of countless tavern battles. They could sense a fight in the making as surely as a sea captain could smell a coming storm. Conversations trailed off, and glasses clinked busily as the patrons drained their spirits while conditions permitted.

As quickly as it came, the threat passed. Looking faintly surprised at himself, Danilo released his sword and fished an embroidered handkerchief from his breast pocket. He wiped his fingers as if they had somehow been sullied by the touch of a weapon, and his vaguely apologetic smile took in both Arilyn and the elf. "Someone you know, I take it?" he said into the inn's sudden silence, gazing down at the elves' joined hands.

Self-consciously, Arilyn snatched her hand away and stuffed both balled fists into her trouser pockets. Before she could issue a scathing rejoinder, her new acquaintance spoke up.

"For a moment, I mistook the *etriel* for an old friend."

Danilo's eyebrows flew up. "By the gods, an original ploy!" he said with great admiration. "I shall have to try that myself next time I see a lady whose acquaintance I should like to make."

The *quessir*'s eyes narrowed at the implication, but Danilo's bland, smiling face betrayed not a hint of sarcasm. For a moment the three stood, unmoving. The moon elf made a curt bow of dismissal to Danilo, then, turning his back on the dandy as if he were of no further consequence or concern, the elf took Arilyn's arm and escorted her toward a table near the fireplace. The inn's patrons sensed that the crisis was past, and the clink and murmur of resumed drinking and conversation filled the inn.

Still aghast at Danilo's rude behavior, Arilyn felt a flood of relief that a fight had been avoided. In the Marsh of Chelimber Danilo had proven himself a remarkably good fighter, but Arilyn did not want to see him take his chances against this elf. As the *quessir* led her to his table, she shot an angry look over her shoulder mouthed *Go away!* at Danilo. She glared at him and silently willed him to leave well enough alone.

If Danilo understood her warning, he stupidly refused to take it. Casually the dandy followed the elves to their table. It was a corner table, big enough only for two to share a bottle and conversation, but Danilo dragged a third chair up and dropped comfortably into it. His smile was arrogantly complacent, as if his presence there had been commissioned by royalty.

"Danilo, what has come over you?" Arilyn snapped.

"What has come over *you*?" he countered languidly, gesturing across the table at the *quessir*. "Really, my dear, accepting an invitation from this, er, gentleman—or would the term be gentle*elf?*—without benefit of a proper introduction." The dandy shook his head and tsk-tsked. "At this rate, how shall I ever induct you into Waterdhavian society?"

Enraged by Danilo's presumption, Arilyn drew in a long, slow breath. Before she could expel it in a barrage of much-deserved abuse, something in Danilo's meanderings struck home. Come to think of it, she realized, the elf had not given her his name. She turned her eyes toward the *quessir*. He was observing the exchange with an alert expression in his amber eyes.

"I make no secret of my identity," the elf said, speaking only to Arilyn. "We were merely interrupted before I could complete the introduction. I am Elaith Craulnobur, at your service."

"Well, damn my eyes!" Danilo interjected in a jovial tone. "I've heard of you! Aren't you known as 'the Serpent?' "

"In certain objectionable circles, yes," the elf admitted coolly.

Elaith "the Serpent" Craulnobur. With an effort, Arilyn kept her face expressionless. She had also heard of the elven adventurer. His reputation for cruelty and treachery was legendary, and Kymil had issued strict and repeated orders for her to stay far away from the moon elf. Her mentor emphasized that Arilyn's reputation, damaged by the unfortunate label of assassin, would be further tainted by association with such as Elaith Craulnobur.

Arilyn, however, refused to be prejudiced by the dark rumors or by Kymil's old-lady fussing. After all, tales of some of her own exploits had come back to her, twisted beyond all recognition. It could be so with this elf. Arilyn turned to face her host, keeping her voice and face carefully neutral. She would judge for herself.

"Well met, Elaith Craulnobur. Please accept my apologies for my companion's unfortunate remark."

"Your companion?" Elaith regarded Danilo with the first sign of interest.

"Thank you very much, Arilyn, but I can speak for myself," Danilo protested cheerfully.

"That's what I'm afraid of," she muttered. "Really, Danilo, I know that seats are scarce, but would you please excuse us? I have accepted Elaith Craulnobur's invitation for a drink. I will join you later, if you like."

"What? You want me to leave? And miss the opportunity to meet such a legend? Not likely. What kind of amateur bard do you think me?" Danilo folded both arms on the table and leaned toward Elaith Craulnobur, smiling confidingly. "Did you know that songs are sung about your exploits?"

"I did not." The *quessir*'s tone did not invite more discussion on the matter.

Danilo missed the unspoken message entirely. "You mean that you've never heard 'Silent Strikes the Serpent?' It's quite a catchy tune. Shall I sing it for you?"

"Another time."

"Danilo . . ." Arilyn warned through gritted teeth.

The dandy smiled apologetically at her. "Arilyn, my dear, I'm forgetting myself again, aren't I? Mark of an amateur, that's what it is: going on and on like this, when a true bard would merely listen and observe. I'll do that, really I shall. Please, do go on with your conversation. Pretend I'm not here at all. I'll be as silent as a snail, really."

Stubborn fool, Arilyn thought, stifling a sigh. She knew that arguing with the dandy usually made matters worse, so she smiled ruefully at Elaith and said, "With your permission then, it would seem that we are three this evening."

"If it pleases you," the elf agreed mildly. He regarded Danilo as one would an overgrown and badly trained puppy. "I don't believe we have met."

"This is Danilo Thann," Arilyn supplied quickly, before the young man could say something more to risk the elf's ire.

"Ah, yes." Elaith smiled with gentle amusement. "Young Master Thann. Your reputation precedes you, as well."

The elf left that remark for Danilo to take as he would, turning his attention to the ceremony of the Elverquisst. With a flick of his long-fingered hands, he tossed a tiny magical fireball toward the candle at the table's center. Arilyn winced as the candle caught flame. At that moment she caught Danilo's curious gaze upon her, and she gravely shook her head to warn him not to interrupt. The nobleman subsided and watched the ceremony in growing fascination.

Elaith Craulnobur cupped his hands first over the candle, then over the decanter of elven spirits on the table before him. The bottle was a marvel, made of transparent crystal that sparkled from thousands of tiny facets. The elf took the decanter in both hands, turning it slowly before the candle, and the bottle grew ever brighter as it absorbed the light. Finally the *quessir* spoke a phrase in Elvish, and the stored light coalesced into thirteen distinct points that glowed like stars against the sudden darkness of the crystal decanter

Arilyn's throat tightened, as it always did, before the sight of the autumn constellation Correlian. To the moon elves, the appearance of this star formation marked the final demise of summer. Elaith and Arilyn joined softly in a chant of farewell, and the light faded from the decanter with the final words of the ritual.

Gently Elaith poured some of the liquid into a goblet, swirling it in a complex pattern that set in motion a play of fairy lights and color. His graceful hands moved through the steps of the ritual with practiced ease. The ceremony's resonant magic had been forged through centuries of repetition, as untold generations of elves celebrated the spiral dance of the seasons.

As she watched, Arilyn almost forgot about Danilo's foolishness and Elaith's reputation, and for a moment or two she allowed herself to be transported back to her childhood in Evereska. The last time Arilyn had shared the Elverquisst ritual had been in her fifteenth year, just before the death of Z'beryl.

Elverquisst itself was a ruby-colored liquor magically distilled from sunshine and rare summer fruits. Utterly smooth, the liquor was nonetheless flecked with gold and had an iridescence of both color and flavor. It was highly prized at all times, but in the autumn rituals it was savored as if it were the gift of one final, perfect summer day.

Elaith completed the ceremony and handed the goblet to Arilyn. She drank it slowly, with proper respect, then inclined her head to the *quessir* in a ritual bow of thanks that completed the ceremony.

With an imperious gesture, Elaith summoned a waiter. "Another goblet, if you please," he instructed the young man. As an afterthought, Elaith turned back to Danilo. "Or perhaps two more? Will you have some Elverquisst as well?"

"Thank you, I prefer zzar," Danilo said.

"Of course you do," Elaith said smoothly. "A goblet of that ubiquitous beverage for our young friend, then, and dinner for three," he instructed the nervous waiter, who nodded and escaped to the safety of the kitchen.

"Now," Elaith said to Arilyn, "what brings you to Waterdeep? The Feast of the Moon, I would suppose? You're here to enjoy the festival?"

"Yes, the festival," she agreed, thinking it the most harmless response.

"An interesting affair. Raucous, gaudy, but undeniably colorful enough to draw a crowd. Like this inn, the city is already full of visitors. Too full for my taste, although the influx of travelers is good for business. I trust you have found a suitable place to stay?"

Arilyn looked to Danilo for an answer. "Were you able to get rooms here?"

"Room," Danilo corrected a bit sheepishly. "One room. The place is full up."

One room, Arilyn thought with dismay. Another night with Danilo Thann. She leaned back in her chair with a faint groan. Her reaction was not lost on Elaith.

"That would be the bad news of which you spoke, I imagine," the elf observed wryly.

"Strange you should find it so," Danilo countered mildly, apparently misunderstanding the gibe. "Sharing a room with a beautiful woman doesn't strike me as a hardship."

"The *etriel*," Elaith corrected pointedly, observing Arilyn's silent fury over Danilo's suggestive remark, "does not seem to share your enthusiasm."

"Oh, but she does. It's just that, you know, Arilyn is the very soul of discretion," Danilo confided, man-to-man.

At that moment the waiter returned with their drinks. Arilyn snatched the goblet of zzar from his tray and thunked it down in front of Danilo.

"Drink this," she suggested sweetly, "and several others. I'm buying."

Taking up the other goblet, Arilyn plunged into the half-remembered ceremony of pouring and offering the Elverquisst. If Elaith found anything amiss in her rendering of the ritual, he did not speak of it. The ritual brought a much-needed change of direction to the conversation, which turned to local gossip, politics and—this being Waterdeep, after all—commerce.

Despite his promise to remain a bardic observer, Danilo continued to verbally spar with the *quessir*. The nobleman scored a good number of hits, any one of which, coming from any other man, could have been considered grounds for a challenge. Elaith let the gibes pass without comment. He really could not do otherwise, for Danilo's barbs, if such they were, were issued with such friendly delicacy that responding with anger would seem as ludicrous as swatting at soap bubbles.

Arilyn sipped her drink, silently taking the measure of her strange dinner companion. Elaith was charming to her, unfailingly polite even in the face of Danilo's foolishness. For someone reputed to be a savage, ruthless killer, he showed remarkable restraint and good humor. Perhaps the rumors are exaggerated, after all, Arilyn mused.

"Ah, dinner at last," Elaith announced. Two waiters appeared, one bearing a well-laden platter, the other a small serving table to augment the overly cozy corner table.

The waiters lay several dishes on the tables: roasted meat, several small fowl still sizzling on a spit, turnips, boiled greens, and small loaves warm from the oven.

The moon elf studied the simple fare with patrician distaste. "I'm afraid this is the best the inn has to offer. Some other time I will offer you more suitable hospitality."

"It is fine. After the rigors of travel, simple food is the best," Arilyn assured him.

She and Danilo tucked in. The meal seemed to improve Danilo's mood even more. Disgustingly cheerful, he again engaged Elaith Craulnobur in conversation, relishing the verbal give and take in the same way a swordsman enjoys a good match.

Too bone weary to take part in the sparring, Arilyn nevertheless kept a keen eye on the room as she ate, alert for anything that might prove a clue in her search. There was some talk of the Harper Assassin drifting about, and even in this safe haven the patrons seemed unnerved by the macabre tales.

"Branded, she was, branded right on her haunch like a prize cow . . ."

"They say that assassin got past the guard in Waterdeep Castle and . . ."

"Now me, if I was a Harper, right about now I'd be melting

that pin down and recasting the metal for a chamber pot."

Arilyn learned nothing of value from the fragments of conversation, but she noted with dismay how the tales of the
Harper Assassin had grown in the telling.

A smattering of applause began in one corner, spreading until it competed with the hum of conversation. Chairs were
scraped across the floor to make way in the middle of the
room. Two of the waiters brought in a large harp, setting it
down in the center of the makeshift stage. A tall, slender man
walked diffidently to the harp and began to correct the instrument's tuning.

"Ah, now we shall hear from a true bard," Elaith noted
pointedly.

Danilo craned his neck around, taking in the scene in the
middle of the tavern. "Really? Who is he?"

"Rhys Ravenwind," Arilyn said. She recognized the bard
from one of her trips to Suzail. Although the man was young
and rather shy, he was very good indeed.

"Hmm. I wonder if he might be up for a duet or two, after
the—ouch!" Danilo broke off with a reproachful look at Arilyn,
then he bent down to rub the spot where she had kicked his
shin.

Arilyn responded by putting her finger to her lips. The gesture was hardly necessary. After the first few notes, every
person in the room fell silent, held spellbound by the power of
the bard's music. Those who had come only to worship the art
of the brewers listened as intently, as delightedly, as the most
devoted music lover. It was customary for a visiting musician
to sing at any inn or tavern, but seldom was the House of Fine
Spirits graced with the presence of such a bard. Even Elaith
and Danilo forgot their baiting long enough to listen to the ancient song honoring the Feast of the Moon. The applause that
greeted the bard was long and loud. With a shy smile, the
young man gave in to calls for another song.

During the second song, a wistful ballad of long-ago love and
adventure, a newcomer drifted into the tavern. He paused in
the doorway for a moment as he sought a place, then he

moved noiselessly across the room and settled at a corner table near Arilyn.

The half-elf noted the man's entrance and studied him with carefully concealed interest. Probably one of the tallest men in the room, he nonetheless moved with the silent grace of a cat. As were most travelers, the man was wrapped against the chill autumn wind. Unlike most, the man did not remove cape or cowl when he entered the warm tavern. His table sat in the shadows just beyond the fireplace's glow, and he kept his cape closely drawn. Considering the warmth of the room, Arilyn found this behavior peculiar indeed.

A barmaid brought the newcomer a mug of mead, and, as he tipped his head up to drink it, Arilyn caught a glimpse of his face. He was a man well past middle life, obviously robust despite his years. His features were ordinary enough, except for the unusually determined set to his square jaw. It seemed to Arilyn that there was something familiar about the man, although she would swear by the whole pantheon of gods that she had never laid eyes on him before.

She watched the stranger for some time, but he did nothing to arouse suspicion. Apparently content to sit in the shadows and listen to the bard, he attended to his dinner and nursed a single mug of mead. Still, Arilyn felt a tug of relief when the bard finished singing and the man rose to leave.

I'm seeing danger in every corner, she chided herself. *Soon I'll be checking under the bed for ogres, like some frightened child. I need rest, and badly.* At that moment, a yawn escaped her, stopping the recently renewed verbal match between Danilo and Elaith Craulnobur in mid-pleasantry.

"It has been a long journey," she apologized.

Elaith raised a hand. "Say no more. It was inconsiderate of me to keep you so long. As an apology, perhaps you would allow me to settle with the innkeeper?"

"Thank you," Arilyn said, again kicking Danilo under the table to keep him from arguing the point.

"We will meet again, I hope?" pressed Elaith.

"Yes," she said simply. She inclined her head and spread

both hands in the formal leave-taking gesture between elves. Taking Danilo by the arm, she dragged him away before he could start up again.

"So, where is this room?" she demanded in a resigned tone.

Danilo led her to a small staircase in the rear of the tavern. "It's not best chamber in the inn—actually, it's the only one that was left—so don't expect luxury."

"As long as it has a bed," she mumbled, almost numb with weariness.

"Funny you should mention that . . ." Danilo's voice trailed off as the pair climbed the stairs.

Elaith watched them go. He speculated, shrugged, then rose to leave. He briefly considered tossing some coins on the table to pay for the meal, then decided against it. Why should he bother? Skipping out on a tavern bill was the sort of thing people expected of him.

For good measure, he picked up the half-full decanter of elven spirits, firmly stoppered it, and openly tucked it into his belt. The decanter alone was probably worth more than the inn would make during the entire festival week.

With a casual nod to the innkeeper, whose ruddy face paled at the imminent loss of the Elverquisst, Elaith glided out of the tavern. Many watched him go, but no one challenged his passing.

The rain had stopped, and the wind whipped the elf's black cloak around his legs as he strode toward the stable. He claimed his horse and mounted, riding swiftly westward toward the Way of the Dragon. There was a stone townhouse there, a particularly fine building fashioned of black granite. Tall, narrow, and elegant, the house was located on the main road between the South Ward and the Dock Ward.

Blackstone House, as it was called, was one of many properties the elf owned in Waterdeep. Elaith used the house infrequently. It was too stark and angular for his taste, but it was ideally equipped for the evening's purposes. He dismounted at the gate of the iron fence that surrounded the property and flung the reins to the young servant who ran out to greet him.

Elaith nodded to the house servants—a pair of highly trusted moon elves—as he entered, then he sprinted up a winding spiral staircase to the chamber in the topmost floor. He shut the door, sealing it magically against any possible interruption.

The room was dark and empty save for a single pedestal. Removing a silk cloth, Elaith revealed a dark crystal globe that floated in the air several inches above the pedestal. He passed a hand over the smooth surface of the crystal, murmuring a string of arcane syllables. The globe began to shine, dimly at first, and dark mists swirled in its depths. Gradually the light increased, filling the room as the image came into focus.

"Greetings, Lord Nimesin," Elaith said to the image, voicing the title with gentle irony.

"It is late. What do you want, gray elf?" the haughty voice demanded, speaking the word "gray" with the subtle inflection that transformed it from the Common term for a color into the Elvish word meaning "dross." Into that one word was distilled the opinion that moon elves were no more than the waste product formed from the long-ago forging of the golden high elves.

Elaith smiled, ignoring the deadly insult. He could afford to be tolerant tonight. "You always pay a good price for information. I have some to impart that you should find most interesting."

"Well?"

"I met Arilyn Moonblade this evening. She is staying in Waterdeep, at the House of Good Spirits," Elaith began. "She is very beautiful and strangely familiar."

"What?" The gold elf's face was livid. "I told you to keep away from her."

"It was a chance meeting," Elaith said smoothly. "Under the circumstances, I could hardly avoid her."

"I won't have her associated with such as you!" Kymil spat out. "I won't have her reputation tainted."

"Oh, come now," Elaith chided him. "Tainted? Gifted she may be, beautiful she certainly is, but there is no denying that Arilyn Moonblade is thought by many to be an assassin."

"She *was* an assassin."

"Have it your way. Oh, yes. She has a companion, a particularly foolish whelp of one of the Waterdhavian noblemen. Danilo Thann. Why she travels with him is not clear. To all appearances, he's something of a pet."

"Yes, yes," Kymil Nimesin said impatiently. "I know all this already."

Elaith continued, undisturbed by the interruption. "But appearances, as we both know so well, can be deceiving. The *etriel's* companion, I'm convinced, is something more than the fool he appears to be. Were you aware that Danilo Thann is related to Khelben Arunsun? A nephew, I believe."

"Blackstaff's nephew?" For the first time, Kymil's face showed a flicker of interest. Just as quickly, the interest was gone. "What of it?"

"Perhaps nothing," Elaith allowed. "But Arilyn Moonblade is reputed to be skilled at concealing her identity and purpose. Is it inconceivable that her companion is similarly gifted?"

The face in the globe twisted in annoyance. "Your effrontery is inconceivable. You forget, gray elf, that I can observe Arilyn Moonblade myself. The conversation at your table tonight was noted. The Thann twit challenged you to a battle of words—notice that I did not say wits—and the match was a draw."

"But he is Blackstaff's nephew."

"So you've said. I see no significance."

"He is well placed and more clever than he pretends to be," Elaith said. "Given her background, surely the Harpers suspect Arilyn of the recent spate of murders. Perhaps this Thann boy is a spy, sent to ascertain her guilt or innocence."

"Ha!" Kymil broke in scornfully. "Danilo Thann is no more a Harper than you or I."

"Perhaps not, but if he were, wouldn't it be amusing if he were to fall victim to the Harper Assassin?"

"You have a peculiar sense of humor."

"Yes, so I've been told," Elaith agreed. "Now, what about Danilo Thann?"

"If you want the fool dead, see to it. One human more or

less is of no consequence to me."

The face in the globe began to fade into mist. "I also saw Bran Skorlsun," said Elaith casually.

Instantly the image snapped into sharp focus. "Yes, I thought that might get your attention," Elaith murmured, a malicious glint lighting his amber eyes. "Imagine my surprise to see our mutual friend again after all these years. Of course, I did not recognize him at first. Humans can age appallingly in—what has it been? Almost forty years?"

Kymil brushed aside the question. "Bran Skorlsun was there? At the House of Good Spirits?"

"Fascinating coincidence, wouldn't you say?" Elaith said casually.

Lost in thought, Kymil again failed to comment. After a pause, he said, "You did well to contact me. I will send you your usual fee."

Elaith had contacted Kymil Nimesin merely to annoy him, but now the moon elf's curiosity was piqued. Any plot involving Bran Skorlsun smelled of adventure, and where there was adventure there was potential profit. He decided to ignore the gold elf's patronizing attitude for now and press for details. Retribution for tonight's insults would come later.

"Is there something further with which I can help you?" Elaith offered.

"Nothing," Kymil said curtly. "Wait. Yes, there is."

"At your service," Elaith replied.

"You can stay away from Arilyn Moonblade."

"Of course. Is that all?"

"Yes."

Kymil's tone held the ring of finality. Elaith was not impressed. He was accustomed to having the last word himself, in his own time and in his own fashion. "As you wish. There is, however, the little matter of my fee," the moon elf pointed out. "The terms have changed. I prefer payment in, shall we say, a less direct form of currency."

"Yes? Well?"

"Danilo Thann," Elaith said flatly.

"Done," snapped Kymil Nimesin. "As I said, it matters not to me whether he lives or dies. Considering the gold you're giving up, your pride has a high price."

As you will learn, Elaith Craulnobur thought, my pride has a very high price indeed.

Nine

"We could share it," ventured Danilo.

"Hardly," Arilyn returned, looking pointedly at the narrow cot that was the chamber's only bed. "A pair of newlywed halflings would find it too crowded. I'll take the floor."

Danilo watched as she settled down on a pallet by the fireside and jerked a blanket over her head. "I should be a gentleman and insist that you take the bed, but I'm too tired to argue," he said.

"Good," came the muffled response.

With a sigh, Danilo sank down on the bed. So what if this was the humblest chamber in a second-rate inn? They were lucky to find a place to sleep. And after the rigors of travel, anyplace would do. Yet it was some time before sleep came to Danilo. Long after Arilyn's faint, measured breathing assured him that his companion had fallen asleep, he lay wakeful on his lumpy mattress.

The encounter with the rogue moon elf troubled Danilo. Back in Evereska, the nobleman had recognized Perendra's sigil on the gold snuffbox. The one-eared thug had acquired

the box from an elf in Waterdeep. It was not unreasonable to
assume that this elf might be a key to the mystery of the Harper Assassin. In Danilo's mind, the Craulnobur rogue was certainly an elf to consider in their search.

Danilo had discovered long ago that when people were put
on edge, they tended to reveal more than they'd intended. He
had done his best to disconcert Elaith Craulnobur. The elf's
dark reputation lent risk to Danilo's strategy, but a fool such as
he could usually get away with many things.

Danilo smiled ruefully into the darkness. It had been one of
his better performances, yet Elaith Craulnobur had been remarkably unaffected by it. The only thing that Danilo had accomplished that evening was further alienating Arilyn. That
bothered him more than he liked to admit. The young nobleman cast a quick glance at the sleeping half-elf.

Half-elf. That was something else to think about. Danilo
laced his fingers behind his head and stared at the cracks in the
ceiling. Since he'd first seen Arilyn's portrait, he'd thought of
her as a human woman. That perception had lingered long after he'd learned her true heritage, and he'd come to consider
her one of the most intriguing women he'd ever met, although
certainly a stubborn and somewhat mysterious member of
that group. Tonight for the first time he'd been forced to see
another side of Arilyn Moonblade. He realized with a jolt of
surprise that she considered herself more elf than human; no
one could watch her face during the Elverquisst ritual and
doubt that. Arilyn's character had been shaped by the elven
culture that had raised her and, Danilo suspected, rejected
her.

The nobleman trusted his instincts about people; they had
rarely led him astray. Many times on the ride to Waterdeep he
had seen in Arilyn flashes of a bitterness too deep for him to
fathom. He remembered the night they'd spent in the traveler's hut and how Arilyn's face had looked as she spoke of the
gold elf who had taunted her about her heritage. For the first
time Danilo wondered what it meant to be a half-elf, never truly a part of either world.

Oh, he could see it in her, the longing for things elven. Arilyn had been drawn to Elaith Craulnobur, charmed by his courtesy and his ready acceptance of her as an equal. An *etriel*, Elaith had called her, which Danilo knew was a respectful term for a female elf who was noble in bloodline, character, or both. Danilo got the impression that Arilyn was not accustomed to such treatment, for she had turned toward the rogue moon elf like a morning glory seeking a sunrise. From what he had learned of Arilyn during the past two tendays, he perceived that this reaction was out of character for her. She took a fierce pride in her ability to stand alone without help from or need for anyone else.

Well, he would keep a close eye on their new acquaintance. If Arilyn's judgment concerning the moon elf was impaired, Danilo would take upon himself the responsibility of maintaining a proper perspective. He was in a better position to consider the matter objectively.

Sure I am, Danilo thought, and a quiet chuckle escaped him. Uncle Khelben had often told him that too little self knowledge made a person dangerous. The good archmage had neglected to mention that too much self knowledge was not always a blessing.

Danilo sighed. Perhaps it was the strange weather that made him so introspective. Now that the rain had stopped, it was a fairly warm night for autumn. The wind had shifted, coming strongly from the south, and it whistled around the old building, causing many a creak and groan. Tonight was the sort of night in which one waited for the other boot to drop, and Danilo could not shake an almost palpable sense of impending . . . something. Anything could happen on such a night. With so many ale-soaked, money-laden guests from which to choose, the inn was an ideal target for a thief or worse. Throw Arilyn's shadow into the pot, and there was more than trouble enough to keep a man awake.

He cast another glance at his slumbering companion. How could Arilyn sleep on such a night? She must put a lot of faith in the moonblade's ability to warn of danger, which it could apparently do in any number of ways. Danilo had seen the thing glow in the Marsh of Chelimber. One night during their journey Arilyn had awakened him and insisted they lay giant snares about their camp. Sure enough, they caught a pair of owlbears. Arilyn had answered his questions only by saying that the moonblade had sent her a dreamwarning. Danilo thought it a fortunate quirk for a magic sword to have. Owlbears were notorious for ferocity, and without the sword's warning he and Arilyn would have had little chance against eight-foot-tall creatures who sported the most lethal features of both bears and owls. Comparatively, why shouldn't Arilyn feel fairly secure within the four walls of the inn?

Danilo rolled onto his side and gazed through the open window into the starless sky. The night matched his mood—eerie, brooding, uncertain. Although the autumn moon was full and round and silver, the night was dark. The brisk wind tossed clouds across the sky, and only occasionally did the moon glimpse though an opening. For lack of anything better to do, Danilo watched the scurrying clouds, idly observing the play of moonlight against the walls of the inn's most humble chamber.

So he lay, counting the hourly chiming of the bells from the nearby temple of Torm, until finally, lulled by the restless moonlight, he drifted into an uneasy slumber.

*   *   *   *   *

A shadowy figure glided silently down the hall of the inn. It moved inexorably toward the chamber at the far end. A heavy door bore the proud legend, "King Rhigaerd's Chamber," commemorating some long-ago chance visit by that past king of Cormyr. The occupant of this chamber was usually the inn's most honored guest. Tonight proved no exception.

The door swung open without its customary creak, and the intruder slipped into the room. Rhys Ravenwind curled under the thick coverlet, one hand flung lovingly against the sound-board of the harp at his bedside. The dark figure crept to the side of the bed, and, taking up one of Rhys's clever, long-fingered hands, pressed a grim object into the bard's palm.

There was a faint hiss of burning flesh. When the sound faded, the assassin opened the window and flitted silently into the night. A gust of wind caught the strings of the harp, and an almost mournful chord was the instrument's farewell to its owner.

*   *   *   *   *

Down the hall, in a small chamber never graced by royalty, Arilyn Moonblade tossed and twisted on her pallet in the grip of a nightmare.

Whenever the moonblade sent her a dreamwarning, Arilyn immediately woke up and prepared to face whatever danger approached. It was practical, efficient. This dream had all the intensity and immediacy of a dreamwarning, yet no matter how hard she struggled to awaken, she could not free herself of sleep. Something was holding her back, something dark and ancient and full of a despair that was partly her own.

Breathing hard, Arilyn found herself sitting upright on the floor of the House of Fine Spirits' most humble chamber. Still groggy, she dug her fists into her eyes, rubbing away the last vestiges of sleep. She stretched noiselessly, then tugged on her boots. Since she could never sleep after such a dream, she decided to take a walk.

Arilyn froze, suddenly not certain that she truly *was* awake. The clouds had parted, and the moon cast its light into the room, revealing a slender, shadowy figure bent over the sleeping form of Arilyn's troublesome companion.

Danilo! Without another thought she snatched her dagger from her boot and leaped to her feet, ready to carve the heart from the intruder. She flung herself across the room at the assailant, dagger leading. To her complete bafflement, the slash that should have killed the intruder merely sliced open Danilo's lumpy pillow. She hit the cot hard, and a cloud of feathers puffed into the air.

Danilo awoke with a startled "oof," and his arms closed reflexively around his attacker.

"Let me go!" Arilyn demanded, pushing herself up on her elbows and away from the bed.

The dandy's eyes widened in shock as they focused on the dagger still in Arilyn's hand, but he merely tightened his grip on her waist. "Good gods, woman, haven't I told you that you don't need that thing? You're welcome enough without it."

Arilyn met his jest with a sharp curse and another attempt to wriggle away. With speed and strength she would not have thought possible, Danilo flipped them both out of the cot onto the floor, pinning her body beneath his. As they struggled amid the lazily drifting feathers, he grasped her wrist and squeezed until her hand went numb and the dagger dropped to the floor.

Arilyn hurled curses at him in Elvish and strained to break free. "Let me up," she growled.

"Not until you explain what's going on."

The steel in his tone startled Arilyn. For whatever reason, Danilo meant what he said. She couldn't stop to talk now, for every instinct told her that the intruder had been the Harper Assassin. Never had she been so close.

Arilyn let her body go limp. Danilo, sensing her surrender, relaxed his grip just a bit.

That was all she needed. Every finely honed muscle in her slender body tensed, and she twisted, violently throwing her captor off. He rolled, but to Arilyn's surprise he did not loose his hold on her wrist. She leaped to her feet and kicked the nobleman on the inside curve of his elbow. For just a moment his reflexes overcame his grip, and Arilyn wrenched her hand free. She headed for the door, snatching up her sword as she went.

Danilo recovered from the blow quickly. He threw himself forward, grabbing an ankle. Arilyn fell flat, and her moonblade clattered to the floor just out of reach. Furious, she lashed out at him with her free foot. She connected hard, catching his jaw with an audible crack. He let go of her ankle, and he swore with a fluency astounding for one of his station.

Arilyn rolled onto her back and leaped to her feet. Behind

her, a dazed Danilo was on his knees, holding one hand to his face and wiggling his jaw experimentally. Satisfied that his resistance was ended, the half-elf bent to pick up her sword.

The persistent nobleman hauled himself upright and lunged at her. They fell to the floor together, rolling and kicking as each tried to gain the advantage. Arilyn struggled for freedom, frustrated by the unexpected strength and persistence of Danilo's attack. He would never best her with a sword, but he was fully her equal in unarmed combat. She simply would not get away from him in time.

"Stop this. He's getting away," she said wildly.

His hold on her only tightened. "Him? Him who?"

"The assassin."

Danilo's expression hardened into skepticism. Arilyn's frantic words rushed out in an effort to convince him, to make him see before it was too late.

"The assassin. He was here. I saw him by your bed, standing over you. He attacked, and . . ." Her words drifted off into horror.

"And?" Danilo prompted.

Arilyn could not answer. What had become of the assailant? One moment the shadowy figure had been in the room, the next she'd been fighting Danilo. Could she have dreamed it? She sat up and pressed both hands to her forehead, dimly aware that the nobleman had released her.

"Arilyn." Danilo's voice was gentle, pulling her back. "Arilyn, my dear, tell me what's happening."

"I wish I knew." In her bafflement, she allowed Danilo to gather her close, as if she were a frightened child.

"Tell me," he urged.

"I had a dream. When I woke—I think I was awake, at least—there was someone standing over you. It was the assassin."

"You're sure?"

"Yes. I can't explain why, but I'm sure. So I drew a weapon and attacked," she concluded. Before Danilo could respond, a sharp knock sounded at their door.

"Lord Thann? Everything all right in there?"

"Damn it to the ninth hell, it's the innkeeper," Danilo muttered. "Yes, Simon, everything's just fine," he called out. "Sorry about the racket. A bad dream, that's all."

"A little noisy for a dream, sir," retorted Simon.

"Yes, well," Danilo improvised, "after my companion awoke from this dream, she required a little, er, comforting. One thing led to another, and so on. My apologies if we disturbed anyone."

"You're sure everything's all right?"

"Never better."

There was a silence and then a brief chuckle. "Seeing that my less fortunate guests have to sleep, Lord Thann, would you mind keeping it down?"

"I assure you we won't awaken another soul."

"Thank you, sir. Have a good night." The proprietor's footsteps thudded off into silence.

Danilo looked down at the half-elf, a little wary of her response. At the moment Arilyn was too preoccupied to be offended by his outrageous explanation. Reassured of his safety, Danilo raised a hand to brush a damp curl of raven hair away from her face.

"It *was* just a dream," he said gently.

"No," Arilyn insisted, pulling away from him. She rose to her feet, hugging her arms across her chest and cupping her elbows in her hands as she attacked the puzzle with fierce concentration. "It was more than a dream. It was more than a dreamwarning."

"Look, you're just a tad overwrought," Danilo said, spreading his hands before him in a gesture of reassurance. "Which is understandable, really! Taking into account everything you've been through recently, nightmares are almost to be expected. Just the thought of those owlbears is enough to make me want to . . ."

His assurances faded, for Arilyn was obviously no longer listening. She stared, relief and horror fighting for mastery of her countenance.

"I knew it wasn't a dream," she whispered.

Danilo followed her gaze. Glowing faintly blue in the palm of his left hand was a small harp and a crescent moon.

The Harper symbol.

* * * * *

The restless clouds parted, and in the fitful moonlight two figures edged along the side of the building. One moved confidently down the narrow ledge, the other clutched at the building and inched painfully behind.

"I take it you've done a lot of second-story work," Danilo murmured, clinging to the wall as he tried to keep up with the more agile half-elf.

"Some," Arilyn replied absently, intent on her goal.

"I just hope that this bard of yours left his window open," Danilo complained. "By the way, you *can* pick locks? Of course you can. Forget I asked. It's just that, well, if you have to pick open the window, you might just as well have done the door, which would have saved us the trouble of crawling across this wall like a couple of damned spiders—"

"Be still," Arilyn hissed, stifling a rising wave of anger. Once again she berated herself for being drawn to Danilo Thann. The man was endlessly frustrating. One moment he was a canny fighter, the next an understanding friend, the very next a worthless twit. The latter condition currently prevailed. If possible, Danilo was acting more scattered than usual, doubtlessly cowed by the attack upon his precious person. She should have left him behind to cower in that dismal room.

Arilyn edged around a gabled window, secure on her tiny foothold, but Danilo stumbled, arms windmilling as he teetered dangerously forward. The half-elf seized his cloak and pulled him back to safety.

"Careful," she snapped. "Are you sure Rhys Ravenwind will be in the end chamber?"

"Very," Danilo huffed, both hands clutching the wall as he peered down into the courtyard below. Although he strove for nonchalance, his voice was decidedly unsteady. "I asked the innkeeper for the King's Chamber—I usually stay there after partaking too freely, you see—and he informed me that the bard already had dibs. Imagine!"

They were nearing the end of the building. Arilyn gestured for silence and crept to the last window. It was open, and the half-elf dropped noiselessly into the room, sliding behind the heavy brocade drapes that flanked the window. There was no sound in the room, no sign of an intruder.

Holding her breath, Arilyn glided over to the bed and lay her fingers on the singer's neck. "Too late," she groaned softly. Danilo climbed unsteadily into the room and joined her.

"Dead?" he whispered. His face was unusually pale.

"Yes." She pointed to the brand on the bard's upturned palm. Rage poured through her veins like liquid fire. "I'm going to kill this monster," she vowed quietly.

"I don't doubt it, but not tonight," Danilo replied, taking her elbow. "We're getting out of here. Now."

Arilyn jerked away. "No! I'm too close."

"Exactly," Danilo said, his voice strained. "Too close for comfort, in my opinion. Look, maybe you're not afraid of this Harper Assassin, but I for one don't look good in blue." He held up his left palm so she could see the glowing blue brand. "Remember this?"

"You can leave any time," she replied.

Danilo ran his branded hand over his hair to pat the wind-tossed locks into place. The movement seemed to throw him off balance, for he grasped the bedpost to steady himself. "Leave? Nothing would make me happier than scampering off to safety," he retorted. "Did you ever pause to think that I might not be able to?"

Arilyn recoiled and looked him over sharply. "What are you talking about?"

"Me. I feel terrible."

"So do I. I knew Rhys Ravenwind from Suzail."

"No, that's not what I meant, although there's also that element. I *feel* terrible. Think," Danilo said, pointing to the dead bard. "What killed Rhys Ravenwind? Do you see blood? Signs of struggle?"

"Nothing," she admitted. "That's part of the problem. All die in sleep, unmarked but for—" Her eyes widened in realization. "Poison," she concluded in a grim whisper. "The brand is poisoned. The Harpers are not branded after their death, as we assumed. They're killed by a magic, poisoned brand."

"That would be my guess," Danilo agreed. "Neither you nor I are equipped to deal with a magic-wielding assassin, even if we should find him. Which I doubt we could."

Arilyn's eyes widened in comprehension. She grabbed Danilo's hand, staring down at it as if she could remove the brand by the sheer force of her will. "Oh gods, then you've been poisoned, too. Why are we standing here? Are you all right?"

He shrugged away her concern. "I think I'll live. You interrupted the assassin before I got much of the poison, but I'm starting to feel a little shaky."

"The roof," she said, remembering Danilo's near fall.

"That's when I figured it out," he admitted with a weak grin. "I've been in and out of windows often enough to have developed excellent balance. I might be a tad rusty, but not that bad. My little stumble made the pieces fit." His voice suddenly hardened. "But that's neither here nor there. You got me into this, you nearly got me killed—again, I might add—and you're going to take me somewhere safe. Now."

Arilyn nodded curtly, frustrated by the assassin's nearness but equally worried about Danilo. Despite his protestations, the young noble did look rather pale. At the rate he was going, he'd never get out of the inn on his own.

"Come on," she said, then added dryly, "Under the circumstances, perhaps we should take the door."

"Oh," he said, turning back from the window. "Good thinking."

Arilyn glanced at the magic sack that hung from Danilo's belt and remembered the spellbook he carried. She didn't like using magic, but she saw no other recourse. "By any chance, do you know the spell for invisibility?"

"No, but if you'll hum a few bars I'll try to fake it," Danilo responded in a slightly dazed tone.

Startled, Arilyn stared at him with open concern. "You must have gotten more poison than we thought. That jest was ancient in the days of Myth Drannor."

The dandy responded with a weak grin. He held up the spell components and motioned Arilyn to his side. "At the moment, I don't feel so young myself. Let's get out of here."

*   *   *   *   *

Within minutes, an invisible Arilyn and Danilo were quietly headed northwest toward the Castle Ward, to the home of the adventurer Loene. It was the safest place Arilyn could think of. Loene's townhome on Waterdeep Way was a veritable fortress, within sight's distance of the guards stationed at Waterdeep Castle. Still, remembering the trail of death that lay behind her, Arilyn hated involving the woman. She did not wish to lead the assassin to Loene's door.

The half-elf felt she had little choice. Danilo's energy had been sorely tasked by casting the spell of invisibility over them and again over their horses, and he seemed to be growing weaker by the moment. She feared that if he lost consciousness, she would never be able to rouse him. Perhaps if she kept him talking? How difficult could that be?

"Are you sure that the innkeeper will not suspect us of the bard's death?" she asked in a whisper.

Danilo nodded his head, an effort that almost tipped him from his horse.

"Why's that?" Arilyn prompted, reaching out and pushing the noble upright in his saddle.

"I left a magical illusion in our room," he muttered. "Before we left to check on the bard. Just in case, you know."

"Oh?"

The shadow of a smirk crossed the dandy's face. "The maid will see a large empty zzar bottle on the table, and two sleeping figures entwined on the cot," he said in a faint voice. "Sated and snoring."

Arilyn's head slumped in resignation. "Bearing a remarkable resemblance to you and me, I suppose."

"Naturally. The illusion will hold until mid-morning. The bard's body will be found before then."

Arilyn had to admire his solution, however twisted. "No wonder you stumbled on the ledge. Casting such a spell must have taken a great deal of energy."

"Yes, but it was fun," he muttered, again slumping dangerously to one side. Arilyn's arm shot out to steady him.

"Hang on just a little longer," she urged. "Loene's house is around the corner. See that huge elm up ahead? It's in the courtyard behind her house."

"Good. I don't feel so well."

Loene's mansion resembled a miniature castle, complete with towers and turrets. It was surrounded by an ornate iron fence as decorative as it was impenetrable. We'll be safe here, Arilyn thought. She quickly dismounted at the gate, helped Danilo from his horse, and draped one of his arms over her shoulders. He leaned heavily on her as she tied the reins of their invisible mounts to the iron fence, then worked the lock free with a small knife.

"Break and enter often?" the dandy mumbled as he watched her deft movements. "What now? Do they fireball us or call the watch?"

"Neither. No problem. Loene knows me. We'll be fine," Arilyn assured him, speaking with more confidence than she felt.

She and Danilo were still invisible, and that could prove a problem. It was hard to convince someone of your integrity if he couldn't look you in the eye, and she wasn't about to let Danilo squander his waning strength to dispel the magic.

Arilyn half-dragged Danilo up the walk. Raising the knocker, she tapped it briskly, using the code taught her by Nain Keenwhistler, a member of the adventuring party known as the Company of Crazed Venturers. The code would certainly be recognized in this household: Loene had been rescued from slavery by Nain, and for many years she had run with the

Crazed Venturers.

The door cracked open. "Yes?"

The raspy tones identified the speaker as Elliot Graves, Loene's servant. No other voice could sound both so pompous and so whisky-soaked. "It's me, Graves. Arilyn Moonblade."

"Where?" The door opened wider, and a thin, wary face peered past into the courtyard. Arilyn didn't doubt that Graves had his mace handy. He was as skilled a fighter as he was a chef, and he didn't look at all pleased that anyone had breached the walled court.

"I'm right here, Graves, only invisible. I've got a friend with me, and he's badly wounded. Please let us in."

The urgency in her voice convinced the servant. "One at a time," he said, opening the door just wide enough for one person to edge through.

Arilyn pushed Danilo before her. He fell face down onto the ornate Calimshite carpet. "That's one," the prone noble observed in a drunken tone.

The half-elf brushed past Graves and knelt by the fallen man. Sensing Arilyn pass, the servant slammed and bolted the door behind her.

"What's all this?" an imperious voice demanded.

Arilyn looked up. Loene was poised on the stairway, wrapped in night robes of pale gold silk and holding a jeweled dagger in each hand. The woman's dark blond hair hung free in a wild mop about her shoulders, and her large hazel eyes darted about the empty hall. Once enslaved as a "pleasure girl" for her exquisite face and form, Loene had become a skilled fighter and adventurer. In middle life, the woman was still both beautiful and deadly. She had the tawny grace of a desert cat, and at the moment she looked every bit as dangerous.

The words tumbled out. "It's Arilyn Moonblade. I've got a friend with me. He's been poisoned."

"Get my potion case," Loene instructed the servant, not taking her eyes from the hall carpet. Graves melted away, still holding his mace at the ready.

"Well, well. Arilyn Moonblade. Since when did you start resorting to invisibility spells?" Loene asked, descending the stairs with catlike grace. She lay down her jeweled weapons on a marble-topped table at the foot of the stairs.

"It wasn't my first choice."

"I'll bet." Loene agreed dryly. The woman twisted the magic ring on her hand, murmuring the command that would dispel Danilo's enchantment. As she did, two outlines appeared on the expensive carpet, gradually filling in until they took the form of a large, prone man and a half-elven adventurer. Loene's lovely, curious eyes met Arilyn's. "Ah. There you are. You look terrible, by the way."

She came forward and crouched at Arilyn's side, touching henna-tipped fingers to the fallen man's pulse. "It's strong and regular. His color is good, his breathing regular. What happened to him? Poison, you said?"

"It's a long story," Arilyn said tersely, her anxious gaze fixed on her companion.

"Hmmm. I can't wait to hear it. Oh, thank you, Graves," Loene said, accepting a box from the servant. "Just who is your friend?"

"Danilo Thann."

"Dan—" Loene's incredulous echo broke off into derisive laughter. "Girl, you picked a strange time to start trusting magic-users. His drawing room tricks misfire more often than Shou rockets. Oof. And he's heavy. Give me a hand here."

The two adventurers managed to roll the young nobleman over. Loene gently lifted one eyelid, then the other. After a moment's speculation, she selected a small blue vial from the box of potions and handed it to Arilyn. "An antidote," Loene said. "Very rare. Works amazingly fast."

The half-elf quickly uncorked the vial, raised Danilo's head, and held the potion to his lips. His eyes flickered open.

"Pretend it's rivengut," Arilyn advised him with a touch of grim humor.

The mention of his favorite libation rallied Danilo sufficiently to sip some of the potion. Somewhat revived, he propped himself up on one elbow and looked around the hall.

"I feel better," he announced, sounding surprised.

"You're sure?" Arilyn pressed.

"Almost as good as new," he promised, surreptitiously showing her his palm. The brand had faded noticeably. Arilyn's shoulders sagged in relief.

Loene sat back on her heels, a speculative smile playing about her lips as she watched the scene before her. She'd known Arilyn for years, and never had she seen the half-elf so rattled. No potion or antidote worked so quickly—Arilyn should have known that—and her usually sharp elven senses should have caught the scent of the apricot brandy that was the vial's only ingredient.

Ah, but there's a story here, Loene thought. If she were to admit to a weakness, it would be her inordinate fondness for interesting and unusual tales. An unexpected bounty had been delivered to her door this night. "I suppose explanations must wait for morning," she said, her voice tinged with regret. "Graves, would you see our guests to their beds?"

"One bed," Arilyn corrected.

"I say. That might be expecting a bit much from the healing potion," Danilo warned her.

Arilyn shot him a look that would have frozen a wiser man, then turned away. "With your permission, Loene, I'll leave Danilo in your care. I must attend to urgent business."

Loene stood and placed her hands on her hips. "Forget it, elf. Of course I'll keep your friend until he can travel," she huffed, "but just you try to leave without telling me what's going on and I'll nail your blue hide to the wall."

Arilyn rose with a sigh of resignation. "All right. At this point, I don't suppose a short delay can hurt too much. You'd better break out the sherry and plan to sit for a while."

"I keep a full bottle on hand, just in case you decide to make one of these impromptu visits," Loene purred, smiling with satisfaction. "See to our other guest, won't you, Graves?"

"As you wish, madame."

The woman and the half-elf linked arms and headed into Loene's study to exchange tales of adventure.

Danilo sat crosslegged on the carpet, watching them go. He noted with a purely personal satisfaction that Arilyn shot a final, concerned look back at him before she left the room. A pointedly cleared throat captured his attention, and he looked up at the servant. The mace still hung at the man's belt, a jarring note amid the elegant furnishings of the entrance hall.

"If you think you can walk, sir, I'll see you to your room," the servant said. When Danilo nodded, Graves bent down and plucked the nobleman from the carpet, none too gently.

Danilo took the servant's arm, making a show of leaning on him as they walked slowly up the stairs. A pair of giant black mastiffs followed them, eyeing Danilo with wary interest. The nobleman fleetingly hoped that the dogs were well fed. He noted that the wiry servant was surprisingly strong, and that the man's raspy, whiskey-drenched voice and eyes the color of cold steel seemed more suited to the battlefield than the Castle Ward. It was a reassuring observation, and Danilo suddenly felt a little better about what he had to do. If he had to leave Arilyn for a time, at least she would be well protected.

The dandy let Graves lead him into a richly appointed guest room and lower him into a chair. "Is there anything else that sir requires?" the servant asked coolly.

"Sleep should do it," Danilo assured him. "That was a dandy potion, really."

"Very good, sir." The servant closed the door firmly behind him.

Danilo listened until the servant's footsteps died away. When all was silent, he rose, reaching into the magic bag at his waist. He took from it his spellbook and a length of rope. He quickly studied the runes on one of the pages, memorizing the complex spell he had to cast. Finally satisfied, he slipped the spellbook back into this bag.

Not a trace of his lethargy remained. The effects of the assassin's poison had faded long before they'd reached Loene's house, although Danilo had maintained a facade of weakness in order to get Arilyn out of the inn and away from an assassin who could disappear from a locked room.

He threw open a window, secured the rope to a bedpost, and lowered himself to the courtyard. After his experience on the ledge of the inn, he was not about to attempt a levitation spell from a second-story window, antidote or not. By the way, Danilo mused, I must find out what was in that concoction. It was quite tasty.

He reached into his sack for the spell components and went through the complex patterns of gestures and chants. After rising into the night and over the wall, he floated down, featherlike, to the street beyond. At last, quietly, he strode to the front of the house and dispelled the enchantment that made his horse invisible.

The edge of the night sky was just beginning to fade to silver when Danilo started west on Waterdeep Way. Just down the street, a few contented patrons were leaving Mother Tathlorn's House of Pleasure and Healing, a combination fest-hall and spa that was very plush and very popular. That was a sure sign that morning was near.

Danilo Thann gave his horse's reins a sharp shake, and he rode quickly toward nearby Blackstaff Tower.

Ten

As he rode, Danilo pondered all that had transpired during the night. He would have given much to have heard Arilyn's version of their story. He did not imagine that he fared well in the telling.

Danilo was accustomed to being thought a fool. Even within his own family, he bore his father's stern disapproval and the scorn of his older brothers. This he accepted as part of his role, but when he saw a foppish Waterdhavian dandy reflected back to him from the mirror of Arilyn's elven eyes, he found that he had little stomach for the charade.

Perhaps it was time to make some changes.

Riding swiftly, Danilo soon reached the home of the archmage. Blackstaff Tower looked impenetrable. It was, but only to the uninitiated. A series of powerful magical wards and devices, as well as a twenty-foot stone wall, protected the tower. By all appearances, the place had no doors at all and windows only on the upper floors.

Danilo dismounted at the gate and muttered a cantrip,

casting an easy spell that would keep his horse tethered. Another quick spell opened the gate. Danilo strode quickly through the courtyard, and, after knocking on the tower and softly speaking his name, he walked through an invisible door into the wizard's reception hall.

Khelben "Blackstaff" Arunsun descended the spiral staircase to meet his nephew. "I see you've finally managed the door," he observed.

Danilo grinned and rubbed an imaginary lump on his head. "Missed it enough times, wouldn't you say?"

"Indeed. Well, come up, come up. I've been waiting for your report," Khelben said, gesturing for Danilo to follow him up to the parlor.

Steaming cups of roasted chicory rested on a small table between two comfortable chairs. Danilo cast his a longing look but insisted, "I haven't much time. Arilyn is at Loene's house on Waterdeep Way. I need to get back before I'm missed."

"Of course." Khelben settled down and took up his cup. "Have you anything concerning the assassin's identity?"

"Not yet. Back in Evereska, Arilyn was followed by a thug from Waterdeep. In his possession was a snuffbox bearing the sigil of Perendra."

Khelben choked on a mouthful of chicory, and Danilo nodded grimly. "In answer to your next question, yes, I'm sure it was Perendra's mark. She was one of the first to die, wasn't she?"

"Yes," Khelben said as soon as he could speak. "Unlike the later victims, she was not marked with the brand. It is possible that her death was not the work of our assassin. Did that man admit to killing Perendra?"

"No. He claimed he'd gotten the box from an elf. He was obviously enspelled to die before he could reveal the villain's name. Arilyn, I assume, intends to track him or her down."

"Good. Stay with her as she does. Now the sword. Tell me everything you can think of."

Danilo perched on the edge of his chair, took a deep breath, and spoke fast. "It's elvencrafted and very old, made of some dull but very strong metal I don't recognize. There are runes down its length—Espruar, I think, though a form I've never seen—and also on the sheath. There's a large gem on the hilt, and it—"

"Stop!" Khelben demanded. Alarm etched itself across the wizard's face as he leaned intently toward his nephew. "There's a moonstone in the hilt? Are you sure?"

"No, it's a topaz."

"Did she say anything about this stone?" Khelben urged.

"Actually, yes. She told me that her teacher, Kymil Nimesin, had it set in the hilt to balance the blade."

"I see." Khelben relaxed. "Good. I didn't know Arilyn was trained by Kymil Nimesin, but it figures. He's one of the best armsmasters in the Realms, and he works for the Harpers from time to time. Go on."

"The sword cuts through metal and bone as if it were slicing a summermelon. Its strike is unusually fast, although I think a good deal of that is Arilyn. According to her, the sword cannot shed innocent blood. Just how it ascertains innocence, I don't know. It warns of danger—"

"How?"

"It glows. It also glows sometimes when Arilyn draws it, but sometimes it doesn't. I can't figure out any kind of pattern to that."

"And if anyone else were to draw it?"

"They would get fried like a flounder," Danilo concluded flatly.

"Of course," Khelben muttered. "It is a hereditary blade, after all." He arched an eyebrow at Danilo. "You didn't find this out through personal experience, I trust?"

"Unfortunately, I did. Fortunately, I barely touched it."

Khelben chuckled at Danilo's droll tone, but quickly sobered. "Anything else?

"It can also warn Arilyn of danger by sending dreamwarnings."

"Interesting. All right, what else?"

Danilo told his uncle what had transpired, starting with the inn near Evereska and describing the mysterious assault at the House of Good Spirits.

"Poison," muttered Khelben, visibly annoyed with his own lack of perception. "Of course. Why do you think the assassin attacked you? Have you reason to think that your alliance to the Harpers is suspected?"

The young man looked a little chagrined. "No, but my sense of chivalry certainly is. There was but one bed, and I had it. The chamber was very dark, and I suppose the assassin presumed that a gentleman would take the floor."

"I see. You're all right now?"

"I didn't get much of the poison. If you're through, I have a few quick questions." Danilo leveled his gaze on Khelben. "Why are you so concerned with Arilyn's sword? What does it have to do with this assassin?"

"It is possible that there is no connection," Khelben admitted. "Given the sword's history, however, it was something that I could not ignore."

"I think it is time for a history lesson. In more ways than one, I have a personal interest in this." The young man spoke quietly, but he held up his branded palm for Khelben to see. "But please, make it quick."

Khelben nodded. "Yes, it's time you knew." He passed one hand over his salt-and-pepper hair and took a deep breath.

"Before you were born, Arilyn's parents inadvertently used the magic of the sword to open a portal between these mountains and the elven kingdom of Evermeet. The damnable gate stayed open, and the best any of us could do was obscure it and move it elsewhere. The elves ordered Z'beryl to dismantle the sword. Arilyn's father took the magic moonstone away with him. As it is today, the moonblade carries potent magic. Restored, it could be used to unveil the gate to Evermeet."

Khelben concluded his terse recitation with a sigh. "So there it is. If there was a chance that someone knew of this gate and was after Arilyn for her sword, we had to know about it."

"I see," Danilo said, though his mind was racing through all that Khelben had told him. Given the fabled riches of the elven kingdom of Evermeet, an open portal would be an invitation to plunder. The elves of Evermeet were fiercely reclusive, and the island was guarded by the powerful elven navy of Queen Amlauruil, by lethal coral reefs, by hosts of mysterious sea creatures allied with the elves, and by ever-shifting energy fields that could reduce an invading ship to ashes and seafoam. In comparison to these defenses, any guard that could be posted at the magic portal would seem a small obstacle. Secrecy was the best protection for the gate to Evermeet, for if knowledge of this portal spread, the last stronghold of the elves would be compromised and the very existence of the dwindling race threatened. Danilo wondered how Arilyn would react to the knowledge that she was in part the keeper of the elven kingdom.

"By the way," Danilo added, "why didn't you tell me that Arilyn was elven?"

"A half-elf. Her father was human, more or less." Khelben said. "Whenever I see her, she's usually passing as human."

"Indeed. She was a Sembian courtesan when we met. Great disguise," Danilo reminisced with a grin. "I managed to recognize her from Rafe Silverspur's ring, and, believe it or not, from your portrait."

Khelben smiled sourly at his nephew's good-natured insult. "Which reminds me: according to your mother, my esteemed brother-in-law is none too happy with his 'shiftless son' for taking off with 'some fancy pleasure girl.' You might check in with him when time permits."

"Another lecture from dear father. The gods know I've been *such* a disappointment to him," Danilo drawled flippantly.

Khelben eyed the young man keenly, sensing a new note in his act. "Thinking of quitting?"

"What, being a disappointment?"

"No. Playing the fool in the service of the Harpers."

Danilo shrugged. "What options do I have?"

"There are always options," Khelben asserted. "After this assignment, if you like, come out in the open. You're a good agent. The Harpers would surely welcome you."

Danilo stood to go, his face more reflective that Khelben had ever seen it. "You know, Uncle, I just might take you up on that."

Moving swiftly through the magic door, Danilo left Black-staff Tower, mounted his horse, and sped back toward the townhouse on Waterdeep Way. To the east, the sun was peeking over the roofs of the city, casting long shadows along the still-quiet streets.

One of those shadows suddenly moved and began to follow Danilo Thann toward Waterdeep Way.

* * * * *

Loene was curled with catlike coziness amid the silken pillows of her couch, her slippered feet tucked beneath her. At the moment, she looked as content as Arilyn had ever seen her. "An interesting tale," said Loene.

"Worth the price of that sherry?" Arilyn asked dryly, glancing at the half-empty decanter on the table that sat between Loene's couch and the more spartan chair she herself had chosen. The half-elf's first glass, which was almost untasted, rested in her hands. The rest of the sherry had been consumed by her host, who was renowned for her ability to hold the stuff.

"And then some," the woman said, raising her fourth goblet for a toast. "Here's to a happy ending."

"Hear, hear," Arilyn agreed, her face turning serious at the thought of what lay before her.

Graves chose that moment to poke his head through the door of the study. "There will be two for breakfast, madame?"

Loene smiled invitingly at Arilyn. "Will you stay? Graves makes the best scones in Waterdeep, you know."

Arilyn was reluctant to delay her search longer, but she needed to eat sometime. "Thank you, yes, but I must leave soon."

"I understand." Loene turned to the servant. "There will be three, then, unless our other guest prefers a tray."

The servant's eyebrows rose. "Our other guest has already departed."

"What?" Arilyn rose slowly to her feet. "Danilo's gone? Are you sure?"

"Oh, yes," Graves said. He held up a length of rope. "By the window, no less," he muttered, shaking his head in self-recrimination. "I let the peacock strut right past me."

"The fool," Arilyn blazed, slamming her fist onto the serving table as she stalked from the room. Loene lunged to save the wobbling sherry decanter, then she followed Arilyn into the hall, clutching the cherished spirits to her as she went.

"Let him go." Loene laid a restraining hand on Arilyn's arm.

The half-elf shook her off. "He's not strong enough to travel."

The woman snorted. "Don't believe it for a minute. That young man was perfectly normal—whatever that may mean in his case."

Arilyn went very still. "I don't understand."

Loene's eyes were compassionate. "My dear, he was fine last night. He did not need that potion."

"How do you know?"

"You really need to ask?" Loene asked. "Unlike you, I have no aversion to using poisons when the occasion demands. I know what's out there, I know the effects and the signs."

"You gave him an antidote," Arilyn pointed out. "Why?

"Apricot brandy. I suspected that your friend wasn't really poisoned, and his rapid recovery proved me right."

"What about that brand?"

"Well, all right," Loene conceded. "Perhaps he did get just a touch of some poison when he was branded, but the effects had certainly faded before he got here. You were too concerned to notice."

Arilyn nodded slowly. It made perfect sense. Danilo was most anxious to reach safety. Having done so, what better way to ensure his continued safety than to sneak away, leaving her and the assassin far behind? Arilyn couldn't blame him, especially after the attack on his life. Why, then, did she feel betrayed? "He is a coward," she seethed. "I'm well rid of that one."

"Granted," Loene said, understanding Arilyn's anger for

what it was. "Forget him, and let's have some of Graves's incomparable scones." She brandished the decanter. "We can wash them down with the rest of this."

"I'm afraid I cannot," Arilyn replied. "I have to leave right away. Danilo Thann has a tongue that wags at both ends. He will spread this tale all over the city by sunset. If I'm ever to find this assassin, I must do it soon."

"You will return and let me know how things turn out?"

"Do I have a choice?"

Loene grinned. "It's so comforting to be understood by one's friends." She handed the sherry decanter to the ever-present Graves and stepped forward to clasp Arilyn's forearms in the traditional farewell of adventurers. "Until swords part, then."

Arilyn absently repeated the words, her mind already on her quest. As soon as Loene released her, the half-elf reached into her bag for a tiny pot and a comb. She spread a dark unguent over her face for a sun-weathered look, then combed her hair over her ears. Laying her hand on the moonblade's grip, the half-elf closed her eyes and envisioned a human lad. Loene's chuckle informed her that the transformation was complete.

It was a simple illusion. Arilyn's shirt and trousers were suddenly a little looser, and they appeared to have been made of the rough linsey-woolsey that was often used for the work clothes of growing lads. A wrinkled cap held Arilyn's hair in place over her ears and shadowed her elven eyes; work gloves concealed her slender hands. The rest was a matter of stance, movement, and voice.

"What a handsome lad you make," Loene teased. "You almost make me wish I were ten years younger."

"Only ten?" Graves asked with a rare flash of humor.

Arilyn's smile of response was quick and halfhearted. "Please be careful, Loene. A visit from me might be enough to lure this assassin. Watch yourself."

"I will," the woman promised.

"As will I," came the servant's quiet voice.

Arilyn met Graves's eyes and nodded her thanks, knowing

that his words held no small assurance. With his thin, ascetic face, sparse hair, and elegant black attire, Elliot Graves was the very picture of a proper majordomo. In truth, the man was gutter bred and raised, a fearsome fighter who could carry a grudge for a dragon's lifetime. He was utterly loyal to Loene, and she would not be better protected by a score of Cormyr's best Purple Dragons.

As Arilyn walked into the courtyard she tried not to envy Loene, but she wondered what it would be like to have a friend as devoted as Elliot Graves. She'd always walked alone, and she wasn't sure that she could do otherwise. Certainly her treatment of Danilo had not been the sort that inspired loyalty.

Resolutely Arilyn put all such thoughts aside. She had long wished to be rid of Danilo Thann, and now she had got her wish. It was time to throw all her effort into ridding the world of the Harper Assassin.

Arilyn circled around to the back of the house. There she agilely climbed the fence that separated Loene's property from Gem Street, a small, lightly traveled alley. She knew better than to try to climb the fence from the other side, which was protected from intruders by magical wards.

Dropping lightly to her feet, Arilyn checked about to make sure she was alone and unobserved. Reassured, she thrust her hands into her pockets and ambled down Gem Street with long swinging strides, a human lad, set on some family errand.

* * * * *

By the time Danilo reached Loene's house, Waterdeep Way was already awake with the bustle of morning commerce. Since he was cloaked by neither darkness nor invisibility, he slipped around the back of the house to Gem Street and quietly dismounted. He spat on his hands and prepared to climb the fence.

The instant Danilo touched the iron, a magical current sped up his arms. He jumped away from the fence with a sharp oath. There had to be another way in. Scratching his head in puzzlement, he squinted up at the guest room window.

His escape rope no longer hung there. "No rope," he said with a soft groan.

So his departure had been noted, probably by that deceptively starched and pressed servant of Loene's. Since Danilo doubted that Graves's silence could be purchased, he would have to talk fast to explain to Arilyn why he'd left by the window. Or better yet, Danilo thought, maybe he could get back into the house and make off with Arilyn before Graves had a chance to inform the women of his desertion.

A large elm shaded the rear courtyard, its branches just of out reach. Fortunately, Danilo had climbed a lot of trees in his youth. He improvised a spell, a simple cantrip meant to move stationery objects. One of the large branches of the elm, responding to the magic summons, bent over the fence and stretched leafy hands out to the young mage. Danilo jumped, and as he caught hold of the branch he released his spell. The branch sprang back to its natural position, flinging the nobleman high into the tree.

He hit hard and tumbled through layers of foliage, grabbing wildly for a hold until his hands closed on a branch. Pulling himself up onto a large limb, he straddled the branch and leaned wearily against the tree's trunk. His face stung from a dozen scratches, and when he brushed a strand of hair away from face his hand came away tinged with blood. Danilo shook his head in disbelief. "Maybe all those people who think me a fool are onto something," he muttered.

Once Danilo's sense of balance was restored, the rest of the ascent was easy. He climbed the sprawling elm and slipped in through the guest room window without further incident.

From the floor below, he heard the clatter of dishes. He'd have to hurry. After pouring some cold water from a pitcher of fine Shou porcelain into a matching washbowl, Danilo dashed the water over his scratched face and raked his hands through his hair to tame it somewhat. Taking a deep breath to steady his wits, he manufactured his most charming and inane smile and stuck it firmly in place. He followed the sounds downstairs and into the dining room.

To his surprise, Danilo found Loene sitting alone at a long table of polished wood, staring absently into a glass of sherry. "Good morning," he said cheerfully as he sauntered into the room. "I see I beat Arilyn down to breakfast. Is she still abed?"

Loene put down her glass and appraised Danilo for a silent moment. "Rough night?"

The nobleman smiled sheepishly. "Cut myself shaving."

"Really. What do you shave with? The talons of a goshawk?"

"Dull blade." Danilo selected a pear from the fruit bowl on the table and took a bite. "You were starting to tell me where I might find Arilyn?"

"Was I?"

Maintaining his facade, not to mention his temper, was getting more difficult by the moment. Danilo took another bite of the pear and chewed slowly. While he was still collecting himself, his hostess spoke again. "Sit down, won't you? I'm getting a crick in my neck staring up at you."

The nobleman obligingly took a seat. Loene stretched out her hand and picked a leaf from of his hair. "By the way," she said in an innocent voice, "would you care for some more apricot brandy?"

Danilo stared blankly for a time. "The potion?"

"Very good."

"I thought that stuff tasted familiar." With a resigned sigh, he held up his hands in surrender. "You win. Now, can we please talk about Arilyn?"

Loene's smile reminded him of a cream-sated tabby. "You can count on it."

"She didn't leave, by chance?"

"By chance, she did."

"Damn. I should have known better than to let that girl out of my sight. I *am* a fool," Danilo chided himself.

"Maybe, maybe not," the woman replied, eyeing him keenly.

"Do you have any idea where she went? Any at all?"

Loene smiled and stretched, catlike. "I might know where Arilyn Moonblade went. I might even be persuaded to tell you."

The true son of a Waterdeep merchant, Danilo did not miss the speculative gleam in the woman's eyes. With a sigh of resignation, he folded his arms on the table and glared at Loene. "At what price?" he asked.

Before answering, his hostess poured another glass of sherry and pushed it toward Danilo. "Arilyn told me her side of the story," she purred. "Why don't you tell me yours."

Eleven

Morning had broken over Waterdeep Way. On the roof of a tall building overlooking the home of the adventurer Loene, smoke from the breakfast fire began to spiral into the sky. In the shadow of that chimney crouched a lone figure.

From his rooftop perch, Bran Skorlsun had a clear view of every angle of the tiny white castle sprawled below. He drew his cape closely about him, shifting his weight to bring some circulation to a numb foot. The morning was chilly, and he was weary to his very core. The road from the Vale of Darkhold had been a long one, and his assignment—to follow Arilyn Moonblade and determine whether she was responsible for the deaths of his fellow Harpers—was turning out to be far more difficult than he had anticipated.

As the Harper watched, the front door of Loene's home was flung open. The half-elf's human companion stormed out, swearing softly and furiously. Bran rose, intent upon following the young man from the rooftops of the closely

163

set houses.

"Why, if it isn't the Raven. How are you, Bran?"

Startled, the Harper whirled to find himself face to face with a beautiful, familiar woman. Leaning casually against the chimney, arms folded over a robe of pale gold silk, stood Loene. Pleasure at seeing his old friend warred with Bran's chagrin at the ease with which she had surprised him.

Loene's hazel eyes glinted with laughter, and she held up her left hand to display a simple silver band. "In answer to your question, I flew. A ring of spell storing is a handy thing to have," she commented lightly. "A gift from the Blackstaff, of course. I trust you've seen our old friend already?"

"No."

"Well, you must stop by Blackstaff Tower. He'll be delighted to visit with you."

"That is unlikely."

Loene chuckled. "I would give a great deal to know what caused the trouble between you two all those years ago."

"Another time, Loene. I must go now."

"Stay," she purred, coming closer and taking his arm. "If you're worried about losing Danilo Thann's trail, don't. I can tell you where he went. By the gods, Bran," she said with genuine feeling, "it's good to see you after all these years. Almost like old times. I've heard about some of your adventures, but I'd given up hope you'd ever return to Waterdeep. I suppose your sudden reappearance is due to this Harper Assassin?"

Bran looked down at her sharply. "I have been charged with finding the assassin, yes. What do you know about the matter?"

The woman preened and smiled coyly. "Plenty. Care to swap tales?" Under the man's steady gaze, her smile wavered and faded.

"Where did the young man go?" Bran asked sternly.

Loene sighed. "He's headed for the Dock Ward, to a tavern on Adder Lane. Tell me one thing," she said, grabbing his arm when he started to turn away, "how did you find out that Arilyn is the assassin's target?"

"Target?"

Loene dropped Bran's arm and stepped back. "What else?" Realization dawned on her face. "Don't tell me you think Arilyn is the assassin?" She shook her head in disbelief. "You don't know her very well."

A flash of pain crossed the man's face. "No, I don't."

"Obviously. Who set you on her trail?"

Bran hesitated. "The Harpers."

Loene's laughter was tinged with irony. "You people really should talk to each other more often. Did you know that Danilo Thann is Blackstaff's nephew? His dear Uncle Khelben has charged him with helping Arilyn find the assassin."

"That young fool?"

"He's not really, you know. Just last month, Blackstaff confided to me that for years now he's been secretly training a young mage. Khelben's not entirely happy with the secrecy. I believe our dear archmage is vain enough to want to spring his protege upon the world with all due fanfare. His most promising pupil, Blackstaff said, with the potential to become a true wizard." Loene inspected her henna-tinted nails. "From what I learned this morning, I would wager a chest of sapphires that Blackstaff was speaking of young Lord Thann."

"I'd heard you'd given up gambling, Loene."

The woman's hazel eyes were serious. "I don't consider it a gamble. Arilyn is *usually* a decent judge of character, and I believe she cares about the young man."

"Why do you say 'usually' in that manner, if Thann is all you believe him to be?"

"I wasn't talking about Danilo," Loene said ruefully. "You might as well know. Arilyn is on her way to talk to Elaith Craulnobur."

*   *   *   *   *

When Arilyn rounded the corner onto Adder Lane she found the street a virtual beehive of activity. The Dock Ward was the busiest and most crowded section of Waterdeep, with com-

merce both legal and illegal taking place at all hours. She
walked the length of the street twice, but there was no sign of
the establishment Loene had mentioned.

Finally Arilyn stopped a dour passerby and asked for the
Rearing Hippocampus Inn. He looked at her as if she'd struck
him. "It was over there," the man said, pointing to a large
wooden structure. Arilyn shot a glance at the building.

"Ah, here you are," the man said glumly, turning away from
Arilyn to address two servants, who carried between them a
wooden sign. On it Arilyn saw the name of the inn she sought,
as well as a crudely carved picture of a hippocampus. The man
sighed, cast a last wistful glance at the building, and set off
down the road. His servants fell in behind him, carrying their
strange banner.

Puzzled, Arilyn walked to the building and peered in through
the open door. Chairs were up on the tables, and a small army
of workers bustled about, scrubbing and polishing every surface of the tavern. Merchants came and went with stocks of
food and drink. In the midst of the commotion, directing it all
with gentle commands, stood Elaith Craulnobur.

"Adder Lane. Quite an appropriate address for the good
elf's new establishment, wouldn't you say?"

Arilyn jumped and turned to face the source of the familiar,
drawling voice. Her jaw dropped in astonishment.

"Hello there," said Danilo Thann, as casually as if they had
never parted company. He looked her over carefully, taking in
her disguise with ill-concealed distaste. "I must say, as disguises go I much prefer the Sembian courtesan. You are con-
vincing, though. For a moment, I mistook you for my
stableboy. He has a cap just like that one, only I believe his is
brown."

Arilyn shut her mouth and glared at the nobleman. "What
are you doing here?"

"Visiting friends?"

"You *have* friends?"

His brows rose in lazy surprise. "Really. That's quite a welcome, considering all the trouble I've gone through to find you."

Arilyn sniffed. "Why did you bother?"

"I'm beginning to wonder about that myself," he murmured. "You don't seem happy to see me."

In truth, Arilyn wished that she weren't quite so pleased to see the dandy again. The half-elf's eyes narrowed. "How did you find me? Your skills at tracking must far surpass your spellcasting or your bardcraft."

"Really my dear, you should reserve judgment until you hear my latest song. It's really quite—"

"Enough!" she burst out. "For once, give me the courtesy of a straight answer. How did you find me? Loene?"

"Well . . ."

"Loene," Arilyn confirmed grimly. "I owe her one. Now, why did you come after me? The truth!"

He shrugged. "All right, but you might not like it."

"Try me."

"I seem to have acquired one of your shadows, my dear," Danilo informed her. "I've come to give it back."

Arilyn drew back. "I don't understand."

"Oh dear. I was afraid you'd say that," Danilo said with a sigh. "Well, let me shed what light I can. As you know, I left Loene's house last night. I've been away from Waterdeep for several tendays, and I simply had to attend to a personal errand of some importance."

"Mother Tathlorn's House of Pleasure and Healing?"

Danilo's shrug made no commitment either way. "Ever since my little trip, something has been following me. Notice," he said pointedly, "that I said some*thing*. I see a shadow out of the corner of my eye, but when I turn around there is never anyone there. It is," he concluded in a prissy tone, "most disconcerting."

The description was familiar. Many times Arilyn had experienced that very feeling, although, she realized, not since they had left the House of Good Spirits the night before. She nodded slowly.

"I take it that you recognize my description of this particular shadow?" Arilyn nodded again. "Oh good," Danilo said wryly.

"Now we're getting somewhere. Let me assure you, I have no intention of dealing with this on my own. The way I see it, if I follow you around for a while longer, perhaps this shadow will return to its original owner, and I can be on my way, unencumbered. Fair enough?"

"I suppose," she said grudgingly. "Come on. Just keep quiet, if that's possible."

"Lead on."

Arilyn walked through the open door of the tavern and into a solid wall of muscle. She fell back a step and looked up into the threatening scowl of one of the biggest men she had ever seen. As square as a castle courtyard, the man literally filled the doorway.

"We ain't open," he growled down at her through a thick curly beard the color of rusted iron.

"We're looking for Elaith Craulnobur," Arilyn began.

"If he wanted to see you, boy, he'd look for you," the giant observed with a nasty smile. "Now git, before I turn you over my knee."

Arilyn drew the moonblade. "I'm afraid I must insist," she said softly.

The man threw back his head and roared with laughter, drawing several other, equally rough-looking men to his side. "He insists," he told one of them, jerking a thumb toward the slender "lad" in the doorway. His companions smirked.

Danilo buried his face in his hands. "She insists," he muttered.

"Nice sword, boy. Antique shop's down the street," one of the men taunted Arilyn. "You might as well sell it, 'cause you don't look like you can use it."

"Stand aside or draw your weapons," she said firmly. "I do not fight unarmed men."

"Right sportin' o' the lad, wouldn't you say?" piped up another. Hoots of laughter followed.

"Well, let's oblige the little chap," rumbled a deep bass voice from behind the human mountain in the doorway.

"Yeah. Show him some steel, boys." The speaker had the

sun-weathered skin and rakish clothes of a Ruathym pirate. He flashed an evil grin—complete with several gold teeth—as he drew a long knife from his bright yellow sash.

With a look of pained resignation, Danilo drew his own sword and stepped to Arilyn's side. The gathered ruffians looked the dandy over from plumed hat to polished boots and burst into renewed mirth.

The elven proprietor, alerted by the commotion, looked up. As he glided toward the door, Arilyn sheathed the moonblade and removed the cap that covered her hair and ears. Elaith Craulnobur's eyes lit up in recognition.

"It's all right, Durwoon," the *quessir* said to the doorkeeper. "Your diligence is commendable, but we must not scare away the customers."

It was a gentle reprimand, but the huge man blanched and melted into the shadows, followed by his chastened cronies.

"What a pleasant surprise," Elaith murmured, pointedly speaking only to Arilyn. "Welcome to my new establishment." Elaith gestured around at the bustle of activity. "I acquired it just two nights past. The previous owner imbibed too freely, I'm afraid, and challenged me to a game of darts. So it goes. We plan to reopen this evening in time for the first night of the festival." He broke off suddenly and took Arilyn's gloved hand, bowing low over it. "Forgive me. I doubt you've come here to discuss my latest business venture. Can I be of some service?"

"I hope so. You know that Rhys Ravenwind was killed the night we met at the House of Fine Spirits," Arilyn began.

"A tragedy," Elaith said smoothly. "What has this to do with you or me?"

"You were there," Danilo pointed out ingenuously.

The *quessir* raised his eyebrows in gentle reproach. "As were you. I assure you, the watch has already made the same dreary assumption, and they are now completely satisfied with my innocence."

Arilyn shot Danilo a quelling glance and turned back to the elf. "May we talk alone?"

"By all means," Elaith agreed, eyeing Danilo with distaste. The elf took Arilyn's arm and drew her into the tavern. Refusing to be insulted or excluded, Danilo resolutely trailed behind.

"I do not presume to tell you your business, my dear *etriel*, but you would be well rid of that one," the elf murmured, too low for the human to hear.

"Don't think I haven't tried," Arilyn returned.

"Really. How very interesting," he mused.

To Arilyn's surprise, Elaith contemplated her offhand remark as if it were a particularly important piece in a puzzle. She would have pressed him for an explanation, but they had traversed the length of the tavern and reached a back room that apparently served as his office. The elf had wasted no time in settling in to what had probably been a storeroom. The room had been swept and newly whitewashed, and the window that overlooked the back alley sparkled in the morning sun. Another window, which appeared to be newly installed, looked out over the tavern. Arilyn remembered that from the other side the window appeared to be a mirror.

Elaith politely seated her in one of the leather chairs that flanked a desk of exotic Chultan teak. Danilo refused a chair. Carefully arranging the folds of his cape, he leaned indolently against the wall just behind Arilyn.

"What do you know about the bard's death?" Arilyn asked, getting right down to business.

Elaith sat down behind his desk and spread his hands before him. "Very little. I left the inn shortly after you retired. Why do you ask?"

"Never overlook the obvious, I always say," Danilo observed brightly.

The *quessir* threw a contemptuous glance in Danilo's direction. The troublesome human hovered behind Arilyn Moonblade as if he intended to protect her, at the cost of his worthless life if need be. It was a humorous notion, but Elaith was not in the mood to be amused. "Young man, don't try my patience. I am not the Harper Assassin, as you so clumsily imply." The elf's scowl faded, and he smiled evilly. "If truth be told, I almost wish I were. He—or she—is very good indeed."

"When next we encounter the Harper Assassin, we'll be sure to pass along your good wishes," Danilo drawled. "I'm sure your approval means everything to him."

Arilyn ignored her companion as she spoke to Elaith. "I have reason to believe that the assassin is someone within the Harper ranks."

"Really?" Danilo broke in, sounding surprised.

She threw a glance over her shoulder at the nobleman. "Yes. Now if you'll excuse me for a moment?" She turned back to Elaith. "This makes any investigation difficult for me. Obviously, I cannot make inquiries directly for fear of alerting the wrong person."

"Obviously," Elaith murmured with a smile. "I am delighted to be of service, but might I ask why you have come to me?"

"I need information, and I'm aware that you have many connections in this city. I will pay whatever fee you require."

"That will not be necessary," the moon elf said firmly. "The Harpers are unlikely to pass secrets on to me, at least not directly, but I have other sources, as well as information not available to the Harpers. I will certainly make inquiries." Elaith opened a drawer and pulled out parchment and a quill. "Why don't you tell me a little more about this assassin. Start with the kill list."

Kill list. Arilyn winced at the elf's choice of words, spoken with such callous ease. Perhaps she was unwise to try to do business with Elaith Craulnobur. As she hesitated, Danilo came up and seated himself in the chair beside her. The noble man took a small snuffbox out of his magic sack and helped himself to a liberal pinch. He sneezed violently and repeatedly, then he offered the box in turn to Arilyn and to Elaith.

"Thank you, no," Elaith said coldly. Arilyn just stared at Danilo. His intention was too obvious to miss: by reminding her of Perendra's snuffbox, he was telling her not to trust the elf. She would not have thought Danilo capable of coming up with such a ruse, and for a moment she was inclined to agree with the dandy. Yet she intended to tell Elaith Craulnobur only what the elf could easily gain from other sources. What harm could there be in that?

Arilyn briefly described the assassin's method and macabre signature. Under Elaith's prompting, she listed the victims, the approximate date of each attack, and the location. Finally she could think of nothing more that she wished the elf to know.

"Very impressive." Elaith looked up from the parchment, and smiled reassuringly at Arilyn. "That should give me enough to start. I'll get right on it and let you know as soon as I learn anything." He rose and held out his palm to Arilyn.

Grateful, she laid her hand over his. "I appreciate your help."

"My dear, be assured that I shall do whatever I can."

"Why?" demanded Danilo bluntly.

Elaith withdrew his hand from Arilyn's and looked the noble over, an amused smile on his face. "The *etriel* and I have much in common. Now, if you will excuse me? I have a great deal to do if the tavern is to open in time for tonight's revelry."

Arilyn nodded her thanks and dragged Danilo out the back door of the office into the alley.

"How did you like that last remark? 'Much in common,' indeed," Danilo echoed derisively the moment the door had swung shut behind them. "I don't know how much more proof you need."

"What are you babbling about?"

"Proof, that's what. 'Much in common'? Think: you're an assassin, he's an assassin. To my ears, that was as good as a confession," Danilo said. Arilyn threw up her hands in disgust. "I take it you don't agree."

The half-elf paused, carefully considering her words. "Whatever else Elaith Craulnobur may be, he is a moon elf *quessir*," she said. "You could not possibly understand what that means."

"Enlighten me," Danilo returned in a flippant tone.

"The term *quessir* means more than a male elf. It is a formal word, with overtones of a certain status and code of behavior.

The nearest equivalent in Common is the word 'gentleman,' but that is not very close, either."

"I would hardly consider him a gentleman," Danilo observed.

"You've made that very clear," Arilyn said. "By the way, since when did you take up snuff?"

Danilo grinned. "Ah! You understood my message."

"It wasn't very subtle," she groused. "What makes you think that the thug in Evereska got the snuffbox from Elaith? He isn't the only elf in Waterdeep, you know."

"I don't trust him," Danilo said flatly, "and I don't like the fact that you do."

"Who said I trusted him?" Arilyn retorted. "Although perhaps I should. Moon elves traditionally have a strong sense of loyalty to each other."

Danilo opened his mouth to say something, then shut it. "On another matter, whyever did you say that the Harper Assassin might be a Harper?"

"Because it's very likely," Arilyn said shortly. "Harpers are a secret organization, and few advertise their membership in the group. The assassin knows his victims too well for it to be otherwise."

"Oh."

Arilyn started off down the alley, and Danilo took off after her. "Where are we going now?"

"We're going to find the elf who had Perendra's snuffbox."

* * * * *

In the tree-lined alley behind the busy tavern, a shadow stirred and prepared to follow Arilyn and Danilo.

"Come, come, old friend. What's your hurry?"

The melodious voice struck a chord, a memory of vile deeds that seemed incompatible with the gentle tone of the speaker. An icy chill stiffened Bran Skorlsun's spine, and for the first time in many years he turned to face the Serpent.

Elaith Craulnobur had changed little over the decades. He

was an elven warrior in his prime, an elegant and beautiful living weapon. Slender and sinuous, he leaned gracefully against the alley's wooden fence. A smile of gentle amusement lit Elaith's handsome face, and his amber eyes were deceptively mild.

Bran knew the elf for what he was. "It's a cold morning for serpents to be about."

Elaith's brows arched lazily. "Hardly a gracious greeting, considering all the adventures we shared in your distant youth."

"We share nothing," Bran said flatly. "The Company of the Claw is no more. Many of its members were slain by your hand."

The elf shifted his shoulders, unmoved. "A commonly held assumption, but one that was never proven. I shall forgive your bad manners. Your years of wandering through parts unknown have obviously dimmed whatever small amount of polish you once possessed."

"Unlike you, I am what I appear to be."

The elf's gaze swept over the human. "That's hardly something to boast about," he observed wryly. "Even so, I must admit that I'm consumed with curiosity at your sudden appearance. Whatever could have brought you back to the City of Splendors?"

Elaith's tone was gently mocking, and his confident smile implied that the answer was already known to him. Bran had no patience or time for the elf's games, so he simply turned to leave.

"Going so soon? We've had no time to talk."

"I've nothing to say to you."

"Oh, but I've a few things to say that you may find of interest. And you need not hurry. The pair you follow should be easy to track . . . unless your ranger skills have become as dismally rusted as your social graces."

"Insults from such as you mean nothing."

The elf's handsome face twisted with rage. "We are not so very different," he hissed. He quickly regained his composure, but his amber eyes held a malicious gleam. "You've fallen as far as I have, but you just can't bring yourself to admit it. Look at yourself! You've been exiled, to all intents and purposes, to wandering the far and forgotten edges of the world. Now you're reduced to lurking in shadows, trying to disprove your nasty suspicions about Amnestria's daughter."

Bran's face darkened at the elf's last words. "You do not deserve to speak her name."

"Don't I?" taunted the elf. "Princess Amnestria and I were friends from our childhood in Evermeet, long before you were even a gleam in your father's eye." He sighed with deep nostalgia. "Such grace, such talent and potential. Arilyn is very like her in those respects. She's got Amnestria's spirit combined with a rather devious mind. Truly a fascinating combination. Amnestria would have been proud of her daughter, as I'm sure you are," he concluded with heavy sarcasm.

"What is your interest in Arilyn?" Bran demanded.

A reflective expression crossed the elf's face. "It is rare— even during the long lifetime of an elf—that one is afforded a second chance. By all that is just, Arilyn should have been my daughter." He paused and gave Bran a measuring look. "Not yours."

The Harper recoiled at the words. Elaith was pleased with the reaction, and an evil smile curved his lips.

"Yes, your daughter," the elf mocked, openly baiting him toward admission. "Interesting, fate's little twists: the oh-so-righteous Harper sires one of the best assassins in Faerun."

"Arilyn is not the assassin," Bran asserted.

"But she *is* your daughter!" Elaith crowed triumphantly, reading the truth in Bran's face and tone. In his opinion, the only good thing about dealing with Harpers was that the fools were generally too noble—or too stupid—to dissemble. The elf's face darkened suddenly. "Does Arilyn know about you? I should hate to have her learn her father's identity when he provides evidence against her in a Harper court."

"It is not your concern."

"We'll see. How is Amnestria?" Elaith asked, changing the

subject. "Where has she been these many years?"

Bran was silent, and a look of deep sadness filled his eyes. "Despite everything, you *are* her far kinsman, and there is no reason why you should not know. Amnestria went into secret exile before Arilyn's birth. She took the name Z'beryl of Evereska. She has been dead for almost twenty-five years."

"No."

"It is true. She was ambushed and overcome by a pair of cutpurses."

The elf stared at Bran. "It does not seem possible," he murmured, dropping his stricken eyes. "No one could fight like Amnestria. Has nothing has been done to avenge her death?"

"The murderers were brought to justice."

"That remains to be seen," Elaith said in a grim tone. When he again raised his eyes to Bran's, hatred blazed in their amber depths. "Another weapon might have killed Amnestria, but it was you who destroyed her. Keep away from Arilyn. The *etriel* has her own life."

Elaith leaned toward the Harper, looking the very picture of a fighter taking an offensive stance. His evil smile openly taunted his foe. "By the way, know you that Arilyn has taken the name Moonblade as her own? Denied family and rank, she made her own name and forged her own code. And she is good. Arilyn has developed skills that would make her Harper sire squirm."

Elaith paused. "To answer your earlier question, my interest in her is both personal and professional."

"I've no use for riddles."

"Nor wit for them, either. In plain words, Arilyn should have been my daughter, *but she is not*. What a remarkable partner she would make, or—" he smiled maliciously "—what a consort. She and I could accomplish much, side by side."

Bran's massive hand shot out, grabbing Elaith's shirtfront and jerking the slender elf up to his eye level. "I'll see you dead first," the man thundered.

"Keep your threats, Harper," Elaith said scornfully. "Arilyn Moonblade has nothing to fear from me. I only wish to aid her and to guide her career."

"Then she is indeed in grave danger," Bran concluded.

Elaith misunderstood Bran's meaning, and his eyes narrowed in menace. "She is in no danger from me," he hissed. "The same, however, cannot be said for you."

With the speed of a serpent's strike, a dagger appeared in the elf's hand and flashed toward Bran's throat. The aging Harper ranger was faster still. He tossed the elf to the ground. Elaith twisted and landed crouched on his feet, wrist cocked in readiness to flick the dagger into his old friend and enemy.

But Bran Skorlsun had vanished. Elaith stood and tucked the dagger back into its hiding place.

"Not bad," Elaith admitted, brushing a bit of dust from his leg as he admired Bran's skill. "You should watch your back, old friend. Watch your back."

Elaith turned back to his new establishment. As entertaining as the encounter had been, he had a myriad of details to attend to before the tavern could open. His eye fell upon the large oak sign, just delivered that morning, that leaned against the back wall of the building. This turned out nicely, the elf mused, moving in for a better look. I must have someone hang it immediately.

He ran his fingers over the raised letters of the sign that would soon grace the front door of the Hidden Blade.

Twelve

In early afternoon Virgin's Square was teeming with activity and bright with autumn sunlight and colorful merchandise. Local legend claimed that an altar had once stood on the site, upon which virgins were sacrificed to dragon gods centuries before Waterdeep was a city. On such a day that dark past seemed distant indeed.

The time for the highsun meal had passed, and delicious scents lingered in the warm autumn air. A large crowd browsed among the stalls of an open air market that offered goods ranging from fresh produce to exotic weapons. On the other side of the square services were sold, and perhaps two hundred persons, representing many races and nationalities, milled up and down the steps of a tiered piazza.

Those who wished to find work flocked to the square. Newcomers to the city, travelers relieved of their purses by pickpockets and in need of passage home, adventurers, servants, mages, sellswords—all gathered to hire themselves out. Services of many kinds could be purchased in Virgin's

Square. There was little overt pandering, but those who made inquiries were assured that discreet introductions were always possible.

Potential employers were there in large number, as well. Caravan-masters stopped in Virgin's Square to acquire the guards and scouts needed for long trips. Since slavery was illegal in Waterdeep, visiting merchants and dignitaries from the southern and far-eastern lands often went there to find hired servants to replace their slaves. Even adventurers wishing to form parties sought each other out in the square.

At the center of this activity sat Blazidon One-Eye. He was, perhaps, the best known among his profession, and he ran a brisk trade matching those who would hire with those who wished to work. The grizzled former adventurer was an unlikely businessman. His clothes were dusty and unkempt, and his body seemed to be made of little more than bone and stringy muscle. The graying beard had probably once been bright red; at present it appeared ale-soaked and in dire need of a trim. A dusty eye patch covered his left eye, and a leather vest lay open over his bare chest.

Blazidon was attended by a clerk and a bodyguard, both of whom were as unlikely as their master. The former was a tallfellow, a rare type of halfling that grew to be somewhat taller and slimmer than most of their kind. A little over four feet in height, the tallfellow maintained thick crops of very blond hair on his head, chin, and bare feet, a color echoed by the lemon shade of his tunic and leggings. His frivolous appearance was greatly at odds with his serious demeanor, for he scribbled laboriously in the book that kept Blazidon's accounts and records, and he counted each fee with the type of intensity that halflings usually reserve for their own treasure. The bodyguard was a tiny but ferocious dwarf whose knotted muscles and keen-edged axe more than made up for his lack of stature.

Arilyn nudged Danilo's attention away from a display of pastries and pointed at the strange trio. "That's Blazidon. If anyone would know our man, it's him."

Danilo nodded. "My family often outfits our caravans

through him. Why don't you let me do the talking?"

Arilyn looked doubtful, then she saw the merit in the dandy's suggestion. Dressed as she was, a human lad of common class and limited means, she seemed an unlikely person to be making the type of inquiries that must be made. The well-dressed Danilo could ask questions without raising suspicions. She nodded and fell in behind Danilo, taking the role of servant to a wealthy merchant.

Blazidon looked up at their approach. "What'll it be?"

"We were rather hoping you could help us find an employer," Danilo began.

The man's one good eye swept over the nobleman and his "servant," and his lips pursed. "Got work for the boy, no problem, if he knows how to use that weapon he carries. Gem merchant needs a couple of hireswords. As for you," Blazidon said, eyeing Danilo speculatively, "I hear there's a lady from Thay what wants a local escort for the festival. Mind you, I usually don't do this sort of hiring, but I can tell you where to find the lady."

Arilyn smirked, but Danilo fell back a step, aghast. "Sir, you misunderstand. I don't seek employment for myself. Rather, we need to ascertain the identity of—"

Arilyn pushed past Danilo and held out a charcoal sketch she'd made of the man who had had Perendra's snuffbox. She was no artist, but depicting a one-eared man with a twisted nose and a lightning-bolt scar was not difficult.

"Do you know this man?" she asked, her voice low.

Blazidon squinted at the picture. "That's got to be Barth. Haven't seen him around for some time." The man's eyes shifted from the picture to Danilo and then Arilyn. "Who am I doing business with, lad? You or your master?"

"Me," Arilyn said firmly.

The man nodded. "Good."

"Can you tell me anything about him?" Arilyn asked.

"No, can't say as I know much to tell. Hamit, his partner, is a whole 'nother story. We go way back."

"Where can I find this Hamit?"

"In the City," the man said bluntly, using the Waterdhavian slang for the City of the Dead, the large cemetery on the northwestern side of Waterdeep. "He must have crossed someone. They found him with a dagger in his back." The man shrugged. "It happens."

"Do you have any idea who might have hired Barth and Hamit recently?"

"That's precisely what *I* was trying to say," Danilo explained plaintively. No one paid him any notice.

"I might," Blazidon said, glancing at the dwarf.

The dwarf stuck out his square hand, palm up. "Fee," he rumbled. Danilo obligingly dropped a gold coin into the upturned paw. The dwarf examined it, bit it, and gave a curt nod to the tallfellow. Blazidon's clerk turned several pages.

"That pair worked for anyone who had money," the tallfellow said, his voice that of a human boychild. "Bodyguard, strongarms, second-story, even an assassination or two, although no one of pith and moment. Barth liked to work on his own, as well. His specialty was sleight-of-hand theft. He worked with one fence in particular."

"The name'll cost you extra," added the dwarf. Danilo dumped a handful of coppers into the dwarf's hand. The bodyguard regarded Danilo so balefully that the nobleman hastily added a gold coin to the pile.

"Jannaxil Serpentil," said the tallfellow. "A merchant and scholar of Turmish descent who runs a folio shop on Book Street. Rather stuck on himself, but if you've got good merchandise, that's the place to go."

"Need anything else?" Blazidon asked.

"I don't think so," Arilyn said. She tucked the sketch of Barth into her sleeve. Unable to resist, she cocked an eyebrow at Danilo and added, "Unless you want to reconsider the offer from the Thayvian woman?"

By now Danilo had regained his equilibrium. "She couldn't afford me," he said grandly.

* * * * *

Clad in a sober dress of deep burgundy silk, Loene laced her fingers in her lap and looked across the parlor at her old friend, the mage Nain Keenwhistler. Times had changed. Once they both had shared adventures as members of the Company of Crazed Venturers. Now they primly discussed trade and politics. "Your plan sounds good, Nain. I'm in."

The man smiled with satisfaction. "You won't regret your investment, Loene. Not only is there a growing market for Chultan teak and mahogany, but our venture will help establish Waterdeep's ties to the island of Lantan. Piracy along the coasts is worsening, and Lantan offers us a port in exchange for some additional protection for their fishing waters."

"You've become quite the politician, Nain," Loene said, deftly cutting him off with a compliment. Tales she enjoyed, but Nain's recital of political matters held little interest. "You've been here since before highsun. Have you eaten? No? Nor I. We can talk over lunch."

"I'd be glad to stay."

"Good." Loene rose from her chair and reached for an embroidered bell pull. "I'll let Graves know."

The servant did not answer the summons. Loene rang the bell a second time, and her face clouded. "Graves is usually so prompt. I think I'll see what might be keeping him."

She made her way to the kitchen, pausing at the doorway, almost like an intruder. After all, she had rarely been near the room since the day she'd bought the tiny castle. Her gaze swept through the meticulously kept room. Not a thing was out of place, except the sole occupant.

Graves slumped over a pine worktable, next to a bowl of apples that awaited peeling and a pastry crust that had long since become dry and transparent. His mace was still hooked on his belt, and a paring knife lay within reach, next to a halved apple.

Fear rose in Loene, and she walked like one asleep across the spotless floor. Reaching for his left hand, she turned it over. On the cold palm of her oldest and most trusted friend blazed a harp and crescent moon.

Loene dropped to her knees beside the kitchen table and gathered the man's thin body in her arms. "Damn you, Elliot," she said softly. "You should have thrown that Harper pin down the sewers years ago."

* * * * *

"Hello, Jannaxil."

The merchant jumped, and the priceless volume he'd been perusing dropped from his hands. Elaith "the Serpent" Craulnobur had entered the room and was seated comfortably in a chair, his legs stretched out before him and his pale hands toying with a small dagger.

"By all means, pick it up," Elaith said, amused.

Jannaxil Serpentil, the owner of Serpentil Books and Folios, did as he was told. In a state a shock, he retrieved the book and put it down on the edge of the table. Until now, the merchant-fence had always felt relatively safe despite his risky business and his location in the rough and tumble Dock Ward. The elf had somehow gotten past the defenses of might and magic that every good fence had in place. Here, in his inner sanctum, Jannaxil had no such protection.

Hoping to get the upper hand on the situation, Jannaxil walked behind the oak table that dominated his private office and lowered his girth into a wide leather chair, doing his best to appear master of his own small world. "How did you get in here?" he asked bluntly.

"Really, my dear man. In your business and mine, there are questions that one simply doesn't ask," the elf replied, crossing his ankles in a leisurely fashion. "I understand that some papers have come into your possession, some correspondence to the Zhentarim leadership at Zhentil Keep regarding a series of assassinations?"

"That is so," the fence said cautiously.

"I should like to see them."

"By all means." Jannaxil hefted himself out of the chair and retrieved a sheaf of papers from one of the shelves that lined the walls of the office. He handed the papers to the elf, who took his time looking them over.

"The asking price is ten silver," the fence said into the silence. He should have asked twice that amount. Bartering was second nature to the man, but today his enthusiasm was tempered by the reputation of his client. He began to wish that he had not spoken of these papers to Elaith Craulnobur's messenger earlier in the morning. To be sure, the elf had spread word that he would pay well for certain types of information, but a good fence should realize that some risks were simply not worth taking. When an assassin started looking into the business of other assassins, it was never prudent to be caught in the middle.

Elaith laid the papers down on the table. Interesting, he mused. There was a connection here, an important one that nonetheless eluded him. As he was wont to do when thinking, the elf toyed with a small ornamental dagger, twirling it idly between dexterous fingers. He did not miss the effect this action had upon the fence.

Jannaxil's eyes followed the jeweled dagger's path, watching each flash and twist with an expression of horrified fascination. Yet the fence's hands rested calmly on the table, pudgy fingers spread wide as if ready to reach for profit, despite the risk.

Greed. Elaith liked that in a human. Jannaxil, one of Waterdeep's best fences, had that quality in abundance. Squat and shrewd, the fat little man could deal with the worst the Dock Ward had to offer, yet he could discuss rare tomes with the most learned sages of several kingdoms. Elaith considered the man a valued contact and did business with him frequently. The elf intended to pay the asking price, but he saw no reason why he should not first amuse himself a bit.

"Very valuable," Jannaxil repeated, this time with less conviction.

"To whom?" the elf asked. "The Assassin's Guild?"

Jannaxil blanched and pointed to the papers on the table. "That is a communication to Zhentil Keep. Those don't come from Waterdeep every day," he sputtered.

"A curiosity," Elaith allowed. The dagger's circling slowed.

"A bargain. They're worth much more than ten silver," Jannaxil insisted, scenting a potential sale.

The dagger resumed its dance. "I don't see why."

"Well, there's probably a reward for the papers."

"Who would offer such a reward?"

"The Lords of Waterdeep might like to know that someone from the city is billing the Black Network for the services of a 'Zhentarim enforcer,' " suggested the fence. He invoked the powerful but mysterious council who ruled the city, hoping to strengthen and legitimize his selling price. After all, there wasn't a broad market for stolen papers of this sort.

"The Lords of Waterdeep?" Elaith broke into genuine laughter. "Will you tell them about this or shall I?"

The human colored a dull red. Unnerved and embarrassed, he muttered, "All right, then, take the papers. You've got more use for the Zhentarim than I do."

As soon as the words left his mouth, Jannaxil realized his error. Too late. Without faltering or missing a spin, the circling dagger flashed toward him. A scream echoed through the empty shop.

Elaith was known for his utter disdain of the evil rulers of Zhentil Keep and the members of the dark network that used the black-walled city for one of its prime bases. To the elf this was less a matter of conscience than of style: the Zhentish and the Zhentarim had neither. Despite the insult and the hurled dagger, Elaith's smile never wavered.

"I *will* take those papers. Thank you for your generous offer." With leisurely movements, the elf moved the sheaf safely away from the bloodstain that was beginning to spread across the table. He tucked the papers inside his cloak and rose to leave. Then, almost as an afterthought, he reached for the hilt of his weapon.

The dagger stood upright, deeply embedded in the wood, and it pinned Jannaxil's left hand firmly to the table.

Elaith curled his fingers around the grip and leaned toward the fence's terrified eyes. Sweat poured down Jannaxil's face as he stared up at Elaith, every bit as mesmerized as if the elf were truly the serpent for whom he was named.

The moon elf slid a gold coin beneath the fingers of the maimed hand. "You may need this for a cleric," he observed.

Chuckling at his own cruel joke, the elf wrenched the weapon free and turned to go. A second, anguished scream followed him out into the alley behind the Books and Folios.

Book Street was busy at midday, and Jannaxil's screams had drawn a crowd to the front door of the book shop. Elaith could hear the Waterdhavians, muttering and exclaiming over what might have happened and what they ought to do about it. The alley was also occupied, as were many alleys in the Dock Ward, by an assortment of scoundrels plying their dark trades. Even the blackest rogues fell back into the shadows at the elf's approach.

*　*　*　*　*

"There's a healthy demand for rare books today," Danilo noted, pointing toward the small knot of people gathered under the modest sign for Serpentil's Books & Folios.

"Most of them are leaving," Arilyn said, noting the wary expressions on the faces of the onlookers and the rapidly diminishing size of the crowd. "Whatever happened in there seems to be over."

The shop itself was an unassuming building fashioned of sandstone blocks. The only extravagance was a richly carved door of some exotic dark wood. As Arilyn drew closer, she saw that the door had in it a second, smaller door, which closed over a window cut near eye level. This small door stood ajar to reveal shelves and cases displaying the merchant's wares, but the door itself was securely bolted. Arilyn rapped loudly on the jamb.

"We're closed," came a voice from the back. "Come back another day."

"My business can't wait."

"Well, it'll have to!"

Arilyn balled her hand into a fist and knocked again, louder this time. The last two people who lingered near the shop exchanged uncertain glances and drifted off.

"Go away!"

"As soon as my business is concluded, I'll be happy to."

Muttering, a short pudgy man came out of a back room and lumbered to the door. Despite his rather undignified size, the man strove for a suave appearance. His clothes were carefully tailored dark garments, over which he wore an open scholar's robe of sober black to emphasize that he was both a successful merchant and a learned man. His black hair had been oiled and smoothed into place, and his round face was wreathed in fat. At the moment he appeared pale and drawn, and one hand had been clumsily wrapped in layers of gauze. His eyes swept disdainfully over Arilyn's peasant boy disguise. "What business of yours could be so important?"

"I'm looking for Jannaxil."

"What do you want with me?"

Arilyn held up the charcoal sketch she'd made of the thief Barth. "Do you know this man?"

The merchant's small eyes narrowed into slits. "He does not look like the sort who purchases books. Neither do you, for that matter. Go away, and don't waste my time."

"Now see here, my good man," Danilo said, his hand toying casually with his pendant so that the Thann family crest was prominently displayed. "We have excellent reasons for seeking this man, and I suggest you cooperate with us."

The nobleman's tone was haughty in the extreme, his stance the overbearing mien of one who was accustomed to obedience. Jannaxil responded with the instincts of a born sycophant. He shot back the bolt locking the door to the shop and ushered them in with murmured apologies and repeated bows that were as low as his pudgy physique permitted.

The fence led Danilo and Arilyn to a back office. The room was lined with shelves of rare books, many inlaid with precious stones and metals. Arilyn refused any refreshments and took the seat offered her in front of the merchant's oaken table.

Danilo refused both, preferring to lounge against a shelf laden with books.

"I'll just browse, if you don't mind," he said to Jannaxil.

"Of course." The fence took a chair behind the table. Arilyn caught sight of a small, jagged hole, made obvious by the polished wood. The fence casually moved an ink stand over the spot and dropped his bandaged hand onto his lap.

"What can I do for the Thann family?" he asked grandly. The unspoken addition "this time" echoed clearly in his tone.

Arilyn drew a gold snuffbox from the folds of her cloak and held it up. "Ever see this before?"

The man shrugged. "It is possible. Gold snuffboxes of that type are common enough."

"Very few bear this mark." Arilyn placed the box on the table before him and tapped the flowing rune engraved onto the top. "Do you know this mark?"

"My field of expertise is books and rare papers," the man said importantly. "I cannot be expected to know the sigil of every mage in Faerun."

Arilyn leaned forward. "I can tell you're a learned man," she said in a pleasant voice. Jannaxil inclined his head in modest agreement. "Otherwise, you could not know that this was a mage's sigil." Her shot found its mark, and a nerve twitched under the man's left eye.

"What else could such a mark be?"

"What else indeed?" Arilyn laid the sketch down beside the box. "You're quite certain you've never seen this man?"

Jannaxil picked up the sketch and studied it. "Hmm. Come to think of it, I believe he did purchase a book some months ago. Paid for it in barter."

"This box?" she asked.

The man smiled suavely and spread the fingers of his one good hand, as if to say, "all right, you've caught me."

"These books must be quite expensive," Danilo said, looking up from an illuminated volume. "I doubt you got the best of that deal."

"It is a most unusual box," Jannaxil said defensively. He

reached for it and raised his eyebrow to ask permission. Arilyn gave a curt nod. The fence opened the box, took a liberal pinch of snuff, savored it. "Ahh. The best I've encountered any-where." He removed a large piece of parchment from a drawer and placed it on the table, then he dumped the rest of the snuff onto it, shaking the box to empty it completely. Then he closed the lid and handed the box to Arilyn. "Have some."

Curious, the half-elf opened the box. It was full to the brim. She set it down.

"You see?" The fence shot a triumphant glance at Danilo. "It is quite a valuable item. The enchantment is very strong."

"It ought to be," Arilyn said. "The box belonged to the mage Perendra." Jannaxil responded to this announcement with deftly feigned surprise. "I don't suppose you received anything else of hers—in barter?"

"It's not likely." The man paused, considered. "Of course, since I didn't know *this* was stolen, it's possible that some-thing else of the mage's came into my hands. I do not know. I deal in books, mind you. And, as young Lord Thann pointed out, many of my books are extremely valuable. On occasion, I do exchange a book for barter, since scholars are notoriously short of cash. I get whatever I can for the goods I receive."

"Funny, I wouldn't have taken our man Barth for a scholar," Danilo said mildly.

"The thirst for knowledge can reside in the humblest of men," the fence said piously. "I have learned to overlook ap-pearances."

"That is wise, I'm sure," Danilo said. He picked up a small, leatherbound tome and glanced at the pages. "What language is this?"

"Turmish." Jannaxil looked sharply at the nobleman. "That book is not for sale." Nodding agreeably, Danilo put the book down and picked up another.

"How did this man happen to acquire the snuffbox?" Arilyn broke in.

"Who can say?"

"Our man said he got it from an elf," Danilo said helpfully.

"Strangest thing, really. He tried to tell us the elf's name, and he died." Danilo shrugged and picked up a book with a cover made of fine inlaid wood.

"An elf?" asked the fence in a dry whisper.

"Yes, that's what he said. Barth also had a partner," Danilo mentioned, looking up from the book. "A man by the name of Hamit. Poor man got a dagger in the back." Jannaxil's eyes widened in pure panic, and the nobleman appeared stricken with remorse. "Oh, I'm sorry. Was he a friend of yours?"

"No," the fence said hastily. A light went on in the man's eyes, and as he glanced down at the hand in his lap his face took on a crafty appearance. "Perendra the mage was slain by the Harper Assassin, was she not?"

"It's possible," Arilyn said.

"What will happen to this assassin, should you find him?"

Arilyn looked steadily at the fence, letting him read her intentions. He looked intrigued, then his round face clouded and his eyes fell to the desk. After a moment he said in a flat tone, "I'm afraid I can't help you. Now, if you'll excuse me?"

Murmuring her thanks, Arilyn rose to leave. Danilo laid down the book he'd been perusing, stretched lazily, and followed her out of the shop.

"We certainly didn't get much from him," the half-elf grumbled as they walked down Book Street.

"Oh, I wouldn't say that."

Something in the dandy's smug tone stopped Arilyn in mid-stride. "What *did* we get?"

"This." Danilo held up a book bound in plain brown leather.

"What's that?"

"Jannaxil's account book."

Thirteen

Arilyn took off her cap and raked one hand through her hair. "Let me understand this. You stole the man's account book?"

"Why not?" Danilo said mildly, stuffing the book back into his sack. "To whom is he going to complain? Let's take a look at it over lunch, shall we? There's a tavern nearby that has the most wonderful fried fish."

"That was a stupid risk to take."

The dandy smirked. "You're just mad because you didn't think of it first."

"You may be right," Arilyn admitted. "How did you get it? I didn't see you take it out of the shop," she said, allowing him to guide her down the street.

"Thank you," he said as if he'd just been complimented. "Ah, here's the tavern. The Friendly Flounder, and aptly named it is."

Danilo ushered her into the small taproom, which was already filled with people and the pungent odors of ale and fried fish. Danilo ordered for them both. He ate quickly, then he carefully wiped his fingers free of grease and took out the book. On it were neat columns filled with some ornate eastern script.

"You can read that?" Arilyn asked.

"Not yet."

Danilo cast a cantrip, a simple spell to discern language. Before his eyes, the flowing lines on the page shifted and wiggled, rearranging themselves into Common. "What do you know!" Danilo said admiringly. "It worked!"

"Resourceful, aren't you?" Arilyn commented, observing him keenly.

"Occasionally, though often accidentally," Danilo said. He turned the pages of the book, taking no more than a glance at each one. After several moments, he looked up. "I don't think you're going to like this."

"Well?"

Danilo slid the book closer to Arilyn and turned to a page near the middle. "Look at this item. Elaith Craulnobur, purchased twenty uncut sapphires." He flipped several pages and pointed. "Here's his name again, as seller of a spellbook. Here he acquired a Cledwyll statue, and on this date he was really in the mood to shop. On the final page, there's a notation concerning an inquiry by Elaith Craulnobur." Danilo looked up and held Arilyn's eyes. "It seems that the good elf is a regular customer."

"That doesn't necessarily mean he's the elf we seek," Arilyn pointed out.

"Don't be too sure." Danilo flipped back a few pages. "On this day the fence received a shipment of rare coins from Elaith Craulnobur. The coins were delivered by a man named Hamit, to whom the fence gave a receipt. Do I say 'I told you so' now, or shall I wait until you're unarmed?"

"All right, you've made your point," Arilyn conceded, "but how did you *do* that? You knew exactly where to turn each time."

"The benefit of having an empty head, my dear, is that you

can fill it with all manner of inconsequential things. I've an excellent memory, in addition to all my other gifts."

"But—"

"Ah! Listen to this! This settles the matter, I should say."

Danilo's tone was so triumphant that Arilyn allowed herself to be distracted. She listened with growing dismay as Danilo read a list of goods received from Hamit, a list that included an enchanted snuffbox. She rose from the table and tossed down a few coins to pay for her uneaten fish.

"Where are we going now?" the dandy asked in a voice heavy with weary resignation.

"To see Elaith Craulnobur."

Suddenly energized, Danilo leaped up from the table and followed the half-elf out of the tavern. "Arilyn, this is not a good idea. He isn't going to like what you've got to say, and they don't call him the Serpent without good cause."

"I've been called worse."

Danilo grabbed her arm and spun her around to face him. "Wait! I've got a better idea. Why don't we just turn the elf in to the authorities?"

"On what proof?"

That stopped him. "Well, what about those two men? Barth and Hamit? They both were murdered, one by magic and one by a dagger."

Arilyn pulled away from the nobleman's grasp and started purposefully back toward Adder Lane. "There is nothing to prove that Elaith Craulnobur was responsible for the death of those men."

Danilo threw up his hands. "What would convince you? A signed confession?"

"Enough!" She snapped, stabbing a finger at him. "I've no time to argue. I'm going. You can come or not as you choose. If you're afraid, stay here."

Danilo sniffed disdainfully. "I'm not afraid of the elf, but I dislike being associated with such a scoundrel."

"You're with a suspected assassin," she pointed out.

"Ah, but there's a world of difference, my dear," Danilo returned with a smug grin. He fell in beside Arilyn, his polished boots clicking along the stone streets as he kept pace with her. "Different planes, altogether. An assassin is colorful, and therefore, almost respectable. At any rate, this adventure shall make for a most interesting song."

"Ever the bard," she mocked.

"I just hope I live long enough to sing this tale," he commented lightly.

There was more than enough truth in his jest to make Arilyn wince. "You've endeavored to deliver my shadow back to me, for which I thank you," she said. "Please do not feel obliged to stay on my account."

"You seem to forget that I, too, have a stake in finding this assassin," Danilo reminded her. "He tried to kill me once, you know. It could well be that he's the persistent type."

"You've run from the assassin already," Arilyn said. "Suddenly you're eager to confront him?"

"Actually," Danilo admitted, "no. I was hoping to be around when *you* caught up with him. It should be quite a show." At Arilyn's derisive sniff, he added defensively, "Well, someone has to be there to record the event for generations yet unborn. Can you think of a better means than a ballad, or a person better suited to the task than myself?"

"Yes."

For once, Arilyn's words seemed to pierce the noble's inch-thick hide. Looking thoroughly insulted, Danilo subsided into silence and allowed the half-elf to tend to business. Quickly they retraced their steps to Adder Lane, pushing through crowds and weaving through the vendors and street entertainers that had cropped up everywhere like mushrooms after a summer rain. When they reached Elaith's tavern, they were greeted by the new sign that hung over the doorway.

"The Hidden Blade, eh?" Danilo murmured. "Very reassuring."

Arilyn did not bother to respond. She stalked through the tavern—this time Elaith's giant doorkeeper did not attempt to hinder her—and threw open the door to the elf's office. He was at his desk, going through what appeared to be bills of lading, and he looked up at the intruders with a chilling glare. Immediately his handsome face arranged itself in a smile of surprised welcome.

Without saying a word Arilyn tossed the snuffbox onto his desk. Elaith gave it a brief glance and said mildly, "Oh, so that's where it went. Do you mind if I ask where you found it?"

"Do you know a man named Barth?" Arilyn said.

"Yes. I rather thought Barth had stolen it from me. He was inordinately fond of snuff and not at all happy with his partner for selling the snuffbox. Barth is dead, I take it?"

"Very."

"Good. I paid a considerable sum for the spell that killed him. It's always reassuring to know that one's money was well spent."

Arilyn exhaled deeply, disconcerted by the elf's revelation. "You had him enspelled to die if he tried to reveal your name. Why?"

"My dear, I should think that would be obvious. One must occasionally employ a man such as Barth, but it is hardly in good form to advertise the fact."

"Appearances must be maintained," Danilo noted without a hint of sarcasm, though the others ignored him.

"Why was Barth following me?" Arilyn demanded.

"It's rather a long story," Elaith said. "Won't you have a seat?"

"No."

"As you will. I believe you're acquainted with a man named Harvid Beornigarth?"

Arilyn straightened and folded her arms. "Sort of."

"I've employed him and his men in the past, on such occasions when finesse is not essential. Several months ago I heard him ranting about an 'elf-wench' who fought with a two-handed grip. He vowed to find you and settle some imaginary score. Since I was curious to learn more about you, I sent along a man of my own with his band."

"Barth."

"Of course."

Arilyn placed both hands on Elaith's desk and leaned forward, her face full of quiet menace. "Why?" she repeated.

Elaith was silent for a moment. "I knew only one *etriel* who fought that way. I thought that you might be Z'beryl."

Arilyn recoiled. Nothing could have prepared her for that answer. She was dimly aware than Danilo's arm had circled her waist, that he was guiding her into a chair. "I think you'd better tell me what this is about," she said in a dazed tone.

Elaith Craulnobur rose and walked to a window. He laced his long-fingered hands behind his back and gazed into the alley as if the answers to his past might be written there. "I grew up with Z'beryl on the island of Evermeet. We are related, although distantly. Many years ago we completely lost touch."

"I don't suppose you can support any of this," Danilo said from his usual place behind Arilyn.

The elf shot a sidelong glance at the dandy. "Of course. I anticipated that Arilyn would be back, and I had certain items brought here to me." He glided over to a wall safe and deftly opened it, taking out two silk-wrapped objects. The first he unwrapped and handed to Arilyn.

A small cry escaped the half-elf. She cradled the small oval frame in both hands, unable to look away from it. Danilo leaned down over her shoulder.

"Your mother?"

Arilyn could only nod. The portrait showed a young moon elf maiden, not quite a mature *etriel*, with long braids of sapphire silk and gold-flecked blue eyes. Beside her was a younger, happier version of Elaith Craulnobur. Both were dressed in ceremonial robes of silver and cobalt blue—betrothal robes? Arilyn raised incredulous eyes to the moon elf. His answering smile held an ancient sadness.

"There is also this," Elaith said, unwrapping an ornate sword and laying it on the table before Arilyn. Runes ran the length of the blade, and a white, blue-flecked stone gleamed in its hilt.

"That's a moonblade!" Danilo burst out, pointing.

"Don't be so surprised, young man. These swords are not all that uncommon to my people. I know many who either carry or own them, although admittedly most of these elves live far away, either on Evermeet or in the far reaches of the Dales, near the old site of Myth Drannor."

"You do not carry the moonblade?" Arilyn asked Elaith.

"That is so."

"I thought that elf and blade could not be separated," she said.

"While that is usually the case, this particular one is dormant. Whatever magic it once held is lost."

Arilyn's brow furrowed. "I'm not sure I understand."

"Z'beryl didn't tell you about moonblades? No, I see that she did not." Elaith leaned against the edge of the table and folded his arms. "Many centuries past, the first moonblade was elvencrafted in Myth Drannor. Although it was a magic sword it had but one inherent property: it could judge character. It could be wielded by only one person, and it was to be handed down from one generation to the next. With each generation, a new magical ability was added to the sword, and this was derived from the needs or nature of the wielder." The elf paused and raised an eyebrow. "This much is familiar to you?" Arilyn merely nodded, not wishing to distract Elaith. "Do you know the purpose behind the moonblades' creation?" he asked. She hesitated, then shook her head.

"I'm not entirely surprised," Elaith said dryly. "You trained with Kymil Nimesin, did you not?"

"What of it?" Arilyn said, a trifle defensively.

"My dear *etriel*, in more ways than one Lord Kymil is of a dying breed. He still mourns the demise of Myth Drannor. Like many of his race, he is unable to come to terms with the changes that have swept Faerun and transformed the destinies of the elven peoples. If Kymil knows the part moonblades bore in this, I doubt he could bring himself to speak of it."

"I'm no scholar, and Kymil knows that. My only interest was the practical use of the sword. Kymil's time was too valuable to waste on history lessons that I wouldn't bother to remember."

"More's the pity," Elaith said, then sighed. "But to continue. The Council of Myth Drannor foresaw that steps had to be taken to ensure the continuation of the elven peoples on Faerun. We moon elves are in many ways most like mankind, and of all the elven races we are the most adaptable and tolerant, and are therefore best able to act as liaison between the more reclusive elven races and the increasingly dominant humans. It was decided that a moon elf family would be ennobled and set up as rulers of the island of Evermeet. Moonblades were used to choose this family, in a process that lasted many centuries."

Elaith picked up the dormant moonblade. "It was a simple process of elimination. As you know, a moonblade can confirm or decline each new wielder. The family who held the most moonblades for the longest period of time showed true nobility as well as a proven line of succession. They became the royal family."

"What happens when a sword declines the chosen heir?" Danilo asked.

"Remember what happened to your finger when you tried to touch the moonblade?" Arilyn asked.

"Ouch." Danilo winced. "A risky inheritance."

"Precisely," the *quessir* agreed. "The risk increases as time progresses, for as a moonblade becomes more powerful, it becomes harder to handle. Few prove worthy of the task. Not every unworthy heir dies upon drawing the sword, however. If he or she is the last member of a line, the sword's task—testing the bloodline's nobility—is completed and it becomes dormant." The elf's hand absently touched the white stone set in his moonblade.

"Such as your sword," said Danilo.

"Such as my sword," Elaith echoed softly. He looked up at Arilyn and admitted, "I am the last in the Craulnobur line, the only child of an only son. The sword came into my possession shortly after that portrait was made." A faint, self-deprecating smile curved his lips but did not reach his eyes. "It would seem that the sword knew more about me than I, at that time, understood about myself."

"I'm sorry," Arilyn said softly.

"So was I. On the basis of the moonblade's choice, my betrothal was nullified. Rather than remain in Evermeet and live with the stigma, I chose to come to Waterdeep and carve out a niche for myself. The rest is a matter of record and—" the elf broke off and made an ironic bow to Danilo "—rumor."

"This is all very touching," Danilo drawled. "It explains your interest in Arilyn but, unfortunately, little else."

"What else would you like to know?"

Danilo picked up Perendra's snuffbox from the table. "Let's get back to this. How did you get it?"

"I bought the snuffbox from a fence."

"Jannaxil."

Elaith's silver eyebrows arched. "Very good, young man. And I suppose you know where *he* got it, as well?"

"From Hamit. Waterdeep seems to be a small city."

"At the moment, I'm inclined to agree," the elf said, eyeing Danilo with distaste. "Yes, at my request Barth and his partner Hamit broke into the mage's home to retrieve one particular item, a spellbook. She surprised them, and they killed her. They made the mistake of plundering the place and selling the stolen items. I learned of this when I saw Perendra's snuffbox in Jannaxil's shop. I purchased the box and took it to my home, then I went to deal with Hamit."

"You killed him," Danilo specified.

"Of course. I would have seen to Barth as well, but while I was taking care of Hamit, he apparently retrieved the box and left for Evereska. Fortunately the spell seems to have done the trick." He paused. "By then several Harpers had fallen to the assassin. Even though Perendra alone had not been branded, I wanted to leave no possibility that her accidental death would be placed on my doorstep, bringing with it the label of Harper Assassin. I do not care to wear that particular mantle."

"You're very forthcoming about all this," the nobleman said with a touch of bewilderment.

Elaith looked faintly surprised. "Surely you've heard that

there is honor between thieves. Assassins have a similar code." The elf turned to Arilyn. "By the way, I have some of the information you requested." He returned to the safe and took out several sheets of parchment, one of which he handed to Arilyn. "I acquired something this morning that belongs to you. You certainly don't want this to fall into the wrong hands."

Not understanding, Arilyn scanned the sheet. "This is directed to the Zhentarim at Zhentil Keep."

"Yes. I came across it while looking into the background of the Harper Assassin."

Arilyn winced involuntarily. Elaith took in her reaction with an amused smile on his face. "Perhaps now, all things considered, we can dispense with the pretense."

"Pretense?"

"Oh, come now," he chided her gently. "Truly, I admire your plan. Quite devious. It wouldn't have occurred to me to arrange my affairs so that I could collect simultaneous fees from both the Harpers and the Zhentarim."

"What are you talking about?" she demanded, aghast.

"Why, your scam, of course." He smiled. "It is brilliant, although not without risks. A Harper agent, working for the Zhentarim. Whatever their other shortcomings may be, the Black Network is certainly known to pay well. As a Zhentarim enforcer, you provide them with a valuable service: culling their ranks of the unruly, the inconvenient, and the inept. The Harpers are pleased to see you ridding the world of vermin." Elaith chuckled. "Harpers and Zhentarim, united at last. What delightful irony!"

Elaith's amusement broke off abruptly. The tip of Arilyn's moonblade was held firmly at his throat.

"I do not work for the Zhentarim," Arilyn stated, her voice bubbling with suppressed rage. "Where did you get such an idea?"

"Well, what do you know?" Danilo marveled. "I've been baying at the wrong raccoon, after all."

Arilyn shot a furious glance at him. "Danilo, this is not the time—"

"Don't you see?" the nobleman persisted. "The elf you're about to skewer is innocent. Well, I don't suppose you can claim that he's innocent, precisely, but on the other hand he's not exactly guilty. Er, that is to say—"

"Out with it!"

"Elaith Craulnobur thinks that *you* are the Harper assassin!" Danilo blurted out. "Which means, of course, that *he* is not."

Fourteen

 Arilyn slowly lowered the moon-blade. Elaith raised a hand to his throat and wiped away a fleck of blood from the spot where she'd nicked him. "Thank you for that stirring defense of my character," he said to Danilo.

Turning to Arilyn, the elf bowed deeply. "It seems that I have made a grave error. Forgive me for misreading your character, daughter of Z'beryl. May I explain how this occurred?"

"Please."

Elaith pointed to the letter Arilyn still held. "I thought that letter came from your hand."

"Why?" demanded Danilo, clearly outraged.

"A detailed bill was sent with it," Elaith said, laying two pieces of parchment on the table. He pointed to the one on the left. "This is the bill. And this," he added, pointing to the other, "is the information you gave me about the Harper deaths."

Arilyn bent over the desk to read, and Danilo leaned over

her shoulder. On the bill to the Zhentarim was a list of names. All of them were known to Arilyn. The last name was Cherbill Nimmt, the soldier she had killed last moon in Darkhold. "This bill lists most of my assignments for the past year," she said in a small voice.

"Yes, I know," Elaith said.

She compared the lists. Like two columns of a merchant's receipt book, the dates and locations lined up in perfect balance. Arilyn froze.

Balance. For each Harper who fell to the assassin, an agent of the Zhentarim was slain by her sword. Neither side gained in strength from the other's loss. As Arilyn considered this aspect of Elaith's revelation, a suspicion crept into her mind, too appalling to contemplate, but too insistent for her to dismiss.

Still absorbed in the study of the two lists, Danilo let out a low whistle. "By the gods, someone is going through a lot of trouble to set you up."

"And succeeding," Elaith added. To Arilyn, he said, "I have reason to believe that the Harpers suspect you and have set someone on your trail. If they get hold of this supposed connection to the Zhentarim, your guilt in their eyes would be sealed. Be careful."

"I will." Arilyn rose and extended her left palm to the moon elf. "Thank you for your help."

"At your service," he said, laying his palm briefly over hers. The half-elf walked to the back door, trailed by Danilo.

At the doorway, Arilyn turned back to Elaith. "One more thing: when we met in the House of Good Spirits, you mistook me for Z'beryl."

"That is so."

"Yet you called me by another name."

"Did I?" Elaith shrugged as if the matter was of no consequence and turned to Danilo. "Oh, by the way, I've made arrangements to have you killed. Just in case I'm unable to rescind my request, you may wish to take extra precautions."

Danilo's eyes bulged. "*By the way?*" he repeated in disbelief.

The elf seemed to enjoy the dandy's befuddlement. "I suggested the idea to an old acquaintance of mine, and he agreed to see to it."

"I don't suppose you'd care to name that old acquaintance?" Arilyn asked. The moon elf merely raised one eyebrow, and Arilyn shrugged. "Just tell me one thing. Is he a Harper?"

Elaith laughed. "Most definitely not."

The half-elf nodded and abandoned that line of inquiry. "By the way, why did you want Danilo killed?"

"*By the way*," Danilo echoed in a dazed voice. "There's that phrase again."

"I don't particularly like him," the elf told Arilyn casually, as if that were reason enough. "Now, if you will excuse me, I have a great deal of work to do before this evening."

Arilyn grabbed Danilo's arm and dragged him out of the Hidden Blade. Evening was nearing, and the late afternoon sun cast long shadows. The dandy looked about nervously. "You don't think the elf was serious, do you?" he asked when they were once again in the safety of the crowded street.

"Of course he was, but I'm sure we can handle whatever his 'old acquaintance' throws our way," Arilyn said evenly, setting as brisk a pace as the crowded street allowed. Danilo's distressed expression did not fade, so she added, "Why so glum? Hasn't anyone tried to kill you before now?"

Danilo sniffed. "Of course. I've just never been *disliked* before now. Well, what's next? Check into the moon elf's old acquaintance, I suppose?"

"No. An adventurer such as Elaith would not live long if he revealed the names of his associates," Arilyn pointed out. "It would do little good, anyway. The assassin is probably within the Harper ranks."

"You said that before," Danilo noted. "Why?"

Because Harpers and their allies work to maintain the Balance, Arilyn thought. Aloud she said, "Like I told you before, Harpers are a secret organization, yet the assassin knows the identity of his victims."

"The assassin also knows a lot about you, it would seem," Danilo said. "I don't understand why someone in the Harpers would do such a thing, or why he would go to such lengths to make you look like the Harper Assassin."

"Neither do I," said Arilyn.

"So what do we do now? Now that Elaith is no longer suspect, we've run out of places to look."

"Then we'll have to make sure the assassin gets back on our trail," Arilyn said. A slender, black-robed mage brushed past Danilo, and the half-elf's eyes lit up. "Tymora's luck might yet be with us," she said softly. "See that young man carrying the huge book? We're going to follow him."

"Why?" Danilo fell in beside Arilyn as she wove through the crowds.

"I'm going to let the assassin know where to find me."

"Oh. Why are you still wearing that disguise, then?"

"Elaith said that the Harpers suspect me. I've got to keep out of sight until I find the assassin and clear my name."

"Ah. What should I do?"

The young mage slipped into a tavern by the name of the Drunken Dragon, Arilyn and Danilo close on his heels. "Have dinner," the half-elf suggested. Obligingly, Danilo found a table near the front door and dropped into a seat.

While pretending to watch an ongoing game of darts, Arilyn observed the black-robed mage as he settled himself at a table. He pulled a bottle of ink and a quill from his bag, then opened his book and began to write. Every now and then he would look up, staring into space and absently chewing the end of his quill, then again take to scribbling.

Arilyn pushed through the crowded room toward the young man's table. On the way, she relieved a passing serving wench of her tray, slipping the servant the price of the ale plus an extra silver coin. The girl pocketed the money, dimpling flirtatiously at the handsome lad Arilyn appeared to be. Having become accustomed to such responses to this particular disguise, Arilyn merely gave the girl a roguish wink and continued on her way.

"May I join you?" she asked the mage, holding out the ale-laden tray.

"Why not? Good company and free ale are always welcome," came the response. He took a mug from the tray Arilyn offered him, drained it, and then gestured toward the book that was prominently displayed before him. "I welcome a diversion from my work. It's not going well tonight."

"I'm sorry to hear that," Arilyn replied, sitting down and taking the cue that the young man so obviously supplied. "What are you working on? Is that a spellbook?"

Beaming with the pride of a father displaying his firstborn son, the young man pushed the tome toward Arilyn. "No. It's a collection of my poetry."

The half-elf opened the book and leafed through it. Written on its pages in slanted, spidery script was some of the most execrable verse she had ever encountered.

"Not my best work," the youth disclaimed modestly.

Even without seeing his best efforts, Arilyn was inclined to believe him. She had read more edifying poetry on the walls of public conveniences.

"Oh, I don't know about that," she lied heartily as she tapped the page, her thoughts drifting back to a certain battle on the Marshes of Chelimber. "This ballad in particular seems quite stirring. If ever you decide to set any of your work to music, I know of a suitable bard." She cast a quick glance at Danilo. He was busily charming a serving wench whose overstated curves strained the lacings of her bodice. Arilyn sniffed. The girl looked like a two-pound sausage stuffed into a half-pound casing.

"A ballad, you say?" The young man brightened at the perceived praise. "I had never thought of doing that," he marveled. "Do you really think some of these poems would make songs?"

Arilyn dragged her gaze back to the young mage. "Why not? I've surely heard worse."

"Hmmm." He pondered that for a moment, then stuck out his hand in a belated gesture of introduction. "Thank you for the suggestion, my friend. My name is Coril."

"Well met, Coril. I'm Tomas," Arilyn replied, clasping the offered hand. She already knew the young man's identity. As well as a terrible poet and minor mage, Coril was an agent of the Harpers. Reputed to be a shrewd observer of people, Coril was employed to gather and pass on information.

"So, Tomas, what brings you here?" Coril asked, helping himself to another mug of ale.

Arilyn waved her own mug in a nonchalant arch. "The festival, of course."

"No, I mean what brings you here, to this table?" persisted Coril.

"Oh, I see. I need some information."

The Harper's face hardened almost imperceptibly. "Information? I'm not sure I can help you."

"Oh, but surely you can," Arilyn insisted, painting disappointment and dismay on her face. "You are a mage, are you not?"

"I am," allowed Coril, somewhat mollified. "What do you need?"

Arilyn unbuckled her swordbelt and laid the sheathed moonblade on the table. The task she intended to place before Coril would surely fall beyond the mage's limited abilities. "There's some writing on this scabbard. It's supposed to be magic. Can you read it?" Arilyn asked.

Coril bent forward and examined the marks with great interest. "No," he admitted, "but if you wish, I can cast a comprehend language spell on them."

Arilyn feigned relief and gratitude. "Such a thing can be done?"

"For a price, yes."

Arilyn fished several copper coins from her pocket. The sum, although paltry, would represent a small fortune to "Tomas." It was too little for even such a simple spell, but offering any more might raise suspicions. So she held out the money and asked eagerly, "Will this be enough?"

Coril hesitated for only a moment, then he nodded and gathered up the coins. He drew out a mysterious substance from some corner of his robes and hunkered down over the sword, muttering the words of the spell.

Arilyn waited through the spellcasting, confident that the mage would fail. Early in Arilyn's training, Kymil Nimesin had sought to decipher the runes through both magic and scholarship. If Kymil's powerful elven magic could not read the ancient, arcane form of Espruar, Coril's spellcasting had no chance of success.

Her purpose in showing the rare sword to Coril was to send a message to the assassin. Since Coril was a conduit for information to the Harpers and the assassin was likely someone within the Harper ranks, word of the moonblade might reach him and put him again on Arilyn's trail. She'd lost the assassin back at the House of Fine Spirits due to Danilo's cowardly pretense, and now she would lure him back with a ruse of her own.

After several minutes, Coril looked up, puzzled. "I cannot read all of it," he admitted to Arilyn.

"*What?*"

Coril's eyebrows raised in surprise at the youth's sharp tone. "There seems to be magical wards on most of these runes against such spells," he said defensively. "Very powerful wards."

"But you *can* read *some* of it?" Arilyn persisted.

"Just this." With one slender finger Coril traced the lowest rune, a small mark about two-thirds down the scabbard.

"What does it say?" Arilyn demanded.

" 'Elfgate.' And this one up here says 'elfshadow.' That's all I can read." He looked sharply at Arilyn. "How did you happen to come by an enspelled sword?"

"I won it in a game of dice," Arilyn said ruefully. "The former owner swore to me that the marks on the sword would give the location of a great treasure, if only I could find a mage to read the runes for me. Are you sure there's nothing on there about a treasure?"

"Very. Nothing I can read, at least."

Arilyn shrugged. "Well, then I guess I lost that bet after all. Next time I'll know better than to take my winnings in magic swords."

Her explanation seemed to satisfy Coril. The young mage looked sympathetic, although not sufficiently so to offer to return the fistful of coppers to the disappointed lad.

Still stunned by Coril's revelation, Arilyn thanked the mage and slipped out of the tavern. Her mind reeled with questions. What was an elfgate, and what was an elfshadow? Why had Kymil not told her of either?

She circled around to the back of the inn, intending to rid herself of her disguise. A large barrel of rainwater stood by the kitchen door. Arilyn discarded her cap and work gloves, then washed the dark stain from her face with the icy water.

It was time to become an elf again. Arilyn took from her bag another tiny jar, this one filled with an iridescent cream. She spread it over her face and hands, and her skin took on the golden hue of a high elf. Her hair she shook out free and full, then tucked it back so her pointed ears would be obvious.

Gripping the moonblade, she formed a mental image of an elven cleric of Mielikki, goddess of the forest. It was a simple illusion, requiring only that her blue tunic take on the appearance of a long red and white silk tabard and the moonblade itself become a nondescript staff such as any cleric might carry. The illusion was complete in the span of a heartbeat. Arilyn adjusted the tabard so that the unicorn-head symbol of the goddess lay properly over her heart, then she returned to the tavern.

Arilyn had long ago learned that elaborate physical changes were not necessary for an effective disguise. Her regular features and an unusually mobile face made her a natural chameleon and the moonblade's illusion power provided her with any necessary costume, but the transformation from human lad to elven cleric was achieved largely in matters of speech, stance, and movement. No one could note the cleric's distinctive elven grace and equate her with the heavy-footed lad who had just left the inn.

So it was that Arilyn glided back into the Drunken Dragon with confidence. She seated herself at the table next to Coril, not drawing a second glance from the mage she had spoken with only minutes before. She ordered dinner and a glass of wine and made a pretense of eating.

Arilyn hadn't long to wait. Shalar Simgulphin, a bard reputed to be a member of the Harpers, entered the tavern and joined Coril. Arilyn eagerly eavesdropped upon their conversation as she sipped her wine.

"Greetings, Coril. What brings you to the Drunken Dragon?" Shalar said, slipping into a chair and acting as if theirs was a chance meeting.

Coril shrugged. "It is a good place for watching people," he said in a noncommittal tone.

The bard's voice dropped. "And what have you seen?"

"Everything and nothing." Coril again shrugged. "I see much, but I have not the *means* to make sense of it all."

A small bag changed hands under the table. "Perhaps this will help," Shalar noted, adding, "There is a little extra this month."

"As there should be," Coril said. "Festival expenses are high. The costs are already being tallied," he added significantly.

Shalar sighed heavily. "I suppose you're speaking of Rhys Ravenwind?"

"And others," Coril added in a dark voice. "The assassin struck again, shortly after daybreak."

"Who?"

"The man has used many names, but most recently he was known as Elliot Graves," responded Coril.

Arilyn's goblet slipped from her fingers, and its contents spilled unheeded onto the table. She had brought this upon her friends. Elliot Graves's death was on her hands, as surely as if she had killed the man with her own sword. Fighting despair, Arilyn mopped at the spilled wine with a linen napkin an attentive servant brought her, and she forced herself to attend to Coril's next words.

"Graves was a former adventurer, now a servant in the house of—"

"Yes, yes, I know of him," the bard broke in impatiently. "How did it happen?"

"The same as the others," replied the mage cryptically. "There were several differences, however. The attack took place during daylight, and the man was awake. He must have known the assassin, for there was no sign of struggle."

Shalar ran both hands through his hair. "It is as we feared. The assassin must be a Harper, one whose affiliation is widely known."

"I agree," said Coril. "Otherwise, how could he approach so many of the Harpers unopposed?"

Shalar nodded, then he reluctantly ventured, "Was there anyone else?"

"Possibly. Do you know an adventurer by the name of Arilyn Moonblade?"

"Yes. At least, I know of her. Is she dead, as well?" the bard asked in a resigned tone.

"I don't know for sure," Coril admitted, "but I think I saw her sword earlier this evening. An ancient sword, set with a large golden stone? It was in the possession of a young man who claimed he'd won it in a game of chance."

Relief flooded Shalar Simgulphin's face. "I would lay odds that the lad you saw was actually Arilyn Moonblade. She is known for her skill in disguises."

"Really." Coril thought that over. "Well, that is good. She is wise to travel in disguise, especially if she plans to stay here at the Drunken Dragon."

"Oh?"

"I believe there is to be a secret meeting tomorrow concerning this assassin, in this inn's council room?"

"That is so."

"Several Harpers have taken rooms here for the evening," Coril explained. "If the assassin were to strike tonight, this would be a likely place."

Shalar nodded in agreement. "It is late to notify the watch of this possibility, but I shall try. At the very least, the Harpers must be warned and alert." He looked around the room.

"I see the druid Suzonia, Finola of Callidyrr, some ranger from the Dales—I think his name is Partrin—and his partner Cal, who is not a Harper, I believe. There are others?"

Arilyn listened with growing horror as Coril added to the list. There were at least six members of the Harpers at the inn. It was rare to find so many in one place. Goldfish in a mug of ale would present a more challenging target.

What a fool she had been! Laying hints for the assassin when he was probably as close as her own shadow, laughing at her pitiful efforts. Arilyn had believed that she'd taken enough precautions to protect Loene and her household, yet Elliot Graves was dead. If the assassin could follow her while she was invisible, he could surely see through her simple disguises. Would he also taunt her with the deaths of all the Harpers in the Drunken Dragon?

With a quick, jerky movement Arilyn rose from the table. If she could not yet confront the assassin, at least she could lead him away. As she neared the door, Danilo seized the hem of her tabard.

"Excuse me, Lady of Mielikki. Is your business here completed?"

Arilyn focused with difficulty upon the dandy. He was working on his second cup of zzar, and the overripe barmaid was seated on his lap.

"I'm leaving," Arilyn announced abruptly. "You might as well stay here and enjoy yourself."

Danilo gently eased the girl off his lap and rose. "I don't want to enjoy myself. I'm coming with you." He made a face. "Oh dear. That did sound dreadful, didn't it? What I meant to say was—"

"Never mind," she said distractedly. "I'm leaving Waterdeep. Tonight. Now. If you plan to come with me, you'd better hurry."

Danilo observed her keenly. "You're not talking to me alone, are you?" he asked in a soft voice.

She shot him a warning look and pushed open the door of the Drunken Dragon, dimly aware that Danilo was close behind her. On the street outside the tavern lamplighters were tending to the street lanterns. In a circle of light stood two men in the black-and-gray uniforms of the Waterdeep Watch. One of the men, whose unicorn pendent proclaimed him a worshiper of Mielikki, respectfully greeted Arilyn. She nodded an acknowledgement, then stopped, her hand frozen mid-way through the gestures of a clerical blessing.

She recognized both men: Clion was a charming red-headed rogue, as light of finger as he was of tongue, and the other man was his constant shadow, Raymid of Voonlar. Almost fifteen years ago, when the men were lads just starting out, she had traveled with them in a company of adventurers. Impressed by their talents, after a time Arilyn had introduced them to Kymil Nimesin. Both men had trained with the elf at the Waterdeep Academy of Arms.

Their presence brought a measure of relief to the troubled half-elf. "It is well that the watch is here," she said to Clion. "Several members of the Harpers have taken lodgings at this inn, and I fear that they might be endangered."

The watchmen exchanged worried glances. "You speak of the Harper Assassin?" asked Raymid. The "cleric" nodded.

"We'll let our watch commander know of your fears," Clion said. "A guard will be sent."

"Sent? You two are not at liberty to stay?" Arilyn asked.

"We can't. The funeral of Rhys Ravenwind is this evening. We are part of the honor guard," said Clion.

Arilyn knew it was not a common practice to send the city watch to a funeral. If the watch was engaged in a search for the assassin, perhaps old comrades could give her some information that would aid her own search.

"A sad night," she commented. "Waterdeep does well to honor such a bard. I trust the murderer has been brought to justice?"

"We are not at liberty to discuss this, my lady," responded Clion in a stiff, official voice.

Arilyn stifled a sigh. She had no time to waste on such formalities. She would probably learn more if they knew who she was, still more if she caught them slightly off guard.

"I am surprised, Clion, to find that you have so soon forgotten me," she chided him, tilting her head to one side and painting a coy smile on her lips. "You who once professed such great admiration for my charms."

The shock on the man's face was almost comical. "My lady?" he stammered.

"Ah, but I am presumptuous," she said with a heavy sigh. "A man whose life is as filled with women as yours! You cannot be expected to remember every one."

Arilyn turned to the other man, who appeared to be enjoying his companion's chagrin. "Surely you remember me, Raymid."

The man's grin disappeared, and he studied her for a long moment before shaking his head. "You look familiar. . . ."

"We have a friend in common," she hinted. "A master of arms?"

Realization dawned on Clion's face. "Arilyn!"

"The same," she said, adding teasingly, "Really, my friend, I thought you had forgotten me entirely."

"Not likely," responded Clion, grinning as he traced a finger along a knife scar on the back of his hand. "I have this to remember you by." He sobered quickly, adding, "It also serves as a reminder to keep my hands out of places where they do not belong."

"Then I do not regret giving the lesson," Arilyn said. "Few former thieves are admitted to the watch. You have done well."

"What brings you here and in such a guise?" asked Raymid, ever one to attend to the business at hand. "Or have you truly become a cleric?" Both men grinned broadly at the jest.

"And changed my race as well? Hardly." Her voice took on a grim tone. "I seek the Harper Assassin, as do you. Perhaps, once again, we can work together?"

Clion shook his head. "Believe me, Arilyn, I wish we had

something to tell you. All we know is that we're to go to the funeral and stand guard. No one seems to know for whom or what we're supposed to watch."

A long shadow fell upon the cobblestone street, unannounced by the sound of footsteps. Raymid looked up. "Ah, good. Here comes our watch commander now."

Arilyn's sharp intake of breath drew a curious stare from Danilo. He had listened to the conversation with great interest, which he now focused upon the newcomer.

The watch commander was a young male elf, probably near the end of his first century of life. The elf's skin was a golden hue, and his hair was a darker shade of gold and bound around the forehead by a band decorated with elven script. His face was narrow, with prominent cheekbones and an aquiline nose, and his long, slender form appeared as graceful and supple as a reed. Danilo noted how human Arilyn, and even the full moon elf Elaith Craulnobur, seemed in comparison with the exotic golden elf. The elven commander held himself apart through bearing that was haughty in the extreme. His black eyes held naked contempt for the three humans.

The elf's obsidian gaze softened somewhat as it fell upon Arilyn's gold skin and red silk tabard. Many elves as well as humans revered the goddess of the forest, and the elf bowed deeply to the cleric.

"Greetings, Lady of Mielikki," he said.

The red-haired man whom Arilyn had called Clion chuckled at the elf's remark. "That'll be the day. Captain, I'd like you to meet an old friend of ours. This is Arilyn Moonblade, one of the best adventurers Raymid and I ever traveled with. Arilyn, Tintagel Ni'Tessine."

With a sudden start, Danilo remembered where he'd heard that name. Tintagel Ni'Tessine was the elf who had tormented Arilyn during her years in the Academy of Arms. He looked at the half-elf. Her face was composed and she met Tintagel's furious gaze squarely, but there was a wariness about her eyes and a taut set to her mouth. "We've met," she said in an even voice.

The gold elf was the picture of outrage. "This is blasphemous! How do you dare impersonate a cleric of Mielikki, not to mention trying to pass as *Tel'Quessir.*" His scornful gaze swept over her. "I can understand your wish to cloak your true origins, but gilding dross cannot create gold."

The two watchmen listened to the elf's harangue with open mouths and dumbfounded expressions. Danilo's palm itched for the feel of his sword, but something in Arilyn's face stayed his hand.

"Well met, Tintagel," she replied calmly. "I must admit that your appearance is something of a surprise, as well. Few of your race wear such a uniform."

The elf's eyes narrowed, and Danilo could only assume that her seemingly innocuous words housed an insult.

"My presence in the watch is a matter of honor," he said, both his voice and expression a bit defensive.

"Really? Although I have utmost respect for the watch, I would not have thought that you would consider it an honorable position."

"By and large, the watch is a pitiful jest," Tintagel said spitefully, not noting the angry scowls this comment brought to the faces of his men. "Someone has to see that it provides a semblance of order to this lawless pile of clinking coins you call a city."

"You're that someone? How fortunate for all of us in Waterdeep," Danilo said, an amused drawl in his voice. There was a certain unintentional humor in the elf's remark. In truth, Waterdeep was well-ruled and orderly, a city whose laws were enforced and respected.

The elf's dark gaze slid over Danilo and dismissed him, then he turned back to Arilyn. "My own father was shot through the heart in the mountains of Waterdeep." His hand drifted to his side and clenched around an arrow shaft that hung at his belt. Danilo caught a glimpse of an oddly shaped black mark on the wood of the shaft. "I devote my life to avenging his death by ridding the city of such vermin as killed Fenian Ni'Tessine," Tintagel proclaimed grimly.

"A worthy quest it is," Danilo said, his tone clearly humoring the elf. "If it's all the same to you, we'll leave you to it now." He took Arilyn's arm and led her toward the stables. The half-elf came with him, her coldly polite expression frozen on her face.

"I'll get the horses," Danilo offered. Arilyn nodded absently, her attention fixed on the long wooden trough near the door of the stable. At one end of the trough stood a hand pump. Arilyn snatched up an empty feed bucket and walked to the well. She pumped water into the bucket and, dipping her cupped hands into the water again and again, viciously scrubbed and splashed the gold stain from her face and hands. There was a sound of ripping silk as she jerked off the tabard, too impatient to wait for the illusion to fade. The half-elf threw the ruined garment aside and stood, wearing her own identity like a defiant banner.

"Much better," Danilo said and handed her the reins of her horse. "That particular shade of gold was not becoming to you, and judging from the specimen we just encountered, the *Tel'Quessir*—whatever the Nine Hells *they* might be—are damnably unpleasant folk."

Fifteen

Against Danilo's better judgment, he and Arilyn left Waterdeep and rode into the night. The bright autumn moon was high in the sky as they headed south along the cliffs overlooking Waterbreak, a small peninsula of rock and sand that jutted into the sea and protected the southern section of Waterdeep's harbor. In the bright moonlight they could see the rocky shoreline below and the promise of safety given by the city walls that lay to their north. An empty promise, Danilo mused, considering the events of the past three days.

He had plenty of time to think of such things during their flight from Waterdeep. Arilyn said very little as they rode, and for once Danilo did not press her. He gave her all the distance and solitude she needed, the better to catch her off guard at the proper moment. Tonight he planned to force a confrontation.

The nobleman was not looking forward to his task, yet if he and Arilyn were to find the Harper Assassin they had to change the direction of their search. The conversation with Elaith Craulnobur had convinced Danilo that Uncle Khelben was right: the moonblade was the key to finding the assassin. Danilo wished he could simply tell Arilyn what he knew of the sword's history, but to do so would dispel his facade.

Since Arilyn seemed so distracted, Danilo took it upon himself to keep eyes and ears alert for danger. For all its riches and splendor, Waterdeep had been carved from a wild and dangerous land. "The Savage North," spiteful southerners called the area, and they were not far wrong. To the north and west of Waterdeep lay noble estates and rich farmland, but the southern path took Danilo and Arilyn into wilderness. As they reached the brush and pines that formed the far edges of the Ardeep Forest, Arilyn reined her horse to a stop.

"We make camp here. I'll hunt, you tend to the horses." Without waiting for a response, the half-elf swung herself down from her saddle, armed herself with a small bow and quiver, and disappeared into the trees.

As he set up camp, Danilo tried to devise a manner of broaching the subject of the moonblade. He considered and discarded one idea after another. Danilo groomed and tethered the horses, then gathered some stones and ringed them. After piling wood in the circle, he trimmed two forked sticks to the same length and thrust them into the ground on either side of the campfire, planning to roast whatever Arilyn's arrow brought down.

Something about the act of preparing a campfire gave him a jolt of inspiration. He had collected bits of information about Arilyn like pieces of a puzzle, and the prospect of fire gave him the final, crucial piece. He sat down near the stone circle and waited for the half-elf.

When Arilyn returned to camp with a pair of partridges, Danilo rose and continued with his chores. He threw a few sticks of wood into the circle, then he reached into his sack for a bit of flint. Keeping his movements slow and exaggerated, he stooped down and pointed the piece of flint at the stone circle. Out of the corner of his eyes he saw the half-elf stop cutting a branch from a bush and fling out her hand as if to stop him.

Deliberately taking no notice of her, Danilo murmured, "Dragonbreath." The flint in his hand disappeared and bright flames burst from the wood, sending a spray of golden sparks into the night sky. After the initial burst, the magic fire immediately settled down and became a cozy, crackling blaze.

"Didn't I tell you not to do that?"

Danilo rose and turned, hands in pockets, to face the furious half-elf. "You might have," he drawled. "I can't imagine why, though."

"I don't like magic fire, that's all." Arilyn settled herself crosslegged on the ground and began to prepare a spit. She removed the leaves from a branch and started to whittle the end of the green stick into a sharp point.

"Can I help with anything?"

The half-elf tossed the partridges to Danilo, indicating that he was to pluck the birds. The nobleman briskly set about the task. When the spit was ready, Arilyn glanced up. "Aren't you done with those birds yet?" she asked sharply.

Danilo handed her the first partridge. The half-elf spitted the bird and rather gingerly put the stick over the fire.

It was as good an opening as any. "Really, my dear," Danilo said as he busily plucked the second partridge, "don't you think that your aversion to magic fire is a little foolish?"

"Foolish!" Arilyn's eyes flared. She sat down and wrapped her arms tightly around her knees. "You are a fine one to use such words. Everything is a game for you. Magic is for parlor tricks, the Harper Assassin is merely a subject for your third-rate songs."

"Perhaps 'foolish' was an unfortunate choice of words," Danilo said.

Seeing that the second partridge was ready, the half-elf took it from the nobleman. Removing the spit from the fire, she put the second bird to roast. When her task was completed she turned to Danilo again. Her face seemed more composed, but her elven eyes burned with anger and remembered pain.

"Magic fire went awry during the Time of Troubles. Many died, many good people . . ." Her voice faded away.

"Someone you knew?" Danilo asked softly.

Arilyn nodded. "I traveled at the time with a group of adventurers called the Hammerfell Seven. One of them was a mage. She attempted to use a fireball spell against an ogre. The whole party went up in flames. Except me, obviously," she concluded bitterly.

"I wonder why you escaped?"

Arilyn ignored his question. "I don't suppose you've ever seen magic fire used in battle. I have. The devastation war wizards create is beyond imagination. You should see what Thay's Red Wizards have done to parts of Rashemen, or what the Alliance's mages did to the Tuigan during King Azoun's crusade against the barbarians. But then, none of the Waterdhavian nobility thought the crusade important enough—" Arilyn broke off and hurled a stick into the fire. "You are so pampered, so protected, so comfortable. You can't possibly understand me, so don't sit in judgment and pronounce me foolish for fearing what you cannot possibly fathom."

For several moments the only sounds were the crackling of the fire and the cry of a hunting owl. "Perhaps you're right," Danilo conceded. "I know little of an adventurer's life. I am, however, somewhat of an authority on women."

His comment surprised an exasperated hiss from Arilyn. "I don't doubt it. Your expertise means little to me. I am not a woman, but an elf."

"A *half*-elven woman. That's close enough."

"Really. Do you care to share any of your profound insights?" Her sarcasm was as sharp as a dagger's edge.

"If you'd like," Danilo said casually, and he pointed to the moonblade. "Take that sword, for example. You're a little afraid of it, aren't you?"

Arilyn drew herself up, as outraged as Danilo had intended her to be. "Of course not! Why would you say such a thing?"

"I've been thinking about some of the things Elaith Craulnobur said. It seems unusual that you know so little about your sword. By all accounts, it should be capable of a great deal of magic, and you barely tap the keg."

"Trust you to use an expression involving ale," Arilyn said with derision.

"Don't change the subject, my dear. Magic—including magic fire—is a fact of life, a reliable and powerful tool."

"Reliable? Ha!" Arilyn's face was tight with fury. "If you'd seen your friends die by fire during the Time of Troubles, you'd change your thinking."

"Waterdeep did not go unscathed during that unfortunate period," Danilo reminded her mildly. "From all accounts, it was quite nasty. Waterdeep suffered street battles with denizens of the underworld, the destruction of a god or two, and the resultant flattening of a good chunk of the city."

"From all accounts?" she repeated. "Where were you when all this happened?"

His eyebrows rose in surprise. "In the basement of the family estate, drinking." She glared at him, and he added defensively, "It seemed the only sane thing to do at the time."

Arilyn sniffed and fell silent. After several moments, she glanced at her annoying companion. He lounged indolently by the fire, watching her. His face was sympathetic, but in the firelight his gray eyes looked uncommonly shrewd.

"Since you don't agree with my observations, allow me to prove that my instincts are correct."

"Go ahead," she said.

"Remove the spit and walk through the fire."

The half-elf gasped. "Have you completely lost your mind?"

"No," he said thoughtfully. "I don't think so. I'm quite certain you can do it without injury or I wouldn't suggest it. I'm so certain, in fact, that I'm prepared to make you an offer. You've been trying to rid yourself of me for some time now, haven't you?"

"How perceptive."

Danilo held up his hands. "If I'm wrong about this, I'll leave. Tonight."

Arilyn stared at him. He looked serious. Nodding, she

abruptly rose to her feet. Scorched boots would be a small price to pay to rid herself of Danilo Thann.

She removed the spit and handed their sizzling meal to the nobleman, then stepped directly into the middle of the campfire and out the other side. The burning sticks crunched under her boot, sending sparks flying around her. A few bits of burning wood and ash landed on the sleeve of her shirt. Arilyn quickly moved to brush them off, but other sparks clung to the legs of her trousers like tiny glowing lanterns. She noted that the fabric did not even blacken.

The half-elf dropped to her knees beside the campfire. She thrust her hand into the flames and kept it there. There was a sensation of heat, but no pain. She sat back on her heels and glared at Danilo. "You enspelled the fire."

In response, the dandy reached into his magic sack and pulled out a pair of gloves. He slipped one on and stuck his hand into the fire. The smell of burned kidskin filled the air. Danilo stripped off the scorched glove and tossed it into her lap. "You owe me a new pair," he said lightly.

Arilyn stared down at the ruined glove. "Do you mind telling me what this is about?"

"Isn't is obvious? You are magically protected from fire. The tragedy of the Hammerfell Seven, not to mention your little stroll through the campfire, proves that. Really, my dear, it's not like you to be so dense."

Her laughter held little amusement. "Oh, that's rich, coming from you."

"Let me put this another way: would you care to repeat the exercise, this time *without* the moonblade?" He crossed his arms and cocked an eyebrow.

After a moment of silence, Arilyn raised her hand in the gesture of a fencer acknowledging a hit. Danilo pressed his point. "Your aversion to magic fire gives you a blind spot. The sword obviously has one ability you didn't consider. Isn't it possible that there are others?"

"I suppose."

"Well, let's find out what they are, shall we?"

Arilyn replaced the spitted birds over the fire with the air of one determined to attend to practicalities. "I have more pressing duties."

"Such as finding the assassin."

"Yes."

Danilo pointedly swept a gaze around their wilderness campsite. "Why are we out here?"

Arilyn's shoulders slumped. "No matter what I do, the assassin keeps following me. Not to kill me—he probably could have done that a dozen times—but as the pawn in some grisly game. I don't understand his motive, but until I figure it out I don't want to be responsible for any more Harper deaths." She hurled another stick at the fire. "There are no Harpers out here to kill."

"Is it possible," Danilo suggested tentatively, "that the assassin wants you for the powers of your sword?"

Bitterness flooded the half-elf's face. "Of course it's possible. The sword and I are inseparable."

"All the more reason for investigating your sword's magic. Once you know what the moonblade can do, you'll be able to figure out the assassin's ultimate motive. Once you know the motive, you have a chance of discerning the villain's identity."

Arilyn stared at the dandy in amazement. There was truth in his words, and more than a little wisdom. "How did you figure all this out?'

"Quite easily. After all," he said grandly, "magic *is* my specialty." Danilo drew back with a melodramatic flourish. "Really, my dear. If you were to advise me as an assassin, I would take your word as that of an expert. I expect you to extend me the same courtesy."

He rose to his feet and flounced off, settling down on a log on the other side of the fire, the very picture of offended dignity. Arilyn grinned despite herself. Generally she didn't find foolishness endearing, but Danilo made it an art form and raised it to a level that commanded a certain respect.

Danilo caught sight of her smile. "What's so funny?" he demanded in a sullen voice. The half-elf blinked. His insight had momentarily led her to assume that his foolishness was an act. Looking at him now, she wasn't so sure.

Arilyn wiped her face clear. "I can't imagine. All right, Danilo, you win. I'll find out everything I can about the sword." She rose to her feet. "Let's go."

"Now?" Danilo protested, with a longing glance at the sizzling partridges.

"I like to keep busy."

They were very busy indeed for the next hour. After they kicked the fire into ash, Danilo placed simple magical wards around the campsite to protect the horses from night-stalking predators. He and Arilyn carefully climbed down the rocky incline that led to the sea, then they headed northward along the coastline of the Waterbreak peninsula. Even with the light of the bright autumn moon to guide them, they had to pick their way carefully along the jagged rocks of the shoreline.

At the very tip of Waterbreak stood a natural formation of black rocks, the lower part of which was submerged in the sea. Small crustaceans clung to the base of the rock, and several jagged points thrust skyward like small turrets. On the whole, Danilo thought, it looked like a drunken mage's attempt at conjuring a miniature castle.

Arilyn reached into a niche in the rock formation and drew out a small leather box. From it she took a silver pan pipe. As a fascinated Danilo looked on, she put the instrument to her lips and played a few notes. The silvery tones rang out over the water, shimmering there like moonlight.

"Nice tune," Danilo observed. "What do we do now?"

"We wait."

Arilyn motioned Danilo toward a pile of rocks some hundred yards away. He obediently withdrew and settled down to wait, and Arilyn stationed herself at the point of Waterbreak and gazed out over the water with elven patience.

The nobleman could not gauge how long they stared out to sea. After a time he noted that a ripple disturbed the still silver surface of the water to the south. Assuming their wait was nearly over, he rose and brushed the lichen and sand from the seat of his trousers. Arilyn flung out a hand to halt him, then she gestured for him to stay back and stay quiet. Again Danilo did as he was bid.

The ripple appeared twice more, each time closer, then the surface of the water was broken by a glossy black head. Danilo watched in amazement as a large seal-like creature emerged from the sea. As it climbed onto the rocky strand beside Arilyn, the nobleman noted that its body ended in legs rather than tapering to the flippers of a seal. The creatures's black eyes shone with intelligence, and it reached out to clasp Arilyn's forearm in the salute of fellow adventurers. In the bright moonlight Danilo could discern that its hands were like that of a man, albeit covered with dark fur and webbed between the fingers.

"A selkie," Danilo breathed. He had heard of the rare creatures, but he had never expected to see one. His wonderment increased a hundredfold as the selkie stepped back from Arilyn and, in the span of a heartbeat, transformed into a human man.

Never had Danilo seen such perfection in a man. The transformed selkie was no taller than Arilyn, but his pale body was perfectly formed and powerfully built. Sleek, dark brown hair fell to his shoulders and framed a clean-shaven face too masculine to be called beautiful.

"Hello, Gestar," Arilyn said warmly. The half-elf did not seem disconcerted by the transformation or by the selkie man's nakedness.

"Well met, Arilyn. It is good to see you, even at this late hour," said the selkie. He cast a suspicious look at Danilo, and the nobleman caught a glimpse of intense eyes the color of fine blue topaz.

"The man over there is a friend of mine and quite harmless," she assured the newcomer. "Can you send a request through the Relay? I need some information from Evermeet, by morning if possible."

"Anything for the elf who saved the life of my mate."

Arilyn smiled her thanks. "I seek information about a moonblade. It belonged to an elf named Amnestria, who left Evermeet about forty years ago. I'm afraid that's all I have."

"It should be enough. I'll see to this immediately and send word in the morning. Since I cannot transform to human shape again so soon, please expect Black Pearl."

"Seeing her again will be a pleasure. Thank you, Gestar." The adventurers embraced unselfconsciously, and the selkie man turned and dove into the sea.

Danilo could contain himself no longer. "That was a selkie!"

Arilyn turned to face him. "An old friend. We'll wait here until morning for the information. If you're cold, make a fire."

The nobleman nodded his agreement. Although he was full to the brim with questions, the night was chill. He began to collect driftwood, aware that Arilyn watched him with an amused smile.

"Go ahead and ask," she said. "I can see the toll your silence is taking upon you."

Danilo cast her a grin. "What is the Relay? And how can it send a message to Evermeet and back in the span of a single night? Is it magic?"

"No, it's not magic. The Relay is a network of selkies, sea elves, and sentient sea creatures that look very much like small whales. All can move at impressive speeds, and sound itself travels three times as fast in water as it does in air. Underwater messages travel swiftly."

"But to Evermeet and back?"

"It may be that my inquiry need not go so far. Those who serve in the Relay are bound to secrecy concerning specific messages, but as you can imagine there is a wealth of accumulated information in its members."

"Oh. Who is this Black Pearl?"

"A sea half-elf."

"That's possible? I doubt I could hold my breath long enough to accomplish such a feat," Danilo marveled.

Arilyn let out a burst of surprised laughter. "Sea elves do not always stay under water."

"Interesting name, Black Pearl."

"You'll understand when you see her. Black Pearl's human

mother came from a land far to the southeast. Her ship sank off the coast of Calimport and she was rescued by sea elves. There are few half sea-elves, and Black Pearl spends much time with the selkies."

"I imagine selkies could understand her dual nature better than most other creatures," Danilo mused.

His perceptive remarks startled Arilyn, who had herself always felt uniquely comfortable with selkies. "That's true," she said, and immediately changed the subject. "Any other questions?"

"Yes. You said that the sword belonged to an elf named Amnestria. Who's that?"

Arilyn paused for a long moment. "My mother," she said, her voice without expression.

"Didn't Elaith speak of someone called Z'beryl? I thought that was your mother's name."

"So did I."

"Oh."

Silence hung between them. "Listen, why don't you get some sleep?" Arilyn asked after a time.

Her question caught Danilo in the middle of a yawn. "Good idea." The shuttered expression in Arilyn's eyes, combined with his own weariness, convinced him of her suggestion's merits.

Danilo awoke when the sky was still silver with the promise of sunrise, to find Arilyn deep in conversation with Black Pearl. At first glance Danilo knew that it could be no other. The sea half-elf's far-eastern heritage showed in the slope of her dark eyes and in the hair that fell to her hips like a length of wet black satin. Her pointed ears were somewhat more rounded than Arilyn's. Although her hands and feet were webbed, her white skin was very different from the mottled green or blue color that distinguished most sea elves. In the early morning light her naked body shone with the pure translucent sheen of a rare pearl.

"After King Zaor's death," said Black Pearl, "Queen Amlaruil became sole ruler of Evermeet. Their daughter Amnestria was sent into secret exile because of some private disgrace."

"That would be me, I suppose," Arilyn said in a low voice. In a louder tone she asked, "Exactly when did Zaor die?"

"At the end of the four hundred thirty-second year of his reign. The event made an great impact in the sea elf community, and I remember it well, young though I was. It was springtime, during the High Tide Festival." The sea half-elf bit her lip and calculated. "That would be the year 1321, as humans reckon time in the Dalelands. I remember the day, as well; the second day of Ches."

"Was the murderer caught?"

"No. Amnestria's human lover shot and wounded the assassin, who nevertheless managed to disappear without a trace."

"Of what race was the assassin?"

The sea half-elf dropped her eyes as if ashamed. "He was elven," she admitted.

"Yes, but what *race*?" Arilyn persisted.

"Oh. A gold elf. Is that important?"

"It might be," Arilyn murmured in a distracted tone. She looked up suddenly. "What did you learn about the moonblade?"

"Little is known of its powers, I'm afraid. It seems that Amnestria inherited the sword shortly before her exile, from a great-aunt whose family spent most of their time away from Evermeet. You would do better to seek the sword's history from sages here on the mainland." The exotic half-elf paused, then added, "I'm sorry I could not bring you the answers you needed."

"You've answered many questions." Arilyn extended her hand, palm up. "Thank you for your help, Black Pearl." The other half-elf smiled and covered the offered palm with her own webbed hand, then she disappeared into the sea with a faint splash.

Arilyn stood looking absently out to sea. When she turned, she seemed faintly startled to see that Danilo was awake. "I suppose you heard."

"Yes."

"We might as well get your questions out of the way now."

"You're catching on," the nobleman said approvingly. He rose and stretched. "First and foremost, don't any of the sea people wear clothing?"

Arilyn raised her eyebrows. "From all that was said, you gained that single insight?"

"Black Pearl *was* rather hard to overlook, Princess Arilyn," Danilo said with a grin. "By the way, Your Highness, should I genuflect before you or will a simple bow suffice?"

"The royal elves were Amnestria's family, not mine," she said curtly. "I don't claim to be a princess." The half-elf abruptly turned away. "Please see to your breakfast and wardrobe as quickly as possible. We return to Waterdeep this morning."

"Oh, splendid." Immediately Danilo began removing garments from his magic sack and considering the merits of each. "Are we going anywhere in particular?"

"Yes."

Danilo looked up from the silken pile with a pained expression and a patient sigh. "Perhaps you could be a trifle more specific? I do so hate to be inappropriately dressed."

"Blackstaff Tower." At her words, Danilo's face took on an odd expression. Arilyn had a vision of him pulling a wizard's robe out of his bag. With a touch of grim humor, she added, "Dress like a mage and you won't live to cast your next spell."

Hastily Danilo snatched up a shirt of pale yellow silk from the pile of discarded garments. "This will do splendidly, really." Within minutes he was ready to go. Sunrise colors stained the sky as they made their way back down the rocky coast.

"Why Blackstaff Tower?" Danilo asked, trotting easily beside Arilyn's long-legged stride as they headed back to their campsite.

"I need to find out what there is to know about this sword. I suppose a learned mage is the best place to start."

"Yes, but there are other mages in Waterdeep, ones with fewer demands on their time."

"I don't know any of them. I do know Khelben."

"Really, now. Khelben Arunsun? He can be most unpleasant," Danilo said.

"Yes, I know," Arilyn agreed, "but if I must entrust my sword to a spellcaster, I suppose it might as well be him. At least he knows which end of a weapon is which."

Danilo smirked. "I wonder how the great wizard would like to hear himself named a 'spellcaster.'" He smiled and held out his hand. "Listen! I've got a marvelous idea. There's no need for both of us to go to Blackstaff Tower. I'll go alone."

Arilyn stopped so quickly that Danilo, trying to follow suit, tripped on a rock. She studied him as he bent and rubbed his bruised shin. "Why should you do that?" she asked.

"Chivalry," he stated, still attending to his injury. "After all you've been through of late, I thought I might spare you an encounter with the old coot."

"Your concern is touching."

"Of course it is," Danilo said, beaming. He straightened and laid a hand on her shoulder. "You wait in town. Take a rest and get your hair done for the festival. Whatever. I'll be in and out of Blackstaff Tower before you know it."

Arilyn threw off his hand, exasperated. "Khelben Arunsun knows me. What makes you think he'd see you?" Danilo paused a bit too long. "Well?" she demanded.

"He's my uncle. My mother's brother, to be precise. Believe me, Mother would have Uncle Blackstaff the archmage drawn, dressed, and roasted if he slighted her baby boy. Formidable woman." Danilo smiled winningly at Arilyn. "Come to think of it, I believe you'd like my mother."

Sixteen

The half-elf's eyes flamed with anger at Danilo's casual revelation. "Why didn't you tell me you were Khelben's nephew?"

He shrugged. "It didn't occur to me. You never told me you were related to elven royalty, either," he pointed out. "Family trees never came up in conversation."

With a hiss of exasperation, Arilyn lapsed into silence. They climbed the rocky incline to their camp and found their horses calmly cropping grass. Without a word the half-elf set about saddling her horse. Danilo did likewise, and once they mounted he reached toward her. "Give me your hand."

"Why?"

"I'm going to teleport us to Blackstaff Tower. It'll save time."

"No!"

It was Danilo's turn to be exasperated. "By the gods, woman, be reasonable for once." He leaned over and snatched her hand.

Immediately they were surrounded by white, milky light. There was no sensation of movement, no sense of anything solid around or beneath them. It seemed to Arilyn that they were suspended in nothingness, a state of being that was outside of her understanding or control. Before the half-elf had time to feel the panic and sickness she expected, the light faded and the dark granite walls of Blackstaff Tower came into focus before them.

"There now, was that so bad?" Danilo asked.

"No, it wasn't," Arilyn said with a touch of surprise. "That's odd. Dimensional travel has always made me very ill, ever since I first tried it with Kymil. . . ." Her voice drifted off.

Danilo did not seem to notice her distraction. He knocked on the gate and was promptly answered by the disembodied voice of a servant. "Arilyn Moonblade to see the Blackstaff," Danilo announced.

Within moments the gate opened and Khelben Arunsun himself came to greet them. "Come in, Arilyn. It's always a pleasure to see you." The mage's gaze fell on her companion. "Oh, it's you, Danilo."

"Hello, Uncle Khel," Danilo replied. "Arilyn needed a spellcaster, so I brought her here."

Khelben Arunsun's brow knit as he turned to Arilyn. "And you listened to my frivolous nephew? I hope this is important."

"It could be." Arilyn unbuckled her swordbelt and handed the sheathed moonblade to Khelben. "I give you my permission to touch it," she said, her voice taking on a hint of ritual. "Just make sure you don't try to take it from the scabbard."

The archmage accepted the ancient sword and examined it with interest. "Fascinating weapon. What's all this about?"

"I need to learn everything I can about this sword and its history. Can you help me?"

"I'm no sage, but a legend lore spell might yield some answers," Khelben said, tucking the moonblade under his arm. "Please follow me."

The archmage led them into the courtyard. When they

reached the tower he motioned for them to follow and disappeared into the wall. When Arilyn hesitated, Danilo unceremoniously pushed her through the hidden door. She glared over her shoulder at him. "I *have* done this before, you know."

"Really? I wouldn't have guessed."

"Hmmph." The half-elf squared her shoulders and stalked into the reception area of Blackstaff Tower.

"Come upstairs," Khelben said. "We'll have a better look at your sword up in my spellcasting chamber."

Arilyn and Danilo followed the archmage up the steep spiral stairway that wound up the center of the tower. When they came to the third and top floor, they stepped into a large, book-lined study. Khelben ushered them through it and opened an oaken door into another, smaller room. A table stood under the chamber's only window, and in the center of the room a scrying crystal rested on a marble pedestal. There was nothing else in the chamber that could distract the wizard from the process of casting spells.

"Wait here," Khelben said. He put the moonblade on the table and disappeared through a door.

"Spell components," Danilo explained to Arilyn. "He keeps his magical supplies in the next room. Very organized, our archmage."

Khelben reappeared carrying several small items. "Stay over on the far side of the chamber," he instructed his visitors, "and for the love of Mystra, Danilo, try to hold your tongue. This spell requires a degree of concentration."

The archmage moved to the table where the moonblade lay and arranged the spell components. Arilyn caught a glimpse of a small white vial that bore Khelben's sigil.

She bit her lip, suddenly chagrined by the boldness of her request. She'd heard that some spells required the sacrifice of an item of value. For the first time it seemed odd to her that an archmage of Khelben's stature would cast such a spell for a mere acquaintance, at such cost to himself.

The wizard moved through the words and gestures of the incantation, his hands sure and his voice filled with the resonance of power. At length Khelben unstoppered a second vial, and the dark aroma of incense filled the chamber. The archmage tipped the bottle and spilled its contents over the moonblade. Instantly the spell components disappeared in a flash of light.

Arilyn felt rather than saw Khelben cross the room to stand by her side. All her attention was focused on the moonblade and on the ghostly mist that rose from it. The mist swirled in a quick spiral and then descended to the floor. It coalesced into the image of an elven bard, carrying a small harp and clothed in the robes of an ancient time. Not taking any notice of the trio, the ghostly elf spoke.

"Let those who hear attend the ballad of the elfshadow." He struck the harp strings and began to repeat a ballad in ringing, rhythmic speech:

> Upon the wings of seven winds,
> Upon the waves of every sea,
> Zoastria the traveler seeks
> The shadow's living elf.
>
> Twinborn she was, and from her birth
> In sisterhood of soul and flesh
> Zoastria and Somalee
> Were destiny-entwined.
>
> The heiress elf a sword was given,
> The younger sailed to distant shores
> To marry as her duty bid.
> Her ship did not reach port.
>
> Zoastria now walked alone.
> Her weeping swelled the rising tide,
> Her longing brought through stone and steel
> A shadow sisterhood.
>
> Call forth through stone, call forth from steel;
> Command the mirror of thyself.
> But ware the spirit housed within
> The shadow of the elf.

The elven bard struck one final chord, then the image and the music faded. "The lyrics aren't bad," Danilo commented, breaking the tense silence that hung in the spellcasting chamber. "The tune could use some work, though."

Khelben turned to Arilyn, who stood pale and still. "Does any of this make sense of you?" She hesitated, then shook her head. "What about you, Dan? Any ideas?"

The nobleman looked astonished. "You're asking me?"

His comment roused Arilyn from her trance. She managed a faint smile. "Why not? Magic is your specialty, isn't it?"

"Dan taught me all I know," Khelben said, echoing the half-elf's dry humor. "Let's go downstairs to my parlor and talk this over." Arilyn picked up the moonblade and followed Khelben down the spiral staircase to a large sitting room, which was furnished with comfortable chairs and decorated by samples of Khelben's handiwork as an artist. Arilyn sank into a chair and laid the moonblade across her lap, but Danilo walked about the room, idly examining the portraits that covered the walls and stood on easels that had been set up in the corners.

"Could you cast that spell again?" Arilyn asked the archmage.

He took a chair near the half-elf. "Not today. Why?"

"I have to find out all there is to know about the moonblade," she said tersely. "If you can do no more today, where do I go?"

Khelben rubbed his cheek and considered. "Candlekeep would probably have the most information. They've a fine library on elven magical objects."

The half-elf's shoulders sagged. "You might as well have said Rashemen," she said ruefully. "The trip to Candlekeep would take months by land. By sea it could take several tendays, more with the winter storms at hand."

"As it happens, that won't be a problem," Khelben said. "I do a great deal of research there, so I had a dimensional door installed between my library and Candlekeep." Arilyn looked dubious, so Khelben added, "Take Danilo with you. The boy could be a help to you in your studies. He's been to Candlekeep with me and he's familiar with their methods. What do you say, Dan?"

Arilyn and Khelben turned toward the young man, who had been engrossed in the study of one of Khelben's portraits. He nodded avidly. "Sounds good to me. There's a rogue elf in Waterdeep devoted to the idea of killing me. I'd just as soon head south until he changes his mind."

Khelben's black eyebrows shot up, but Danilo dismissed the mage's unspoken question with an insouciant shrug. "By the way, what is an elfshadow?" the young man asked.

"I don't know," Khelben admitted. "The answers given in response to a legend lore spell are usually cryptic."

Arilyn suddenly recalled that the mage Coril's spells had interpreted two runes on the moonblade: elfgate and elfshadow. At the time, it had seemed strange that Kymil Nimesin had failed to do this. Now Arilyn also wondered why Kymil had not attempted to cast a legend lore spell.

She turned to Khelben. "The spell you just cast," she said abruptly, "is it very difficult?"

He spread his hands. "These things are relative, but I suppose you could say it is difficult. The spell components are expensive, and the spell is not widely known. Few can manage it."

"It's beyond me," Danilo said, offering his support as if the archmage's word required bolstering.

"I see," Arilyn murmured absently. "Is it possible that the sword is warded against elven magic?"

"I doubt it. Why?"

"Just a thought," she said. Squaring her shoulders and firming her resolve, she looked up at Danilo. "If we must go to Candlekeep, we might as well start now."

"You'll need a letter of introduction," Khelben said. He rose and walked to a small writing table. Seating himself, he scratched some runes on a piece of parchment, rolled it into a tight scroll, and sealed it with his sigil. He scrawled a note on another scrap of parchment, then handed both messages to his nephew.

Danilo glanced at the note. He slipped it into his breast pocket and dropped the scroll into his magic sack. "Uncle Khel, might I have a few words with you in private? A family matter, I'm afraid, and of a personal nature."

"This is hardly the time. Is it important?"

"I think so. You might not, of course."

The archmage glowered, then relented. "All right. Come up to my study. If you'll excuse us?" he asked Arilyn. She nodded absently, and the two men disappeared up the spiral stairs.

As soon as Khelben had shut the door to the study, Danilo stated bluntly, "A group of Harpers are having Arilyn followed. They seem to think that she's the assassin. Did you know that?"

The archmage was clearly surprised. "No, I didn't. How did you learn of it?"

"She's been followed since we met in Evereska. Of that I'm fairly certain. At first I assumed that it was the Harper Assassin, then a rogue elf by the name of Elaith Craulnobur claimed a Harper ranger was on Arilyn's trail. How he learned that, I don't know, but the elf seemed to know a great deal about Arilyn."

"Elaith Craulnobur, eh? You said she suspected an elf was involved, didn't you? He'd certainly be a likely candidate."

"No," Danilo said firmly. Khelben looked curious, but the young man shook his head and refused to elaborate. "Can you find out anything from the Harpers?"

Khelben nodded and laid a hand on the scrying crystal. The globe began to glow, and the archmage's face grew distant as his thoughts turned inward and traveled to places far away.

The nobleman waited impatiently. When Khelben turned to him, the archmage was more disturbed than Danilo had ever seen him. "A complication has arisen."

"Oh, good," Danilo said, crossing his arms. "This assignment has been altogether too easy thus far."

Khelben ignored his nephew's sarcasm. "Your elven informant was right. A small group of Harpers in Cormyr believes that Arilyn is the Harper Assassin. They intend to prove her guilt and bring her in for trial."

Danilo's face paled. "Go on."

"They've sent Bran Skorlsun to follow her." Khelben's tone implied that this was a grave matter indeed.

"Who's he?"

Khelben started to pace about the study, clearly agitated. "Bran Skorlsun is a Master Harper, one of the best rangers and trackers the Harpers have," he admitted grudgingly. "The secret nature of the organization makes it possible for rogues to use the Harper name to further some scheme or another. For almost forty years now, Bran has been tracking false and renegade Harpers, mostly on the Moonshae Isles, but occasionally in other remote areas. He is devoted to keeping the Harpers' ranks pure."

"Forty years, eh? The man must be getting rather old by now," Danilo observed. His casual tone masked his growing concern, for it was unlike Khelben to stray so far from the main point.

Khelben shot a glance at Danilo. "Bran Skorlsun comes from a long-lived family."

"Indeed."

The archmage's jaw tightened. "He's also Arilyn's father."

Danilo slumped against the wall and raked both hands through his hair. "The poor girl," he murmured.

"Poor girl!" snapped Khelben. "Let's not lose sight of the broad picture, Dan. Have you forgotten that Arilyn's father carries the moonstone? The last thing we need is for stone and sword to become one again."

"There's that, too," Danilo admitted. His face hardened. "How is it that such a thing could occur?"

"The Harpers are a secret organization," Khelben repeated testily.

"So everyone keeps telling me. Must that mean the right hand doesn't know what the left is doing?"

"Certainly not. In this particular matter, it was deemed best that no one person know all the details concerning the dimensional door, or elfgate, as it came to be called."

"All things considered, do you still think that a wise course?" Danilo asked. "It seems to me that it's time to compare notes. You have a good idea what the assassin wants. Arilyn might have some notions as to who and why."

Khelben suddenly looked very interested. "Does she know the assassin's identity?"

"I'm not sure. I don't think so."

"Well, we'll have to wait until we know. We must find out whether this involves the elfgate."

"Blackstaff Tower is warded against magical observation. Why not tell Arilyn the whole story, here and now?" Khelben was silent for a time, and the young nobleman's face tightened. "Wait a minute. You don't trust her either, do you?"

"The issue is not whether I trust Arilyn or not. When the Harpers and the elves worked together to resolve the elfgate danger, I gave certain assurances." The archmage paused. "I pledged not to tell this tale to anyone, with the exception of my probable successor."

The young man lowered his head, stunned by the implication of the archmage's words. "You can't be referring to me," he murmured.

"Perhaps this is not the time to speak of such matters," Khelben said sternly, "but I would not make such a suggestion to you if I did not mean what I said. Neither would I break the pledge I made some forty years ago."

Danilo conceded with a nod. "I understand your position, but Arilyn is now searching openly for the moonblade's secret. What happens when this mysterious assassin decides she's getting too close?" His uncle did not speak, but the silence between them held the answer. "If the cause is sufficiently noble, the sacrifice is justified. Is that about right?"

Khelben's face was grim. "In the main, yes."

The young nobleman walked slowly to the door of the chamber. Doorknob in hand, he paused and spoke with his back still to the archmage. "With all due respect, Uncle Blackstaff, I'm not sure that I want to be your probable successor." He slipped through the door, closing it firmly behind him.

"Let's go," Danilo said to Arilyn as he descended the stairs. She rose and belted on the moonblade.

"Wait a minute, young man," Khelben called from the floor above. "You're leaving from the library, remember? The dimensional door?"

Danilo stopped at the foot of the stair, and his foolish grin was a little uncertain. "Oh. Right."

"Did you ride? Then you'll need to stable your horses here. I'll walk out with you and help you bring them around," Khelben said firmly.

When they reached the street, the archmage said, "By the way, Dan, the dimensional door from Candlekeep will not return you directly to Blackstaff Tower. You'll return to a place called Jester's Court, just off the corner of Selduth Street and the Street of Silks. The door is one-way and invisible, and it stands between the two twin black oak trees on the north side of the garden."

"I'll bear that in mind."

"I want you both to report back here before sunrise tomorrow. Is that clear?"

"Crystal," Danilo answered flippantly. Without further discussion he and Arilyn led their horses to the stables behind Blackstaff Tower and returned with Khelben to the second floor library. The archmage slid a bookshelf to one side, revealing a narrow black portal where the wall should have been.

"Before we leave for Candlekeep, I have one more question," Arilyn said to the archmage. His readiness to help had raised her suspicions. Could it be that the archmage knew something about the moonblade, something that he kept from her? A test came to mind: if a minor mage like Coril could decipher some of the runes on the scabbard, surely Khelben could at least do likewise. Arilyn drew the moonblade and ran her finger along the runes. "Can you read any of these?"

Khelben leaned closer and studied the arcane marks for several moments. "No. I'm sorry."

"You do know what they say, though," she stated, her tone posing a question.

The archmage's face was inscrutable. "How could I know such a thing?" He motioned toward the portal. "Good luck on your trip."

"Thank you for your good wishes," she said in an overly sweet voice. "Since we will be traveling in the dark, we certainly have need of them."

Khelben glowered at the disrespectful and far too perceptive half-elf. She merely raised her eyebrows, took Danilo's arm, and disappeared into the velvet blackness of the dimensional gate.

The archmage smiled faintly. Arilyn is sharp, he mused as he walked down the stairs to the parlor. A flash of green caught his eye. Danilo had left a scarf behind, draped over a small portrait that rested on a table easel. Even as Khelben reached for the bright silk, it faded from sight.

"An illusion," he said softly. "That boy's getting far too good." Khelben instantly realized why the portrait had been covered. It was a sketch of four friends, one he had drawn from memory many years ago. The archmage picked up the portrait for a closer look. His own face looked back at him from the past, that of a young mage whose hairline had not yet begun its northward migration. The man beside him also had dark hair, curly and full, and implacable stubbornness was written in the set of his jaw and the steadiness of his eyes. Seated before the men were Laeral the mage and Princess Amnestria of Evermeet.

Khelben gripped the portrait. Laeral sat with her hand clasped in that of her friend Amnestria. The archmage could see why Danilo did not wish Arilyn to see the pencil sketch; without the vivid difference in their coloring apparent, Amnestria and Arilyn looked so much alike that the half-elf could not have failed to recognize her mother. If she had seen the picture of the four friends, she would have surely raised questions that Khelben was not prepared to answer.

Laeral. The mage's gaze returned to the pert, smiling face of the young adventurer. It had been quite some time since he'd seen his lady. She returned to Waterdeep from time to time, and

Khelben still kept chambers for her in the top floor of his tower. But Laeral had developed a taste for travel and continued a life of adventuring, and Khelben found himself trapped in Waterdeep more and more often, pursuing politics and diplomacy. Both had become powerful mages, both worked with the Harpers. There was no real quarrel between them. How then, Khelben mused, could it be that they were drifting apart?

The archmage found himself pondering Danilo's angry words. How much had he himself sacrificed on the altar of a noble cause? Even for a man who strove for self knowledge, it was a disturbing thought.

*   *   *   *   *

In his villa not far from Blackstaff Tower, Kymil Nimesin leaned back from his scrying crystal. His angular face showed deep concern. Perhaps he should have heeded Elaith Craulnobur's warning concerning Danilo Thann.

Even if the young nobleman was indeed the fool he appeared to be, he had led Arilyn to Khelben Arunsun. Of all those connected to the Harpers, the Blackstaff was most likely to know the secrets of Arilyn's moonblade. Since Kymil could not magically observe the half-elf in Blackstaff Tower, he had no idea what she had learned from the archmage. At least the mage had been foolish enough to mention the pair's destination outside the tower. Candlekeep. Kymil cursed. He could not spy on her there either. If his plan was to succeed, he needed to move now. Kymil turned to his assistant.

"Filauria, summon the mercenary team."

The lovely *etriel* at Kymil's side went without question to do his bidding. Soon she returned, leading a contingent of human adventurers from the chambers where they had awaited Kymil's summons, swilling ale and playing dice.

For a long moment, Kymil regarded the men whom Elaith Craulnobur had recommended for the task. They were led by Harvid Beornigarth, an uncouth one-eyed giant of a man. The unfortunate result of a barbarian rampage, Harvid owed his size to his father's race and his eye patch to Arilyn Moonblade. The fighter's huge arms were knotted with muscle, and he was known to wield his spike-studded mace with skill. The four men with Harvid were equally strong and unkempt, to all appearances a wild and formidable force. They were precisely what Kymil needed.

"Well, Harvid, it seems that you shall finally have the opportunity to avenge the loss of your eye," Kymil began, steepling his fingers in a gesture of satisfaction.

The man hefted his mace in anticipation. "Where is the gray wench?" he snarled.

"Let us hope your skills match your enthusiasm," Kymil said dryly. "Your chance will come before the sun rises again. Behold."

Kymil waved his fingers over the scrying crystal and an image of a garden courtyard appeared. A few people wandered about, enjoying the bright autumn morning. "This is Jester's Square. Do you know it? Good. The half-elf and her companion, Danilo Thann, will arrive here before daybreak. There are but two ways to leave the courtyard." Kymil pointed to a large gap between two buildings. "This would be the mostly likely exit. You are to block it. Use whatever you can find. You will lie in wait for them here, in this alley."

Kymil looked up at the mercenaries, his face grim. "And you will kill them both." A gasp of surprise came from the elven female who stood attentively behind the armsmaster's chair.

Harvid Beornigarth had his own doubts. He grimaced and scratched at his eye patch with a large, grimy finger.

"Is there a problem?" Kymil asked calmly.

"Well, yes," Harvid admitted. "I know young Lord Thann."

"Yes? So?"

"I don't want to kill him."

"Really," chided Kymil. "I had thought you beyond such sentiment."

"It's not personal. I just don't like messing with nobility. His family is powerful."

"Is that all." Kymil sniffed. "Believe me, the Thann family will recover from the loss. Danilo is a sixth son, a wastrel and a fool by most measures." The elf's voice hardened. "You will kill Danilo Thann. That is the price I demand for giving you Arilyn Moonblade's life."

The gleam returned to Harvid's good eye. "I'll get the gold you promised when I bring you her sword?"

"Of course," Kymil said smoothly. "Now go."

Filauria watched the mercenaries clomp from the room. "I have seen the half-elf in battle. Those men are as good as dead."

Kymil patted her hand. "Of course they are, my dear, but they are nothing if not expendable."

The *etriel* looked puzzled. "If Harvid Beornigarth and his men cannot kill the half-elf, why do you send them?"

"I do not want Arilyn dead. I merely wish to restore her sword to its full potential," Kymil said mildly. "Harvid Beornigarth is the means to that end. At first glance, he looks dangerous, and he and his men should give Arilyn a good fight. Bran Skorlsun will certainly come out of the shadows if his daughter's life appears to be endangered. With him comes the moonstone."

* * * * *

The first thing Arilyn noticed about Candlekeep was that the air was considerably warmer than that in Waterdeep. No wonder, she thought dazedly. She and Danilo had materialized several hundred miles to the south of the City of Splendors.

Before them towered the library, a massive citadel of pale gray stone that was ringed by walls and perched on a rocky seacoast. Although the setting was austere, the air, even in late autumn, was balmy, tempered by the strong breeze that blew in from the Sea of Swords.

"State your business," boomed a powerful voice. For the first time Arilyn noticed the small gatehouse that stood at the entrance to the wall ringing Candlekeep. From it came a tiny, wizened apparition of a man.

The Keeper of the Gate was stooped and thin, and his skin was as dry and yellowed as ancient parchment. The aura of power about the man, however, was such that Arilyn doubted he was ever challenged.

"We request entrance to the libraries. The archmage Khelben Arunsun of Waterdeep sent us to seek information about a magic elven weapon." Danilo handed the scroll to the keeper. The old man glanced at the sigil and nodded.

"Who might you be?"

Danilo drew himself up. "I'm the Blackstaff's apprentice," he said with a mixture of pride and becoming modesty. "Danilo Thann, accompanied by an agent of the Harpers."

Arilyn leaned close to Danilo. "Nice cover," she murmured. "Remind me never to play cards with you." The nobleman smirked.

Not noticing the exchange, the keeper broke the seal and scanned Khelben's letter of introduction. "You may enter," he said. Immediately the gate opened and a robed man came out and bowed to the keeper. "Moonblades," the old man said tersely, and the newcomer bowed again.

"I am Schoonlar," the man said, turning to Arilyn and Danilo. He was of medium height and slender build, with unremarkable features and hair, and garments the color of dust. "I will aid you with your studies. If you will follow me?"

He led them into the tower and up a narrow spiral staircase. They passed floor after floor filled with scrolls and tomes, illuminators and scribes laboriously copying rare books, and scholars delving into the accumulated lore of centuries. Located about halfway between the two largest cities on the coast, Waterdeep and Calimport, and lying directly east of the lower Moonshae Isles, Candlekeep was a repository of knowledge for all three regions: the North, the desert lands of the south, and the ancient island cultures.

Finally they reached a floor near the top of the tower. Schoonlar brought out a large tome and laid it on a reading table. "This book may be a good place to begin your search. It is a collection of tales about elven owners of moonblades. Since few bearers of these blades chose to broadcast their swords' abilities, we rely in the main upon the writings of observers."

Schoonlar turned to an index that comprised several pages in the front of the book. "To your knowledge, who was the earliest wielder of the blade in question?"

"Amnestria," Arilyn said.

Obligingly Schoonlar ran a finger down the list of names. "I'm sorry. She is not listed."

"What about Zoastria?" Danilo suggested.

The scholar's face lit up. "That name is familiar." He quickly found the passage and then scurried off in search of more information. Danilo began to read aloud.

" 'In the year 867 by Dalereckoning, I, Ventish of Somlar, met the elven adventurer Zoastria. She sought information concerning the whereabouts of her twin sister Somalee, who disappeared during a sea voyage between Kadish and the Green Island.' "

Danilo looked up. "Kadish was an elven city on one of the Moonshae Islands, I believe. Long since vanished. Evermeet was once known as the Green Island."

"Go on," Arilyn urged him.

" 'Upon occasion, Zoastria was seen in the company of a female elf who was as like to her as a reflection in a pool. She once confided that she could summon the elf to do her bidding, something she did with less frequency during the time I knew her.' " Danilo paused and pointed to the small writing under the passage. "This note was added by the scribes who compiled this volume:

" 'Zoastria died without issue, and the moonblade passed to the oldest child of her younger brother. The heir's name was Xenophor.' "

Danilo flipped back to the index, found an entry bearing that name, and turned to it. He scanned the brief passage and grinned.

"Well?" Arilyn asked impatiently.

"It seems that Xenophor had a difference of opinion with a red dragon, and the beast tried to incinerate him. The chronicler notes that Xenophor was unharmed by the blast and was thereafter impervious to fire." The nobleman gleefully nudged Arilyn's ribs with his elbow. "I told you so."

"Keep reading."

"Here is something you might find interesting," broke in Schoonlar. He handed Danilo a cracked, ancient parchment. "It gives the lineage of the sword of Zoastria."

Danilo accepted the scroll and carefully unrolled it. With a feeling of deep awe, Arilyn looked down at the fine writing. Before her were the names of her ancestors, elves who had carried the sword that was now strapped to her side. The half-elf had grown up without knowledge of her family, and the scroll represented the elven heritage that had been denied her. With a sense of reverence she touched a finger to the runes, gently tracing the thin lines that connected the elves. Danilo allowed her a moment before he resumed.

"Here's something. This says that Dar-Hadan, Zoastria's father, was a mage rather than a fighter, so he imbued the sword with blue fire to warn of physical danger."

"We know that already. Keep going."

They worked all day and long into the night, aided by the attentive Schoonlar. A fascinating picture emerged, a saga of elven heroes and the response the magic sword made to each. Finally they traced the line to Thasitalia, a solitary adventurer. The dreamwarning evolved so that she could sleep alone on the road without fear. From the date of Thasitalia's death, they gathered that she had been the great-aunt who had passed the sword to Amnestria. There was nothing about Amnestria in any of the records.

"The night's drawing to a close," Arilyn grumbled, "and we're no closer to finding the Harper Assassin. A waste."

Danilo stretched languidly. "Not entirely. We know what power each wielder granted your sword, with the exception of you and your mother."

"I will never add to the moonblade's magic," the half-elf

said. "The moonstone is missing, and all magic originates in the stone and is gradually absorbed by the sword. I'm not sure whether my mother added a power—" She broke off.

"What's wrong?" asked Danilo, suddenly alert.

"Elfgate," Arilyn said softly. "That has to be it."

Danilo looked thoroughly bewildered. "I beg your pardon?"

The half-elf drew the moonblade and pointed to the bottom-most rune. "When we were in the Drunken Dragon, the mage Coril deciphered this mark to read 'elfgate.'" Her face grew more animated as she tapped the ancient scroll laid out before them. "This traces the moonblade's history from its creation until it passed to my mother. There were seven wielders, and we know seven of the sword's magic powers: rapid strike, glowing to warn of coming danger, silent warning of danger present, dreamwarning, fire resistance, casting illusions over the wielder, and elfshadow." As she spoke, she counted off the powers on her hand.

"Go on," urged Danilo, catching some of her excitement.

"Look at the sword," she said triumphantly. "There are *eight* runes. The final one, elfgate, must refer to the power my mother gave the sword. That has to be it!" The half-elf turned to Schoonlar. "Can you check and see whether you have any information concerning something called elfgate?"

Their assistant bowed and withdrew. He returned almost immediately, looking deeply troubled. "The files are sealed," he said without preamble.

Arilyn and Danilo exchanged worried looks. "Well, who can unseal them?" Danilo asked. Schoonlar hesitated. "Surely telling us the names can do no harm," Danilo said persuasively.

"I suppose not," the man conceded. "The only persons who can open the files are Queen Amlauril of Evermeet, Lord Erlan Duirsar of Evereska, Laeral the mage, and Khelben Arunsun of Waterdeep."

Arilyn's face darkened. "I knew it. Khelben already has the answers, doesn't he?"

"I wouldn't be surprised if he's got most of them," Danilo admitted.

"Why send us here?"

"Like everyone else allied to the Harpers, Khelben likes to keep secrets," the nobleman said. "He also likes to collect them. If there's one puzzle piece he lacks, he's probably hoping we'll find it."

"Such as?"

"Well, such as who's behind the assassinations, I imagine."

"That I know," Arilyn said sadly.

Danilo sat up straight. "You do?"

"I'm pretty sure. What I don't know is what the elfgate is or how it could possibly be connected to the assassinations."

Danilo suddenly became very still. "Bran Skorlsun," he said quietly. "By every god, that has to be the connection." He rose abruptly from the table. "Come on. We've got to get back to Blackstaff Tower. Immediately."

Seventeen

 By the time the courtyard of Jester's Square firmed beneath her feet, Arilyn had recovered from her uncharacteristic attack of docility. She stepped out from between the twin black oaks that flanked the invisible dimensional door and turned to face Danilo, blocking his way. "Just before we left Candlekeep, you spoke a name. Who is this Bran Skorlsun, and what does he have to do with me?"

"My dear Arilyn," Danilo said in his lazy drawl, "it is not yet daybreak, and you wish to stand here and chat? I don't like being on the streets at this hour." He cast an uneasy glance over her shoulder at the deserted square. "By the gods, doesn't Uncle Khelben know of a dimensional door with a tonier address?"

The half-elf blinked, stunned by the sudden and complete change in Danilo's behavior. "What has come over you?"

"I'm sure I don't know what you mean," he said lightly, trying to brush past Arilyn into the square.

She would not be budged. "Who are you, Danilo Thann?

What manner of man hides beneath those velvets and jewels?"

"A naked one," he quipped lightly. "But please feel free not to take my word on the matter."

"Enough!" said Arilyn violently. "Why do you present your-self as you are not? You've a quick mind and a strong sword arm; you show promise as both scholar and mage. I will no longer accept that you are a fool, and I will not allow you to treat me as one!"

"I would not," he said gently.

"Oh no? Then stop this nonsense and answer my question! Who is this Bran Skorlsun?"

"All right." The noble leaned close and spoke as quietly as he could. "He's the Harper ranger of whom Elaith Craulnobur spoke, whose business is to track down false and renegade Harpers."

"Really. How would you come by such information? Perhaps you are also employed by the Harpers?"

"Me, a Harper?" Danilo stepped back and laughed immoderately. "My dear girl, that jest would inspire much mirth in some circles."

"Then you won't mind if I read this." Arilyn deftly plucked from Danilo's pocket the note Khelben Arunsun had written. She read aloud. "Candlekeep is protected from magical observation. You need only maintain your facade enough to convince Arilyn."

The eyes the half-elf raised to Danilo's face were blazing with anger and accusation. "Sing me a song, bard, a song of a man with two faces."

Before Danilo could parry her demand, a cat's squall erupted from the alley behind them, followed by a muffled oath. Danilo cast an uneasy look toward the dim alley and glanced down at the moonblade. It glowed with a faint blue light. He grasped Arilyn's shoulders and firmly turned her around, urging her forward.

"We'll talk about this later," he said in a low voice. "I think someone's following us."

Arilyn laughed derisively. "That, Lord Thann, is old news indeed."

"So are you, gray elf," growled a voice from the alley.

Her anger forgotten, Arilyn whirled toward the alley, sword in hand. Harvid Beornigarth stepped out of the shadows, closely followed by a pair of his thugs. The lamplight reflected off his bald pate and rusty armor; were it not for the lout's vast size and his confident air, his appearance would have been more comic than threatening. He folded his arms across his rusty chain mail shirt and leered down at the half-elf with malevolent satisfaction.

"See? I told you so," Danilo murmured. "Does anyone ever listen to me? Of course they don't."

Arilyn glared at the huge adventurer. "Haven't you had enough?" she asked, her voice edged with contempt. "You should have learned by now that you can't win."

Rage washed over the man's face, and he raised one hand to his eye patch. "You'll not get the best of me this time," he vowed, shaking a spiked mace at her.

"Apparently he's a slow learner," Danilo remarked.

Harvid Beornigarth's scowl deepened. He barked a command, and two more ruffians stepped out of the alley.

Danilo let out a long, slow whistle. "Five-to-two. Maybe I shouldn't have said anything!"

The half-elf merely shrugged. "Coward's odds."

Her insult swept away the last of Harvid Beornigarth's restraint. With a roar, he charged at her like a maddened bull, swinging his mace wildly. Arilyn nimbly dodged the swing, and the battle was on.

Fury gave speed and power to Harvid's mace. Cursing and roaring, he swung at the half-elf again and again. His slender opponent was forced into a defensive position, putting all her strength into dodging and blocking the onslaught.

As soon as she could, she cast a glance toward Danilo. The nobleman was not faring well. Harvid's four thugs had surrounded him; apparently Harvid had instructed them to leave Arilyn to him.

Dread chilled the half-elf. She knew that Danilo, although skilled in the ways of classic swordplay, could not hold off four streetwise fighters for long. She would have to come to his aid, and quickly.

Even as the thought was being formed in her mind, one of the men slipped through Danilo's guard. A blade glanced off the jeweled hilt of the nobleman's sword and cut a deep gash in his forearm. Danilo's sword fell from his hand with a clatter, and a bright stain of blood blossomed on the yellow silk of his shirt. One of the thugs grinned and kicked the fallen weapon out of reach.

A cold fury swept through Arilyn, and in an instant she transformed into an elven berserker. She broke free of her battle with Harvid Beornigarth and turned on Danilo's attackers. Her moonblade cut down the nearest man with gory efficiency. The half-elf hurled herself over the body, violently shoving Danilo into the small space between the twin oak trees. She whirled, placing herself between the three fighters and the unarmed and wounded nobleman. They advanced, and Arilyn's flashing sword caught the first rays of morning as she held off the three ruffians.

Abandoned by his quarry and cheated of battle, Harvid Beornigarth stood alone and unnoticed. His mace dangled at his side, and his jaw hung slack over both of his chins. He watched the fight for a long moment, a stupefied expression on his face. His one good eye narrowed, and he hefted his mace and moved in for the kill. It took but a moment for him to realize he could not get at the half-elf without knocking his own men out of the way. He wasn't averse to killing his men, if the situation demanded, but if he did so he'd have to face the elven berserker alone.

Damn the wench! Harvid sank down on a handy crate, sucking in a long, angry breath. Then his wits—such as they were—returned to him. He exhaled in a leisurely fashion and settled himself comfortably on the crate. He might as well sit back and enjoy the show. Truth be told, Harvid Beornigarth had little desire to join his men in the Realm of the Dead. Let the elf wench spend herself and her berserker rage on the destruction of his faithful army. All he cared about was seeing her killed. If his men couldn't manage the job, at least they could tire her out. Once again Harvid Beornigarth's hand rose to his eye patch, and he sat, biding his time.

Arilyn had no thought for the lout or his plans. All her will and strength was being poured into the fight with the three men. The odds usually would not trouble her, but she had slept little in the three nights since she'd come to Waterdeep. She was nearing exhaustion, and her sword arm felt as if it were moving through water.

One of the men brought his blade high overhead and sliced down at her. As she parried that attack another man made a low lunge for her unprotected body, his long knife leading. Arilyn kicked out viciously, catching the man's arm and sending the knife flying. The moonblade sliced cleanly across his throat.

The man's death cost Arilyn. One of the remaining thugs landed a blow on her right arm. The half-elf willed aside the searing flash of pain and feinted a stumble to the ground, letting the moonblade fall to her feet. Two men closed in, confident that they could easily finish off the unarmed half-elf.

Arilyn surreptitiously pulled a dagger from her boot and threw herself upright, using her momentum to drive the dagger hard under the ribs of one attacker. From the corner of her eye, she saw the other man swinging his sword toward her neck. She dove to one side, and the blade sliced harmlessly into the man she had just killed.

As she rolled aside she snatched up the moonblade, then came catlike to her feet. In three quick strokes she finished off her last attacker, and the fight was over. She could not see Danilo, so she assumed he'd escaped the square somehow. The courtyard of Jester's Square tilted crazily, and the half-elf rested her sword on the cobblestone, leaning heavily on it. Her wound was not serious, but her sleepless nights had taken a toll. She heard in the back of her mind the sweet, insistent call of oblivion. . . .

The sound of slow, measured applause called her back.

"Quite a show," came Harvid Beornigarth's cynical observation. He hefted himself from the crate and strutted toward her, mace grasped in one beefy fist. Halting just outside the reach of her sword, he sneered, "Time to even the score."

Harvid lifted the mace high, swinging down with all his considerable strength. Arilyn rallied enough to bring the moonblade up to deflect the mace, but the impact of the blow drove her to her knees. A jolt of pain shot through her wounded arm and sent silver sparks through her field of vision. Resolutely she blinked aside the lights and the pain, in time to see Harvid, an evil grin splitting his face, raise the mace for a killing blow. She threw her remaining strength into rolling clear.

The dull clash of metal on wood echoed through the square. Arilyn looked up. Where she had stood just a moment before was a tall, dark-cloaked man. His stout staff had turned aside the descending mace. Harvid reeled back, astounded by the appearance of the tall fighter. Arilyn's rescuer advanced. He drove the end of his staff under the lout's too-short chain mail and deep into his belly. With a guttural noise Harvid bent double. The staff circled and came down hard on his neck. There was an audible cracking of bone, and Harvid Beornigarth dropped to the ground.

Arilyn struggled to her feet. Her first reaction was annoyance that someone would interfere in single combat. "I could have handled that myself," she snapped.

"You're welcome," came the cold response.

At that moment Danilo emerged from between the trees, looking dazed and clutching one hand to his head. In her surprise to see him, Arilyn turned away from the tall newcomer. "I thought you had run away."

"No. I was merely senseless. More so than usual, that is. Are you all right?" he asked, looking at her torn and bloodied sleeve with concern.

"A scratch. You?"

"Somewhat more than a scratch, but I think I'll live." The nobleman removed his hand from his forehead to display a large, bruised knot. "By the gods, Arilyn, you're more dangerous than those cutthroats! You didn't have to hurl me into the tree like that. If you wanted me to get out of your way, you just had to ask." He glanced up at Arilyn's rescuer. "Who's your friend?"

The tall man turned to face Arilyn, pushing back the deep cowl of his cloak as he did. He was older than his fighting prowess and his raven hair led one to believe, with a face that was deeply creased and weathered by the passing of years. Arilyn recognized him to be the stranger she had noticed in the House of Fine Spirits, the night that the Harper bard had been slain.

"Merciful Mystra," Danilo said softly. "It's Bran Skorlsun."

Before Arilyn could reply, a blinding flash of blue light engulfed her, and she was flung to the ground. Instinctively she threw up her arms to protect her eyes.

The sound of renewed battle rang along the street, but Arilyn had been temporarily blinded by the flash. She dug her fists into her eyes, trying to free them of the dancing spots that obscured her vision. Her elven infravision cleared first, and she saw the multicolored heat image of the tall Harper, thrusting and parrying with his wooden staff. The night rang furiously with the clanging of wood upon metal.

Yet she could see nothing else. Bran Skorlsun was fighting something, but nothing of flesh and warmth. As her vision returned more fully, the shape of the second fighter began to grow clear.

Slender, dark, somehow insubstantial, the assailant was definitely an elf in form and agility. Arilyn's heart thudded loudly in her ears as she held her breath and waited for a look at the fighter's face.

The battle shifted, and the elven fighter spun toward her. Arilyn released a long, shuddering breath. Oh yes, the fighter was familiar indeed.

"She looks exactly like you," Danilo said, coming up behind Arilyn. "By the gods! That's the elfshadow from the legend lore poem, isn't it?"

"Shadow and substance," Arilyn murmured. "But which of us is which?" Rage and bitterness lent new strength to the half-elf. Raising the moonblade high, she charged at the elfshadow. Her first stroke should have cleaved the creature in two. The moonblade passed right through it, but Arilyn continued to flail at her shadowy double. Again and again the moonblade swished harmlessly through the elfshadow and its flashing sword.

"Arilyn, stop," Danilo shouted, circling around the wild fight and trying without success to get the half-elf's attention. Since he couldn't stop her without getting himself killed by one of the three fighters, the young mage turned and sped to a wooden bench. A rusty nail protruded from the wood, and Danilo wretched it free. He pointed it at Arilyn and rapidly moved through the chant and gestures of a spell.

The nail disappeared from his hand, and Arilyn froze in midstrike, moonblade held high. Danilo leaped forward and grabbed her around the middle, dragging her away from the battle. Her body remained as rigid as a statue as the nobleman propped the magically paralyzed half-elf against one of the elms.

"Listen," he said earnestly. "I'm sorry about this, but I had to stop you before you accidentally killed the Harper. Trust me, you wouldn't want to do that. This is not your fight, Arilyn. You can't hurt that thing with the moonblade. It *is* the moonblade, don't you see? Now, if I let you go, will you promise to behave?"

Arilyn's eyes were murderous in her immobile face. "I didn't think you would," Danilo said with a sigh. Since there was nothing else he could do, he stood next to the immobile half-elf and awaited the outcome of the fight between the strange warriors. As he did, he wondered if Arilyn would see the strong resemblance between the elfshadow—her mirror image—and the aging Harper, who was also her father. The young nobleman prayed that she would not.

Indeed, her elven eyes held not recognition but the fear of a trapped animal. Danilo felt a surge of remorse.

"Willow," he muttered, and Arilyn was released from the spell. The half-elf's uplifted sword arm fell heavily to her side, and the moonblade clattered to the cobblestone. Arilyn took no notice, for her gaze remained fixed on the tableau before her.

The strange pair fought fiercely, sword and staff twirling and clashing. The elfshadow brought its blade around in a broad arc, aiming for the Harper's knees. Surprisingly agile, the man leaped up. His cape opened and floated upward as he fell, revealing a large, glowing blue stone hanging from a chain.

The elfshadow's eyes widened at the sight of the stone, and its features, so uncannily like Arilyn's, contorted with triumph. The moonblade—as if it were a living thing—skittered across the cobblestones toward the elfshadow. In the span of an eyeblink the elfshadow snatched up the sword with one hand, then it lunged forward with its own ghostly blade to tear the moonstone pendant from Bran Skorlsun's neck.

Blue light flared from the moonblade, and an answering flash came from the stone. The two streaks of magic light met between the elfshadow's hands with the sound of a small explosion, and a fierce crackling energy filled the sky. The air churned wildly around Jester's Square, becoming a magical storm that swirled autumn leaves into dizzying eddies, overturned crates, and rattled the armor of Harvid Beornigarth's fallen men. In the midst of the maelstrom stood the elfshadow in a halo of blue light. Its eyes met Arilyn's and for the first time it spoke.

"I am whole again, and I am free," the elfshadow said triumphantly, its clear alto voice ringing above the tumult. "Listen well, my sister. We must avenge wrongful deaths. We must kill the one who misled you and enslaved me!"

The magical current built into an inaudible scream around Arilyn and Danilo, whipping their hair and capes around them. The nobleman pulled the dazed half-elf to the ground, shielding her as best he could with his cape and his own body.

There was a second flash of light, and an explosion rocked the street and sent everything into blackness.

*   *   *   *   *

"This way!" shouted Siobhan O'Callaigh, brandishing her broadsword as she gestured for her men to follow.

Drawn by the sound of the explosion and the sulfurous scent of smoke, a detachment of the city watch charged through a small alley toward Jester's Square. They skidded to a stop, stunned by the sight before them.

Captain O'Callaigh had not seen so bizarre a battlefield since the passing of the Time of Troubles. The courtyard looked as though an angry god had gathered up the contents of the square, shaken them, and cast them onto the cobblestones like a handful of dice. Huge branches had broken off a pair of stately elms, benches and flowerboxes had been tossed about, and crates and rubbish had blown in from the alley. Several twisted bodies lay nearby, some of them in pools of blood. The macabre scene was dominated by the glowing sword that lay in a blackened circle in the center of the courtyard. Wraithlike wisps of blue smoke still swirled about it, drifting lazily upward in the early morning light.

As the watch stared, one of the bodies stirred. A blond man sat up slowly, the fingers of both hands gingerly pressed to his temples. As he moved, his cape came away from the crumpled form of a half-elven female. Kneeling with his back to the watch, the man bent protectively over the pale figure and thrust one hand into the sack hanging from his belt. From it he drew a silver flask. As he held it to the lips of his companion, the unmistakable almond scent of zzar drifted into the air. The half-elf sputtered, coughed, and sat up.

"What happened here?" Siobhan O'Callaigh demanded in gruff, official tones. The blond man turned to face her, and the watch captain groaned in dismay and thrust her broadsword back into her belt. "Danilo Thann. By Beshaba's bosom! I should have known you'd be a part of this mess."

"Captain O'Callaigh." Danilo rose unsteadily to his feet. "You're looking particularly lovely this morning. Interesting oath, too. Quite visual."

She snorted, completely unmoved by the young man's flattery. "What have you been up to this time?"

"Is the Harper alive?" interrupted the half-elf in a dull, dazed voice.

"I am." At the far side of the courtyard, a tall, dark-cloaked man rose to his feet and walked slowly toward the watch.

Siobhan O'Callaigh threw up both hands. "Tell me, is *anyone* on this battlefield going to stay dead?"

"I certainly hope so," responded Arilyn in a grim voice. She accepted the hand Danilo Thann offered her and rose to her feet. "I'd hate to have to kill them all over again."

"All right, since you admit to killing these men, perhaps you'd better tell me what happened," Captain O'Callaigh demanded.

The tall man intervened. "I am Bran Skorlsun, a traveler to your city. I was passing and saw ruffians ambush these two. The young pair fought only to defend themselves. I gave them what aid I could."

"Looks like you did all right, old man," one of the watchmen said, crouching down beside a large, chain mail-covered form. He heaved the body over onto its back, then gave a grunt of recognition. "Well, I'll be an orc-sired cyclops. I know this one. Harvid Beornigarth, a half-barbarian sell-sword. Nasty piece of work, but not a common cutpurse. Likes all kinds of political intrigue, he does. Or did." The man cocked an eyebrow at Danilo. "What business would he have with the nobility, I'm wondering."

"None," Arilyn said firmly. "His business was with me."

"And who might you be?" O'Callaigh growled. She crouched down to get a better look at the fallen man, swatting one of her own red braids out of her way.

"Arilyn Moonblade."

"She's a Harper agent," Danilo added significantly, as if invoking the mysterious and highly respected organization would somehow mitigate the destruction around him.

Every member of the watch froze. In unison they turned to Arilyn, and several pairs of gleaming eyes fixed on the half-elf.

"A Harper agent?" Siobhan O'Callaigh questioned eagerly. "You were the one who was attacked?

Arilyn responded with a curt nod, and the men exchanged incredulous glances with their captain. One of the watch gave words to their excited speculation. "You figure one of these pieces of buzzard bait to be that Harper Assassin?"

"Look good on our record if it turned out that way, now wouldn't it?" returned Siobhan O'Callaigh, grinning.

"No. None of these men is the assassin."

The captain and her men again looked up, surprised by the steel in the half-elf's grim voice. The captain pressed for an explanation, but Arilyn stubbornly refused to elaborate.

O'Callaigh's face turned red with rage, and she looked to Danilo to vent some of that anger. "What caused all this?" she demanded, sweeping a hand toward the general devastation.

Danilo grinned sheepishly. "My fault entirely, I'm afraid. I'm not much on the sword end of a battle, don't you know, so I tried to help things along with a spell. Something sort of, well, sort of went wrong," he concluded lamely.

"Sort of went wrong?" O'Callaigh snorted. "What else is new? Young man, you still owe the city for damages done the last time your spells misfired."

"On my honor, I'll pay for all the damages in full," swore the nobleman. "May we go now?"

The captain glared at Danilo. "Maybe you think it's that simple, being Lord Thann's son and all. From my corner of the pasture, I see things differently. There are five dead men to cart off and identify, a city square to clean up before the start of business, and a miscast spell to report."

"Oh, must you report it? I'm afraid news of this little mishap is not going to enhance my reputation as a mage," Danilo said ruefully.

"Good. The Mage's Guild is not going to be happy about this," said O'Callaigh, thrusting a finger at the young man. "They're putting pressure on the watch to curb irresponsible uses of magic. It's about time you started answering to them. When that group gets done with you, you won't even be able to scratch your backside with your magic wand."

"I don't use a wand. May we go now?" Danilo asked patiently.

Siobhan O'Callaigh smiled unpleasantly. "You sure can." She turned to her men. "You! Ainsar and Tallis. Take these three away and lock them up. The rest of you, clean up this mess."

"That was not exactly what I had in mind," Danilo protested.

"Too bad. You can have it out with the magistrar, *after* he's had his breakfast. I'm sure he'll be very interested to hear whatever this closed-mouth half-elf knows about the Harper Assassin."

The two men gestured for the trio to follow. Arilyn stooped to pick up the sword, staring fixedly at the blue and white moonstone that now glowed from its hilt. She started to rise to her feet and stopped abruptly, her attention drawn by another stone, blackened and still smoking. She picked the hot stone up, oblivious to the pain it caused her fingers, and turned it over. Her shoulders sagged as she slipped the stone into the pocket of her trousers.

"Take their weapons," O'Callaigh commanded. The man she'd called Ainsar reached out to take the moonblade from Arilyn. He jerked his hand back with a sharp curse.

"By the way, no one but Arilyn can touch it," Danilo explained casually.

Exasperation flooded the captain's face. "All right, let her keep the sword, but make sure you take all their other weapons. Now get them out of here."

She dismissed the trio and their guard with a curt wave of her hand, and turned her attention to the corpses littering the landscape. The sun was on the rise, and her men would have to hurry to clear the street before the start of business. Her commander took a dim view of anything that slowed the wheels of commerce. By Beshaba, O'Callaigh swore silently—seeing Danilo Thann always brought to mind the goddess of bad luck—why did these things always seem to happen on her watch?

*   *   *   *   *

Arilyn Moonblade sat alone in her small, dark cell, holding in her hand a blackened topaz. Again and again she passed her finger over the sigil engraved on the stone's underside, as if to convince herself that it was not truly Kymil Nimesin's mark. She had suspected that her old mentor was behind the assassinations ever since she had seen the lists of dead Harpers and Zhentarim, the lists that balanced each other as precisely as a clerk's account book. The elfshadow's words had removed all doubt.

Balance. Kymil had preached it constantly, stating that good and evil, wild and civilized, even male and female were relative terms. The ideal state, he claimed, was achieved by maintaining a balance. Even in this dreadful, incomprehensible scheme of his, the elf strove to maintain the Balance.

The question of why Kymil was arranging the deaths remained to haunt the half-elf. What injustice, what imbalance, demanded the lives of innocent Harpers? Why had Kymil deceived her, an *etriel* he had befriended and trained from childhood? And the Harper, Bran Skorlsun, what part did he play in the twisted tale of the Harper Assassin? No matter how she approached the matter, no answers came to her. Exhausted and heartsick, Arilyn fell asleep on the cell's narrow cot.

*   *   *   *   *

Five elven clerics labored over the charred form of one of Waterdeep's most respected elven citizens. Their prayers rose in a combined chant of power to Corellon Larethian, the Ruler of All Elves.

Weaving through the chant was the voice of a circle-singer. Filauria Ni'Tessine possessed that rare elven gift, usually used during an ecstatic night dance to bind elves in their mystical union with each other and with the stars. Now her magical singing wove the prayers of the clerics into a single thread, an enchanted cord of incredible power.

Pale as death, Filauria sang on and on, her iridescent eyes
fixed upon the elflord she had vowed to serve. With every fi-
ber of her being and with all the force of her inherent elven
magic, she poured life and strength into Kymil Nimesin.

The sun climbed into the sky and the morning slipped away
unheeded as the clerics prayed and the circle-singer wove her
magic. Just as they had begun to despair, the *quessir's* blackened skin sloughed away, revealing the yellow-rosebud hue of
a healthy gold elf infant.

Still weakened but definitely healed, Kymil Nimesin fell into
a healing sleep. The chanting and the song faded into a collective sigh of relief, and Filauria slumped with exhaustion.

"Impossible," muttered the youngest of the clerics, looking
from Kymil to Filauria with awe. Although the elven cleric's
power was great and his faith strong, he had truly thought
Kymil Nimesin beyond healing. What Filauria Ni'Tessine had
accomplished was the fabric of myth and song. Word of the
circle-singer's feat would spread throughout the elven nations.

Another, older cleric regarded Filauria with sympathy. The
young *etriel's* devotion to Kymil Nimesin was well known.
"We will watch over him while he sleeps. You must rest," the
elf urged her kindly.

She nodded and rose. Numb as a sleepwalker, Filauria left
Kymil's chamber and walked through the connecting room. It
was the room in which the scrying crystal had once stood.

As she regarded the devastation, Filauria thought it a
marvel that Kymil had lived through the backlash of the explosion. The walls of the scrying room had been blackened, the
windows and frames blown out. As she left the chamber, her
feet crunched on tiny pieces of charred amber.

The scrying crystal, Filauria realized. When Kymil recovered, he might be able to magically restore it. The *etriel*
dropped to the floor, and with shaking fingers she began to
faithfully gather together the blasted shards.

* * * * *

The jangle of keys interrupted Arilyn's exhausted slumber long before she was ready to awaken. She sat up and pushed her hair out of her eyes as the door of her cell swung open. "What time is it?"

"Almost highsun. You're free to go," announced the jailer. Her hunting bow, arrows, dagger, and knife clattered to the stone floor of the cell—they had "allowed" her to keep the moonblade with her but had taken her other weapons. Arilyn rose and gathered up her steel.

"You three must be pretty important," the jailer observed. "The Blackstaff himself sent word that we were to let you out, and he even sent your horses around for you. They're out front. You're to go to Blackstaff Tower at once."

Arilyn gave a noncommittal murmur and strode into the sunlight. Danilo and Bran Skorlsun were already there. The nobleman, perfectly groomed and clad in forest green, peered into his magic sack as if taking inventory. "Everything seems to be in there," he announced with deep satisfaction.

He looked up at Arilyn's approach. "Ah, good. We're all here now. Bless Uncle Khel for putting in a good word, eh?"

"Be sure to give him my regards." She mounted a chestnut mare and pressed her heels to its side. The horse set off toward the east at a brisk trot. The two men exchanged puzzled glances.

"Where are you going?" Danilo called after her.

"To find Kymil Nimesin."

Bran Skorlsun's face clouded. "The armsmaster? What has he do to with this?"

"Everything," she said.

In a heartbeat both men mounted their horses and sped after Arilyn. "Kymil Nimesin is the Harper Assassin?" Bran asked in disbelief as he and Danilo pulled up on either side of the half-elf.

Arilyn did not slow her pace. "More or less."

"Shouldn't we tell the authorities?" demanded Danilo.

"No." Her voice was implacable. "Leave the authorities out of this. Kymil is mine."

Danilo threw up his hands. "Be sensible for once, Arilyn. You can't bring this man down alone. And you shouldn't."

"He is not a man. He's an elf."

"So? That makes him your sole province?" Danilo argued. "If he's the Harper Assassin—even more or less—you should leave him to the Harpers. You've done enough."

She spoke without looking at Danilo, and her voice was low and bitter. "Yes, I have, haven't I?"

"Then—"

"No!" She faced the nobleman. "Don't you understand? Kymil isn't the Harper Assassin. He created the assassin."

"My dear, please don't talk in riddles before dinner," Danilo pleaded.

"Kymil trained me. He set my feet on the path of an assassin's life, then he encouraged me to become an agent for the Harpers." Arilyn laughed without mirth. "Don't you see? He made me to order."

Danilo was stunned by the guilt and anguish on his companion's face. He reached out and grabbed the reins of her horse, bringing her to a halt. "Stop talking like that. You're not the Harper Assassin."

"With your memory, I imagine you can recall the ballad of Zoastria," Arilyn said.

Danilo scratched his chin, startled by the seeming non sequitur. "Yes, but—"

"Recite the part about calling forth the elfshadow," she insisted.

Still looking puzzled, Danilo repeated the passage:

"Call forth through stone, call forth from steel.

"Command the mirror of thyself.

"But ware the spirit housed within

"The shadow of the elf."

"Don't you see?" Arilyn said. "Kymil Nimesin called the elfshadow and bid it become the Harper Assassin. Here is the stone I carried in my sword for many years," Arilyn said, producing the blackened topaz from her pocket. "This is Kymil's sigil. I imagine that the stone was enspelled so that he could call and command the elfshadow *through the stone*, as the ballad says."

"So that's how he kept such a close watch over you," Danilo said. "Your carrying an enspelled stone would make scrying very simple." He paused and sternly waved a finger at Arilyn like a schoolmaster reprimanding a pupil. "Kymil Nimesin betrayed you and misused your sword's magic, but that doesn't make you the Harper Assassin."

"Doesn't it?" she retorted bitterly. "I am Arilyn *Moonblade*. Where does the sword end and where do I begin? If guilt belongs to the elfshadow, and the shadow is the moonblade's reflection of me, how can I be unstained by guilt?"

Bran Skorlsun broke his silence at last. "I have seen the elfshadow before, although at the time it wore another face. It's merely the entity of the sword, and the sword is yours, Arilyn Moonblade."

"That's right," Danilo agreed, "and now the elfshadow is yours to command, as well. Whatever his purpose, Kymil Nimesin failed when the elfshadow broke free of his control."

Arilyn's laughter was hollow. "Twenty and more Harpers lie dead. How did Kymil fail?"

"We three are alive," the nobleman said grimly, "and Kymil does not possess the moonblade."

* * * * *

By highsun, Kymil Nimesin was fully recovered from the backlash of the magical explosion. He sifted the bits of blackened crystal through his long slender fingers, furious at his inability to reconstruct the priceless scrying globe.

The crystal had been shattered when the magical link binding it with the enspelled topaz broke. In the moment just before the magical explosion, one image had burned itself into the gold elf's memory: the tantalizing, infuriating picture of the moonblade, once again whole but beyond his reach.

Why the elfshadow had not retrieved the restored

moonblade, Kymil could not begin to fathom. For over a year the entity had followed his every command. So accustomed was Kymil to obedience that it had not occurred to him that the elfshadow might break free once the moonstone was returned to the sword. Inexplicably, his elfshadow assassin—his finest magical achievement—was no longer under his control. It had failed in its final, most vital task.

Kymil resisted the urge to fling the useless bits of broken crystal across the room, instead calling for his assistant. Ever attentive, the *etriel* glided into his room.

"Filauria, send word to the Tel'Quessir Elite." He waved a hand over the pile of charred fragments. "Obviously I can no longer reach them through the crystal. I shall meet them at the academy, and we teleport at once for Evereska."

The *etriel* bowed and left Kymil alone to fume over the unexpected failure of his plan. He didn't have the wretched sword. According to his sources in the watch, Arilyn Moonblade, Bran Skorlsun, and Blackstaff's nephew still lived and were under arrest in Waterdeep castle. If those three put their resources together, they would be able to discern his goal. His plan had gone fully and truly awry.

He would have to fall back on his contingency plan.

Kymil smiled. He understood his half-breed student well. Skilled though she was, Arilyn believed herself under the shadow of the moonblade. She would take upon herself the guilt of the Harper Assassin, and she would come after him to redeem her name and her sense of honor. No one would be able to talk her out of it. Of that he had no doubt.

And she would bring him the moonblade.

Eighteen

 The bright sun of mid-afternoon set the forest ablaze with color as the three riders approached the gate of the Waterdeep Academy of Arms, the prestigious training school that was set several miles to the west of the city's walls. Arilyn, who had been strangely quiet during the ride, dismounted and strode up to the gatehouse. The two students who stood guard eyed the approaching half-elf with interest and presented their best imitation of seasoned warriors.

"State your business," one of the lads growled in an uncertain baritone.

Seeing that Arilyn was prepared to do so at the point of a sword, Danilo came forward and took over. "We are three Harper agents. Our business is with one of your instructors."

The students held a whispered consultation, then the future baritone made a respectful gesture and let them pass. The other lad called for someone to stable the horses, then offered to escort the visitors to the headmaster. Danilo accepted with thanks.

"Three Harpers?" Arilyn muttered to Danilo as they walked. "*Three?*"

He shrugged. "It got us in, didn't it?"

Arilyn responded with a measured look and lapsed into silence. The student led the unlikely trio of avowed Harper agents through a labyrinth of halls to the office of the academy's headmaster.

Headmaster Quentin was a burly gray-haired cleric who wore the brown robes and hammerhead symbol of Tempus, god of war. Still broad-shouldered and ham-fisted in his early old age, Quentin looked as if he would be much more at home on the battlefield than in an office. At the moment, he was seated behind several piles of parchment, sadly at odds with his sedentary task. He looked up when the trio came to the door, and his face lit up at the offered reprieve.

The student guard spoke up. "Brother Quentin, these Harpers seek audience with you."

"Yes, yes. I'll take over from here," replied Quentin, rising from his desk and striding forward. He dismissed the student with an impatient gesture.

"It has been too long since the Raven flew to these parts," Quentin said heartily, clasping Bran's forearms. Arilyn's head snapped up to look at Bran Skorlsun, and a peculiar expression crossed her face.

"What brings you here, Bran?" continued Quentin. He slapped the Harper on the back with the familiarity of an old comrade. "Can you stay long enough to share our evening meal and perhaps tip a few mugs?"

"Another time, I would be glad to," Bran replied. "My companions and I seek one of your instructors. Kymil Nimesin. Is he here?"

The headmaster's forehead creased. "No, he took a leave of absence. Why?"

"Did he say where he would be going?" Arilyn demanded.

"As a matter of fact, he did," Quentin remembered. "Evereska, I believe."

"Evereska . . ." Arilyn repeated softly, looking thoroughly

puzzled. "Was there anything out of the ordinary about his request for leave?"

Quentin thought that over. "Well, Kymil did take several of
our best students with him."

"What can you tell me about them?" Arilyn asked.

The headmaster retrieved one of the piles of parchments
from his desk—a large pile—and began to thumb through it.

Arilyn shifted her weight impatiently from one foot to the
other. "Ah, here it is," Quentin exclaimed happily, brandishing
a piece of parchment. "Kymil's request for leave. He took
with him Moor Canterlea, Filauria Ni'Tessine, Caer-Abett
Fen, Kizzit Elmshaft, and Kermel Starsinger."

"Some of those are elven names," Danilo commented.

"All of them," Quentin corrected. "All gold elves, come to
think of it. Every one of them personally recruited and trained
by Kymil Nimesin. An impressive lot, I must say."

"You have personal records on these students, I imagine.
May I see one of them?" Arilyn asked.

"Of course. Which student?"

"Ni'Tessine. Filauria."

"Ah, yes," Quentin said. "Fine student. I understand she
had a brother in the academy some years back, but that was
somewhat before my time."

"It was twenty-five years ago," Arilyn said softly as she accepted the parchment the headmaster offered her. "He and I
were classmates."

"Is that so? What did you say your name was?" Quentin
asked with friendly interest. Arilyn told him, and his bushy
brows lifted. "This is odd. Kymil left a note for you." The
headmaster produced a small parchment scroll and handed it
to Arilyn.

She quickly scanned the note, then without comment she
slipped it into the pocket of her cloak and turned her attention
back to the records of Filauria Ni'Tessine. As Arilyn had anticipated, the gold elf had followed custom and listed her family
history in some detail. Among Filauria's siblings was Tintagel
Ni'Tessine, alumnus of the Academy of Arms, member of the

Waterdeep Watch. Her father's name was Fenian Ni'Tessine, deceased as of 2 Ches, 1321 Dalereckoning. Interesting, Arilyn thought, that the elf died on the same day King Zaor of Evermeet was assassinated.

Abruptly Arilyn handed the paper back to the headmaster. "Thank you."

"Always ready to aid the Harper cause," Quentin said heartily. "I don't suppose you could fill me in on what's happening?"

"Gladly, but at a later time," Bran said.

"Just tell me one thing," Quentin pressed, "is Kymil Nimesin in any sort of danger?"

"Count on it," Arilyn promised in a grim tone.

None too gently, she ushered Bran and Danilo out of the room. Once they reached the academy courtyard, she turned to confront the Harper. "Why did the headmaster call you Raven?"

The Harper drew back a step, a little surprised by the intensity of her question. "My given name, Bran, is the word for raven in an ancient language of the Moonshae Isles. Why do you ask?"

"Hearing it just then brought to mind something I'd almost forgotten," Arilyn said slowly. "I trained at the academy with Filauria Ni'Tessine's brother, Tintagel. He carried the broken shaft of an arrow with him like a talisman. A tiny brand—a raven—was burned into the wood of the arrow shaft. Tintagel said it was to remind him of his purpose in life. I learned from one of Tintagel's friends that his father, Fenian Ni'Tessine, was killed by that arrow." Arilyn glanced up at the Harper, her face wary. "Was that arrow yours?"

"I cannot say. The name Fenian Ni'Tessine is not known to me," Bran said quietly. He reached back into his quiver for an arrow and handed it to Arilyn. "Is this the mark?"

She examined the brand and nodded. "Does it help to know that Fenian Ni'Tessine was killed on the second day of Ches, in the year 1321? The year before I was born." She spoke the last statement in a barely audible voice.

"No. I'm sorry."

"Perhaps this will help you remember: King Zaor was assassinated that day by a gold elf, who was in turn shot by my mother's human lover." She lifted her guarded eyes to the Harper's. "Moonstones are not commonly worn by humans, and the gem you carried fit my mother's sword. Am I wrong in thinking that you are the one who killed Fenian Ni'Tessine?"

"I did not know his name, but it would seem that you are right," Bran admitted. The lines of pain and regret that creased the Harper's face answered Arilyn's unspoken question, as well. Their gazes clung for a moment in silent acknowledgement. She handed Bran back his arrow, then turned away, deeply shaken.

Danilo, who had followed this exchange in silence, let out a long, slow whistle. "That means Bran Skorlsun is—"

"Arilyn's father." Bran said quietly. He turned to the half-elf. "I would have told you in time."

"You waited a bit too long," Arilyn observed in a faint voice. Her face hardened and she said, "But you *can* tell me why you had the moonstone."

"In truth, I cannot," Bran admitted.

"More Harper secrets?" Danilo said with a touch of sarcasm.

"Not on my part, at least," the Harper said. "A tribunal of elves from Evermeet and Master Harpers decreed that I must carry the moonstone until the day of my death, but I was never told why."

"Then let's get back to Blackstaff Tower and find out," Arilyn said flatly. She turned on her heel and headed for the academy's stables.

"A woman of action, your daughter," Danilo observed to Bran as the men fell in behind her. The Harper nodded absently.

A chatty family, Danilo thought wryly. A hint of a smile lit the young man's face as he contemplated the murderous expression he'd seen in the half-elf's eyes. To his way of thinking, Uncle Khelben had it coming.

They rode back into the city in virtual silence. "You wait here," Danilo instructed Arilyn and Bran when they reached the wall around Blackstaff Tower. "It's well past sunset, and Uncle Khelben expected us hours ago. It's probably been quite some time since someone kept the archmage waiting, and he's sure to be frantic. Give me a moment to calm him down." So saying, the young nobleman walked through the courtyard and disappeared into the solid granite wall of the tower.

After a few moments Arilyn moved to follow him, but Bran put a restraining hand on her arm. "Wait. It is difficult to use invisible doors without the guidance of a mage."

Arilyn shook off his hand. "I can see faint outlines. Secret doors are difficult to hide from an elf."

"A half-elf," he corrected quietly and pointedly.

His words were meant to bring about confrontation. Arilyn tensed. She was not yet ready to acknowledge the relationship that bound them, and she struggled against the strength of her anger.

"All of my life, my mother grieved for you," she said finally. "I never had a father and I feel no need of one now, but how could you—how could anyone!—turn away from Z'beryl?"

"He had no choice."

Startled, Arilyn and Bran looked up. Standing before them was Khelben Arunsun, with Danilo close behind.

"Well, it would seem that the wandering Harper has returned," the archmage observed coldly. "Bringing trouble, as usual."

Bran returned Khelben's glare with a calm, steady look. "Many years have passed. We cannot go back and relive our youth, but must we discard the friends who shared it? Laeral and I have come to an understanding. Cannot we do the same?"

The wizard's face darkened at the mention of his lover. "What has Laeral to do with this?"

"Not enough, it would seem," Bran said sadly. "Our paths crossed shortly before I left the Moonshaes. She was on her way to Evermeet." Bran's brow furrowed suddenly, and he glanced at Arilyn. "Laeral is my friend, but it seems not right that she should be accepted by the elves when their half-elven kin are not."

"Your concern is belated, but touching," Arilyn observed with cold scorn.

"Enough of that, Arilyn Moonblade," Khelben said irritably. "You have every right to dislike the man—Mystra knows *I* do—but not to misjudge him. As I said, he had no choice but to leave your mother. She took that choice out of his hands. At the time, he didn't even know about you."

"It is true," Bran said sadly.

"You see?" Khelben asked Arilyn, who listened, unmoved by the explanation.

"No."

The wizard raised his eyes skyward in exasperation over her stubbornness, then beckoned them toward the tower. "Come in, come in."

Once they were inside the reception area, Arilyn faced down the archmage. "You knew about this all along."

"I had suspicions," he admitted, "but I was not free to discuss them with you. Dan says you know who the assassin is. Who?"

"In time," Arilyn said grimly. "First, tell me why my . . . why Bran Skorlsun carried the moonstone."

"It was decreed by the elves of Evermeet," Khelben said.

"To what purpose?"

The archmage glanced from Arilyn to the aging Harper. "Have you two talked?"

"She knows," Bran said.

"She also knows that her mother was the Princess Amnestria," added Danilo.

Khelben nodded to Arilyn. "Good, because there's no way for me to explain this otherwise. Amnestria married a human and carried his child. The elves don't look kindly on that sort of behavior in their princesses." He let out his breath in a deep sigh. "In an unconscious attempt to span her two worlds, Amnestria added a potentially dangerous power to the moonblade. The moonstone was removed before the power could be fully absorbed into the stone."

"That would be the elfgate," Arilyn broke in. When Khelben leveled a glare at Danilo, she raised her eyebrows and added, "Your nephew did not give away the game. The elfgate is a dimensional door between Evermeet and Waterdeep. How else could the elf who killed King Zaor on Evermeet be found dead in Waterdeep that same day? Not an easy feat."

"Impressive. You've put all the pieces together," noted the archmage.

"No," Arilyn said. "I still don't understand why the moonstone was given to Bran."

"Punishment," Khelben said. "Amnestria was sent into exile and pledged to protect the elfgate. She knew that as long as Bran carried the stone, they could never be reunited."

"Why was I not told any of this?" Bran demanded.

"That knowledge would put the key to the elfgate in your hands," Khelben said. "The elves of Evermeet did not have that much faith in you. Since they did not think that a half-elf could inherit the moonblade, they did not foresee the possibility of a father and daughter reunion."

"Kymil made sure we met," Arilyn stated bitterly. All three men looked puzzled, so the half-elf turned to Bran. "Who hired you to follow me?"

"Some Harpers from Cormyr contacted me," he said.

"Lycon of Sune? Nadasha?" Arilyn asked tersely. Bran nodded. "It figures. Kymil often worked with them, but they never fully trusted me. I imagine it was easy for Kymil to convince them that I was the Harper Assassin and that they should put you on my trail."

"So Kymil Nimesin arranged the death of Harpers to lure Bran to you, hoping to reunite the stone with the moonblade. Appalling," Khelben muttered. "But what would he want with the elfgate?"

Arilyn's smile was chilling. "I'll be sure to find out before I kill him."

"You can't go after Kymil," Khelben protested. "Now that the moonstone is back in the sword, the moonblade's very presence could help anyone—particularly an elf—find and use the hidden portal."

"She could meet Kymil before he finds the portal," Danilo suggested.

"Too late. He's already there," Arilyn said. "He left a message for me telling me where to meet him."

"Where—Oh, yes. Evereska," recalled Danilo. "He left word that he was going to Evereska. Well, let's go get him."

"Don't be a fool, Dan," Khelben snapped. "The moonblade must stay far away from Evereska. I take it you've already guessed that the elfgate was moved there," he said to Arilyn.

"Yes. Perhaps the moonblade can't go to Evereska, but I can." She unbuckled her sword belt and offered the magic sword to Khelben. "Here. The thing will be safe enough in your vault."

Khelben shook his head. "You can't go to Evereska without the sword, either. With the moonstone set in the hilt once more, the link between you and the weapon has been finalized. A wielder can't be separated from an active, intact moonblade for any length of time and live."

Arilyn regarded the sword in her hands for a moment, then hurled it across the room. It landed with a clatter. "So be it. If I can live long enough to meet and overcome Kymil Nimesin, I'll be content."

"Why?" Danilo demanded. He took her shoulders and shook her. "Why would you throw your life away?"

She met his eyes, defiant and resolute. "My life has never been completely my own, so it's not mine to keep or throw away. I must make amends for my misused sword." Her voice was firm and wholly devoid of self-pity. "I'll do so, but on my own terms. I may be a half-elf and a half-Harper, but I refuse to be half a person. I will not be the moonblade's shadow any longer."

"That has never been the case. You command the moonblade, not the other way around," Bran told her.

"If that were true, then I could choose to leave it behind," she said stubbornly.

"I don't suppose it would do any good to try to dissuade you," Khelben said.

"None."

"Then I'll keep the moonblade for you. You're right, the sword should stay here," the archmage conceded. "So should you, for that matter."

"Thank you, Khelben. I would ask one more thing from you. Can you lend me transport to Evereska? A griffon, perhaps, with a speed enchantment?" she asked.

"Very well," Khelben agreed. "If you insist upon going to Evereska, I'll get you there. But with one condition. Danilo goes with you."

"No." Her tone was implacable. "I go alone."

Khelben glared at Bran as if this were somehow his fault. "She is your daughter, beyond a doubt." He turned back to Arilyn. "All right, you've got transport. An enspelled griffon should suit as well as anything."

"Good. Where do I need to go for it?" Arilyn demanded.

"The stables are on the top of Mount Waterdeep." The wizard went to his desk and scrawled something on a bit of parchment. He pressed his signature ring to the note, and his rune magically burned onto the paper. Khelben handed the note to the half-elf. "Give this to the griffon master. He'll give you everything you'll need."

"My thanks." She started toward the tower's exit.

"Arilyn."

She froze at the sound of Danilo's voice but did not turn around. "You'll need a new sword." He faltered. "Permit me to lend you mine."

Arilyn nodded and accepted the blade Danilo offered her, then she stepped through the magic door.

Danilo watched her go, swearing under his breath. "Did either of you see that coming?"

"I should have," the Harper replied. "It's too much like something I would have done at her age."

Before the archmage could respond, a sharp rap that seemed to come from the center of the room drew his attention. "Piergeiron's timing is about as good as usual," the wizard grumbled, stalking to the door that led to the basement and the secret tunnel to the palace of Waterdeep's lord. "Wait here," Khelben instructed his visitors.

Danilo paced back and forth before the door, muttering imprecations against the Lords of Waterdeep and their preoccupation with protocol. Danilo had little patience for the processes of law and order. He worked independently and under cover so he could keep free of the sacred cords of propriety that bound all aspects of Waterdeep life. Never mind that Kymil Nimesin ran free, that the elven kingdom's safety had been compromised, that Arilyn was walking willingly into what was surely a trap. The Lords of Waterdeep were probably consulting Khelben about a new monument or some such foolishness.

To the impatient young noble, Khelben's whispered consultation with the messenger seemed to take an eternity. Finally the Blackstaff returned with an official-looking parchment in his hand. His face was deeply troubled.

Khelben was not given to preambles. "This is from the Lords of Waterdeep. Arilyn Moonblade has been identified as the Harper Assassin, a rogue adventurer in the employ of the Zhentarim."

"What?" exploded Bran. "By whom? I was the one assigned to make that judgment."

Khelben held up a hand for silence and continued. "Piergeiron says that the evidence is overwhelming. An anonymous source sent papers to Waterdeep Castle, precisely balancing each assassination with documentation on Arilyn's whereabouts. There was also a letter billing the Zhentarim for an assassin's services. The dates coincide with each Harper Assassination."

Danilo's eyes turned cold. "Elaith Craulnobur sold her out. He'll die for that."

Khelben looked worried. "She was working with the rogue elf, wasn't she? By Mystra, that won't look good when she comes to trial."

"A trial." Danilo slumped into a chair. "It will come to that? Can't you do anything?"

"I can speak in her behalf."

"There's no truth in this accusation," Danilo protested. He winced and amended, "At least, not much truth."

"One thing I learned long ago," Bran responded, "is that truth often has little power to sway opinion. It seems that the Harpers have never completely trusted Arilyn. Any hint of involvement with the Zhentarim will color opinion further. You must admit that with her background as an assassin, she is a credible suspect."

Even Danilo had to concede the logic in that. "Surely, when the full story is known . . ."

"The full story can never be told," Khelben stated in an uncompromising tone. "Evermeet would be endangered if news of the elfgate became widespread. The secret must be protected."

Filled with fury, Danilo flew to his feet and faced down the archmage. "Even at the cost of Arilyn's life?"

"Even so."

Their eyes locked like horns, Danilo's blazing with condemnation, Khelben's fixed on his commitment to duty. The younger man broke away first.

"I'm going after Arilyn," he said abruptly.

"Be reasonable, Dan," growled Khelben. "How will you find her? Did she tell you where the elfgate is?"

"In Evereska, that's all I know." Danilo's eyes narrowed. "Wait a minute. Don't *you* know?"

"Evereska's a big city," Khelben snapped. "And I wasn't the one who moved the gate."

Danilo shook his head in disgust. "All right, who *does* know? Or can you relinquish your vows of secrecy long enough to part with that information?"

"Watch your tongue. Laeral devised the spell that moved the elfgate. The only others who know its exact location are Queen Amlauril and the elven lord of the Greycloak Hills, Erlan Duirsar. Perhaps the elven council of Evereska knows by now, too. By Mystra, this mess will set back ties with the elves a century or two," the Blackstaff concluded in a mutter.

"You deal with the politics, Uncle. If you can't help me, I'm going to Evereska alone."

"I'm going with you." Bran Skorlsun's quiet voice was as inflexible as tempered steel.

"You're as bad as your daughter," Khelben said. "What makes you think the elves will let you near Evereska, Bran? Elves have long memories, and they're not overly fond of humans who ruin their princesses."

Bran met the archmage's glare. "Who else could track Arilyn to the site of the elfgate?"

"It's out of the question!"

Danilo laughed without mirth. "Oh, come now, Uncle. Aren't you just a little curious to know where this elfgate is? Now that the cat's in the creamery, so to speak, I imagine you'll have to move the thing sooner or later." Khelben's eyes widened.

"Another thing," added Bran. "If we wish to help Arilyn, we must bring in Kymil Nimesin. In her current frame of mind, I fear that she will kill the elf."

"Let her," Danilo retorted. "Forgive me, but I cannot shed many tears over the fate of Kymil Nimesin."

"As much as it pains me to do so," Khelben put in, "I must agree with Bran. Arilyn is a former assassin. Kymil Nimesin is a highly respected armsmaster. Kymil must be brought in and magically questioned. Without such evidence at the trial, without Kymil's actual presence, Arilyn looks very much like the Harper Assassin. She would stand a much slimmer chance of acquittal if she kills Kymil."

"So you agree that we should go, Uncle Khelben?"

"Given our options, yes." The wizard turned to Bran. "If you will excuse us, I need to have a few words with my nephew before you leave. Come up, Dan."

Khelben and Danilo climbed the tower's staircase to the magical supplies room. Once the wizard had shut and warded the door, he got right down to business. "You were right. The elfgate must be moved again," Khelben said bluntly.

"Oh, marvelous. With Laeral off cavorting with the elves of Evermeet, who's going to accomplish this miracle?"

Khelben fixed a steady gaze on his nephew. Danilo shook his head and whispered, "Surely you're not serious."

"I am very serious."

The wizard stalked to his scroll library, a large shelf that covered the length of one wall and kept the vast collection in order. Its tiny, round compartments held hundreds of magic scrolls, making the shelf looked like an oversized honeycomb or at the very least an impressive wine rack.

Pressed for time, Khelben muttered a spell. Instantly one of the compartments glowed with green light. Khelben drew the scroll from the glowing niche, blew the dust from it, and removed the magic wards that sealed it.

"Here is the spell, Dan." Khelben spread the scroll out on a table and fixed the young man with a steady stare. "I've pledged not to cast the spell, so you'll have to." Danilo paled. "You can do it. I've been working with you since your twelfth winter, after that last tutor quit in despair. You have the ability. Do you think I would endanger your life by insisting you cast a spell you could not control?"

"You're willing enough to sacrifice Arilyn's," Danilo said.

"Tread carefully, young man," the archmage warned. "Few things in life are as simple as you would make them. When you have carried the burdens and responsibilities I have known, then you can sit in judgment upon me. Will you cast the spell or not?"

Danilo nodded and bent over the scroll. One glance at the arcane symbols that formed the powerful spell, and Danilo knew that the task lay on the untried edges of his magical ability. Few mages would attempt such a spell. That Khelben would expect this of him was a measure of the wizard's trust. Or perhaps his desperation.

As the young mage struggled to read the spell, pain shot through his head like shafts of lightning, making the arcane

symbols cavort on the parchment. With fierce concentration,
Danilo forced himself to focus on the spell, and after a time the
symbols slowed their dance. As they arranged themselves into patterns, their meanings started to become clear. Danilo
began to memorize the complex gestures and the strange
words that formed the incantation.

After a moment he closed his eyes. He saw the runes em-
blazoned in gold upon a field of black. Once he had truly
learned a magic spell, he could see the symbols in his mind.

Danilo opened his eyes and nodded. "I've got it."

"Already? You're sure?"

The nobleman grinned at his uncle. "The spell, I'm afraid, is
going to be the easy part."

"Don't be cocky, boy."

"It's true! Compared to keeping Arilyn from chopping Kymil
Nimesin into carrion?"

Khelben smiled reluctantly. "Perhaps you have a point.
Even without the moonblade, Arilyn is a formidable force."

To Danilo's ears, the wizard's words lacked conviction. "You
don't think she can win, do you?"

"I'm sorry, Dan. Without the moonblade, she'll be lucky to
live until sunset tomorrow."

"Then Bran and I had better be on our way."

Khelben removed a silver band from one of his fingers and
handed it to Danilo. "A ring of transportation. On an enspelled
griffon she could get to Evereska by late afternoon tomorrow."

"Thank you," Danilo said, accepting the ring. He removed a
large, square-cut emerald from one finger to make room for it.
Khelben rolled up the spell scroll and handed it to his nephew,
who slipped it into his magic bag. As Danilo did so, a daring
plan suggested itself. He stared at the magic sack for a moment, considering. "I suppose I'm ready," he said at length.

"I don't see that you have any other choice."

Khelben and Danilo descended the stairs to the parlor
where Bran waited impatiently. "Ready to go?" he asked the
young nobleman.

Danilo blinked. "I just had a bad thought. Since Arilyn is flying to Evereska on a griffon, she must land somewhere outside the city and arrange other means of transport." He turned
to the archmage. "Would it be possible for you to contact the
Griffon Eyrie? Perhaps she told the keepers there what destination she had in mind."

"Good thinking, Dan. I'll be back in a moment." Khelben
Arunsun retraced his steps to the spellcasting chamber to
make inquiries through his crystal.

Danilo removed a pair of gloves from his magic sack and listened intently for the sound of a door closing. He moved to the
corner of the parlor. Arilyn's moonblade still lay where she had
hurled it. The young man hesitated for just a moment, then he
willed himself to accept the pain and picked up the sheathed
blade. As he expected, a current of magical energy shot up his
arm, and the acrid smell of burned flesh filled the chamber.
Danilo quickly dropped the moonblade into his magic sack and
slipped the glove over his blackened hand. He sped through
the gestures and chant of a spell that would create an illusion.
When he was finished, the moonblade, to all appearances, still
lay where Arilyn had abandoned it.

He turned to Bran Skorlsun and said quietly, "Arilyn needs
the moonblade, and I plan to take it to her. If you speak of this,
you are a dead man."

A faint smile curved the Harper's lips, and he laid a hand on
Danilo's shoulder. "Young man, I like the way you think."

Khelben Arunsun wrinkled his nose in disgust when he entered the room again. "Merciful Mystra! It smells terrible in
here."

"Your cook is busily burning lentils, no doubt," Danilo said.
"Did you find out where Arilyn is headed?"

"Yes. The Halfway Inn, just outside of Evereska."

That was precisely what Danilo had expected to hear.
"Good. We're on our way, then." The nobleman and the Harper exited Blackstaff Tower with rather indelicate speed. Grinning like two schoolboys savoring a prank, the two men left
the courtyard for the darkness of the street.

"Hello, Bran," said a musical, faintly amused voice.

The Harper pulled up short. Standing in the shadow of a milliner's shop was Elaith Craulnobur. The elf stepped into the light of the street lamp. "I was beginning to wonder whether the Blackstaff had invited you to take up residence in the tower. I see that his nephew is with you, so I assume Arilyn is nearby?"

Danilo's eyes narrowed. He reached for his sword, but remembered that he'd given it to Arilyn. The moon elf laughed. "Your scabbard is as empty as your wit. Don't worry, dear boy. You've nothing to fear from me."

"Is that so? I thought you were going to have me killed."

"Not a matter for concern."

"That's easy for you to say," the nobleman retorted.

The elf's eyebrows rose in amusement. "Would it comfort you to know that the attempt has already been made?"

"The House of Good Spirits," Danilo said, suddenly understanding. His eyes narrowed. "So you knew all along who was behind the assassinations."

"If I did, I wouldn't have had to spend an obscene amount of money on bribes to the Zhentarim. They're quite willing to betray their own, but the price of friendship is high," Elaith said. He held up the documents he had shown to Arilyn two days earlier. "Where is Arilyn? I must speak with her about these."

Danilo calmed himself. "Someone sent copies of those papers to Waterdeep Castle. I thought it might be you."

"Good gods, no. It was Kymil Nimesin. He's the one who originally sent the bill to the Zhentarim. Working both sides of the fence, he's been amassing a tidy sum." The moon elf shook his head, and a grim expression replaced his usual facade of gentle amusement. "I'd like to know what Kymil plans to do with those funds. He should be quite a wealthy elf by now, and he's ending the scam by serving up Arilyn as the Harper Assassin."

Danilo looked up at Bran, his expression worried. "That would be a convenient way for Kymil to explain Arilyn's death, wouldn't it? The noble armsmaster slays the half-elf assassin?" Bran merely nodded, never once taking his eyes off Elaith's face.

"All the more reason for Arilyn to deal with Kymil at once," the moon elf agreed. He handed the papers to Danilo. "Please give her these."

The nobleman glanced at the papers. "I don't understand."

"It is always wise to have a contingency plan," Elaith said. "With this letter, Arilyn can turn the Zhentarim against Kymil. An amusing end for the villain, wouldn't you say?"

"Arilyn would not work with the Black Network!" Bran thundered.

"My dear Raven, do try to be practical for once." Elaith took the itemized bill from Danilo's hand. "There are a number of names on this list, people for whom the Zhentarim had no further use."

"Yes? So?"

"So, just suppose there were *more* names on this list, including some individuals who *are* important to the Zhentarim leadership."

Bran still looked outraged, but a tiny smile of comprehension tugged at Danilo's lips. "I see. Pad the bill a bit?" asked the young nobleman.

"If you chose the right names, it could raise some hackles," Elaith agreed mildly. "I've already looked into the matter. As usual, there have been several unexplained deaths in the network's ranks of late. If an explanation were suddenly presented . . ."

"Very clever," Danilo admitted, "but I doubt Arilyn would want the Zhentarim doing her work for her. Don't give the matter another thought. She'd prefer to handle Kymil Nimesin herself."

"You're probably right." Elaith inclined his head.

Bran observed the moon elf with suspicion. "This is hardly the behavior one expects from the famous Serpent."

Elaith let out a ripple of cynical laughter. "Do not make the mistake of thinking me noble. I am not."

"What do you want from Arilyn?" Bran demanded.

"Taking your fatherly duties a bit seriously, aren't you?" the elf mocked. His smile faded abruptly, and his amber eyes suddenly seemed dull and empty. "Don't concern yourself, Harper. I realize that Amnestria's noble daughter is beyond my reach. If Arilyn were in truth the devious assassin I once thought her, it would be another matter."

"Then why do you help her?" Bran asked, puzzled.

"Unlike the *etriel*, I have no compunction against letting others do my work for me." Suddenly Elaith's voice hardened, and his amber eyes met Danilo's. "Kymil Nimesin has insulted me too many times. I want him dead. Unless I miss my guess, Arilyn is going to kill him. It is that simple. Though she and I may be very different, where Kymil Nimesin is concerned we both want the same thing."

Danilo held the deadly elf's gaze for a moment, then he nodded. "Revenge," he said softly.

"We understand each other at last," said the moon elf with a strange smile. He melted into the shadows and was gone.

"Merciful Mystra," Danilo said softly. "Keeping Kymil Nimesin alive may prove to be more difficult than I thought."

Nineteen

"By Mielikki, this is no way for a ranger to travel," Bran Skorlsun grumbled, shaking his head free of the travel spell's confusion. The Harper stamped his feet several times as if to assure himself that he once again stood on solid ground. The action was greeted by the crunch of fallen leaves. He and Danilo had teleported into a mist-shrouded forest. Night was deepening around them, and the nobleman pointed toward some lights flickering through the bare tree branches.

"The Halfway Inn is up ahead. Let's go," Danilo urged, crashing off through the fallen autumn leaves with an appalling lack of woodcraft. More skilled in such things, Bran followed him silently. Urgency quickened their pace.

In minutes Danilo and Bran arrived at a large clearing. Laid out before them was a complex of wooden buildings clustered around a large stone inn. Both elven and human merchants bustled about, busying themselves with the care of their animals, or bartering with other traders, or storing their goods for the night in one of several warehouses. Contented nickers wafted from the large stables, and the clinking of crockery could be heard through the windows of the tavern's kitchen. The odors of the evening meal gave a pleasant warmth to the autumn air.

"The Halfway Inn was where I first met Arilyn. She left her horse here, and even without Khelben's inquiries to the Griffon Eyrie I was quite sure she'd return for it."

"How far are we from Evereska?" Bran asked.

"Not far at all," Danilo assured him. "We're just to the west of the city. The ride takes an hour, maybe two. Let's make sure that Arilyn's horse is still here."

The men slipped into the stable. Danilo had no trouble finding Arilyn's gray mare. "Let's go to the main tavern and find someone who'll sell us some horses of our own," the nobleman suggested.

"Fine." Bran pulled the cowl of his cape over his head and followed Danilo toward the sprawling stone building. As the nobleman hung his lavishly embroidery cape on a cloakroom peg, the Harper peered into the large, crowded tavern. He laid a restraining hand on Danilo's arm.

"Who is that elf behind the bar?"

Danilo looked. A small and solemn moon elf stood at one corner of the bar, bent over what appeared to be an account book. "Him? Myrin Silverspear. He owns the place." Danilo answered. "Why do you ask?"

"I met him once before, many years ago, on my one and only trip to Evermeet," Bran murmured. "Odd that a captain in the palace guard should become an innkeeper." He turned to Danilo. "You go in alone. It's unlikely that he would recognize me, but it's best that I stay out of sight." So saying, the ranger slipped out of the cloakroom and melted into the shadows of the night.

Danilo sauntered toward the bar. The proprietor looked up at his approach, regarding the nobleman with silver eyes that gave away nothing. "Lord Thann. Welcome back."

"Thank you, Myrin. I would say it's good to be back, but

I've had a bit of bad luck. Ale, please."

The elf produced a foaming mug, and Danilo settled down on a bar stool and took a couple of sips. "I just lost my horse in a game of chance," he said. "I need to purchase two new mounts. Fast."

"The horses or the transaction?" asked the proprietor without a touch of humor.

"Well, both, I suppose. I'd like to take care of it now, since I don't bargain well after too many of these." Danilo lifted his half-empty mug.

The elf studied Danilo in silence. "Several of my current guests can oblige you. I would be happy to make the introductions."

Myrin Silverspear summoned a barmaid, a slip of a moon elf whose black hair and blue-tinted skin reminded Danilo of Arilyn's. After a few words of instruction, the girl disappeared. She returned within moments with an Amnish merchant.

Danilo took one look at the merchant's well-oiled smile and prepared to part with most of his ready cash. The man was obviously a horse trader in every sense of the term. As were most natives of Amn, the merchant was short, thick, and dark. He wore colorful clothing that was ill suited to the chill autumn winds of the north, as well as an impressive amount of gold jewelry and an equally flashy smile. The lust for gold shone in his eyes as plainly as his gold teeth lit his smile.

For the sake of saving time, Danilo made only a pretense of bartering, giving the delighted merchant nearly his asking price. He also accepted the man's assurances that a merchant train would leave for Evereska in the morning. With such horses, the merchant fervently swore, the young lord could sleep away the effects of many mugs and still have time to catch the caravan.

After the merchant left the taproom for the horses, Danilo cocked at eyebrow at the elven proprietor. "Not to impugn the man's integrity, but truly, is a merchant train leaving tomorrow?"

"Three caravans plan to leave in the morning. Several more

will probably pass through during the day. If you wish to enter the city, you should have no problem persuading one of them to count you among their number," the elf said, shrewdly responding to Danilo's unasked question.

The nobleman nodded and rose to leave. "Good. Well, I might as well see what kind of horses I squandered my father's money upon."

The Amnish merchant had brought the horses to the tavern door, and Danilo was pleased to note that they were indeed fine animals, black and spirited, worth almost half of the amount he had paid for them. As he led his two new mounts toward the stables, Bran fell in behind him. They found an empty stall near Arilyn's mare, and settled down in the hay to await the half-elf's arrival.

*   *   *   *   *

Throughout the night and well into the next day, Arilyn's enspelled griffon flew toward Evereska. By late afternoon, the half-elf saw beneath her the misty foothills of the Greycloak Hills. Her heart quickened at the thought of returning to her childhood home. As the hills grew into mountains, she watched eagerly for the verdant fields and deep, soft forests of the Vale of Evereska. The hands that clenched the reins of her griffon steed relaxed somewhat, and she nudged the magical creature into its descent. Enspelled for enhanced speed, the creature was capable of covering large distances. Even without the magic enhancement, it was an extraordinary beast with the strong, tawny body of a lion and the head and wings of a giant eagle.

Arilyn knew better than to try to fly directly into Evereska. The city was so well guarded that she would have little chance of surviving such a flight. Outposts dotted the mountains surrounding Evereska, and sharp-eyed elven watchmen would spot her within five miles of the city. If she should try to fly above the range of their vision, she would likely encounter the patrols of giant eagles who circled in the skies. The elven archers who rode these mounts were known never to miss a target.

So Arilyn steered the griffon clear of the walled city and the surrounding vale, instead swooping low over the western forest. She saw a familiar clearing, dominated by a large stone building and ringed with wooden structures and bustling merchants.

Since a griffon could not land in the middle of the busy merchant town without causing a stir, Arilyn urged her winged mount toward a nearby glen. The beast's enormous wings curled in an arch like that of a giant hawk, and it descended to the earth in a tight spiral. The pads of its lion's paws touched the ground, and with great relief Arilyn dismounted. With a final shriek, the griffon took off for Waterdeep, and Arilyn strode toward the stables of the Halfway Inn.

Her mare was there, sleek and well-conditioned. Arilyn patted the horse with genuine affection. She wished that she had time to seek out and thank Myrin Silverspear, but he would understand that she could not. Arilyn left a small bag of coins in a pre-arranged place in the stall as payment for the horse's care.

The golden light of late afternoon lit the sky as she turned her horse toward the city. After the enspelled griffon, her fleet mare seemed to move far too slowly, and her progress was hampered by the seemingly endless merchant caravans that monopolized the tree-lined road. As she wove her way through the swarm of wagons and riders, she took no note of the two riders on Amnish stallions who followed her through the crowd, tracing her steps toward the elfgate.

* * * * *

An insistent flurry of coos erupted outside the window of Erlan Duirsar's study. The elflord's face betrayed his apprehension as he turned to an aid. "Let the messenger in," he commanded sharply.

The young elf threw open the window sash to admit the messenger. Onto the window sill hopped a gray dove, which tilted its head as if politely requesting admittance. A small scroll was tied to one leg with a bit of silver ribbon.

"Lord Duirsar will see you," the aid told the bird. The tiny messenger flew directly to the elven lord of the Greycloak Hills and perched expectantly before him.

A wave of trepidation swept through Erlan Duirsar. It had been some time since he had received a message from the western outpost. Myrin Silverspear was a proud elven warrior who preferred to take care of most problems himself. A matter had to be grave indeed before the "innkeeper" would pass it on to Evereska. Erlan untied the scroll. As he read it, his face grew troubled.

A polite chirp, the avian version of a cleared throat, drew Erlan's attention back to the messenger. The bird awaited his reply, its tiny head cocked at an inquisitive angle.

"No, there will be no response," Erlan told it. "You may go." The bird bowed its head and chirped an unmistakably respectful farewell, then it dissipated into a scattering of tiny lights.

"My lord?" questioned the aid.

"Summon the council immediately. Make it clear that we are to meet at once and in the utmost secrecy."

"Yes, Lord Duirsar." The urgency in the lord's voice was not lost on the aid. He bowed and hurried to the silver globe that would send the silent summons. Each council member wore an earring that was magically attuned to provide transport directly to Lord Duirsar's halls.

Erlan Duirsar gazed out the window to the courtyard below, a vast square ringed by buildings of enspelled pink crystal. Elvencrafted with the whimsical asymmetry and solid practicality that characterized the work of moon elves, the buildings housed most of the lords and ladies who sat on the council. Both the duties and privileges of government were shared by all in Evereska, and the common elves frequently gathered in the square for ritual, festivity, or contentious town meetings.

It was his voice, however, that issued the final word on such matters as now confronted the city. Erlan Duirsar kept this thought before him as he strode into the meeting hall to address the council. A powerful and proud group, the elves studied him with varied degrees of curiosity and impatience.

"I know that you all have important business elsewhere, but I must ask that you remain here in counsel this night. Evereska may need the special talents of each elf here."

"What's going on?" demanded the head of the College of Magic.

"Bran Skorlsun has come to the Greycloak Hills," said Erlan Duirsar simply.

It was explanation enough.

*   *   *   *   *

The stars were beginning to wink into light as Arilyn entered the central garden through its maze of rose-entwined boxwood. Before her stood the statue of the Hannali Celanii, as radiantly beautiful as Arilyn remembered.

The half-elf drew a small parchment scroll from her pocket and held it aloft. "You told me to meet you at my mother's statue. Let's get this over with."

Arilyn's voice rang out through the empty garden. There was a moment's pause, then Kymil Nimesin stepped out from behind the statue.

"Arilyn. You cannot know how delighted I am to see you," he said, his patrician tones rounded with satisfaction.

"Let's see how quickly I can change your opinion on that matter," Arilyn said, as she drew Danilo's sword in challenge.

Before the steel had scraped free of its scabbard, several elven warriors emerged from their hiding places amid the boxwood hedges. Weapons in hand, they formed a semicircle behind Kymil, ready for his signal to attack.

"Need help these days, do you?" Arilyn asked.

Kymil regarded her weapon with dismay. "Where is the moonblade?" he demanded.

"If you're here, the elfgate must be nearby. Surely you didn't think I'd bring the moonblade with me."

Kymil stared at her, not sure whether to believe her or not. His noble plan, his grand design, could not be thwarted by a mere halfbreed. It was impossible. His handsome bronze face gleamed with righteous wrath. "Where is the sword?" he repeated.

"Where you cannot get it," Arilyn responded, smiling.

The gold elf's narrowed eyes glittered with malevolence as he changed his tactics. "This is a surprise. You've been so malleable all these years. Who would have thought that you could be as stubborn and stupid as Z'beryl?"

The comment caught Arilyn off guard, just as Kymil had intended it to do. A cold hand of sorrow clutched at her heart. "What do you mean?"

"What else could I mean?" he taunted. "After I learned the secret of the moonblade, it took me fifteen years—fifteen years!—to discover that Amnestria and the elfgate were in Evereska. I might still be looking, had I not encountered some students who had studied under Z'beryl of Evereska."

"I doubt any of Mother's students knew her identity. I can't believe any of them would betray her," Arilyn said.

"Not intentionally, perhaps. In their admiration for your departed mother, they tried to mimic her unusual two-handed fighting technique." He spread his arms wide. "Imagine my chagrin to finally find elf and sword, only to learn that the moonstone was gone and the elfgate still denied me. Naturally, your mother refused to tell me where the stone was, so I ensured that the blade would pass to someone who promised to be more reasonable."

The color drained from Arilyn's face. "You killed her."

"Of course not," Kymil retorted, his voice tight with self-righteous scorn. "She was, as the watch reported, killed by a couple of cutpurses, though perhaps I sold the men some enspelled weapons. Perhaps I also informed them that she carried a heavy purse."

Arilyn hurled an elven curse at Kymil Nimesin like a javelin. He curled his lip in a show of disdain. "If you must be vulgar, by all means speak in Common and do not sully the elven language."

"You filthy murderer," she spat. "Now I have one reason more to kill you."

"Don't be tiresome. I did not kill Z'beryl," Kymil reiterated calmly. "I merely passed on some information to the cut-purses who did. Of course, I don't mourn the use they made of that information." Kymil paused and swept a hand toward the gold elven fighters behind them. "Soon you will join her in whatever afterlife awaited her."

Arilyn saw a familiar face among the elves. "Hello, Tintagel. Still Kymil's shadow after all these years?"

"I follow Lord Nimesin," Tintagel Ni'Tessine corrected her with cold disdain, "as did my father before me."

"Making a family business out of being assassins, are you?"

"Can one use the term assassination to refer to eradication of gray elves? Extermination would be a more likely term," he sneered.

"That is apt," Kymil agreed. "Once we open the gate, my Elite will slip in and kill every member of the so-called royal family. With the moon elf usurpers gone, the proper order and balance will be restored."

"I see," said Arilyn slowly. "And Kymil Nimesin will reign in their stead, I imagine."

"Hardly." Kymil gave a patrician sniff of scorn. "The high elves, the true *Tel'Quessir*, do not require the vulgar trappings of royalty. I will restore the ruling council of elders, as it was in the days of Myth Drannor."

"Will you, now?" Arilyn taunted him. "It seems to me that you'll have to get to the moonblade first. How you're going to remove it from Khelben Arunsun's safe is a marvel to me."

"That is a lie," the *quessir* snapped. "You cannot lay aside the moonblade on a whim. With the sword whole once more, you are tied to it like mother and newborn. If the sword were truly so far away, you would be dead."

"What can I say?" Arilyn returned with a flippant shrug. "It's amazing what one can do when properly motivated. I refuse to die while you still draw breath." Her face hardened.

"Maybe you're right about the moonblade, and it could be that neither of us has long to live. I challenge you, Kymil Nimesin, to single combat. May the gods judge between us."

"Your pretension is almost amusing," said Kymil. "The student cannot possibly hope to vanquish the master."

"It has been known to happen."

The elf regarded her for a moment, then he noted in a condescending manner, "My dear Arilyn, you cannot fight a duel with that lifeless blade."

In reply, the half-elf raised Danilo's sword to her forehead in challenge.

Kymil merely laughed and turned to the Elite. "Kill her."

* * * * *

Khelben Arunsun stood by a window of Blackstaff Tower, gazing out into the gathering night. Try as he might, he could not rid his mind of Danilo's words. In the matter of the elfgate, the wizard had done what he thought best. The Harper council had decided that secrecy was the only real protection for the elven kingdom, and they had guarded the secret by dividing it up like so many chunks of bread. At the time, it had seemed to be the most prudent course to take.

Now Khelben was not so sure. Harpers worked in secret, always collecting information and using their talented members to subtly thwart evil or correct imbalance. In the matter of the elfgate, the very veil of secrecy that the Harpers employed, usually with great success, had been turned against them by an elf they trusted. Therein, Khelben knew, lay the dilemma. Bran Skorlsun had been kept busy for almost forty years tracking down pretended Harpers and an occasional renegade Harper. What other disasters could occur if these false Harpers had access to Harpers' secrets?

Danilo had been right about many things, Khelben acknowledged silently. The archmage had knowingly and deliberately endangered Arilyn's life. Without the moonblade, she was unlikely to live through the night. Khelben's heart ached for his nephew, who obviously cared deeply for the half-elf.

The archmage abruptly left the window and walked to the corner of the room where the moonblade still lay. To his knowledge, Arilyn had not named a successor. To whom, then, should he send the blade? Absently he reached for the ancient scabbard, and his hand closed on air.

"What!" Snapped from his introspection, Khelben sped through the words of a cantrip to dispel magic. The moonblade faded, although its faint outline hung in the air a moment longer as if silently mocking him.

"An illusion," he murmured. "Danilo took the sword and left an illusion." The boy's getting too good to keep under wraps, the wizard thought, unable to suppress a small smile of pride.

He passed a hand over his forehead. His sympathies were with Danilo, but how could the boy be foolish enough to endanger the elfgate? Both Danilo and Bran Skorlsun were risking their lives to help Arilyn. Khelben was not sure whether he ought to be angry or ashamed. Perhaps they could do it. Perhaps Danilo could move the gate without a problem, and perhaps Arilyn could defeat Kymil Nimesin. Perhaps I should let them try, the archmage mused.

The weight of responsibility pressed upon Khelben Arunsun, and suddenly he felt very old. He walked the staircase to his spellcasting chamber to alert Erlan Duirsar. The elven lord of Evereska would not be pleased to learn that the moonblade was again whole and on its way to the site of the elfgate.

*   *   *   *   *

The sounds of battle rang through the temple gardens, drifting down the labyrinth of footpaths that wove their way to the top of Evereska's highest mountain. Two men broke into a run, the taller of them leading the way. Swiftly and surely the aging Harper raced to the top of the mountain. There, in the very center of the garden, was a sight that chilled him to the soul.

Before the statue of a beautiful elven goddess stood his

daughter, fighting for her life against four gold elves. The rising moon reflected from their flashing blades.

Awe filled both Bran and Danilo, who had now reached the garden. It held them, immobile, in its spell. Never had they seen such fighting. In any company, each of the agile gold elves would be considered a rare champion. Although two of their number had fallen to Arilyn's sword, the remaining four wove a dance of death around the half-elf. Off to one side stood another gold elf, a tall slender *quessir* who awaited the battle's outcome with an expression of self-righteous confidence.

At that moment, one of the fighters managed to knock Arilyn's borrowed sword from her hand. In the bright moonlight, Danilo could see the triumphant sneer on the face of Tintagel Ni'Tessine. Panic struck the nobleman, and with it a moment of indecision. He had not intended to reveal the moonblade until he'd found the elfgate and moved it to safety.

Tintagel Ni'Tessine raised his sword arm across his chest, preparing to deliver a backhanded strike to Arilyn's throat. Danilo made his decision swiftly.

"Arilyn!" he shouted, thrusting his wounded hand into the magic sack. A second blast of pain ripped through his arm as his fingers closed around the magic sword. The startled elves looked toward him, and Danilo hurled the sheathed blade toward Arilyn.

A flash of blue lightning ripped through the garden like an explosion. Magic thunder shook the ground, and the gold elves were knocked to the ground by its force.

Arilyn stood at base of the statue with a glowing sword in her hand, a powerful figure of magic and vengeance. Smoke from the explosion flowed toward her. Before Danilo's stunned gaze, the writhing smoke swirled and twisted, forming a faint circle behind the half-elf that glowed with an eerie blue light.

"The elfgate!" shouted Kymil Nimesin, pointing. "You must get past her and into the elfgate!"

The elven fighters rose to their feet and exchanged uneasy glances. Danilo took one look at Bran Skorlsun's puzzled face and immediately understood what troubled the elves. They could not see the gate.

Some dimensional doors were visible only to powerful mages. Of all the people gathered in the garden, only Danilo could see what Kymil Nimesin was pointing to.

The nobleman grabbed the spell scroll from his bag and prepared to move the elfgate. With a start, he realized that Khelben had not told him where the gate should be moved. An ephemeral smile touched his lips when an answer presented itself. Conjuring a mental picture of the elfgate's new location, the young mage began the lengthy chant and gestures of the spell.

"For the honor of Myth Drannor!" shrieked Kymil, galvanizing the elves into battle. Three of them circled Arilyn. Wielding his staff, Bran raced to aid his daughter, but was stopped by Filauria Ni'Tessine. The tall Harper and the elven circle-singer made strange opponents, but Filauria held him back with astounding skill.

"Your sword cannot shed innocent blood," Tintagel reminded Arilyn smugly. "It is worthless against me."

"Times have changed. Care to chance it?" she asked. Tintagel confidently advanced, and in three strokes Arilyn's moonblade had found his heart. The elf's eyes widened in disbelief as he slumped to the ground. With a keening wail, Filauria fled the battle and dropped to her knees beside her brother's body.

"The time to mourn our martyred dead will come later," raged Kymil. "You must get through the elfgate."

Arilyn slashed viciously at her two elven attackers, intent on preventing them from following Kymil's orders. The moonblade found the heart of one elf, killing him instantly. With her next stroke, Arilyn gutted her final opponent. His sword fell to the ground as he clutched at his spilling entrails. Arilyn slipped on the spilled blood and fell to the ground.

"Show me," Filauria demanded. Kymil pointed her in the direction of the elfgate and shoved. The *etriel* ran, leaping over Arilyn's prone body and into something she could not see.

At that moment Danilo completed his spell. The scroll disappeared from his hands, and a second magical explosion rocked the garden. The survivors stared in horror. Only half of Filauria Ni'Tessine had made it through the elfgate.

A scream of frustration echoed through the temple garden. Kymil Nimesin's patrician reserve had vanished along with the hope of fulfilling his lifelong quest. With quick, jerky movements, the elf formed the gestures for the teleportation spell that would take him away from the scene of his failure.

"Wait!" Arilyn shouted. As Kymil glared murderously at her, she rose to her feet. "You haven't lost yet."

Kymil's obsidian eyes fixed upon Arilyn, hatred somehow making their black depths even darker.

"Don't speak in riddles. You haven't the wit for it," he snarled in scornful response.

Arilyn came closer, facing down her former mentor. "I renew my challenge to single combat, to continue until one of us is disarmed or disabled. If you win, I will reveal to you the gate's new location."

A flicker of interest showed in Kymil's black eyes. "And in the unlikely event that you win?"

"You die," she said succinctly.

"No!" Bran shouted from across the garden. "Many think of you as the Harper Assassin. You've got to bring Kymil Nimesin to trial or you may hang in his place."

"I'll take that risk," she said steadfastly.

"Maybe you will, but I won't," declared Danilo. "Unless you promise me that you won't kill that skinny orc-sired wretch, you'll have to fight me to get at him."

Arilyn cast an exasperated look at the nobleman. In response, he stripped off his gloves. The moonlight revealed a badly burned hand and a face haggard from the effort of casting the spell. "If you fight me, you'll have to kill me," he added softly. "I shouldn't think it would be too difficult."

His implacable tone convinced Arilyn he was serious. "I think I liked you better as a fool," she said.

Danilo would not be distracted. "Swear it!"

"All right. You have my word. I shall leave enough of him to take to trial. Agreed?"

"Done," Danilo said. "Go get him."

Arilyn again addressed the elf. "Well? What will it be?"

"The mere knowledge of the gate's location will do me little good," Kymil pointed out, bargaining, testing the limits of Arilyn's resolve.

"If it comes to that, I'll take you to it myself. I'll bring the moonblade and open the damned gate for you. I'll even throw you a farewell party before you leave for Evermeet," she said.

"Agreed." Kymil drew his sword and raised it to his forehead in a contemptuous salute. The elf and the half-elf crossed blades, and the fight was on.

Scarcely remembering to breathe, Danilo Thann and Bran Skorlsun watched the duel in awed silence. Both men were skilled fighters, both had seen and done much during their lives, but the battle that raged before them was something completely beyond their experience.

It was an incredible, mesmerizing dance of death, with individual movements almost too quick for the humans' eyes to follow. With elven grace and agility, Arilyn and Kymil faced off, each stretched to the limit by the other's skill and impassioned resolve. Evenly matched in height and strength and speed, at times the combatants were distinguishable only by color: Arilyn a white blur against the dark sky, Kymil an incongruous streak of golden light.

Elven swords flashed and twirled, and sparks from the clashing weapons shot upward into the darkening sky so rapidly that the incredulous Danilo was reminded of festival fireworks. The ringing blows of sword on sword came so quickly that the echoing clangor blended into one reverberating, metallic shriek. A small sound separated itself from the unearthly howl, and a voice began to focus in Danilo's mind. The voice spoke not with words, not with sound, and not to him. Irresistible as the song of the lorelei, the magic voice soared above the din of battle: entreating, insisting, compelling. It called for vengeance. It called for death.

With a start, Danilo realized that it was the voice of the elf-shadow. The moonblade began to glow as the revenge-bent entity of the sword struggled to escape unbidden. Even to Danilo, its demands were nearly irresistible.

Arilyn can't give in, Danilo thought frantically. He watched the moonblade trail blue light as it traced a semi-circle and an upward thrust. The movements themselves were too fast to discern, but the sword's lighted paths lingered in the air, luminous blue ribbons against the night sky.

Suddenly there was silence, and the tangle of blue lights began to fade. Kymil Nimesin rose slowly to his feet; the splintered shards of his sword lay scattered around him.

"Praise Mielikki, it's over," Bran said gratefully. With a sigh of relief, Danilo and the Harper came forward. The look on Arilyn's face stopped them, and dread again seized Danilo as he comprehended that the battle was not yet done.

As if it moved of its own accord, the moonblade drifted upward in Arilyn's hands. It leveled at Kymil Nimesin's throat and glowed with a malevolent blue light. The half-elf trembled with the effort of holding back the sword, and her face twisted against the urge to kill her former mentor. Kymil Nimesin stared defiantly at the blade and waited for death.

"Fight, Arilyn," Danilo pleaded. "Don't let the elfshadow and your own need for vengeance command you."

The magical current began to grow, as it had on the streets of Waterdeep. Again the air swirled madly around the battle's survivors in a tangible outpouring of the elfshadow's rage. Only Arilyn managed to remain standing against the gale-strength force.

"Come forth!"

Arilyn's commanding voice rang above the tumult. The angry current of magic energy faltered, then rapidly began to compress. In the span of two heartbeats the elfshadow stood before Arilyn.

"Have done," the half-elf insisted sternly. "We are not the only ones Kymil Nimesin has wronged. The Harpers have the right to bring him to trial. He must live for that."

"It is a mistake," protested the elfshadow, glaring at Kymil's prone form with undisguised hatred.

The half-elf's chin lifted. "Perhaps so, but it is mine to make." She lifted the moonblade, and for a moment Arilyn and her shadow faced each other.

At last the elfshadow bowed slightly and spread her hands, palms up, in the elven gesture of respect. The shadow faded into blue mist, which in a small quick vortex disappeared into the sword's moonstone.

Arilyn slid the moonblade back into the scabbard at her side and walked toward her companions. Bran had helped Danilo to his feet, and the young man was busily fussing over his once-fine clothing.

"Danilo."

He looked up at the half-elf. Her clothing was torn and bloodied and her face was nearly gray with exhaustion. To his perceptive gaze her elven eyes spoke as clearly as words. Finally, Arilyn was at peace with herself, and she was mistress of the moonblade.

"*Now* it's over," she said.

Epilogue

"Did I sing you the ballad about the Marsh of Chelimber?" Danilo asked the Harper.

"Twice," Bran Skorlsun said.

"Oh."

Arilyn chuckled. "Did you notice that the number of goblins and lizard men grows with each rendition? I expect that next he'll throw an orc or two into the pot for spice."

Arilyn, Danilo, and Bran lingered over sparkling wine at the House of Good Spirits, the night speeding by as they talked. The tavern emptied around them. Chairs went up on tables; barmaids slipped away to seek their beds. The innkeeper dozed behind the bar, his pockets weighted down by the gold Danilo had slipped him.

Despite their shared adventures and the various ties that bound them, they knew little of each other. The three were greedy to learn more of their companions' histories, dreams, and plans. By sunrise, they had made a start at that.

Inevitably the talk turned to the events of the day before. "Now that your good name is restored, what do you plan to do?" Bran asked Arilyn.

A thoughtful expression crossed her face. "The Harper tribunal found me innocent, but that does not necessarily restore my name. I should be able to find work, but it could be years before I regain my reputation."

"As an assassin?" Danilo said ingenuously.

Arilyn cast her eyes skyward and sighed. "Thank you for putting things back in perspective."

"How about you?" Bran asked Danilo. "Do you still believe that Khelben and the Harpers were wrong in their manner of dealing with the elfgate?"

Danilo chose his words carefully before answering. "For a time I did. When I tried to think of a better way, however, I couldn't come up with one. I might not approve of all that Khelben has done, but I was not the one who had to face his decisions."

"What about the dangers inherent in secrecy?"

"They remain," Danilo admitted, looking slightly troubled. "Again, I see no real alternative. Working for good and maintaining balance are often matters of small degrees. If you wish to shape a bush you must prune it gently, not take a scythe to it."

Bran smiled. "We have need of insight and talent such as yours." The Harper reached into an inside pocket of his cape and drew out a small box. Inside gleamed a Harper pin, the tiny crescent moon and harp rendered in fine silver. "This pin is a pale thing next to most of your finery," the older man teased gently as he handed the box to Danilo, "but it is a sign of rare value. It is my pleasure to offer it to you, along with a place among the Harpers."

When the young man hesitated, Bran urged, "Take it and wear it with pride. You deserve to be known for what you truly are."

"I am honored by your trust, do not mistake that," Danilo assured him. "In the role of village idiot, I've been fairly effective. I cannot continue my work if I am a known Harper."

"You may have little choice in the matter," Bran pointed out with a touch of humor. "Your own ballad will spread your fame."

Arilyn laughed. "Your role has served you well, Danilo, but isn't it time you outgrew it? You should get the respect that you deserve, and you are resourceful enough to develop new methods."

"Uncle Khelben did suggest something like that," Danilo reflected.

Bran smiled again and held out the emblem. "This is a pleasure indeed. Khelben will not like it that I have usurped his privilege, and it is rare that I am handed such an opportunity to irritate the good wizard." The Harper joined in with Danilo's laughter, then he put the box down in front of the young man and clasped him by both forearms: an adventurer's salute to a fellow and an equal. "You are a good man, my son," Bran concluded.

Deeply moved, Danilo accepted the pin. "Thank you. You have already given me a greater gift. Such acceptance I've never received, not even from my own family."

"That's got to end, too," Arilyn decreed. "The Thann family will hear of everything that you have done, if I have to sit them down one at a time and make them listen at swordpoint." Her face softened, and she laid a hand on Danilo's shoulder. "I am glad for you. You deserve this honor."

"Do not think that I have forgotten you," Bran said to Arilyn. He removed his own weathered pin and offered it to her.

Arilyn drew back. "I can't take that," she protested.

"Why not? I've never met anyone more deserving."

"But it is your own—"

"All the more reason why you should have it," Bran said. "The gods know, I have given you little of myself."

Arilyn looked at the Harper, surprised by the sadness in his voice. "I do not fault you. We all do what we must. You did no less." Her voice took on a businesslike tone. "I accept. You know, however, what the giving of a Harper pin means?"

"Of course," Bran responded with a puzzled smile.

"You will be expected to vouch for me, to supervise me until I am accepted as a Harper in my own right," continued Arilyn as if she had not heard him. "Given my past and the notoriety this trial has afforded me, that will not be a pleasant task and it could take some time. Will you be around to do this or do you plan to again disappear to the far corners of the world?"

The Harper's heart warmed to the appeal that lay behind Arilyn's words. The prospect of getting to know his extraordinary daughter made his remaining years beckon to him with a lure that the road had ever held.

"I will remain," he said. "There is more than enough work for rangers in the North. Perhaps in time I shall retire to Waterdeep."

"Oh, good," said Danilo with a grin. "Uncle Khelben will be so pleased."

"Speaking of the archmage, we must consult him concerning the elfgate," Bran said. "Safeguards must be arranged, and its new position must be secured."

Arilyn made note of the young man's smirk. "What is it, Danilo?"

"What? Oh, just agreeing with the good Harper." He rose from the table reluctantly. "I must be going now. It will take me several hours to explain my extended absence to my family, not to mention the various new scandals I've brought upon the family name of late. Father will merely be quietly disappointed, but my mother's reaction would do credit to a red dragon."

Arilyn stood, too, her eyes blazing with battle light. "I'm coming with you."

"Truly?" Danilo asked, looking vastly pleased. "I thought you were jesting."

"I seldom do."

Her tone was grim, and Danilo threw back his head and laughed. "By the gods, this should be worth watching."

The trio left the tavern and retrieved their horses. Arilyn mounted and regarded the nobleman for a moment. His green velvet cape and extravagant jewels seemed a bit inappropriate for a newly made Harper. "Do you need time to change before we leave?"

"Whatever for, my dear?" Danilo drawled. With an indignant huff, he fussed with the floppy plumes on his latest hat. "I'll have you know that this ensemble is considered the height of fashion in Waterdhavian society. At least," he amended, "it *will* be once I've been seen wearing it."

"Whatever you say," she said, humoring his foolishness. "As long as I never have to hear that wretched ballad again, I'm content."

Danilo smirked in Bran's direction and swung himself into his saddle. "The lady has taste, it would appear. At least," he amended as his gaze swept pointedly over her travel attire, "she has taste in matters of music."

Arilyn looked down at her usual clothes: boots, trousers, a loose white shirt, and a dark cape. Her only ornamentation was a weathered Harper pin. "What's wrong with what I'm wearing?"

"I had hoped we could celebrate properly after we vanquish Lady Cassandra Thann. Forgive me, my dear, but that outfit simply will not do."

"I like it."

"Yes. Well. As it happens I managed to do a little shopping after the trial." Danilo reached into his magic sack and drew out a cloud of diaphanous sapphire silk. He held it up, displaying a day gown of rare beauty.

Arilyn regarded him soberly. "I can see your hands through the fabric," she commented.

His only response was a broad smile.

"Tell me, Danilo, how much of the dandy is real and how much is contrived?" she asked, his contagious smile catching her lips, too.

"One must keep up appearances," he said, returning the garment to the sack. "I take it you don't like the gown."

"Good guess."

"Let's see, what else would suit you? Have you ever considered a blue velvet gown, perhaps cut down to about here? No? Then at the very least, a blue shirt. Deep blue silk, with just a sprinkling of gold jewelry. Perhaps a cape of matching velvet. Yes!" Danilo exclaimed. "As it happens, I know this marvelous little shop, right on the way, that—"

Arilyn reached over and smacked the flanks of Danilo's stallion. The horse let out an offended whinny and took off down the road, and the rest of Danilo's words drifted into the wind.

Arilyn looked down at her father. Slowly she extended her hands, palms up, in the elven gesture of respect. Tears held unshed for many long years glistened in the Harper's eyes as he returned the salute. His daughter gave a sharp shake to the mare's reins and sped off after Danilo Thann.

"One mystery remains, Danilo," Arilyn noted as they rode together through the streets of the city. "Where did you put the elfgate?"

Danilo gave her a solemn look. "I moved it to the safest place I could imagine."

"Well?"

"Blackstaff Tower."

"*What?*"

Mischief broke over Danilo's face like a sunrise. "Can you think of a safer place? Or a man more inclined to keep secrets?"

"No, but—"

"There's more," Danilo said. "I put the elfgate in Laeral's chambers. Since the good lady mage spends much time in Evermeet, I thought I might make it more convenient for her to stop by and visit Uncle Khelben more frequently. Do you think that might improve his disposition?"

Arilyn's laughter rang out. "It might. There is one problem, though. When the elfgate was in Evereska, I always felt drawn to the temple of Hannali Celanil. Does this mean I'll feel compelled to visit Khelben Arunsun?"

After sharing a chuckle with Arilyn over the picture she'd painted, Danilo sobered. "Actually, the location is appropriate. The elfgate created many imbalances. Moving it to Blackstaff Tower might help remove the wedge its creation placed between Evermeet and the Harpers."

"You're already talking like a Harper," Arilyn teased him. "Do you also plan to give up your frivolous ways?"

Instead of answering, Danilo removed the Harper emblem from his silken tunic. He folded back his cape and securely fastened the silver pin to the lining. The smile he turned on Arilyn was the lazy, vacant smirk of Waterdeep's celebrated fashion plate and most notoriously inept mage.

"Me, a Harper?" Danilo laughed. "My dear girl, that jest would inspire much mirth in some circles."

Arilyn smiled faintly. "So that's the way things will be."

"I think it's best," he said lightly. "What about you?"

"When I began my training, Kymil Nimesin told me that the moonblade set me apart. I've always felt that I had to stand alone, that I was a shadow to the sword's power. But the moonblade is *mine*, and things must change."

Arilyn drew the sword and pointed to the line of runes. "There are nine runes now; this new one is mine." She paused and chose her words carefully. "It is not so much a power, but the removal of certain restrictions." She turned the moonblade and offered it to Danilo, hilt first.

His gray eyes filled with understanding. Arilyn was offering him far more than her sword. Deeply moved, he accepted the symbol of her friendship and cradled it in his burned hands. "A rare and precious thing," he murmured, looking not at the moonblade but at the half-elf's face. "You honor me by sharing it."

Their gaze clung for a long moment, then Arilyn's eyes slid away. Her uncertain expression tugged at Danilo's heart. To lighten the moment, he assumed a cocky grin and returned the magic sword to its master. "Things of value should always be shared. Your beauty, for instance." He drew the translucent gown from his bag with a flourish. "Now, about this gown . . ."

Arilyn's smile brightened her face. "Don't push it."

Fantasy Adventure

The Cleric Quintet

R. A. Salvatore

Book One
Canticle

High in the placid Snowflake Mountains lies a little-known conservatory for bards, priests, clerics, and others. Cloistered among his colleagues, a scholar-priest named Cadderly must contain a malevolent, consuming essence that's been uncorked, before his own brethren can turn against him. Cadderly must put his studies to the test and enter the catacombs far below to save his brothers and himself.

On sale in November 1991, Canticle is the first in a new five-book series of novels entitled The Cleric Quintet, set in the FORGOTTEN REALMS fantasy world from TSR, Inc. R. A. Salvatore is the author of the bestselling Icewind Dale and Dark Elf trilogies.